The Cut

The Cut

C. J. DOTSON

ST. MARTIN'S PRESS
NEW YORK

This book is dedicated to Marcia Frank—when you encouraged your elementary school class to write our own fiction for the first time, a fire lit in me that has never gone out. You helped shape the course my entire life has taken. From my heart and forever, thank you for that.

First published in the United States by St. Martin's Press, an imprint of St. Martin's Publishing Group

www.stmartins.com

Library of Congress Cataloging-in-Publication Data

Names: Dotson, C. J., author.
Title: The cut / C. J. Dotson.
Description: First edition. | New York : St. Martin's Press, 2025.
Identifiers: LCCN 2024028715 | ISBN 9781250335449 (hardcover) | ISBN 9781250336569 (ebook)
Subjects: LCGFT: Horror fiction. | Novels.
Classification: LCC PS3604.O868 C88 2025 | DDC 813/.6—dc23/eng/20240809
LC record available at https://lccn.loc.gov/2024028715

First Edition: 2025

10 9 8 7 6 5 4 3 2 1

A Moonless Gloom

The beach looked different by night.

A man stood at the bottom of a steep concrete staircase, one hand on the metal railing, a rough patch of peeling paint pressing into his palm. In his other hand, he held a leash looped around his fist, clip swinging free.

Earlier, with a pristine blue sky and bright sun glittering off the expanse of Lake Erie, with the cry of seagulls and the indistinct voices of people going about their day, and with Rosie sniffing the sand and splashing out into the water as far as her leash would let her, he never could have imagined how unsettling it would feel here after dark.

Clouds had swept in sometime between sunset and the dog's escape from his yard, casting the night into a moonless gloom that should have swathed the beach in shadows. Instead, white light blazed to the right. Floodlights, belonging to the power plant, merely ugly during the day, now a hulking presence crouched over the sand and water. Behind him a shallow shale cliff stood about twice his height, the trees and scruffy bushes lining its edge, giving it the appearance of a more forbidding stature. Their autumn-dry leaves rattled in the wind coming off the lake. Just visible above the branches, the top floors of an old hotel overlooked the lake with the dead-eyed blank stare of windows either dark or curtained and impersonal.

"Rosie!"

At his call, the crickets in the scruffy grass bordering the beach fell silent, but only for a moment. The movement of the tiny almost-waves against the sand sounded like an admonishing hush. *Sshh, sshh, sshh,* over and over.

He ignored the warning and shouted once more, a little louder, *"Rosie!"*

There—in the water. What was that?

A shape moved on the surface, low and dark, bobbing near the end of the rocky pier jutting out into the lake.

"Rosie?"

Splashing rose above the soft susurrus of wind and wavelet.

"Rosie!"

Toeing off his shoes, he stepped from concrete to soft, cool sand. He crossed the beach in a rush, bracing for the shock of cold as he ran into the lake, surprised to find it warmer than the night air.

Wet jeans clung to his shins, then to his knees. The shape on the surface drew nearer.

"Come on, Rosie-girl! Come on, baby, let's go home!"

The farther out he waded the harder it became to hurry. The water climbed up under his shirt now, and with the depth came some of the chill he'd expected.

"You want a treat, Rosie?" he called, half out of breath.

Rosie barked. He knew his dog's soft *boof-boof* anywhere. Relief flooded him, but under it ran a current of almost wary confusion; that bark had come from somewhere behind him. Somewhere on shore.

Nowhere near the low, dark shape splashing nearer to him.

Even as he turned, Rosie barked again, a little softer or a little farther away.

He pursed his lips and whistled. "Rosie, stay! C'mon, girl, wait—"

The faintest hint of light swirled in the corner of his eye and he turned back. Nothing. Lake Erie looked like ink beneath the dark sky. Had he imagined that glimmer? No, there it was again, barely discernible under the weak reflections of the floodlights. If the clouds hadn't moved in, he never would've noticed it at all.

There, again. Nearer. Just like that shadow floating on the surface, which . . . which—which was gone.

Dread—unexpected and unreasoning but total—coiled in his gut, as cold as he'd thought the water should've been.

The shore waited but too far away, the water too deep to run through. The pier, he had to get to the pier instead, clamber up onto the rocks, and then he could run. Yes, then he could run, but from what? Nothing he understood, and this nebulousness gave the fear teeth, a sharp scrape under his skin, in his bones.

Something brushed his ankle. He barely had time to feel it before the touch tightened. He drew a sharp breath but had no chance to cry out—before disappearing beneath the surface.

From farther away Rosie barked again.

The lake whispered against the shore. The wind hissed in the leaves. The clouds hid the moon. Nothing more broke the stillness of the night.

CHAPTER ONE

At Least Appear Confident

Though it was a handful of minutes past three in the morning, the idea that the bathroom doorknob might turn at any moment made the skin on the back of Sadie Miles's neck prickle. Still, while she waited the two minutes for the pregnancy test to show its result, she didn't lock the door. She'd made that mistake when Sam had first hit her—opening the floodgates of his rage for the first time—and then never again.

It had been easy to ignore the weight settling down around her anytime she thought about marrying Samuel Keller. The wedding wasn't until next September, eleven months away, and though Sadie had never allowed herself to scrutinize the thought, she'd reminded herself more than once that plans sometimes change. Anything could happen. And even if nothing changed, she couldn't imagine life beyond the wedding day anyway—beyond Sam smiling for the guests as he read his wedding vow to Sadie and a new-stepparent vow to Izzy. Her thoughts always turned away from the days and months and years that would follow.

Now her imagination finally kicked in, finally showed her not the night-dark bathroom she sat in nor the white-dress fantasy of the wedding, but her future.

The unborn baby held hostage through the whole pregnancy.

New motherhood again, adjusting to having a toddler and an infant while dancing around Sam's whims.

Sam giving up the charade of caring about Izzy.

Sadie taking the blame for every bump and bruise Sam's baby collected while learning to crawl or walk. Hiding her own bruises.

Sam realizing the baby would be all the hold over Sadie he'd ever need.

Her phone lit up, the two-minute timer on silent. She used the screen's light to look at the test, her heart lurching faster.

Two lines.

"I'm pregnant," Sadie whispered, and she heard the fear in her voice a second before it swelled cold and thick in her chest and tight in her throat.

She sank to her knees in the dark, feeling her way through the bathroom cupboard. Her trembling fingers closed over her tampon box, and she withdrew it quietly. Breath caught in her throat, she tucked the positive pregnancy test underneath the neatly wrapped cylinders and then closed the flap with delicate care. Only after she slid the box back into the cupboard did she examine what she was doing.

Because if she had a child with Sam Keller, plans would never change enough to let them escape.

That word struck her like a blow. Sadie froze on the floor as if afraid the mere thought of it would summon Sam and all his wrath. But he never came, and when she dragged herself back to lie awake in bed that single word lingered and grew in her mind all through that dark, dismal night.

Escape.

For three days, Sadie carefully avoided even glancing at the walk-in closet where they stored the suitcases. For three days, that one word chased itself around her mind while she cleaned the living room, while she braided Izzy's hair, while she shared Sam's bed, while she cooked, while she read her book club's monthly pick, helped Sam with his tie for a formal appearance as Finney-town's mayor, went to the store, checked the mailbox.

On the fourth day, she woke with the knowledge that if she didn't act now she never would. She moved through that morning with electricity buzzing under her skin, her face stiff and cold, every breath thin and strained. But Sam noticed nothing, said nothing, even as she forced a smile and held stone-still while he kissed her cheek and then stepped out into the garage.

Sadie scurried to the front window and didn't breathe as she watched, carefully obscured by the curtains and blinds, while Sam pulled his low-slung purple coupe out of the driveway and onto their quiet street. The thinning shade of trees already losing their leaves slid over his car as he accelerated. He slowed at the stop sign, then turned left.

He drove out of sight.

Sadie's lungs burned. She didn't inhale yet. Counted to ten.

Then she sucked in a shaking gasp and whirled. She didn't look at Izzy's toybox in the living room as she hurried past it to the hallway. They'd have to leave a lot behind. Too much. Right now, her toddler sat buckled into a booster seat, cheerfully crushing blueberries with her thumbs instead of eating them, but confusion and hurt waited in Izzy's future. The thought nearly pushed Sadie's breath right back out of her.

She'd find a way to make it right. She would. She could, if they got out *now*.

Her steps grew faster. Sadie twisted her engagement ring off her finger. As she crossed into the hallway she broke into a run, scrambling for those suitcases.

Sam wouldn't be home from city hall until dinnertime, but Sadie didn't have a second to lose.

Four days and nearly two hundred and fifty miles later, Sadie surveyed the truck stop's public shower stall—ill-lit and dingy in spite of the lingering odor of bleach—and a dizzying swell of pride nearly lifted her off her feet.

She'd gotten them this far.

She shut the door and twisted the dead bolt, then turned to Izzy and warned her, "Don't touch anything in here yet, stinker."

The sudden buzz in her pocket wiped the smile off Sadie's face. A thread of tension pulled her shoulders stiff. Sam? Or maybe only Mr. Drye calling about the interview this afternoon. If not for that possibility, she'd have put her phone on mute and tried to forget all about it. Sadie let go of Izzy's hand and angled herself to hide the worry in her eyes, then checked her phone.

Sam's name lit up the screen. Sadie's stomach twisted and her chest tightened. She turned the phone over and set it face down on the counter next to the door without swiping to ignore the call. Giving him even that much attention would be a mistake.

Sadie pushed her red hair back from her face and ran her fingers through it, snagging on a couple tangles. She closed her eyes and focused on her breathing for a few seconds, settling herself.

When she opened her eyes, Izzy sat tracing the lines between the tiles with her fingers.

"Isabelle Miles," Sadie said with an exasperated sigh. "*What* have I told you about touching the floor in bathrooms?"

"No."

Sadie hesitated. Was *no* the answer, or a refusal to answer? At three years old, Izzy had entered a contrary stage. Maybe if Sadie reacted the right way, she could encourage better behavior today.

"That's right, stinker. No sitting on the floor in bathrooms. Stand up for Mommy, please?"

Izzy jumped to her feet with a smile, and Sadie breathed a sigh of relief. Even with permission, showing up to her interview with a toddler in tow felt risky. Showing up with a toddler set on tantrums and misbehavior would be disastrous.

"Let's get undressed, baby. We need to get all clean before we go meet the hotel man, okay?"

"I'm all clean already!" Izzy protested.

"Well, let's get double clean, okay?" Sadie helped Izzy pile their clothes, along with her own purse and glasses, away from possible splashes or puddles, and opened the shower stall.

Within, the smell of bleach intensified. Sadie wrinkled her nose. Just like when she'd been pregnant with Izzy, her nose had given her the first clue this time as well. Sadie tried to ignore it as she started their shower.

"Are we going home soon?" Izzy's innocent question broke Sadie's train of thought. She'd asked the same thing each day they'd spent at the motel in Columbus, now a three-hour car ride behind them, never mind that Sadie had told her every time that they were going to find a new home as soon as they could.

Sadie rinsed herself off and decided to roll with Izzy's question this time. With a gentle hand she tilted Izzy's head back to shampoo her hair while answering, "Kind of, stinker. We're going to a nice hotel today to see if I can get a job there for a little while, and we'll find somewhere good to stay close to there, okay?"

"Okay, but no more car, Mommy."

Rinsing accomplished, Sadie shut off the water and moved quickly to wrap Izzy in a towel before she had time to fuss about the cold.

"A little more car," she said. For a three-year-old, Izzy had been an angel during the two hours they'd spent driving from Finneytown, Ohio, to Columbus, and again during the longer drive north from Columbus all the way up to the run-down lakeside town of Walton. "If you're good, after Mommy's interview we can go see the big lake, okay?"

"Opay." Izzy's tone held the warning tremble of an incoming tantrum.

Something close to panic fluttered in Sadie's chest, but she kept it out of her voice as she toweled herself off. "Mommy needs you to be good today, okay? I need the job at the nice hotel or—" She paused, sucking in a breath and holding it for an instant before letting it out again. The money dwindled day by day, and Sadie had watched enough special reports and true crime shows to be wary of withdrawing more or using her credit card. Burdens like that didn't belong on Izzy's little shoulders, though. She knelt next to her daughter and unwound the smaller towel enough to help her dry off. "I need the job so I can take better care of us. That means I need the people I'm going to talk to today to like me. Can you be a good girl for Mommy, to show them how nice we are? Will you help me?"

After a moment, Izzy's impending pout turned into a bright grin. "Opay!"

Some of Sadie's nerves eased, but not all. She knew better than to trust the fickle moods of a toddler. Especially a toddler in the middle of a total life upheaval. Sadie had no choice, though. So she tried to get a handle on her anxiety as she helped her daughter get dressed in a clean unicorn-patterned outfit before pulling on a cream turtleneck sweater dress and dark purple leggings. She could have showered and bathed Izzy at the motel, could have dressed herself and her daughter in their nicer clothes before they got in the car, but she didn't want to risk spoiling or wrinkling them with the long drive—these presentable outfits represented the only clothes from what she'd haphazardly thrown into her suitcase that might pass for interview-worthy.

Another worry: their clothing. Most of Izzy's winter clothes wouldn't fit her this year. And though Sadie's pregnancy wasn't showing yet, in only a few short months she'd need at least a few new outfits. Sadie added that concern onto every other burden and fear slowing her steps and speeding her heartbeat and then shoved them all as deep down as she could manage. She and Izzy emerged from the shower room, clean and put together and ready to at least appear confident.

Until she buckled Izzy into her car seat, slid behind the wheel, and started the car. She watched the needle on the fuel gauge rise by the tiniest fraction and let out a muttered curse as it stopped to hover just on the line over E. They barely had enough gas to reach their destination.

"I better get this job," she sighed. If worse came to worst, she didn't want to find herself stranded at L'Arpin Hotel.

CHAPTER TWO

Welcome to L'Arpin Hotel

An angry shout rang through L'Arpin Hotel's lobby, the first thing Sadie heard as she pushed the double doors open and stepped inside. It made her heart race, her mouth dry. Izzy's little grasp tightened on Sadie's fingers, and Sadie's chest ached.

"... damage to my facilities! I know your hotel is behind it. If you don't put a stop to it, I will!"

Sadie resisted the instinctive impulse to lower her eyes, to shift her weight to her back foot and make herself look smaller.

The hotel had a small lobby, so close as to almost be cramped. The desk stood opposite the entrance, a dark green rug stretching along the space between. Two hallways flanked the desk, both dimly lit. A small, glittery light fixture hung from the center of the ceiling, but most of the light in the room came from a pair of windows to either side of the door. A brick fireplace took up the right wall, filled with unlit jack-o'-lanterns in place of logs. The polished wooden mantel boasted historical photos and framed pages from antiquated newspapers. The wall to the left sported an elevator next to a few armchairs. In one of those sat a wisp of a little old lady, pretending to knit while shamelessly watching the drama unfolding at the front desk. She caught Sadie glancing at her and offered a conspiratorial wink before a quieter murmur from the front of the lobby drew both women's attention back to the confrontation.

Two men stood across from each other at the counter. The man behind it had tidily brushed brown hair shot through with gray, and faint frown lines drawn onto his otherwise mild face. He wore a jacket with L'ARPIN HOTEL embroidered on it in gold cursive lettering, and he squinted over the top of his glasses at a man with his back to the lobby. The second man, dressed in worn jeans and a gray shirt with a yellow safety vest over top, let out a harsh, angry laugh. He clenched his fists on the countertop, his body rigid.

"I don't make threats, Drye, I take action."

The old woman gave a tiny snort. Izzy shifted and shuffled her feet, moving in slow increments until she stood behind her mother's legs, and Sadie focused on keeping a calm grip on her daughter.

"What you can take is yourself—out of my hotel, Bill." The man behind the counter, presumably Mr. Drye, who would be interviewing Sadie momentarily, spoke with quiet authority. Sadie hoped his composure meant the altercation wouldn't leave him in a sour enough mood to bias him against her.

Bill snarled, then spun on his heel. Dark brows and a thick beard lent intensity to his scowl as he stormed across the lobby.

Sadie stepped quickly to her right, pulling Izzy along behind her, but Bill's shoulder collided with hers. He didn't spare a glance for her as he snapped, "Watch it, lady."

"You hit my mommy!" Izzy shouted, full of all the indignation of a three-year-old witnessing an adult breaking the rules.

At the sound of her strident little voice, Bill's step slowed for just an instant and he looked down at her. Sadie wouldn't have believed his brow could furrow farther, but it did. She frowned at him over her glasses. If he shouted at her little girl, Sadie would have words for him. The kind that would cost her the job, almost certainly, but the thought of somebody treating Izzy poorly ever again weighed heavier than her sparse wallet.

Instead of shouting, Bill snorted but grumbled a snide, "Pardon."

Then he shoved the doors open and exited, leaving the lobby feeling bigger and echoingly empty. Sadie watched him through the windows for another moment, her shoulders tight. Bill crossed the parking lot and into the grass at its edge, marching across toward a power plant that marred the view of Lake Erie just a few meters beyond.

Sadie took a slow breath to try to dispel her lingering, queasy tension. Then she turned and knelt in front of Izzy. "Can I hug you, stinker?" Izzy nodded, and Sadie gave her a tight squeeze. When she leaned away she said, "Listen, Izzy. I love that you wanted to help. You're a brave girl. But when grown-ups are breaking rules, you have to let other grown-ups handle it, okay?"

Izzy frowned. "He hit you."

"He did, but that is for Mommy and other grown-ups to worry about, okay? You don't have to worry about grown-up problems until you're big, okay?"

"I *am* big!"

Sadie bit her tongue for a single second, stifling a little spike of irritation. She smiled. This conversation needed to end now; she had an interview to try not to bomb. "I know you're a big girl. I meant even bigger. Be good for Mommy now, stinker?"

"I will."

"Great, good job, thank you."

Sadie stood and took Izzy's hand again, leading her to the desk.

"Good afternoon, and welcome to L'Arpin Hotel," Mr. Drye said, flashing a smile. From here, the wall behind him showed itself to be taken up by little cubbies housing old-fashioned silver keys. "I'm very sorry you had to see that. How can I help you today?"

"I'm here to help you, actually," Sadie answered, holding out her hand. "I'm Sadie Miles. I'm here for the housekeeping interview with Mr. Drye?"

"Ah, very good. I'm Henry Drye."

He shook Sadie's hand, his palm a little damp but his grip firm.

He did not, Sadie noticed, invite her to call him Henry instead of Mr. Drye.

The bell above the door behind Sadie rang, and she tried not to flinch. She half expected to hear Bill returning to cause another scene. She told herself she absolutely didn't think it might be Sam, but of course a part of her thought just that, no matter how impossible it was. Her breathing all but stopped until she glanced over her shoulder to see a tall young woman with ice-white hair lugging a baby-blue suitcase into the hotel.

"I'm sorry to ask you to wait," Mr. Drye said, drawing Sadie's attention again. "But I should check my guest in. Please, feel free." He waved toward the armchairs and end tables. With a hint of humor in his voice, he said, "I'm sure Ms. Harper will be happy to keep you company."

Sadie settled into a chair, pulled Izzy onto her lap, and immediately fell prey to a jitter of pre-interview anxiety. She swallowed hard and tried to find something else to think about.

Some*thing* else leaned over to introduce herself at that moment. "Hello, there, young lady," the old woman said, speaking to Izzy rather than to Sadie.

It used to surprise Sadie how often adults would talk to a baby without greeting her mother first, much less checking to see if such attention was welcome. These days it hardly bothered her, and not at all in this specific instance. This woman wore a kind smile, laugh lines wreathed her face, and her voice carried none of the saccharine condescension Sadie hated hearing even when it was directed at a toddler.

"Who might you be?" the old woman asked.

"My name is Izzy, and this is my mommy!"

"Sadie," she introduced herself quickly before the woman could jokingly call Sadie *Mommy* as well. Sadie harbored intense dislike for anyone who thought that was cute or funny, and she didn't want to give this woman a chance to put herself in Sadie's bad graces. "Sadie Miles. Mr. Drye said you're Ms. Harper?"

"Ms. Harper!" Her laughter startled Sadie, louder and richer than she'd expected from someone so wizened. "Some people are born with a silver spoon in their mouth, but I'll eat my slippers if poor Henry there wasn't born with a stick up his bum." Sadie flushed and resisted the urge to turn around and make sure her hopefully future employer hadn't heard the insult. "Please don't call me Ms. Harper. I'm Gertie. It's very nice to meet you, Izzy and Sadie. I couldn't help but overhear you telling Henry you're here for an interview?"

Sadie would eat *her* slippers if this old lady didn't overhear as much of the goings-on around her as possible, at all times. Still, she smiled. Gertie's gaze held a certain earnest sweetness despite her eavesdropping.

"That's right, a housekeeping position."

"And are you looking for a job, too, little lady?"

"I'm not *lady*, I'm *Izzy*."

"Izzy's very particular about her name," Sadie said with an indulgent smile.

"No, I'm not! I'm just Izzy!"

"That's what I meant, stinker. Gertie asked if you're getting a job like a grown-up."

Izzy laughed and shook her head. "I'm a kid."

"Well, I hope I'll be seeing more of you around the hotel," Gertie said. She sat up straighter, addressing Sadie now. "I live here in L'Arpin, you know. Henry calls me a *long-term guest* but that lacks a certain amount of romance, don't you think? Although I'm as much a fixture of the hotel as that fireplace there, and there's nothing romantic about *that*, either."

Sadie eyed the oversized fireplace, the clean bricks and the ornate fire screen and the history lined up along the gleaming mantel. "It looks plenty romantic to me, Gertie."

The old woman chuckled and patted Sadie's knee. "I like you, Sadie. Oh!" She glanced around, gaze sharpening as if she'd just thought of something. "But surely you're not here alone? Is your daddy around, Miss Izzy?" Two and a half years had dulled the pang in Sadie's chest when anyone asked that question, but not erased it. "Who's going to keep you company while your mommy has her interview?"

"My daddy's gone," Izzy said in the matter-of-fact voice of a child who couldn't remember her father. Sadie's throat tightened. How could one snowy intersection have relegated August to three emotionless words? Then Izzy added, "And my stepdad is still at our house."

Sadie's grief curdled to nervous discomfort, and she leaned down to her daughter to whisper, "No, honey, remember? He's not going to be your stepdad anymore. He's at *his* house, it wasn't really ours. And if you need to talk some more about that later, we can, okay?"

Mimicking her mother's whisper, Izzy said, "Opay, Mommy."

When Sadie straightened and glanced at Gertie, the older woman had gone back to her knitting, pretending not to notice the private exchange. Gratitude swept Sadie in a surprisingly powerful rush.

"Izzy's going to watch the interview. Not many three-year-olds get to see how a grown-up gets a job." No amount of effort or false cheer could actually make that sound fun, but damn if Sadie wasn't going to try.

"Nonsense," Gertie said, looking up again as if the mere idea startled her. "It's hard on a little one, you won't be able to pay any attention to her during the interview. What will she do while you're busy?" Before Sadie could answer that she'd brought a coloring book and some crayons, Gertie turned and asked, "Izzy, would you like to keep me company while your mommy talks to Henry?"

"Oh. Thank you, but that's not—"

"Yes!" Izzy interrupted, clapping.

"I'm sorry about the delay, Miss Miles." Mr. Drye reappeared at the worst moment, just as Sadie drew a sharp breath to make an indignant response. She let the breath out in a rush but then hesitated, the halted momentum leaving her temporarily at a loss for words.

"And you should be sorry, Henry, making these poor girls wait on you."

"It's okay, really," Sadie interjected with a smile. She stood and smoothed her sweater dress, then reached for Izzy's hand. Hoping to brush off the kind but misplaced offer, she casually said, "Tell the nice lady bye-bye, Izzy."

It didn't work.

"You're not going to make this young lady go to your interview with her *daughter*, are you, Henry?"

"I am going to *let* her bring her child, Ms. Harper; she is new to the area and hasn't found a sitter yet—"

"Well, she has now." Gertie turned to Sadie. "You've found a sitter now, don't you worry. I'll watch Izzy."

"I don't want to trouble you," Sadie said, keeping her smile carefully in place, trying to sound grateful even as she demurred.

She reached again for Izzy's hand, but her daughter slipped her grasp and grabbed the arm of Gertie's chair. "I want keep me company!" Izzy shouted, repeating Gertie's words of only a few moments before.

"Miss Miles," Mr. Drye murmured, leaning a little nearer to Sadie. "Ms. Harper is a permanent guest at L'Arpin, and I personally vouch for her—she's a sound, responsible woman."

Sadie hesitated. Employers wanted to hire flexible people, right? But this wasn't an issue with schedule availability or on-the-job training, it was her daughter.

Her daughter, who might outgrow her winter clothes before winter even got here, who ought to eat something other than ramen with frozen peas thrown in. Sadie needed this job, and Mr. Drye vouched for Gertie. The hotel manager would hardly risk the reputation of his establishment for the sake of one interview. Sadie swallowed and tried to will the rising tide of unease away.

"You be a good girl for Ms. Harper, okay, stinker?" Sadie said, crouching down to bring herself to eye level with her daughter.

"Opay, Mommy."

Sadie stayed on the floor for one extra moment, not sure what else to say but certain there was something. But Mr. Drye was waiting for her, and the quicker Sadie finished the interview, the quicker she could collect her daughter and quell her nerves.

When she stood, she reached into her purse and found an empty gum wrapper and a pen nearly out of ink. She wrote her number down and handed it to Gertie. "If there's an emergency, call me and let it ring once, then hang up. I'll come right out." Turning to Mr. Drye, Sadie added, "I won't answer any call that lasts longer than one ring, but I will need to have my phone on during the interview. I'm sure under the circumstances, that won't be a problem?"

Mr. Drye's gaze flicked to Gertie, as if assessing her competence as a babysitter, or possibly reminding himself that Sadie had only just met this woman and had a right to be cautious.

"Shoo, shoo," Gertie said.

"That'll be fine," Mr. Drye answered Sadie at nearly the same moment. He led her to the front desk and then behind it, through a door to the left of all the keys.

The small office featured a battered chair pulled up to a huge antique desk whose splendor hid beneath three piles of papers and binders, coffee rings marring the otherwise polished surface. Two smaller, uglier chairs faced the desk from the other side, and Mr. Drye waved Sadie toward one as he went around to his seat.

"So," Mr. Drye began, reaching for one of the piles and shuffling the papers until he found a printed sheet. He squinted at it for a moment and then looked up at her. "Sadie Miles."

"It's nice to meet you, sir," Sadie said, one of her practiced lines that didn't quite fit now that she'd met him already in the lobby.

"Likewise. Tell me a little about yourself, Sadie."

If this were a social icebreaker she'd talk about Izzy, maybe mention losing August. She wouldn't talk about Sam, and she wouldn't reveal her pregnancy so soon. But emphasizing her single-parent status didn't seem like the best move—Mr. Drye didn't exactly give off the vibe of a man overly motivated by sympathy. Bland basics, then.

"I went to school for early childhood education, and I used to teach. I'm originally from Wisconsin, but I moved to Cincinnati when I was twenty and I've been living in Ohio for just over a decade."

"Hmm. What brought you so far from home?" Mr. Drye's mild question hid a sharpness that didn't entirely surprise Sadie. Why hire someone, after all, who had no local ties and might not stick around?

An understandable question didn't necessarily mean an easy one to answer. She'd have to let the barrier of impersonality slip a bit. Discomfort shifted in her chest as she took a breath. "My late husband. He got a job in Cincinnati right after we were engaged. My family is all still in Wisconsin, but we're not very close." What an understatement; her parents had been furious when Sadie told them about the move, cool and unfriendly at the wedding, too nosy during her pregnancy with Izzy, and the way they'd acted after August died . . . But this wasn't the time or place for that. Sadie made herself smile and said, "Anyway, I like it better here. I grew up close to the Minnesota border, and I've never seen any water as big as Lake Erie before. I'm really looking forward to summer."

Mr. Drye smiled at the mention of the lake, an expression so genuine that by contrast alone Sadie realized how forced he'd been before. The smile widened a fraction at the word *summer*. Then Sadie stopped talking and Mr. Drye looked back at his paper. His face stiffened once more into forced friendliness.

"Very nice. Summer is fine on the lake. You have no previous housekeeping experience. You said you used to teach?"

"That's right."

"What qualities do you have that would make you a good house-keeper in spite of your lack of experience?"

"I'm a fast learner, and I'm willing to listen and find answers if I need them. Early childhood education requires fastidious organization and, if you want to avoid getting sick all year, impeccable hygiene. I'm very accustomed to keeping track of my supplies and to holding to high cleaning standards." The answer sounded formal, well rehearsed, but Sadie thought it was a good one nonetheless.

Mr. Drye asked a few more basic questions that felt to Sadie like rephrases of the first three, and she gave answers as varied and thoughtful as she could. Yes, she'd looked up OSHA regulations. Of course she would be happy to learn how to complete tasks outside of her position (especially, she thought but didn't add, if extra responsibilities came with extra pay).

"Tell me what you would do in a situation where a client is unsatisfied with your work."

The simple prompt sent a spike of adrenaline buzzing through Sadie.

(*"If you're not lazy, then you're stupid. Which is it? Come here. Come here and look at this. Does it look clean? Now answer me. Are you lazy or are you fucking stupid?"*)

She smiled through it; such moments of panic gave away too much, and she'd grown good at hiding them. No client would be unsatisfied with her work. Sadie knew how to make sure of that.

Mr. Drye wouldn't like that answer, though, so instead she said, "I would apologize and try to fix it myself. If the problem remained in spite of my best efforts, I would bring it to the attention of a supervisor and follow their lead. Then I would learn from the mistake and take care not to repeat it."

Mr. Drye nodded and asked a few more standard questions, but Sadie could tell the interview neared its end. After only a handful of minutes passed, the hotel manager smiled and stood. He leaned over his massive desk to offer Sadie his hand to shake again.

"Welcome to L'Arpin Hotel, Miss Miles."

A flood of relief nearly swept Sadie off her feet.

CHAPTER THREE

Disturbance

"Well?" Gertie asked, her bright eyes moving from Sadie to Mr. Drye, a warm smile seaming her wrinkled face.

"We're very pleased to welcome Miss Miles onto our staff, Ms. Harper," Mr. Drye answered. Then, as Sadie had hoped he would, he made what she was sure was a show of solicitation in front of the long-standing guest, turning to his new employee with a kindly expression. Sadie picked Izzy up as Mr. Drye spoke. "Do you have any questions, Miss Miles? Is there anything I can help you with right now?"

"Actually, yes," Sadie said, trying not to look at the little old woman and give away the manipulation she hoped to pull off. "Gertie mentioned that she's a permanent guest here, and I was hoping you might have another room tucked away somewhere that Izzy and I could use for a few days?"

She didn't imagine the way Mr. Drye's eyes darted from Sadie's face to Gertie and back.

Before he could answer, she rushed on. "I'll be able to focus on learning the ropes more quickly here if I'm not looking for an apartment at the same time as I'm getting used to my duties."

"I dunno, letting any old riffraff live in the illustrious L'Arpin seems a bit shady if you ask me."

If the words, spoken from over her shoulder, had not been delivered with such obvious humor, Sadie would have twisted herself up over them.

Mr. Drye, something between exasperation and amusement crossing his features, gestured behind Sadie. "Miss Miles, this is L'Arpin's full-time, on-site chef, Jordan Mishra."

Sadie turned, putting a polite smile on as she shifted Izzy's weight to her left hip in preparation to free her right hand to shake. Behind her stood a tall man with neatly combed black hair and a thick but tidy beard that didn't hide his good-natured grin, the white of a chef's coat standing in contrast to his warm brown skin.

Mr. Drye went on. "Mr. Mishra—"

"Call me Joe," the chef said to Sadie.

"—this is Miss Sadie Miles, a new addition to our housekeeping staff. Mr. Mishra lives on-site as well, so I suppose there's precedent . . ."

"Well of course, Henry," Gertie interrupted. "Look at her sweet child, how can you even think of saying no?" The old woman smiled at Izzy and added in an overly cutesy voice, "Oh, I would just love to see some little ones playing around here."

"Yeah, of course, Henry," Joe put in, not quite talking over Gertie as he gently mimicked her.

"Certainly," Mr. Drye said, and how much of his acquiescence came from Gertie's presence, Sadie didn't know or need to know. "Certainly, that sounds reasonable to me."

"Hah!" Joe exclaimed. "Now you owe me."

"Excuse me?" Sadie asked, although a hint of a laugh rippled in her voice.

"Yeah, you wouldn't have got this old grump to agree if I hadn't pitched in. Right?"

Before Sadie could respond, Mr. Drye gave Joe a pointed

glance. "Don't you have preparations to make for dinner, Mr. Mishra?"

Joe gave Mr. Drye a cheery salute, winked at Sadie, and sauntered off.

With an air of distraction now that the business was settled, Mr. Drye showed Sadie to their new fourth-floor room and left them to their own devices. The room had one bed, a fold-out couch, a dresser, and a desk with two chairs squeezed into it, and no trace of grime or dust and it kept out the deepening late autumn chill. A minifridge took up half the space under the desk, a microwave and coffee maker half the space atop it. The pale blue wallpaper had no bubbles or peels, the complimentary darker blue upholstery and bedding bore no suspicious stains. Nothing fancy, but nice.

The day passed quickly, and only a few hours later Sadie stood tucking Izzy's blanket more tightly around her warm little body, fingertips lingering for a moment to feel the slow rise and fall of her daughter's back.

She straightened and eyed the pull-out sofa bed, the removed rectangular cushions wedged between the arms of the sofa and the hinged mattress frame to form a bit of a guard against falling. Izzy hadn't been out of her crib and into her toddler bed for very long before they'd left Sam's house, but this should be okay.

More than okay. A safe place to stay—for free!—for at least a week was more than just okay. She had known that to leave Sam would be to drag Izzy through homelessness and disaster and poverty. She had known it because Sam made sure she knew it.

And yet they'd landed on their feet in a good place, and Sadie had done that by herself.

A knock at the door doused Sadie's warm reverie. She cringed, gaze snapping back to Izzy. For a toddler, Iz took it easy at bedtime, but waking suddenly in the night always spelled disaster.

Sadie scrambled across the small space to peer through the peephole. She yanked the door open fast, just before Gertie could knock again.

"Room service," Gertie said, her voice a touch too loud. In one wrinkled, slender hand she held a bottle of wine, and in the other two plastic cups.

Sadie smiled but put a finger to her lips then jerked her thumb over her shoulder. Gertie looked past her at the little pull-out bed, widened her eyes, and pulled an excessively apologetic face. Sadie slipped out into the hallway with Gertie, closing the door behind her.

"I thought a little housewarming gift would be nice," Gertie whispered, shaking the bottle, "since we're neighbors now."

"Neighbors?"

Gertie pointed at the door next to Sadie's and said, "I asked Henry to put your room next to mine. The top floor is the only place to stay if you're here longer than a night or two. No guests above you stomping around."

"Well, thanks for thinking of us," she said, reaching behind her for the doorknob. The long, green-carpeted hallway stretched to either side, lit by fixtures set at intervals just a little too far apart. Sadie and Gertie stood in one of the pools of resulting shadow. The dim quiet combined with the long day, bowing Sadie's shoulders under a weight of fatigue.

"Oh, don't go yet," Gertie protested, a tiny current of desperation running under the cheery surface of her voice. "Here, here." She thrust the plastic cups into Sadie's hands. When Sadie's gram was about the age Gertie looked, she would've needed help opening the bottle, but Gertie managed just fine and poured a generous amount into each cup.

"I should really—" Sadie gestured to her door with her elbow, her hands busy with the cups.

"Nonsense. We'll be quick."

Sadie forced a smile. The pregnancy was too new even to herself; she hadn't really finished processing it, couldn't possibly yet share it with anyone. Especially some stranger. But she didn't want to seem rude. How hard could the hotel's only permanent guest make Sadie's life if she took a dislike to her? Not that the nice little old lady seemed the type, but then everybody had the capacity for surprises.

She lifted the cup to her lips and pretended to take a small sip.

Silence stretched between the two women. From somewhere near the far end of the hall came a *pat . . . pat . . . pat.* Sadie glanced in that direction but could find no source. Water falling drop by drop on the carpet, perhaps. A leaky pipe, maybe. Maintenance must be a monster of a job in a hotel built in the 1800s.

When Sadie thought enough time had passed, she pretended to sip again, then turned back to find Gertie holding her own cup, wine half-gone, staring right at her. The awkwardness sharpened dramatically. Sadie had to say something.

"I bet you know all the hotel's ins and outs, hm?"

Gertie gave a soft laugh. "Hotels aren't like houses," she said at the end of her quiet mirth. "They're like people. You *can't* know all their ins and outs, but you can get used to 'em pretty well, I guess. Oh! Before I forget to tell you, I talked to Jordan—our chef, you met him today. Remember?"

"Of course," Sadie said.

"I told him to send dinner up to you a few times a week."

"Oh, I can't. I mean thank you, but—"

Gertie held up a hand. "Don't you worry about it for a moment."

After only another moment of hesitation, Sadie nodded. She would have a private word with Jordan—wait, he'd asked Sadie to call him Joe, hadn't he?—with Joe, then, and tell him this wasn't necessary.

Before she could think of what to say next, her phone buzzed in her pocket. Sadie pressed her lips together and tried not to stiffen, her heart lurching.

Oblivious to Sadie's discomfort, Gertie asked, "What will you do with Izzy while you're working?"

The water dripping onto the carpet suddenly sounded exactly like footsteps. Sadie glanced down the narrow, ill-lit hall, half expecting Mr. Drye to materialize in time to hear her less than ideal answer.

Still empty.

"Mr. Drye gave me a midmorning shift. Tomorrow I'm going to get some things to babyproof the room and a walkie-talkie. I'll leave the connection open so I can work while Izzy plays."

"What? All *day*?"

"I'll come up and check on her through the day, and I can get her down for a nap at the end of my lunch break and just use the walkie-talkie until she wakes up. It's not great, but it'll work. Just until I can afford a daycare."

Not great. That was a hell of an understatement. It was a terrible idea, but Sadie was up against the wall.

Her phone buzzed again, a quick one-two and done. A voice-mail. Sadie fought the urge to let her muscles wind up all tight and hunch her shoulders.

"Nonsense," Gertie said, shaking her head, pulling some of Sadie's attention back to her. "If Henry finds you doing that, he'll turn you out on the street! Do you want me to—"

"Thank you," Sadie said, cutting off whatever offer Gertie wanted to make. "That's very kind, but we're fine."

The old woman frowned. "That just won't work. Not at all. You knock on my door at the start of your shift, I'll keep an eye on little Izzy until her nap. I won't take no for an answer. *Just* until you can afford a daycare, now."

"I—" Sadie hesitated. She rebelled against putting herself in debt to anyone, relying on the goodwill of a stranger, and trusting Izzy's safety to a woman she barely knew. But could all that really be worse than leaving Izzy alone for most of every working day? Could it be worse than losing the job and winding up on the street with her child?

No.

It twisted her guts to do it, but Sadie made herself accept. "That would be very kind, Gertie. I can't thank you enough. Just until I can afford a daycare, I promise."

"Wonderful! If you'll excuse me, Sadie, I really ought to go to bed. It's getting a bit late for me." Her tone implied that this little encounter had somehow been Sadie's doing. Before Sadie could respond, Gertie pushed the half-full bottle of wine into Sadie's hands, glancing down into her cup as she did so. "Why, you've hardly drank anything."

"Oh, ah . . ." Sadie groped for some excuse, tilting the cup toward herself as if she could obscure the view of its undrunk contents after the fact. "Yeah, no, I just don't want to have a hangover."

"One cup of wine never gave anybody a hangover," Gertie said. "Come now, we're being neighborly, dear. We're celebrating!"

She made a self-deprecating face, half smiling, and shrugged a little. "Maybe it's silly," she said in a light voice, "but I'd rather play it safe."

"Well." Gertie hesitated, eyeing the wine bottle she'd forced into Sadie's left hand and then the full cup in her right. She turned her gaze up to Sadie's eyes, gave her a long and searching look, then tutted but smiled and said, "You keep that, then. You can have it some other night." She patted the bottle and Sadie's hand, then turned toward her door. Before she'd turned all the way, Gertie paused again and gave Sadie one more penetrating look before adding a cheerful, "Have a lovely evening, now."

Sadie watched Gertie make her way to the room next door. The dripping water, still unseen, *patted* all the louder for a moment, and the back of Sadie's neck crawled.

(*"Oh, Jesus Christ! Keep nagging me and see what happens."*

"I wasn't nagging, I just—"

"Ask me one more time if I need a plumber's phone number, Sadie. One more time."

"I thought—"

"Bullshit. I know just what you thought. *I said I'll fix the faucet. I'll fix it. When I'm good and ready to."*)

Sadie turned to look down the other end of the hallway, suddenly sure she'd find someone watching her. The alcoves lining the hall, each holding a pair of doors side by side, gathered shadows even near the brighter spots. If one of those doors eased open only a crack, would she ever realize? The thought made her shiver. Down the center of the floor, the green carpet had worn thin, scuffed to a dingy gray.

The few areas of poor illumination revealed here and there faint yellow streaks running down the walls, old stains. In places, the pale wallpaper pulled away from the walls. But Sadie spied no dark patches of fresh damp on the walls or floor. Wherever the slow-dripping leak came from, whatever wet spot it must be making on the carpet, had to be in one of those shadows.

And she remained utterly alone in the corridor. No one. Nothing.

The emptiness didn't make her feel safer.

The strange new environment and the discomfort of knowing what kind of voicemail awaited her had come together to make her feel spied upon. Nothing more. She took a deep breath and for the first time noticed a faint, mildewy-wet smell to go along with the soft, persistent drip.

Old building, old pipes, that was all.

And in the long run, Sadie thought as she slipped back into her room, not her problem. She'd never tell Mr. Drye, but as soon as applications for the next school year started opening up again, she'd get a new teaching position, then take Izzy and leave this hotel behind. Unlike Gertie, Sadie knew that a place like L'Arpin should only be a stepping stone.

She went into the bathroom to pour the rest of the wine down the drain, covering her nose as the scent unexpectedly triggered a wave of morning sickness. She put the bottle and the cup in the trash. She took her phone out of her pocket, set it face down on the counter, and put her hands on either side of it.

Ignoring Sam's calls hadn't stopped him from calling. She ought to delete the voicemail without listening to it. She flipped her phone over and turned on the screen, then stared at the voicemail icon at the top for long enough that the phone went dark again.

This time when Sadie picked up her phone, she unlocked it and tapped that icon. She could delete it the moment it started playing, could never listen to a word of it.

"Sadie, it's me. I mean, I guess you know it's me." He sounded so sad. Sadie'd thought he would rage, full of indignation and threats. Her eyes burned and she swallowed hard. She should have expected this. "And I guess I know why you left the way you did. I was . . . I was so mad at first, but I thought about it. I get it now." The worst thing about Sam was that he wasn't always dangerous—he knew how to flatter, he could make anyone laugh, and remorse always dragged him down into a miserable part of himself after he hurt someone. Hurt Sadie. "I want you to know how sorry I am—" His voice thickened and then choked off. Not a trick, not an act—this was *Sam*, the sweet, sincere part of him that initially drew her in and lured her into making the first excuses. It just wasn't *enough* of him, and Sadie would never again be dazzled by the Sam she'd first thought and then wished he was. "I hate myself, Sadie. I miss you and Izzy so much it hurts. Please call me."

The message ended. Sadie deleted it before she could make the mistake of listening to it a second time, and slid her phone into her pocket with great delicacy, as if it might break. Or as if she might. Her fingers trembled and she pushed them against her lips. Were her hands cold or was her face hot?

"I'm not going to cry," she whispered to herself, then took a breath that shuddered with the very tears she denied. "I'm not going to cry. Not over Sam Keller. Not ever again." She stood in the bathroom for another handful of minutes, and if a few tears did burn her eyes and slip down her cheeks, she could wipe them away quick enough to pretend they'd never been there.

When Sadie left the bathroom, her surface was as calm as still water. The inside of her trembled, though, disturbed. Turning, she leaned her back against the door to the hallway so her gaze could wander over the little room she'd secured for herself and Izzy. She focused on her body, on loosening her tight shoulders and un-clenching her jaw and shaking out her crossed arms. She'd go to bed soon, but for this moment she wanted to make herself find some peace in the quiet, the relative solitude.

The muted tap of water dripping onto carpet intruded into the thoughtless drift of Sadie's mind. She frowned. A pipe with a bit of a leak shouldn't be audible through her door. The sound certainly hadn't been there a moment ago. It grew in both volume and fre-quency, less a *pat* and more a *patter*.

Could someone be sneaking around out there? Her heart lurched so hard she twitched. Sam. Prowling up and down the hall, check-ing room numbers. Trying to be quiet, careful not to disturb the guests. Careful not to look angry.

Sadie had made sure to use for references only old friends who hadn't yet met Sam, friends from Wisconsin who said things like "let's plan a visit" every half a year or so and never did. Nobody who'd tell Sam where she was if Mr. Drye actually called her ref-erences. But what if he'd done a background check and reached out to Sam himself? What if she'd miscalculated and one of those friends had sent Sam a message? What if—?

Breath shaking, scalp tightening, Sadie turned and pressed her eye to the peephole. The fish-eye view let her see fairly far up and down the worn-out corridor.

Still empty.

The dripping water didn't cease, though, and Sadie's heart raced to match its patter.

A soft noise from behind her made Sadie's guts turn to water. She hunched her shoulders and spun, her hands to her mouth, arms tucked tight. Wild-eyed, Sadie's gaze locked onto Izzy—still asleep—before scanning the rest of the room in fast, darting glances that always came back to rest on her daughter. Just as Sa-die straightened, taking a shaky breath, the noise came again.

This time, Sadie recognized the sound. A soft splash, almost furtive, beyond her window and muffled by the glass.

Adrenaline buzzed under her skin, making her cautious as she crossed the room to the window. She stood far to the side and pushed the curtain ever so slightly. Peering out, she found the source of the sound.

The woman she'd seen checking in earlier that day had opted for a nighttime swim in the hotel's small pool. Why would anyone want to swim in October? Why little laps down there, in water cloudy from poor maintenance or some kind of chemical imbalance, when the lake stretched to the horizon mere yards away from L'Arpin?

The white-haired young lady broke the surface with another splash, and Sadie's uncertainty burned away in an instant. The woman in the water wore street clothes, no swimsuit. Her arms flailed, uncoordinated. Her mouth opened as if to gasp or maybe call out, but she sank again.

Electrified, Sadie leaped away from the window and bolted across the tiny room. She shut the door behind her, heedless now of waking Izzy, and raced down the hall.

She skidded to a stop in front of the single antiquated elevator and jammed the button. Stairs might be faster, but she couldn't waste time finding them. The doors slid open and she all but fell inside. She mashed the starred lobby button.

Enclosed alone in the elevator, Sadie finally remembered her phone. Before she could pull it out and start dialing, the doors opened on the first floor and she burst out. Calling for help could wait. She had to get the woman out of the water first. Where was the pool from the lobby? Sadie spun in a fast circle, breathing hard, wide eyes scanning the empty space. A small placard on the wall pointed to another dark hallway and Sadie ran again, panic flooding her. The hall ended in a door that Sadie threw open, barreling out into the night.

The small in-ground pool lay five or so feet before her, the water glowing from lights set into the sides beneath the surface. The very smooth surface. What few ripples danced there came from the wind off the lake and nothing else. From here the pool seemed less cloudy—not crystal clear, but no visibility problem. Sadie scanned the bottom.

Totally empty.

Sadie bent over, hands on her knees, trying to catch her breath as her mind spun. Across from her and to her right, at the far corner of the pool, water darkened the pale concrete. The damp trail led toward the gate separating the courtyard from the parking lot.

Had the young woman dragged herself from the water? Had someone helped her? Why would she go out through that gate? Sadie stood, her breathing controlled but her hands trembling. She didn't know anything about near drowning. Could that girl be so disoriented that she'd wander off?

Sadie circled the pool, lingering unease prompting her to give it plenty of space, and peered through the bars of the gate. The wet trail didn't continue over the parking lot's blacktop. Sadie pulled, but the gate rattled rather than opening. Locked.

Puzzlement grew in place of waning panic. Sadie turned on her heel and hurried back the way she'd come, no longer at a frantic run. As she crossed the threshold back into the hotel a shudder crawled over her, the back of her neck tingling.

Someone was watching her.

She jerked around again, looking back out over the courtyard.

Still quiet.

Still empty.

Taking a shaky breath, Sadie went inside and let the door close behind her with a bang. She paused at the end of the short hallway, the soft sound of a page turning drawing her eye to the front desk. Hadn't the lobby been empty before? Mr. Drye sat behind the desk, a single lamp with a green shade casting warm light onto a book in his hand but sickly shadows over the rest of the small, key-filled alcove behind him.

"Mr. Drye?" Sadie said, her voice ragged with the aftereffects of her fright.

He looked up, mild concern in his eyes. "Miss Miles? Is there a problem?"

"The girl—the young woman, I mean—who checked in today before my interview?"

"What about her? Has something happened?"

"Did she come through here recently? Out to the pool?"

"No. Why would anyone go to the pool in October? Sadie"—the sudden switch to her first name seemed condescending, but Sadie bit her tongue—"are you well?"

"Did someone go lock the gate to the pool recently?"

"No one has been in the lobby or the pool area all evening. Why do you ask?"

"I thought I saw—I *did* see someone in the pool. Fully dressed and struggling."

Finally, alarm crossed Mr. Drye's face. He stood and left the desk, bustling past Sadie. After a moment's hesitation, she followed him.

The cool wind from the lake had picked up strength, pushing Sadie's curly hair away from her face and chilling the sweat on her brow. She wrapped her arms around herself and watched Mr. Drye circle the pool, his eyes moving from the wind-choppy surface to the locked gate. The wet spots on the concrete hadn't dried entirely, but they were barely noticeable now.

"Everything appears to be in order, Miss Miles," Mr. Drye said, standing near the gate. He turned a little away from her. Looking at what? The parking lot? The power plant? Lake Erie beyond that? "I'm not sure what you thought you saw, and I appreciate your willingness to leap to the aid of a guest, but I do think that we can just turn in for the night." Sadie frowned, unsure if she'd just been scolded or not. "I hope you can put your scare behind you, Miss

Miles." He resumed his place behind the desk, already turning away from her. "Good night."

"Uh. Thanks. Yes, good night."

Sadie pushed the elevator's button and stepped back inside, hiding her frown until she was alone. Then she crossed her arms and scowled, chewing her lip. Frustration pricked her, a splinter she couldn't quite pick out. Something Mr. Drye had said? Not the near scold, something before that.

Before Sadie could grasp the thought, the doors opened onto the long, darkness-pooled hallway. Even from here, even through the closed door to their room, the sound of Izzy's restless fussing swept other worries from Sadie's mind.

CHAPTER FOUR

In for a Penny, in for a Pound

Sadie kept her walkie-talkie turned off and out of sight in a pocket under the apron Mr. Drye had given her the previous day. She'd tried leaving the connection open, but it picked up everything Gertie and Izzy said, and every tinkling tune from Izzy's toys. So, she would just have to check the walkie-talkie periodically, ideally while alone in a room, cleaning.

". . . right here, but the bigger bags are on that top shelf up there." Sadie blinked at the other housekeeper, Melanie, a round-faced nineteen-year-old woman she'd met only moments before. The young woman stood shorter than Sadie, but with her wide brown eyes and big, toothy smile, and the animated way she talked, she didn't seem diminutive.

The light above them flickered every few minutes, each time letting out a soft, grating buzz. She and Melanie stood close together in the narrow, cobwebby supply closet on the ground floor, off the same hallway as the exit to the pool. Sadie tried not to think about that pool, or the night before, but the memory of that desperate splashing kept intruding, breaking her concentration on the supply closet tour. And the absurd height and unusual depth of the dusty shelves meant she probably *should* concentrate.

"I'm sorry, Melanie, I was lost in thought. What were you saying?"

"Just Mel's fine. I was saying, if you need bigger trash—"

"Talking about me, are you?" Joe popped around the doorway into the supply closet, winking at Mel. He flashed a grin at Sadie and added, "Settling in? Have a good first night?"

Frantic splashing, gasping lips, wet clothes.

Sadie blinked to banish the image. "Yeah, thanks," she said. "Listen, Gertie told me she asked you to give me food?" Joe nodded, grinning. "You don't have to do that."

The smile fell off Joe's face so fast Sadie stepped back, her breath catching, but when he spoke his voice carried no anger. He sounded hurt. "You don't think you'll like it?"

"It's not that, but I can't pay for—"

"Oh, hey." Joe's good cheer returned in a flash, and he gave her an exaggerated wink. "Don't you worry about that."

"I don't want to get in trouble," Sadie said. "I can't lose this job. My daughter, we have— I just need this job."

"I'll talk with Drye before I send a single bite your way, how about that?"

Sadie hesitated. If she had *permission* to get free food, well, that would be different. And Joe seemed very invested in his cooking— he'd sounded like a kicked puppy when she said she didn't want his food.

"Well . . . all right. Thank you, then."

"Good!" With that settled, Joe turned his attention elsewhere. "Now, Mel, look at this." He pulled his phone out of his pocket and swiped it open. "Which shirt should I wear tonight?"

"Ooh, seeing that girl again?"

"Yeah, I'm taking her to the place on Howe, the one with the good patio."

Sadie stood to the side watching their casual ease, a swell of discomfort filling her. When had she lost the ability to banter and get acquainted with people?

Her phone vibrated in her back pocket and she nearly gasped. She should just turn it off, but then any emergency could happen and she'd be out of reach. As Joe and Mel kept chatting, Sadie checked the screen. Sam again. As she watched, the call rang through, and a handful of seconds later, the phone buzzed twice more.

Sadie glanced at her coworkers. It sounded like Joe was mimicking someone they both knew, his voice dropping in pitch and taking on a whine that made Mel double over with laughter. They wouldn't notice if she stepped into the hallway for a second to listen. It hadn't taken Sam long to leave the message, so she'd only need a moment.

"It's me again." He sounded less soft and melancholy now, and Sadie bit her lip. Should she feel relieved or worried by the change? The uncertainty always made her stomach sour. "Did you get my message yesterday? You must not have. Or you'd have called me back, right? I said I'm sorry, Sadie. Please don't do this to me. Call me, okay? Call me today."

Sadie deleted the message and stared at her blank phone for a moment. She ran her free hand through her hair and closed her eyes, then shoved her phone back into her pocket. Sam could cycle through whatever moods he wanted. She was gone from him now. Safe. If only she could make her body believe that—her breath hitched and her knees wobbled a little as she slipped back into the supply room.

"Anyway," Joe was saying, apparently done with the jokes, "I need to borrow one of the vacuum cleaners."

"For what?" Mel asked, her voice growing a touch sharper.

"You break *one* vacuum and suddenly everyone's suspicious." Joe rolled his eyes. "I spilled some rice in the kitchen."

"Go for it," Mel said. Joe grabbed a beige monstrosity that looked older than Sadie, and on his way out, Mel added, "Bring it back in one piece, Mishra!" He didn't answer and she didn't seem to expect him to, immediately turning back to Sadie. "Anyway. What was I saying?"

"Um . . . bigger trash?"

"Right, the big trash bags are on the top shelf. There's a stepladder over here."

Mel wrapped up her tour, then the two women wheeled their carts out to the lobby. They stopped at the check-in counter to collect a pair of skeleton keys from Mr. Drye, who made them sign the keys out in a small book that he tucked into his pocket.

He handed a sheet of paper to Mel, then cleared his throat. "Miss Ross?"

Mel paused and turned to him. "Yes, Henry?"

"Mr. Drye, please, Miss Ross."

"Sorry, Mr. Drye." Mel didn't sound sorry.

"I'd like you to let Miss Miles shadow you for a room or two. Show her the most efficient way to do the work. Move on to separate rooms when she's ready. Use your best judgment."

"Oh, man, I was planning on using my worst judgment today."

"Very funny." Mr. Drye didn't smile. "Go on now. And remember your hairnet."

Mel paused to tuck her long black ponytail into a hairnet as Sadie hastily stuffed her red curls into one of her own. Before Sadie had quite finished, Mel nodded for her to follow and headed down the hallway leading to the first-floor guest rooms. As soon as the two women rounded the corner, Mel looked at Sadie and rolled her eyes.

"What an asshole," she whispered.

Sadie snorted. Mr. Drye's stuffy formality had seemed merely exasperating yesterday afternoon. After the pool incident last night, annoyance had given way to budding mistrust, and she couldn't put her finger on exactly why. She started to replay the evening again, but Mel distracted her.

"This is our rooms list for the day." She tapped the paper Mr. Drye had handed to her. "We keep a copy in the supply room, too, but sometimes there're last-minute changes, so we always get the list at the front desk at the start of the shift. These are guests staying over, these are vacant rooms that need a spot check, and these are checkouts."

Mel gave Sadie the paper, explained the timing of the cleaning schedule, then let Sadie follow her into a room to watch "the most efficient way to do the work." They left the door open behind them, and Mel chatted as she cleaned. They talked about commonplaces for a while before Mel trailed off and turned to shoot a furtive glance at the open door.

"So, anyway," Mel said when she turned back to Sadie, her voice dropping into a conspiratorial murmur, "there's this party on Halloween." Mel must have mistaken Sadie's blank look, because she elaborated, "You know, on Tuesday. You'd be welcome to drop by, my friends are chill. And, y'know, if you wanted to bring some beer—*not* that I'm only inviting you for that, you know? You'd be welcome either way. But *if* you wanted to bring some beer, that'd be cool."

"Oh, hey, thanks for the invite," Sadie said, trying to sound genuine. She could think of few things more uncomfortable than crashing a party full of people a dozen years younger than her. "My daughter, though. I can't leave her alone in the room all night." She didn't try to pretend that she'd planned for trick-or-treating with Izzy; costumes had been far from Sadie's mind, and at three, Izzy probably wouldn't even realize what she was missing this year.

"Oh, for sure," Mel said, her breezy tone failing to hide evident disappointment. "But if you change your mind, we'll be down at the Cut most of Halloween night."

"The Cut?"

"The beach down past the power plant. I don't think it has an official name, everybody I know just calls it the Cut." Mel shrugged. "Anyway, I think you've got the basics. I'll give you an easy room to start. You take one-forty-one, it's been empty a few days so you should just need to dust and do a spot check. I'll be right across the hall."

Sadie fitted her skeleton key into the lock on the door Mel pointed her to. It stuck briefly; she had to rattle it before it finally turned. Sure, the hotel had been built in the 1800s, but why couldn't Mr. Drye or whoever was in charge beyond him have replaced the locks with key-card entry by now?

Sadie propped the door open and switched the light on, then maneuvered the cart into the room and rummaged for a cloth to dust with.

A damp smell permeated the room, stronger near the entrance. In layout it resembled Sadie and Izzy's room on the fourth floor, the same bed and fold-out couch, the same little desk with two chairs, and a dresser that held a coffee maker, a microwave, and a small TV. Instead of blue tones, the dingy greens of the rest of L'Arpin dominated this space. Had the carpet been nice when it was new? Sadie couldn't picture it—in her mind, L'Arpin had always looked faded and dismal and somehow waterlogged even where it was dry.

Or maybe that was just the wet scent getting to her, the way it clung in her nose and her throat, made her belly flip with morning sickness again.

The bathroom lay in darkness behind her, and as she straightened with the cloth in hand, the skin on the back of her neck tightened. She turned quickly. A deeper shadow in the gloom shifted. Sadie's unsettled stomach twisted. She sucked in a sharp breath, stumbling back against the cart.

The startle passed, and a hot flush of embarrassment replaced it as Sadie realized she'd been given the wrong information. "God, I'm so sorry," she said, voice tight. "I was told the room was vacant."

No answer came.

If it was just an error Mel made, just an occupied room, why would a guest be in the dark in the bathroom?

Sadie swallowed around a tightness in her throat as her fear surged again.

If it was a guest, where was their stuff?

"Is someone there?" she asked, and this time her voice came out quieter, rougher. The subtle shifting motion came again. Sadie's chest tightened. Without taking her eyes off that shadowed doorway she groped behind herself until her fingers found the handle of the broom attached to her cart.

"Answer me," she said.

She slid the broom free and repeated herself. *"Answer me."*

If she slipped out to get Mel, whoever hid in the bathroom might have just enough time to sneak away. They'd go somewhere else in the hotel. Maybe they'd stay nearby, maybe they'd keep watching her, maybe—

With a half-suppressed yelp, Sadie lunged forward and jabbed into the dark room with the broom in one hand. Her other hand slapped the wall, searching for the light switch. In the instant before she found it, she imagined the feeling of a hand grabbing her instead. The childish fear shouldn't have struck her so *hard*.

Finally, her fingers found the switch. The light snapped on and a figure to her right jumped out at her. Sadie gasped, swinging the broom.

At the last second, she pulled the blow before she could shatter the mirror. Her reflection. No one had leaped upon her at all. She turned, eyes darting frantically.

No one lurked in the bathroom, and the source of the movement became apparent. The shower curtain, pushed far back, shifted in an air current from a vent on the nearby wall.

Sadie propped the broom against the countertop and tucked her arms close to herself, one hand curled near her throat and the other covering her mouth. She forced several deep breaths, letting them out slowly. The wet smell from the main room was different here. Not an unclean scent, not offensive, but organic and somehow disquieting.

The burst of adrenaline ebbed. Her heart slowed, but as she calmed herself, Sadie found the emptiness of the bathroom less and less comforting. Peculiar details struck her instead. Like the warmth, and the sound. For a moment Sadie couldn't place the tiny, near-musical notes tapping out in a slow, even rhythm. Water dripping, that was it. But she checked the faucet in the sink, the faucet and the showerhead in the tub, and none leaked. And the lingering moisture in the air—

Mel *had* said this room was unoccupied, right? Had been unoccupied for days? Why did it sound and feel exactly as if someone had just taken a shower?

Sadie took her glasses off and wiped the lenses, then took a small step closer to the tub and leaned to peer in.

It was bone dry. Even the stains around the drain.

The back of Sadie's neck still prickled, and she cast a quick glance around again before crouching to get a better look. She'd seen it enough times—something the school custodian missed after a little kid took an unexpected tumble, something she'd missed when cleaning up the kitchen after Sam stormed out to clear his head—to recognize old blood.

"Melanie!" Sadie shouted, forgetting all about her broom as she lurched to her feet. She scrambled out of the bathroom, out of the guest room, and into the hallway. "Mel! There's blood in the tub!"

The younger housekeeper took her time appearing in the doorway of the room across the hall. "How much blood?"

"What? I don't know! Isn't any blood enough?"

"Let's see." Without a trace of fear, Melanie went into the room she'd tasked Sadie with cleaning. She stepped into the bathroom and peered at the tub. "Nah, that's not too much blood."

"What?"

"I mean, I've seen way worse. This is fine."

"This is fine?" Sadie repeated, incredulous. "Dried blood in the bathtub?"

"Dude. People bleed so, so much. There's always blood. It's everywhere," Mel said. "No sweat."

Mel's nonchalance doused Sadie's growing hysteria, and chagrin rose in its place. After all, there were perfectly legitimate reasons for blood to be in a bathroom. A nick while shaving, menstruation, even an accident with a nail trimmer. She had to get a handle on her overactive imagination.

"Does it look clean enough in here to you?" Sadie hadn't done a thing to the room, she just wanted to be done with it.

Mel glanced around and shrugged. "Looks fine to me."

Relief washed through Sadie. Mel made her way back across the hall to the room she'd been working on. Sadie shut the door to the bathroom but then lingered for a moment. She pulled her walkie-talkie out and opened the channel, listening to Izzy and Gertie chat while a squeaky voice in the background sang the alphabet song.

Reassured, she hid the walkie-talkie again and pushed her cart out into the hallway. After locking the door behind her, Sadie glanced up and down the corridor. This close to the lobby, some sunlight from the windows by the door still illuminated the space, but the farther along the hallway ran the deeper it sank into gloom. At the far end, the shadowy spaces couldn't be distinguished from her own ill-lit hallway at night.

Mel's voice drifted through an open door in an irritated mutter. Really, Sadie shouldn't care about what some teenager thought of her. Nevertheless, the idea that she'd already pissed off her only close coworker made her cringe. She stepped into the doorway.

"Mel?"

"What's up?"

"I hope my nerves didn't throw your day off."

"What? Oh, nah. I thought that sort of thing was weird when I started, too." No trace of the irritation Sadie had heard in Mel's voice a moment ago remained now, but she might just have been good at faking cheer.

"You sounded annoyed a second ago."

"Ohh, no, that wasn't about you. It's this guest. She was supposed to check out this morning, but look at all the junk she left here. I dunno if she left and forgot, like, all her stuff?" Sadie stepped farther into the room, eyeing the scatter of clothing and toiletries. Mel continued, "Or if she's checking out late and she'll be back for all this."

A baby-blue suitcase sat open in the corner. Sadie frowned at it.

"She overflowed the toilet or something, too," Mel added, her tone aggrieved. "She didn't even try to clean up."

Where had Sadie seen that suitcase before?

"What room number is this?"

"Hm? One-forty. Why?"

Room 140. Sadie did recognize the suitcase. She'd heard Mr. Drye say 140 before he'd taken the young lady from the lobby—the young lady from the *pool*—to her room the day before. And now she was supposed to be checked out, but all her stuff remained.

"Does L'Arpin have security cameras?" Sadie asked.

Mel hesitated, giving Sadie a puzzled frown, before slowly answering, "A couple. At the exits and in the lobby. Why? Planning a heist?"

"Yep," Sadie answered, breezily covering her growing anxiety with humor. "C'mon, show me where the security feed is." She backed into the hallway, beckoning Mel to follow her, trying to grin, trying to make this seem funny.

She didn't check behind her, and ran right into someone.

"Watch what you're doing, there!" a man's gruff voice exclaimed.

Sadie rebounded and spun, putting on an apologetic expression. A short, solidly built man in his midsixties scowled at her. Dirty gardening gloves hung half out of one pocket in a faded green canvas vest he wore over an outfit otherwise entirely composed of well-worn denim.

"Sorry," Sadie said, layering a hint of self-deprecation into her tone and trying a slightly ingratiating smile. "Clumsy of me. I'm surprised I don't walk into the walls sometimes. I'm Sadie."

His scowl eased fractionally. Before he could speak, Mel followed Sadie out into the hall and pointed at the man's boots. "Lewis

McCann!" she scolded. "What is *with* you and tracking mud all over the hotel every single time I'm working?" His frown deepened with every word she spoke.

"You've gotta vacuum the halls anyway, doncha? Give me a break. I was looking for you. Need to borrow your key."

"Ask Mr. Drye."

"I don't wanna talk to that prick, I just wanna get an extra bag of mulch outta the shed. He'll only bitch about it." Lewis glanced at Sadie. "What were you asking about security cameras for?"

How long had he been standing in the hall, listening in on their conversation?

Figuring the attitude of conspiratorial joking wouldn't work on Lewis, Sadie shrugged. "I thought I saw something weird last night. Just want to check it out. Where would I do that?"

Mel opened her mouth as if to reply, but Lewis answered first. "You wouldn't."

Mel heaved an intentionally loud sigh. "If I let you borrow my key, will you mind your own business, Lewis?"

A woman materialized from the shadows shrouding the far corner of the hallway. Her step faltered when she saw the three L'Arpin employees clustered together in the hall, and Sadie's heart sank. She didn't need a customer complaint about laziness on her first day. Then the woman passed through one of the circles of light, and her uniform, sturdy coveralls in dark blue with a matching baseball-style cap, as well as her similarity to Lewis became apparent.

"Bothering Mel, again, Dad?" the woman asked, her voice low and gently teasing. She drew even with the small group. "Or are we having a hallway party? Somebody better be on the lookout for Drye."

"Lewis was just asking to borrow my key."

"You don't go meddling with security issues, girls." Lewis shot his daughter an exasperated look, clearly expecting sympathy. "They're trying to get at the security cameras."

"Why's that?" Lewis's daughter asked, frowning at Mel.

"I just wanted to see if something I thought was weird last night showed up," Sadie said, trying her best to sound reasonable and casual.

The woman turned to Sadie and gave her an appraising once-over. Sadie thought her eyes held a strange, cool depth, until she smiled. The aloofness swept away and she held her hand out to Sadie. "I'm Beth, head of maintenance. You'd be Sadie, right? Drye mentioned you and your little girl are staying here awhile. Welcome to L'Arpin." She shook Sadie's hand and then turned to Lewis. "Come on, Dad. Tell me why you needed Mel's key."

Mel handed Lewis her key, and Beth led her father away. Sadie watched them go, breathing hard through a tightness in her chest. She shook the feeling off and turned to Mel. Attempting to recapture the humor of the moment before she'd bumped into Lewis, she said, "So, heist time?"

Mel hesitated a moment, then grinned. "Tell you what. Say you *will* bring beer to the Cut on Halloween, and I'll show you. Mr. Drye doesn't know I know how to access the cameras, but they're good for timing extra breaks."

The weight of what had happened the night before sat heavier in Sadie's mind, on her shoulders, than the risk she'd take providing beer to a bunch of minors she didn't know. So Sadie made herself laugh. "Not just a heist but blackmail and slacking off, too?"

"In for a penny, in for a pound," Mel said with a grin.

"Deal. Let's go."

Mel took the lead for the short walk back down the hall toward the lobby and paused just before rounding the corner to look back at Sadie. She grimaced, and Sadie glanced over her own shoulder, alarm spiking through her. Had they been caught leaving their duties?

"Sadie," Mel hissed. Sadie jumped and turned back toward the younger woman, her mouth dry. Mel didn't look even a little worried. In fact, she seemed amused. "Stop acting like you're sneaking," she said.

"But . . . we are sneaking?"

"Yeah, but don't act like it."

Sadie tried to emulate Mel as they resumed their walk into the lobby. As a result, she felt more conspicuous than before, a thirty-two-year-old woman trying to walk like a cocky nineteen-year-old. Fortunately, when they turned the corner, the lobby stood empty before them. Mr. Drye must have been helping a new guest, or taking a restroom break, something that took him away from his desk.

The empty desk . . . "That's *it*."

"What's what?" Mel asked, slipping around behind the desk and letting herself into the office where Sadie had been interviewed the day before.

Sadie hurried after Mel. "Uh, nothing, I just remembered something."

As Mel sat down at the single screen behind Mr. Drye's desk, Sadie shut her eyes and wracked her mind. When she'd run to the pool the night before, hadn't the lobby been empty then, just like now? And later, Mr. Drye had said . . . Sadie rubbed her temples. What had he said, exactly? He'd reassured her that no one had gone that way all evening. Had he told her he'd been there the whole night, or only implied it?

"What'd you want to look at?"

"The guest who checked into one-forty yesterday was there around four. She made Mr. Drye late for my interview. Can you see if she went back through the lobby at any time last night?"

Mel frowned but didn't argue, enlarging the feed for the correct camera before finding the right timestamp. The empty image of the lobby populated itself.

Mr. Drye stood behind the counter, Sadie and Izzy sat in a pair of chairs near Gertie, and the white-haired young woman approached the desk. Mel clicked a command and the feed sped up. In fast motion, Mr. Drye left, returned, and led Sadie away. A second or so later they emerged, Sadie collected Izzy, Joe made his appearance, and then everyone dispersed. Mr. Drye returned alone, and for the next few sped-up hours he attended to the handful of guests who came and went. The light waned quickly, the chandelier seemed to brighten by comparison. Mr. Drye spent most of his evening behind the desk, leaving only twice. The second time he was gone—*had* he told Sadie he'd been there the whole time?—Sadie flashed back into view, leaping from the elevator and running to the opposite hall.

The missing guest had never reappeared.

"Bring it to the present?" Sadie asked.

"Sure." Mel increased the speed again. The feed caught up to itself and returned to the present moment. The young woman never reappeared. "Huh," Mel said as the fast forward lurched abruptly to real time. "She must've left without checking out."

"Can we check the feeds for the cameras on the exits?"

On the now-current screen, a shadow darkened the hallway to the pool. Mel hissed and moved to close the window. "We're fucked if Drye catches us!"

"No, look, it's just Beth!"

The video image of Beth glanced around and then made for the desk. Mel shut down the feed and jumped away just as the door opened and the head of maintenance joined them in the office. "Here's your key back, Mel. I saw Drye on his way here. You two probably want to make yourselves scarce."

"Thanks, Beth," Mel said, plucking the key out of Beth's fingers as she slipped past her and scurried out to the main part of the lobby.

"Yeah," Sadie said, trying not to sound annoyed about Beth's bad timing. "Thanks."

Sadie hurried after Mel, frustrated and flustered. She'd hoped the cameras would help her clear things up, but confusion and a thread of nervous jitters tugged at her. She'd have to keep a sharp watch on things here, and on Mr. Drye.

Because whatever had happened last night, Mr. Drye obviously wanted her to think nothing strange went on in L'Arpin Hotel.

CHAPTER FIVE

Warm Waters

No one else knew about Sadie's pregnancy yet, but guilt pricked her anyway; she kept her hands off her belly while paying for a case of the lowest ABV beer at a gas station near the hotel, along with bug spray for a walk down to the beach that night, a banana for Izzy, and a case of bottled water (soon she'd have to stop carrying such heavy things by herself) for their room. After hearing the leaky drips in her hallway and seeing the stains in the tub, and after catching herself wondering what else L'Arpin never updated in over a hundred years if they hadn't even figured out key cards by now, the idea of her and Izzy drinking water from the hotel's pipes made Sadie wary.

The idea of hauling a case of beer down to that beach, the Cut, to give to a bunch of underage partiers on Halloween night made her wary, too, but she'd agreed, and she wanted to keep coworker relationships congenial.

Sadie stowed the beer in her trunk until later but carried the water up to the room immediately. She finagled the door open while holding the unwieldy case, and a fishy scent that probably wouldn't have been so overpowering if not for her pregnancy-enhanced sense of smell wafted out. When she wrinkled her nose and hauled her burden through the door, she found herself face to face with Gertie, who had insisted that Izzy would be happier waiting with her than running an errand. Sadie would have refused, but Izzy started whining the moment Sadie demurred.

Giving in to incipient tantrums would spoil Izzy rotten, but Sadie couldn't risk a scene getting them kicked out of the hotel. Once Sadie got a new teaching position and got out of L'Arpin, once they weren't just barely scraping by anymore, there'd be time then to reverse the damage of giving the little girl her own way a few too many times here.

"What's that for?" Gertie asked, frowning at the bottled water.

"It's just water, Gertie," Sadie answered, perplexed by the older woman's suspicious face. "It's for drinking."

"What's wrong with the water we got here?" Gertie said.

Sadie hesitated. Gertie had been living in L'Arpin for a long, long time, and sometimes people grew unreasonably defensive of things in or about their homes.

"Izzy gets a sensitive tummy sometimes," Sadie said, keeping the lie vague and simple. "I think the bottled water helps."

"There's nothing wrong with the water here. I drink it every day!"

"Of course, it's just Izzy's tummy."

"My tummy's too full, Mommy!" Izzy interjected then, scrambling off the couch. Brown smudged the corners of her mouth, telling Sadie exactly what her tummy was too full of. Gertie must have brought it over herself; Sadie kept little in the way of sweets around, even when they could afford goodies.

"You better still have some room in there for dinner, stinker," Sadie said, setting down the water and scooping up her little girl.

Izzy wrapped her arms around Sadie's neck, put her face close to Sadie's, and whispered, "I won't."

"Oh, *speaking* of dinner, I had Jordan bring something up for us," Gertie said, pointing at a closed takeout box on the small desk. That explained the smell. Joe made a lot of seafood for L'Arpin's little on-site restaurant. "But Izzy wouldn't eat a bite of it. I'll leave it here for when her little tummy isn't so full." Gertie's voice turned almost admonishing as she added, "You make sure you eat enough now, too, Sadie dear. It's important."

Before Sadie could settle on a response—the urge to remind Gertie not to feed Izzy things Sadie hadn't approved warring with gratitude for the older woman's help and obvious care—her phone double-buzzed in her pocket. She swallowed around a sudden tightness in her throat and pulled the phone out just enough to tilt the screen and glance at it. Just an app notification.

Blocking Sam would take away this gut punch of anxiety whenever her phone did anything, but it also felt too much like blinding herself to any advanced warning of his behavior. And if he figured out she'd blocked him, what might he do? No, these acid-belly moments of anxiety were better.

"Sadie?"

"What?" Sadie's gaze snapped from her phone to Gertie, who stood by the door. She blinked fast and put on a smile. "Right, you're heading out. Well, see you in a few hours. And thanks again for listening for her so I can step out later."

"It's no problem," Gertie said on her way out the door. "I never sleep much anyway."

The hours passed slowly. Izzy seemed bored in their single room, stomping from one side to the other and picking up then discarding the few toys Sadie had thrown into her daughter's suitcase. Sadie had tried joining a neighborhood group online, hoping to find things to occupy her daughter, but all the posts had been people trying to sell old furniture or hire contractors for insultingly low rates, plus a surprising number of lost-pet flyers, and she'd deleted it again. For now, she and Izzy had to make do without much to keep themselves entertained.

The toddler's fussiness crept under Sadie's skin, and she found herself sitting in silence on the couch as Izzy worked herself up bit by bit. Sadie's shoulders tightened, her eyes moving between her daughter and the door, her daughter and the door.

("*Keep your kid quiet or I'll give her something to scream about.*"
"*She's not screaming—*"
"*You're not talking back to me, are you, Sadie?*"
"*No! No, I'm just saying, she's—*"
"*Then you shut her up, or I will.*")

"Where's doggy guitar?" Izzy asked, pulling her mother's attention back to the room in L'Arpin and the seconds that passed in slow drips.

"Oh no," Sadie muttered, then caught herself and put on a nonchalant smile, hoping to encourage her daughter's behavior by example as she said, "We couldn't bring it with us, honey."

Sadie hated "doggy guitar," but she hadn't left it behind on purpose. She wouldn't ever, because Izzy—

"I want doggy guitar! My best, *best* doggy guitar!"

"I'm sorry, honey," Sadie said, sliding off the edge of the couch to kneel next to her daughter. "It's not here."

"Go get it!" Izzy wailed.

Sadie's stomach clenched at the very idea. "We can't, baby."

"Go *get* it!" Izzy cried again. "Right now!"

Someday, Sadie knew Izzy would figure out what had happened in these early days of her life. The new baby would have questions about its father, and Izzy might dimly remember Sam, and when they were both older and came to her with it, she'd tell them as much of the truth as wouldn't burden them.

But Sadie had no way to explain to a three-year-old that she couldn't return to the home of her abuser for a single noisy plastic toy.

"I'm sorry," Sadie murmured over and over, holding Izzy close, stroking her hair away from her increasingly wet face. Sweat, tears, and snot combined into a mess that Izzy smeared on Sadie's shirt, a small price to pay for comforting her daughter and for muffling Izzy's screams enough that she probably wouldn't annoy the guests.

The tantrum passed but left Izzy's mood fragile and volatile; the guilt Izzy's sadness had churned up in Sadie's gut didn't fade so easily. Bedtime came as a relief to Sadie, and once her little girl's breathing had deepened into the rhythm of true sleep, some of Izzy's earlier restlessness seized Sadie.

Maybe Mel's party wouldn't be so bad. Sadie crept around the room as she changed her shirt and pulled her hair back into a loose ponytail, careful not to wake her daughter. She slipped out to the hall, checked the walkie-talkie's connection, then tapped at Gertie's door.

"Thanks again, Gertie. You're a saint. I owe you."

"So long as you don't forget it," the old woman said, smiling.

Sadie made her way down the long corridor toward the elevator, moving into and out of the shadows, passing alcove after alcove with their closed doors. The dripping sound from the first night hadn't returned, but the old building made other noises. In the strange, quiet limbo of the hotel hallway, each little disturbance sounded intentional and furtive. The peepholes in those closed doors gleamed in the low light as she passed. Anyone could hide behind such a door and watch. Anyone could step out around the dark corner far behind her and creep down the green carpet on silent feet, drawing nearer and nearer. Or ease a door open and leave it behind them, and creep up behind her and reach out and—

Losing her composure meant losing control. Dangerous. Trying not to let herself run, Sadie nevertheless hurried her steps. Heaviness in her chest eased when she reached the elevator.

Just as she touched the button a loud, wet *slap* nearly made her scream. She spun, eyes wide, lifting her hands to protect herself from . . . from an empty hallway.

Nothing moved down the dim green length, no figure obscured

the sparse lights or huddled in the shadows. Her pulse fluttered in her throat and thundered in her chest. Her breath came in rapid gasps. But worse than that, embarrassment bubbled up from her gut, her cheeks burning.

When the elevator *dinged* behind her, Sadie yelped and then slapped a hand over her mouth. She turned and hurried in, jabbing the button for the lobby.

Sadie backed up and slumped until she'd fitted herself into the corner of the elevator. She tilted her head up and closed her eyes. Exhaustion weighed her down, first-trimester fatigue combined with a near-constant twinge of morning sickness. Those discomforts alone would have been a trial in familiar surroundings, without the spike of fear every time her phone buzzed. Together, it was enough to fire anyone's imagination into unpleasantness. She needed to get a handle on herself, try to make the best of things. Straightening, she rubbed her face, fingers sliding under her glasses. She dropped her arms and shook her shoulders. It had been a terrible couple weeks. Anybody would be stressed out.

Maybe the little party would be good for her.

When the elevator opened onto the lobby she couldn't help it— she leaned forward and peeked out before exiting.

"Everything all right, Miss Miles?" Mr. Drye asked from behind the desk.

Seeing him alone there, the glittering light fixture not quite up to the task of alleviating the growing gloom as evening settled in, Sadie couldn't help but think of the night with the pool. She'd get a chance at those security cameras again, but until then, she could do nothing more than remain wary.

"Just going for a walk." Telling her employer she was heading out to join a bunch of nineteen-year-olds drinking beer on the beach didn't exactly appeal to her good judgment.

Mr. Drye frowned. "Your daughter?"

A wave of irritation washed over Sadie—who was this man to try to second-guess her parenting?—but she smiled through it with the ease of practice. "Izzy's asleep." Mr. Drye's frown deepened. Sadie went on, "Gertie's listening for her, she has my phone number."

The annoyance vanished from Mr. Drye's face and he nodded. "Well, you have fun, then," he said, waving her away. "Remember, you have work in the morning."

Sadie had not been planning to stay out very late until that exact moment. She'd had a curfew as a teen, and she'd had a terrible weight of expectations to obey when she lived with Sam. Mr. Drye did not, and could not be allowed to, have any such hold over her time when she wasn't on the clock.

"Happy Halloween, Mr. Drye." Sadie turned to stride out of the lobby and across the parking lot, toward her car and the case of beer stowed in the trunk.

Mel hadn't really given Sadie directions, just "down past the power plant," so Sadie figured it must be the nearest stretch of Lake Erie shore. She left her car behind and hurried across the lot, pausing once at the strip of dry grass separating it from the power plant's employee parking. She turned to regard L'Arpin Hotel.

Little more than a large brick square with minimal exterior lights, it looked its age. Sadie imagined candles and lanterns casting the light from within the windows, pictured horse-drawn carriages rolling to a stop before the white pillars and double layer of balconies taking up the front of the otherwise plain building. The pool courtyard at the western corner of the building strained the illusion, and so did the blare of a car's horn somewhere nearby. When Sadie let her gaze wander toward the sky, the light from nearby Cleveland washed away almost all the stars.

Turning dispelled the illusion of timelessness entirely. The power plant hulking between L'Arpin and Lake Erie could be mistaken for nothing but a modern beast. Rows of tiny windows, dark now after hours, marched along the sides of the building. The lot near Sadie was open, but closer to the building a high fence topped with razor wire ran around the property. Tall, brilliantly white lights blazed on the parking lot, casting an excavator and a bulldozer into sharp relief but failing to properly illuminate the building itself. Scaffolding seemed drawn on in lines of shadow, and four huge smokestacks stretched toward the sky like fingers. Sadie couldn't help but ascribe animosity to the power plant, squatting there, waiting for something.

To her left the sun had set not long before Izzy's bedtime, but beyond the increasingly bare silhouettes of the trees, the faint hues of red and purple still clung to the sky. Ahead, the gentle hush and swish of water drew her attention. Small trees tangled with thick underbrush to separate the lake from the parking areas. A single opening in the foliage must be the way to the beach Mel had told her about.

In spite of the unfriendliness the power plant exuded, the lights in its parking lot shone brighter than those at L'Arpin, and the break in the trees lay beyond that stretch of asphalt. Sadie hesitated, then snorted at herself. Was she going to forgo the easier, safer parking lot because she didn't like the way its building looked?

She made it only halfway before a door in the side of the building opened and a man came charging out. The angry man from her first day at L'Arpin, who had yelled at Mr. Drye. What had Mr. Drye called him? Bill? Bill something. Why was he here so late? Did power plant employees typically work such irregular hours? Such considerations fled Sadie's mind when she realized the man was heading not for any car, but in her direction.

"What're you doing out here?" he barked when he drew near.

"Excuse me?" Sadie's voice came out soft and light, high in tone but not in volume, as nonconfrontational as possible.

This did not mollify Bill, who skidded to a stop in front of her as if to bar her way. "What are you doing in my parking lot? You're from the hotel, aren't you?"

"I'm just walking—"

"Trespassing! This is a private lot."

"I wasn't trying to," Sadie said, moving back a step and holding her free hand up in a pacifying gesture.

"Not trying to trespass? Just accidentally marched onto plant property?"

Sadie shook her head. "I'm sorry," she said. "I'm just going to the beach."

"*Sure.* You have any idea how busy I am? A plant overseer doesn't have time to leave work and come out here to chase trespassers off the property. I'm on a tight schedule. So if you'll see yourself off my lot?" He gestured pointedly at the strip of grass separating the power plant's well-lit space from the shadowy parking area surrounding L'Arpin.

"Sorry," Sadie repeated.

"Sorry doesn't put me back on schedule."

She would have apologized again, but the angry overseer had already turned to hurry back into the power plant. Cheeks warm and the back of her neck prickling, Sadie backtracked to the narrow no-man's-land between the two parking lots and hurried on her way. When she stepped into the break in the trees and bushes she'd spied before, she found the beach spread out below her, with a concrete stairway leading down from where the ground gave way in a small shale cliff.

The scene below contrasted so thoroughly with the barren parking lots and the hulking buildings that the tension in her jaw and shoulders eased, the embarrassment not forgotten but easier to relegate to the back of her mind.

At the top of those steps, the voices that had been hiding beneath the gentle lapping of tiny waves became clear. A group of fifteen or so people stood together or sat around in the sand. Sadie had expected a bonfire, but the power plant looming above the beach rendered flames unnecessary. The same dazzling white lights from the parking lot shone down onto a stretch of beach separated by another length of fence and razor wire. Though the illumination aimed only at that small area, plenty of ambient light spilled over to the rest of the beach. A large hole, too smooth and round to be natural, broke the face of the shallow shale cliff. Visible mostly as a dark streak and a furtive reflective gleam, a thin stream of water ran from the hole, cutting a channel through the sand to the lake. Three shadowy figures bobbed and splashed in the wavelets near the shore. Sadie shivered on their behalf; why would anyone want to go swimming in the lake at this time of the year? To the left, the beach gave way to a tumble of stones that formed a pier, flat and dry in the center but uneven and slick to the sides, stretching out over the water.

Sadie had never been here before, had never met these people, but she knew this scene. Ease and friendship, carefree laughter, sidetracked conversations wandering into surprising depths.

Her throat tightened and dull pain squeezed her chest. When had she last had this? Not just since before Sam, but further back. Before August had died. She'd lost most of her friends when she'd lost her husband. Her eyes burned. She missed this.

"Sadie! Happy Halloween!" Mel's voice rose above the rest, and a hush fell. Sadie waved with her free hand and made her careful way down the stairs. Mel met her at the bottom, catching her in an unexpected hug before relieving her of the case of beer with a bright grin. "I'm glad you came, thanks *so* much! Come and meet everybody." Mel turned and led the way back to the group, raising her voice again. "Hey, guys, this is Sadie, she works with me and she brought beer." She sang the last few words out, lifting the case, to a chorus of impromptu cheers.

The voices all sounded so young. Sadie didn't let herself cringe, didn't let herself show it, but no, this hadn't been the right decision. She pasted on a smile and followed Mel to where the largest cluster of people chatted. Mel made introductions, but each name fell out of Sadie's head the moment after she heard it.

A high, irritating whine hummed near her ear. At almost the same moment, one of Mel's friends slapped her own arm with a curse.

"Oh!" Sadie said, opening her purse. "I have bug spray." She took it out and stepped a little away from the others before spraying herself. But when she offered it around, Mel and her friends declined. Something so simple shouldn't have made Sadie feel so old and out of place. Still, whether it was the smell sensitivity of pregnancy or the way self-consciousness made her hyperaware of it, the stink of the bug spray overwhelmed her enough that she made an excuse about never having been to the lake before and wandered away from the group.

Stopping just shy of the water, Sadie eyed the three swimmers. She crouched down to touch an incoming tiny wave, and found it comfortably warmer than the chill evening air. Straightening again, Sadie remembered the hole in the low cliff. Its thin stream of water hadn't seemed enough to make a change like this. She looked along the water toward the power plant. There, beyond the fence, a second round shadow in the shale wall let out another small and quiet, but steady, stream of water that cut its own channel into Lake Erie. Sadie guessed the plant used the water to cool the machinery, but she also had no real image of what the inside of the power plant would look like or how or where it would need to be cooled. Either way, she suspected the power plant caused the warm waters.

Sadie turned back and made her way to the pier. She walked down the center, leaving the too-young voices behind in favor of the gentle hush of water rising and falling over stone and the wind in her ears.

The lake stretched before her, meeting the sky at an impossible distance. On and on. The farther from shore, the more motionless it looked.

That far-off stillness, however illusory, seemed all at once intentional, the patient quiet of a predator.

Sadie didn't like it. And she didn't like Mel's little party. "I'm going home," she whispered, meaning L'Arpin but not meaning that the hotel felt like any kind of home, and the dissonance between what she'd said and what she felt combined with the water and the sky and the gentle dripping on the rocks behind her, filling her head up.

Dripping on the rocks?

The hair on the back of Sadie's neck stood up, a painful tingle. She froze. Had something crawled out of the unnaturally warm waters of this corner of Lake Erie and dragged itself onto the rocks, dripping and dripping and—

And this was just the upstairs hallway all over again, wasn't it? She'd turn and find the pier running away from her like the corridor ran away from the elevator door, and just as innocent.

She turned.

Mel and her party seemed farther away than Sadie would have guessed. She'd only imagined that dripping. And if a puddle formed a dark stain on the stones behind her, well, she was on a pier on the lake.

Still, Sadie edged around the wet spots as she made her way back toward the shore. Stepping from stone to sand, the melancholy nostalgia that had struck her atop the stairs came back with the force of a blow. Sadie closed her eyes to stop a swell of tears. Was this just the grief hitting her, like it had on and off since August died, or was it the pregnancy pulling her emotions with a strength she was too tired to resist? Either way, time to leave.

"You're going?" Mel called out as Sadie mounted the first of the concrete steps again.

Sadie hesitated. The disappointment in the younger woman's voice caught her by surprise. It hadn't even occurred to her that Mel would notice when she left. She nodded.

"But you just got here," Mel protested, hesitation making her words almost sound like a question.

"My daughter's asleep in our room," Sadie said, turning to where the rest of the party—just kids, from where Sadie stood— went on without her. Only Mel lingered a little apart. Sadie hated to seem unfriendly, but she didn't belong in this scene. Saying so would prompt a tide of overly hearty reassurances, kindly meant but more awkward than just bailing, so Sadie added only, "She's three."

"Aw, what a fun age," Mel said, and Sadie resisted the urge to give her a patronizing smile in return.

"Yeah. Restrictive on the social life, though. Thanks for inviting me, but I oughta go."

"Well, thanks for coming out for a minute, anyway. See ya at work!"

Sadie waved as she turned to climb the stairs.

The wide parking lots between the beach and L'Arpin stretched empty all around her as she crossed the flat pavement. As the quiet sounds of the beach faded behind Sadie, she imagined soft dripping following her back to the hotel entrance.

Mr. Drye still stood in the lobby, facing a woman wearing L'Arpin's uniform. Her thick black-and-gray hair was pulled into a tight ponytail, and she'd rolled her sleeves up past her elbows. The skin on her hands looked dry and pink. Her voice, though not loud, buzzed with irritation.

". . . wonder he left without checking out, Henry, you should see the state of the bedding. I've never seen so much sand in a bedsheet, it had to have been intentional."

"It's nothing to worry about, Miss Danbury," Mr. Drye replied, but out of the corner of her eye Sadie thought she glimpsed the hotel manager turn a meaningful gaze in her direction. Sadie reached up to adjust her glasses as an excuse to block her eyes from him.

She hurried past without glancing again at Mr. Drye or this night-shift coworker she hadn't met yet. Taking care to keep her face neutral, Sadie slipped into the elevator. Another guest had left unannounced—or had disappeared?

Sadie chewed her lip as she rode the elevator up. Did secrets hide behind *every* door in L'Arpin? Behind her own door, her daughter slept, so small and trusting. Sadie couldn't afford that trust. She had to learn the truth.

CHAPTER SIX

Paranoid

". . . The least you can do is talk this out with me like an adult. Call me, Sadie. I deserve that much."

Sadie's heart sped up a pace rather than squeezing with guilt—Sam's voice had sounded more aggrieved than wounded. She deleted the voicemail, put the phone back in her pocket, and leaned on her loaded cleaning cart, elbows on the handle, head in her hands. Behind her, in the supply closet, Mel clattered around, humming to herself. Listening to these voicemails at the beginning of a shift might not be Sadie's best idea, but she wouldn't play them in front of Izzy and she couldn't make herself wait until after the little girl's bedtime.

Sadie straightened and pushed her cart out to the lobby. Halloween had been only the night before, but already the fireplace along one wall no longer held jack-o'-lanterns. A small pilgrim-Thanksgiving-dinner display had been set along the mantel—Mr. Drye must have cared more about classic holiday themes than historical accuracy.

Sadie pushed her cart toward the far hallway, trying not to be too obvious as she eyed the middle-aged blond man behind the checkout counter. Joe leaned against the front of the counter, arms crossed atop it, chatting with the unfamiliar man, who looked exasperated.

"No way. I'm not going to let you borrow my shoes."

"Oh, come on, do me a solid, yeah? I think I'm gonna get serious with this girl, I wanna put my best foot forward tonight."

"Not in my shoes. Who asks to borrow a coworker's shoes?"

"They're very nice shoes."

"Thank you."

"So I can—?"

"No."

Mel bustled out into the lobby at that moment and pushed her own cart right up to the desk, giving Sadie the chance to follow without feeling like the one interrupting.

"Hey, Dan, this is Sadie," Mel said, gesturing behind herself. "Sadie, Dan."

"And don't ever ask him for a favor," Joe put in.

"Ask me for favors that aren't weird," Dan countered with a small laugh.

"Yeah, yeah." The cook snorted, his good-natured tone softening his dismissive words. He turned to Sadie. "Did you like the dinner the other night?"

True to his word, Joe had sent boxed meals up to Sadie's room a few times already, with smaller portions for Izzy. Unfortunately, every last dish had been some kind of seafood, usually fish but occasionally crawdads or mussels. The pregnancy wasn't going easy enough on Sadie's stomach to let her even smell the fish, and she'd never eaten a single mouthful of the food Joe sent her. Izzy, in a particularly picky phase, wouldn't touch it, either.

But Joe wouldn't ask unless the answer mattered to him, so Sadie didn't tell him she'd thrown it all away. She smiled and said instead, "You're a wizard in that kitchen, Joe."

"Damn right," he said, preening, and took his leave of the lobby with an exaggerated swagger. Mel giggled as he went, and Sadie smiled, shaking her head.

"He's exhausting," Dan said, apparently oblivious to the good cheer Joe had left the others with. Mel and Sadie exchanged a quick, amused glance. But with Dan's interjection, the moment of levity passed, and Sadie recalled why she'd been interested to see this stranger manning the desk today.

"No Mr. Drye today?" She kept her voice mild to mask the sharpness of her curiosity and the hope it carried—this might be an opportunity.

"He takes Wednesdays and Thursdays off," Dan said, pulling the skeleton keys and their logbook up from beneath the counter. "You'll see me here instead." He smiled as he handed over the keys.

"Thanks," Sadie said, thinking fast. Mr. Drye's absence might provide the best chance for Sadie to get back into the office, back at the security camera feed. She flashed a friendly smile at Dan and added, "I hope he doesn't try to make you adhere to his weird no-breaks schedule while you're here."

"He did at first," Dan said, rolling his eyes. "But I reminded him about Ohio's labor laws and haven't heard a word about it since. 'Course, that was also when he dropped me down to two shifts a week."

"He's an asshole." Mel shook her head. "I'd quit, but this place works best around my class schedule. See ya later."

She wheeled her cart off, her steps a little slower than usual, her face a little pale. Sadie didn't follow her right away, watching for a moment as she tried to shake off a hint of guilt. She shouldn't have brought the beer to that party last night. When Mel had rounded the corner into the hallway, Sadie turned back to Dan.

"I heard another guest checked out and left a bunch of stuff behind," she said, deliberately mistaking the details to obscure the keenness of her interest. "Sounds like a pain for me and Mel today. Which room was that?"

"You mean the guest who *didn't* check out, just left behind a huge mess?" Dan said, rolling his eyes. "People these days are so entitled."

Sadie hid a grimace and said only, "Uh, yeah, I guess so."

"Room one-twenty-seven," Dan said. "And good luck. The laundry shift last night were pretty mad about it."

"Thanks," Sadie said, then pushed her cart out of the lobby and after Mel, hastening her steps to catch up with the younger woman. "How're you feeling?" she asked.

"You mean, am I hungover?" Mel whispered. She smiled a little and went on, "Yeah, but it was fun anyway. I wish you could've stayed."

"Sorry. I had to get back to Izzy."

"I bet you're a good mom. I should've used that bug spray you brought. How does a person even get a mosquito bite on the bottom of their foot? It's driving me crazy."

"Ugh, I'm sorry, that sounds annoying."

"Yeah. Hey! Are you on TikTok?"

"Facebook," Sadie said.

"Oh, no, Sadie. Facebook is for old people. I only have it to keep in touch with my grandma."

"I guess I'm old people, then," Sadie said with a chuckle.

"You got your phone on you?"

"Always." Who in this day and age didn't have their phone with them? Well, perhaps some people. But Sadie had needed it when she'd been with Sam, had needed to keep an eye out for his texts or calls, and she hadn't broken the habit of keeping it near at hand. She pulled it from her pocket. When Mel held her hand out for the phone, Sadie checked first and dismissed three missed calls with the swipe of a finger before passing it over.

"Friend request sent . . ." Mel murmured at her own phone, then switched her focus to Sadie's. "And . . . accepted." She handed Sadie's phone back with a grin. "One of my friends took a really pretty picture of you last night when you were out on that pier. Is it okay if I tag you in it?"

"Oh." Sadie paused. She and her family kept up with one another only over social media, and if a picture of Sadie at a party full of nineteen-year-olds suddenly interrupted their regular Izzy content, they'd make such snide comments. Besides, Sadie had made her Facebook private and had blocked Sam, but she didn't trust that to stop him from finding a way to snoop. Sadie couldn't even contemplate explaining any of that to Mel. She didn't want the other woman's judgment or pity.

"Sadie?" Mel prompted her.

"Uh, yeah, no," Sadie said. "Please don't tag me in any photos."

"Oh. Sure, no problem."

The conversation petered out after that, dampened by the combination of Sadie's quiet, lingering discomfort and Mel's hangover. Mel showed Sadie which rooms to clean before going off to clean her own. Sadie stood at the first door and pretended to fiddle with the key in the lock again, watching the younger housekeeper in her peripheral vision.

As soon as Mel had opened a door and gone inside, Sadie tucked her key back into her pocket and grabbed the handle of her cart again. She tried to wheel it quietly down the hall, eyes on the door numbers as she went. There, 127, the room Dan had mentioned.

With a quick glance up and down the hall, adrenaline vibrating in her chest and tingling under her skin, Sadie pulled her key out of her pocket and fitted it into the lock. For once, it slid smoothly in and turned on the first try. Swallowing hard, Sadie pushed the door open fast.

Or tried to.

With a rattle and a noise that could not have been as loud as Sadie imagined, the door jerked to a stop beneath her hand. She glanced up toward the source of the sound.

The door chain near the top had been locked from the inside.

That made no sense. Hadn't the laundry staff gotten the linens from this room? Hadn't they said it had been abandoned?

Even knowing it would not work, that it was designed not to work, Sadie slipped a hand inside and reached up, trying to disengage the chain. She felt along the chain and the slot its end fitted into. Unable to see her own hand on the other side of the door, her flesh crawled with imagined touch. Creeping unease overwhelmed her. She yanked her hand back out of the room.

Her clandestine excitement soured, the hum of adrenaline becoming a buzz that made her fingers tremble. Her heart beat harder, faster, and the back of her neck tightened. Caught, she was going to get caught doing something she shouldn't be. Snooping where she shouldn't snoop. Other peoples' business. Going where she didn't belong.

(*"Don't lie. Why are you really in my office? Did you go through the drawers? Mess with my files? Did you touch my computer?"*

"No, really, I was dusting, look—"

"I said don't *lie to me! Get over here!"*)

Sadie rubbed one hand over the back of her neck and paused, forcing herself to take a slow breath. That fear wasn't hers, not really. Sam had given her that fear, and as she'd told herself when she left every bit of her jewelry behind, she would take nothing with her that he'd given her.

Risking an extra moment, risking a relaxation of vigilance, Sadie closed her eyes and made herself take another three slow breaths. When she opened her eyes she half expected to see Mel or Dan or even Mr. Drye in the hallway, ready to ask what she was up to. But she still stood alone in this dim green stretch of corridor.

Calmer now, Sadie tried one more time to release the chain, then gave up and pulled the door closed again.

What now?

Sadie tried not to think about the chained room as she pushed her cart back to the one she should have been cleaning. She moved quickly through the chore, skipping anything that at least looked clean, and emerged into the hallway at the same time as Mel. The two housekeepers spent the morning in quiet work, Sadie's preoccupation with the locked room pushing away such concerns as small talk or worrying about whether Mel was only feeling unwell, or offended.

Sadie spent her lunch break in her room with Izzy and Gertie. She smiled at Izzy, at the way her daughter's red curls caught light from the window and glowed like fire, and at the curve of her cheeks. Her lively animation almost drove Sadie's preoccupation with locked doors out of her head. Izzy was beautiful the way every baby seemed beautiful to their mother—heartbreakingly so. Sadie's throat tightened with a tumble of love and fear and then more love. Something novel, too, something like eagerness and something like dread, when she thought of the new baby. Under the desk, unseen, Sadie pressed her hand flat against her belly, no larger yet, and wondered how Izzy would take to being a big sister, and thought about how the new baby's head would smell, and ached already at the sleepless nights to come.

Amid all that, the image of the chain across the door rose stark and bright to her mind again.

The mystery didn't simply distract her from the moment, it washed the warmth out of her. She and Izzy and whoever the baby would be needed L'Arpin Hotel, needed the paychecks, the time to get back on their feet, and the safe place to stay.

But only if it *was* safe.

Maybe the conversation with Mel earlier, the way it'd brought her family to mind, made them drift to the surface now. Sadie glanced at her phone not with fear of Sam for once, but with a bitter kind of longing.

If she called her mother right now, if she said things were hard and she needed somewhere to go—it would be just as bad as when Sadie brought Izzy to Wisconsin for a few months after August died. Her brother's snide comments and her father's chilly disapproval would be nothing compared to the way her mother would try again to take control of parenting Izzy, and with a new baby on the way it would be flat-out dangerous if she pulled another stunt like that "chickenpox party" she'd tried to sneak Izzy to last time.

No, Sadie couldn't call her parents. Not for something like

this—not for anything short of the end of the world. She had to land on her feet, on her own. She had to keep Izzy safe without having a safety net herself.

And to do that, Sadie had to look in that room.

Ten minutes before her break ended, she stood, turned to Gertie, and smiled apologetically. "I'm sorry, I just realized I forgot to clean the bathtub in one of the rooms. I'm just going to run down and do that now, while I have time." The lie came out smooth and easy, her tone saying what the words never did: *Nothing to worry about, don't be upset.*

"Well, of course, Sadie, you wouldn't want to leave a task half-finished," Gertie said just a little sharply, as if she'd been the one to discover Sadie shirking and needed to scold her. "I'll put your leftovers"—she cast a pointed look at yet another unopened to-go container from Joe in the kitchen—"into the fridge for you. We wouldn't want to be wasteful."

Sadie wiped up the mess Izzy had made of her lunch, kissed the little girl atop her head, and swept out of the room. In the elevator, she tied her apron back on, but on the first floor instead of returning to her cart, she headed out through the lobby. She expected Dan to ask where she was going, but the space behind the counter was empty. Sadie breathed a sigh of relief as she stepped out into the crisp, unseasonably bright day and turned to take the sidewalk leading along the side of the building.

As she walked, she tried to picture the layout of the hotel. Glimpses in the windows helped a little at first—there she passed the window into the lobby, here the small dining room, that window showed a linoleum-floored stairwell—but then she came to the first of the guest rooms. Although this part of the hotel didn't face the power plant, most of these rooms still had drawn curtains. The few that didn't, Sadie glanced into with increasing trepidation. The idea that someone might look back out through one of those windows and take her for a creep made her cringe, unpleasant heat crawling up her neck. Still, she at least knew when the windows had become guest rooms, and she counted them by twos as she walked.

At room 127's window, she paused, chewing her lip. Uncomfortable possibilities swirled around her. Had she miscounted? Had she misremembered the layout and forgotten something vital? She didn't think so.

Setting her jaw, Sadie glanced up and down the sidewalk and then behind her, at the parking lot. Then she stepped over a row of flowers she couldn't name, doggedly hanging on to life this late in the season. The thick mulch gave under her weight, more pleasant than the concrete. She pushed between two bushes and leaned close to the window. The curtains were drawn here, too, but the gap in the middle should give her at least a peek. Sadie raised her hands to either side of her face, blocking out the reflection of the parking lot behind her to better let her see into the room.

Rumpled bedding, a pillow on the floor, and a towel in the doorway leading into the bathroom gave Sadie pause. Hadn't the laundry staff been complaining about this room? Why was the bedding still there? Indistinct shapes on the nightstand on the far side of the bed might be personal belongings, but however hard Sadie squinted she couldn't make it out for sure. A streak on one wall caught her eye, the wallpaper darker near the door, and the carpet, too. If it was a stain, it could have been there for ages, but what else—

"What're you doing there!" Lewis McCann did not ask the question so much as shout it, and Sadie let out a high yelp as she spun to face him. Her foot slipped on the mulch and she grabbed the brickwork framing the window behind her, scraping the heel of her right palm. Her heart raced and her stomach twisted. She schooled her expression to one of calm, but not before the gardener's eyes narrowed at whatever he saw on her face—guilt, perhaps, or fear?

"Well?" he asked.

"What?"

"What are you doing peeking in that room?"

"It's—it's an empty one. Someone left without checking out again. I tried to go in to clean it, but the chain was across the door."

The chain, yes. That was why she was out here. Forgetting Lewis for a moment, Sadie turned to peer in again. The chain no longer barred the door. Was this the wrong room?

". . . into guest's rooms, snooping around, I don't know who—"

"Sorry," Sadie said, cutting off the gardener's angry muttering. "Sorry, I was trying to help." She sidled back out between the bushes. "I'll get out of your way. Sorry."

"Don't trample my flowers!" Lewis called after Sadie as she hustled away, trying not to look hurried. Once around the corner and out of sight of the gardener, she broke into a brief sprint. The moment she reached the lobby doors she paused, composed herself, and pushed through them into the hotel.

She crossed the dim lobby fast, keeping to a speedy walk until she reached the part of the hallway that she thought she remembered as being out of range of the camera. Then she ran again, skidding to a stop only when she reached room 127. This time when she unlocked the door it opened with ease. Before Sadie stepped in she glanced around the corner, peering at the window, making sure Lewis wasn't still in line of sight from outside. Then she turned her attention to the room itself.

It appeared just as it had seemed from the window. Bedding, pillow, towel. Sadie stepped down the little hallway leading from the door into the room proper and leaned out to peer around the corner. The nightstand came into view, and the items on it. A pair of glasses and a metal water bottle.

Turning back to the doorway, the dark stain Sadie had seen before caught her eye. She drew nearer, and light from the hall glimmered across it. Dark because it was wet. Sadie leaned forward with the idea to smell it, to see if she could tell what it might be without having to touch it. Before she drew too near, though, something other than reflected hallway light gleamed within the stain. Sadie blinked and the impression vanished, but left enough unease behind that she leaned away again.

She had to see the security feed.

Skittering out into the hallway, Sadie didn't bother to shut the door behind her this time. She ran back to the lobby, heedless of the startled exclamation Mel let out as Sadie flashed past her. Dan had still not returned from wherever he'd gone—maybe his break, but that hardly mattered. What mattered was that, though Mel followed her, calling her name in a concerned voice, no one stood between Sadie and the security feed.

Of course, once she got into the office Sadie abruptly remembered that she wasn't sure how to access the footage, much less pull up the correct dates and times or speed up the frame rate. She turned to call out to Mel for help when the younger housekeeper hurried through the door, and the two women collided. Sadie held her nose where Mel's forehead had bashed her, breathing against pain that made her eyes water.

"Video footage, not just the lobby, all the exits," she said, breathing so hard she nearly gasped. "All day yesterday."

"This was kinda fun and all the first time, but maybe—"

"Please, Mel? I won't ask again, I'll watch how you do it this time, okay?"

Mel took a breath as if to speak, then held it a moment before letting it out sharply instead. "Fine. Then will you get back to work? I don't want Mr. Drye writing us both up because you've got some weird obsession."

"Yes, absolutely."

Sadie watched closely as the younger woman clicked through menu options, trying to memorize the sequence and commands she used. Mel pulled up the security feed for every camera Sadie requested, splitting the screen, and played through the previous day in fast-forward.

Tiny people zoomed in and out of frames, entered and left the hotel. Sadie tried to look for any male guest wearing the glasses she'd seen on the nightstand, but several of the people in the footage wore glasses and the resolution didn't allow her to pick out enough detail to identify any one of them. A weight of futility settled in the pit of Sadie's stomach. She wouldn't learn anything this way. It wasn't like the guest she'd seen in the pool. She didn't know what to look for. Instead of trying to pick out an individual, Sadie had to look for anything untoward in the footage.

Anything at all. *Anything.*

Nothing.

All this running and panicking had been for nothing. The heaviness in her gut didn't ease, the tangle of suspicion twisting her thoughts didn't loosen. Finding nothing didn't mean nothing had happened. It meant the opposite, Sadie was sure. But it also meant she still had no proof. No certainty.

"Are you done?" Mel asked.

"I'm done," Sadie said. "Sorry."

"It's cool. Let's just chill on the paranoia for now, okay?"

An unexpected twist of pain and struggle for breath caught Sadie by surprise.

(*"Why would I do that? You sound like a psycho." "That's not what happened." "You're imagining things." "You're making shit up." "I'm worried about you, this paranoia isn't healthy."*)

Paranoia.

"Right," Sadie said, keeping her tone light. The younger woman's voice had not been unkind, had been jocular even, but Sadie couldn't bring herself to mirror that humor. "Well, let's get back to work, I guess."

The word echoed in Sadie's head as she went back to work. She cleaned rooms on autopilot, mechanical and inattentive. Paranoia.

Was the lack of evidence in the tapes evidence itself?

Or was she being paranoid?

No. No, she was being observant. She'd missed all the signs, all the red flags, before. And god, had she paid for that—living in a single tiny room with her toddler felt like freedom after the mistakes she'd made. She had to learn from those mistakes, didn't she?

But Sadie's thoughts spiraled through a lifetime in which she really did turn paranoid. Always jumping at shadows, always trying not to run down any ill-lit hallway. Teaching Izzy that fear, teaching it to the new baby. Never trusting, and leaving that as her legacy. What kind of life would her children have, if she had only that to give them?

No evidence was simply no evidence. She *was* being paranoid, wasn't she? And she owed it to Izzy—owed it to herself, but that always felt dim and distant—to let go of something so poisonous.

By the end of her shift, Sadie's conviction that L'Arpin harbored some sinister secret seemed vaguely shameful. The exhaustion of running on adrenaline and high emotion dragged at her. Going through the motions, wrapped up in self-recrimination, Sadie fretted through microwaving dinner.

What if she'd damaged her working relationship with Mel? What if Lewis accused her of peeping through windows? What if Gertie stopped watching Izzy? What if Mr. Drye remembered to kick her out of the hotel after the agreed-upon duration of their stay?

That worry she came back to the most, like a wave washing over a stone—except it never lost its sharp edges, never smoothed like a stone from the lake would smooth.

Even if she did everything right, if Mr. Drye remembered to tell her to leave, she and Izzy would still be in her car with nowhere to go.

While Izzy ate SpaghettiOs with most of the sauce drained off, Sadie picked halfheartedly at a canned-chicken sandwich, scrolling forrent.com and apartments.com on her phone. What kind of place could she afford if she lost L'Arpin? At best a dirty, poorly maintained apartment that would take up all her funds and leave her with no way to save or find daycare for Izzy, no way to do anything at all.

After putting Izzy to bed, Sadie ran a shower. She forced herself to bathe slowly. She forced herself to ignore the way the back of her neck crawled, the cold in her gut that hot water couldn't ease. If nothing else, the heart-pounding certainty that someone watched her as she washed herself proved to Sadie that her fears absolutely were out-of-control paranoia.

When she went to bed, her hair still damp and smelling of cheap hotel shampoo, Sadie resolved to put all this nonsense behind her.

Until she started her shift the next morning and glanced reflexively up and to the right, toward the lobby's security camera. Fear sour in her mouth, Sadie tried to be casual as she checked the exits, one after another, and the pool.

The cameras had all been removed.

CHAPTER SEVEN

Places to Let Go

Sadie chewed the end of the pen she'd found in a drawer in her desk, staring from her phone to a notepad she'd discovered with the pen. A column of numbers ran down one side of the page, a jumble of scribbled notes filling the other. Hunched over, her elbow resting on the little desk, Sadie ran one hand through her hair and let out a long breath.

"I wanna help you, Mommy!" Izzy piped up, and Sadie hid a wince. Budgeting was nothing that should worry a toddler.

"I'm all right, stinker, I don't need any help. Thanks, though." Sadie leaned back in her chair and stretched, trying to ease the tension that had crawled up her spine and settled along her shoulder blades. "You can sit in the other chair with your coloring book."

"Opay."

Sadie helped Izzy get settled, equally glad for the distraction and frustrated by it, then returned to her seat.

"See? I am helping you," Izzy said as she grabbed her first crayon in one fist and scrawled a scribble across the page.

"Thanks for helping," Sadie said, watching her daughter with a smile for a moment before turning back to her finances and her phone. She tapped the filter icon on forrent.com's website and switched from searching for three-bedroom apartments to two-bedroom.

It made the difference Sadie needed. She scratched out old numbers, scribbled in new, and then ran her finger down the list of figures, double-checking. If she looked for two-bedroom places instead of three, she should have enough by the end of March to get herself and Izzy out.

Sadie tapped her pen on the desktop. Izzy copied her a moment later, hitting the desk with a purple crayon, giggling. "I'm just like you, Mommy!"

"You sure are, stinker," Sadie said. She gave the budget one more long, sour look, then folded it up for later and tucked it away on a shelf Izzy couldn't reach. She'd get into a more detailed apartment search later. It was enough—for now—that she'd gotten her timeline and saving goals worked out. Late March.

They could be out of L'Arpin before April if everything went okay.

When a knock at the door caught Sadie's attention a few moments later, it didn't startle her into a fearful freeze. She knew Gertie's quick, light tap by now. Sadie opened the door to see Gertie dressed for chilly weather, her smile bright.

"I'm going for a walk and I was hoping you'd come with me?" Gertie said, bustling into the room. "Do you want to bring your mama and go for a walk with Gertie, Izzy?"

"Walk!" Izzy cried, jumping up and running for the little closet.

It was on the tip of Sadie's tongue to demur—she liked to plan outings better—but Izzy had been getting so restless lately. And how much of Gertie's invitation to join them was about being sociable and neighborly, and how much was need? Maybe Gertie felt hesitant to walk alone. What if she fell?

"Sounds good," Sadie said, and ten minutes later the three of them stepped out of the elevator and into the lobby.

"Good morning, ladies," Mr. Drye called from behind his desk.

"Oh, one moment," Gertie said to Sadie, then turned and raised her voice a little, still addressing Sadie but making the words for Mr. Drye, "I need to discuss something with Henry."

Mr. Drye's expression turned a little apprehensive for an instant, then smoothed. Sadie took Izzy's hand and led her to linger by the door. When Gertie reached the desk, she leaned closer to Mr. Drye, but she didn't lower her voice as much as she probably thought, and the lobby carried sound well.

"Have you looked into what I was telling you about?"

"I'm sorry, Ms. Harper, I've been busy, and . . . well, I honestly don't see the need."

"Oh, don't you, young man?" Gertie's voice lost its quaver, turning sharp instead. "Too busy, are you? Well." The older woman paused, perhaps taking a deep breath, then went on in something closer to her normal tone. "I don't care whether you see the need or not. I'm right." Gertie lowered her voice further, perhaps keeping her scold private to avoid embarrassing Mr. Drye in front of an employee. Between her softness and Izzy's fidgeting, Sadie caught only a handful of words. "Every . . . ought to . . . at least one . . . if only . . . guests with babies . . . You wouldn't . . . that oversight . . . you?"

Mr. Drye held himself with stiff attentiveness—Sadie guessed he wanted to tell Gertie to leave the running of L'Arpin to him but didn't quite dare disrespect a guest as profitable as she must be. Sadie suppressed a smile to see her boss discomfited for a change, all over a mostly sweet old busybody who thought she needed to tell everybody how to attend to their own business.

"Of course, Ms. Harper," he said, and only the barest shade of insincerity in his voice told Sadie he was humoring Gertie.

Gertie herself seemed not to catch the tone, because she nodded and patted Mr. Drye's hands, and in a louder, more cheery voice she said, "Wonderful, Henry. Thank you." Turning back to Sadie and Izzy, she smiled and made a shooing gesture. "Out we go. Out we go."

Outside, the older woman struck off not for the sidewalk next to the street but in the direction of the Cut. "All the cars make me nervous," Gertie said over her shoulder.

Sadie held her daughter's mittened hand tightly as they went down the concrete steps, eyeing Lake Erie spread out before them. Her daughter had never seen anything like this, and as Izzy gasped, Sadie's discomfort dwindled.

"See that rock thing? It's called a pier. If you promise to hold Mommy's hand and walk slowly and be so careful, we can walk out on it and see the lake from out there."

"Yes!"

At the bottom of the stairs, Sadie touched Gertie's shoulder. "I'm going to walk her out to the end of the pier. Can you—I mean, do you want to walk out with us?"

"I'll just wait here."

Sadie nodded and led her daughter out onto the stones. "Watch your step, Iz."

"Opay, Mommy."

The wind sounded hollower and wilder the moment they stepped up onto the pier. Sadie probably only imagined the difference, and she couldn't tell whether she found it exciting or nerve-racking.

At the end of the pier, Sadie glanced down at her daughter, who studiously kept her eyes on her boots, and chuckled. "You can stop watching your step, stinker. Look up. Look at the lake."

Izzy looked up and gasped. "It's so, *so* big!"

Before them, Lake Erie spread, huge and steely gray. The smooth, low cloud cover above the lake didn't carry the dark depth of the water's tone, but still the gray-on-gray vista invited a certain lack of focus, as if Sadie might take off her glasses and soften the whole world.

Water lapped stone behind them. Somewhere in the tumbled rocks of the pier were gaps where the slabs didn't quite fit or where the relentless motion of the lake had carved niches; occasionally, a tiny wave would surge a little higher than the others, and from under their feet or behind and below them an echoing *gla-thunk* replaced the water's normal slap and splash. The sound made

Sadie think of bigger hollows than she knew were possible—not holes but caves. Not caves but hiding places. Places to watch from. The shiver that danced over her skin had little to do with the chill November air. Maybe walking all the way out here hadn't been her best idea.

In the week and a half since the security cameras had vanished—removed, Mr. Drye explained, because the monthly service fee to the security company outweighed their usefulness—Sadie had felt watched everywhere in L'Arpin. Now her unease had followed her to the beach. She tried to quell the unpleasant tightening in her gut.

"Why's it all gray?" Izzy asked.

"It only looks that way in this light."

Gertie's thin voice called from back on the beach, "Lake Erie used to be thinking about freezing up by now, when I was young."

How her voice carried all the way out to the end of the pier, over the water and wind, Izzy's excited shouts, and the piercing cries of a few seagulls flapping in agitation on the other side of the razor-wired fence, Sadie didn't know. She had thought of seagulls as summertime birds, not November birds. The way they squalled and squabbled over some prize hidden in the sand and scrubby growth made her uncomfortable.

"Let's head back, Izzy. Gertie must be lonely back there," Sadie said, lifting her daughter. Only nine weeks pregnant now, Sadie still wasn't showing, and she wasn't experiencing any of the looseness or pain in her joints that would come later, but still as she lifted Izzy she wondered if she ought to start encouraging her daughter's independence a little more. The idea stung her with a melancholy kind of pride, and she kept her eyes on her feet as much to hide the tears she blinked away as to watch for uneven stones or slick puddles.

"I love you, stinker."

"I love you, too. Who's over there?"

"That's Gertie, waiting for us on the beach."

Izzy's mood changed in a flash, as it did almost every time she'd been misunderstood. "*No!* Not onna beach! Who's—that—over—*there!*" She squirmed in Sadie's grasp, stiffening her legs and lifting her arms in a way that always made her harder to hold, and Sadie stopped walking to clutch her daughter more tightly.

"Hey," Sadie said, pitching her voice low and soothing, "I didn't understand. I'm sorry. I can't understand if you're screaming, either. Can you use your calm voice for me? It will help Mommy understand you."

At Izzy's age, Sadie didn't know if her tone and the continuous soft litany of her voice calmed her daughter, or if the simple logic appealed to Izzy. She thought Izzy listened better when Sadie explained her reasoning, but it might have been that Sadie remembered to stay calmer herself when she used this method of soothing her child.

Either way, Izzy stilled and stopped struggling in her mother's arms, going limp in a way that always made Sadie want to hug her tight and never let go.

"Can I kiss your cheek, stinker?" Sadie said, and when Izzy nodded, she did, then said, "Okay. What did you want to tell Mommy?" She started walking again, suddenly aware of Gertie on the beach, watching Izzy's flash tantrum, maybe judging Sadie, maybe reconsidering her position on babysitting the toddler so much. Sadie didn't look in Gertie's direction.

"I saw a man looking at us," Izzy said, still sniffling a little.

Sadie's heart skipped, then raced. Her arms tightened around her daughter. But when she snapped her gaze to the end of the pier, the familiar figure of Sam Keller did not block her path back to the shore. He didn't stand atop the stairs. He didn't pace the sandy beach.

Of course not. Of course. If it had been Sam, Izzy would have *said* Sam. She knew him.

Who had Izzy seen watching them?

Sadie swallowed hard and started walking again, placing her

feet carefully, and took care to keep her voice normal when she said, "Where did you see someone watching us, stinker?" She realized her mistake immediately and added, "Tell me with your words, don't—"

Too late, Izzy had already leaned back from her mother's body and pointed away, across the water, across the sand, toward the power plant. Sadie followed her daughter's gesture and frowned. A figure stood on one of the walkways running outside the building overshadowing the beach. From here, Sadie could pick out no features, but his build, as well as the hostility in his crossed arms and wide stance, struck her as familiar. That yelling man from her first day at L'Arpin, the one who had run out to chase her off his parking lot.

From the beach, Gertie called out again, her voice carrying surprisingly well over the waves once more, "Don't pay any mind to Bill Viago, he's a sour good-for-nothing."

Sadie glanced at the older woman, standing half-turned away from them as if she'd followed the direction of Izzy's point as well. When Sadie looked back toward the plant, Viago—now Sadie had a last name to go with the unpleasant fellow—had turned his back, making his way down the walk toward an open door. When he disappeared into his plant, the lingering sensation of being watched didn't ease in the slightest.

Sadie and Izzy rejoined Gertie on the beach, and Sadie set her daughter down on the sand, away from the water's edge.

"You said something about the lake freezing?" Sadie asked, reaching for some normal topic of conversation to distract her from her racing heart.

"When I was a girl I used to wonder what it would be like to try to walk all the way across Lake Erie to Canada. That was before the boating accident that took my family. I was the only one who made it back to shore."

Gertie spoke without a trace of grief. Would decades and decades give her that same detachment when she spoke about August?

"I'm so sorry." Sadie reached for the older woman's hand, and Gertie gave her a brisk pat.

"After that, when the water froze, I hated it. This damn power plant is good for that, at least. This beach almost never freezes. The rest of the lake seems to take longer each year to ice over, too, though. I like it better this way."

Sadie almost let the words run out of her then, almost said *I lost my husband* and *Izzy was a year old* and *she will never remember him* and *god, sometimes she looks just like him*. The lump in her throat choked the words off, and she turned instead to watch her daughter kicking sand at the water, looked from there out over the lake again. She imagined it iced over, white and solid and dormant, and didn't find the comfort Gertie seemed to feel at the thought of the lake never freezing.

Izzy squatted and dug her hands into the sand, mittens and all. Sadie let out an exasperated noise but didn't tell her to stop—the damage was done.

Perhaps mistaking Sadie's exasperation, Gertie said, "Look at her trying to leave her mark. That's another thing I like about the lake, how it erases anything we do here. Beaches feel like places to let go." Gertie's voice took on an almost conspiratorial tone, and when Sadie turned to the older woman, she found her watching with an expression that looked warm and patient.

Places to let go. To Sadie's surprise, she found she didn't mind that Gertie seemed to know she would find meaning in the phrase. In fact, she felt easy enough to say, "I like that, too."

Gertie patted her shoulder and said, "Sometimes everybody needs to remember we can let go."

How much did Gertie guess about Sadie and Izzy? About their past, about how near it loomed in Sadie's thoughts?

The old woman went on, "Moving forward gets easier with time, you know, Sadie."

Maybe Gertie guessed a lot. She didn't pry, though, taking her hand away at that moment and shuffling across the sand to Izzy, where she leaned down and picked something out of the little hole the girl had dug. Izzy exclaimed in delight, and Sadie smiled, grateful for the old woman.

In that moment of letting go, of smiling and forgetting the cloud of worry and suspicion she'd tried to leave behind with Sam in Finneytown and found again instead at L'Arpin, there came a furtive sound of slipping and dragging. Sadie turned toward the noise, her smile drying up. It came again from the other side of the pier.

She cast a quick glance at her daughter. Izzy and Gertie remained occupied with Izzy's little hole in the sand, a safe distance from the water. The sound came again—dragging, sliding, *slick*. Moving silently on the sand, Sadie crossed toward the rocks. Nearer, soft drips of water joined the dragging sounds.

A gasping gurgle rose above the other noises, and Sadie's fear transformed from suspicion to panic. Not some nebulous unnamable *thing* on the rocks, but a person, a person drowning and dragging themselves up out of the water and choking on the lake and needing help *now*, and Sadie was crossing the rest of the distance to the pier at a run.

She put a foot wrong on the first stone. Gasping, she stumbled, one knee and both palms striking the rocks. The wet choking sound came again, shorter and sharper. Something slithered. Something splashed.

Sadie scrambled up the side of the pier and to the flat path in the center. There was another splash, and Sadie hurried down the length of stone, following the sound. Halfway out she stopped and looked down the other side.

The stones there gleamed, wet. Amid the motion of the small waves, ripples spread from just near that spot. Even as she watched they settled, stilled.

"Mommy?" Izzy's voice drifted from behind her, curious but not alarmed.

"What are you doing, Sadie?" Gertie asked, her tone concerned.

Sadie didn't answer. She scanned the water, her breath coming fast and hard. She imagined someone sinking, reaching, drifting.

Nothing. No one.

No, wait.

A shadow? Something . . . something far down in the murky lake, maybe even all the way at the bottom. Sadie sat in a cold puddle, yanking at her shoelaces. "Hold Izzy's hand, Gertie!" she shouted without turning.

The shadow moved.

It didn't just move, it rippled.

And light flowed within that ripple. Greenish, faint tracing outlines, like pointillism dabbed into the lake.

Sadie's jaw fell open. She stared, wet butt and half-removed shoe forgotten. The shape, too large to be a person as she'd feared, shivered again. Then it shot away, hugging the lake floor. It moved so *fast*, Sadie lost it after a mere second. She rose slowly to her feet. The water before and behind her moved slowly, steadily, and with what suddenly looked very much like intent.

Surrounded.

Sadie didn't let herself run back down the pier, but only because the thought of slipping and falling into all that gray, menacing water filled her with crawling dread.

"Everything okay, Sadie?" Gertie asked as Sadie neared.

"It's fine."

"Mommy?"

"It's time to go, Izzy."

"I don't *wanna* go!" Izzy wailed.

Sadie did not pause to calm her child. She scooped her up in her arms and hauled her up the stairs and off the beach, ignoring wails that became screams, ignoring her shame at the thought of Gertie following silently behind them, and completely unable to ignore the itching, creeping sensation of being watched.

CHAPTER EIGHT

Snooping Around

Sadie stared at the ceiling, one pillow under her head and one wrapped tight in her arms. Beyond the window the few birds remaining so late into the year began their morning chorus before the sun even lightened the sky.

Izzy's night-light illuminated the room well enough for Sadie to trace the shape of an old water stain on the ceiling while she replayed a moment from the previous afternoon.

After fleeing the beach, with Izzy writhing dangerously in Sadie's grip all the way up those concrete stairs, she'd finally paused to look behind her. She'd meant to check for some sign of what frightened her, for pursuit. Instead, she'd seen only Gertie, far below, still laboring up the steps alone with both hands on the rust-spotted rails to either side.

Shame churned in her gut. A whisper of danger—less than that, even, a *figment*—and she'd run off and left a little old lady to fend for herself. Alone in bed, alone in the dark, Sadie could admit to herself that if she didn't rely so heavily on Gertie's goodwill, she might have run on. The thought made her sick.

Actually sick. Nausea swelled abruptly.

Suppressing a gag, Sadie pushed her pillow away and stood in a hurry. She clapped a hand over her mouth and hustled silently to the bathroom, not even bothering to turn on the light. She dropped to her knees by the toilet and had barely lifted the lid and seat up before she vomited. She spat, then vomited a second time, bringing less up. She dry heaved twice after that, spat again, then leaned back from the toilet with a disgusted grunt. Pregnancy nausea. She sure hadn't missed that.

She needed to flush that mess and brush her teeth but didn't want the light or the noise to wake Izzy. Still without flipping the switch, Sadie pushed herself to her feet. Just before she could shut the door, a soft sound came from behind her. Sadie went still and listened, her sour mouth drying. Maybe she hadn't heard anything. Maybe she had, and it was just a normal hotel noise. L'Arpin's age caused it to make lots of strange noises.

There it was again.

The hair on the back of Sadie's neck stood up. Her breath caught. The sound had come from the tub. Not a drip, not like if she'd left the faucet on just a tiny bit after Izzy's bath.

A splash.

Sadie's skin went cold as she turned toward the tub. She knew she'd drained the water after Izzy's bath last night because she'd taken a shower after putting Izzy to bed. There shouldn't be enough in the tub to splash.

Even so, the sound came again. Quiet. Sneaky. Something hiding under the surface in a tub that should have been empty.

Sadie tried not to think of the rippling shadow sliding away along the bottom of the lake a few hours before, but she couldn't shake the memory. Would she find something rippling here, something dancing with its own light in the darkness of the bathroom?

Swallowing unpleasantly, Sadie crept closer to the tub. She reached with trembling fingers for the shower curtain. Just before her fingers brushed the cheap plastic, something *squelched*.

Sadie jerked her hand back with a little cry, then covered her mouth again. That sound had come not from the tub but from the direction of the door. Stumbling in her haste, Sadie spun and hurried back into the main room. Even as she started toward Izzy, she picked out the sleeping shape of her daughter lying undisturbed in the night-light's glow. The *squelch* came again, slightly muffled.

The hallway.

Turning slowly, Sadie flinched as the sound repeated, louder. Nearer. Sadie crept slowly at first but faster with every step, until she'd closed the last of the distance in a rush and had to pull up short to avoid running into the door. The squelching continued, slow and steady and increasingly faint. Something moved away down the hallway outside her door.

Advancing with slow care, she set her hands gently on either side of the peephole. And then she froze. Her breath came faster, harder. Her skin crawled, scalp tight. If she leaned forward and put her eye to that peephole she would see whatever made that sound. What could make a sound like that in the hallway? What if she looked and saw something so horrible she had to act?

Wouldn't it be easier not to look?

Sadie shook herself once, hard, and then before she could stop herself she leaned forward and put her eye to the peephole.

Too slow. A shadow slipped out of the range of her peephole's fish-eyed view just as she looked. The *squelching* faded and faded. The green, shadow-dappled carpet had a long, dark stain running down its worn-thin center, gleaming in the pools of illumination under the sparse lights. Wet. Not just wet, but *sopping*. No matter how she strained herself, though, Sadie could see nothing else without opening the door.

Out of the question.

A loud creak and a thump made her flinch. Sadie rarely used the stark and somehow perpetually chilly stairwell, but she'd heard the door leading to it slam shut often enough to recognize it. Whatever—no, *who*ever—well, they weren't in her hallway any longer.

Still, Sadie stayed pressed against the door, breath shallow, listening hard. No new drips or splashes, no new damp, horrible squishing.

No birds.

Their songs and calls outside simply stopped.

Sadie spun and slipped through the room to the window, a little less dark than it had been before. She reached for the curtains, then drew her hand back instead and dropped into a crouch so only her eyes peered above the level of the windowsill. Then she parted the curtains just enough to peek through.

From this angle she could make out nothing more than the towering stacks of the power plant and a sky tinged with gray. Reluctance weighing her down, Sadie hunched up a little higher, stopping once she could see down into the parking lot.

Shadows. They moved low to the ground, with a gait Sadie couldn't identify—too smooth. She might almost have imagined them rolling, but that didn't quite fit, either. Their pace made no sense, either—faster one moment and slower the next, on and on.

Sadie's sharp, fast breath fogged the cool glass in a cloud that grew until she had to wipe it away to keep watching.

Wet and dragging, like whatever happened at the pier the day before, the shapes pulled themselves in the direction of the power plant and the scrubby trees beyond its brightly lit grounds.

Sadie's eyes widened. All the strangeness, all the quiet, watchful menace—could it all come not from L'Arpin itself but the plant? Anxiety fluttered in her stomach. So what? The unsettling goings-on wouldn't be erased. If the power plant somehow held the key to it all, that changed nothing.

Nothing except Mr. Drye and that surly gardener, Lewis, were harmless. Nothing except L'Arpin held no dangerous secrets itself. Which meant, really, it changed everything.

Sadie had to know.

She turned and bent over Izzy's fold-out bed, pausing with her hands extended. She shouldn't leave her daughter alone in the hotel room. But she *couldn't* bring her daughter to investigate a frightening mystery in a power plant.

Whispering so low she barely heard the words herself, Sadie implored Izzy, "Please stay asleep."

Then she snatched her key from the dresser and let herself out of the room, taking time only to ease the door shut before running down the hall. Her bare feet slapped through the water left in the middle of the carpet as Sadie made for the stairs. Little though she liked them, the elevator let out into the lobby. She couldn't be seen like this.

She burst through the door to the stairwell and blinked hard. Harsh fluorescent light replaced the dim half-illumination of the rest of the hotel. She let herself hesitate for only a moment before starting down.

The steps proved treacherous. Whatever had soaked the long green carpet in the corridor left a trail down the stairs as well, water that seemed to gleam oddly in the too-bright light. Sadie's heel came down in a puddle and slipped out from under her. She grabbed both banisters as her tailbone struck the steps, drawing a pained gasp from her. She slid a couple feet down, wrenching her shoulder.

Heart in her throat, she allowed herself half a second to sit still, trying not to imagine what would become of Izzy if Sadie fell down the stairs and cracked her skull open. She blinked hard, throat tightening, then swallowed and finally pulled herself upright again. After that, she kept to the sides of the steps, moving with more care and less speed, cursing the necessity of it.

Two doors stood at the ground floor, one an exit to the parking lot and one leading back into the hotel proper. Sadie slammed into the bar and shoved the outer door open. The cold mid-November morning wind off the lake nearly took her breath away. Skirting around the wetness, Sadie ran in the direction of the power plant. Her butt and her right heel and her shoulders ached, but Sadie knew how to conceal a limp, how to move without letting pain slow her too much, and she crossed the parking lot in only a moment.

She slowed a little at the edge of the painful lights of the power plant, squinting against the glare for whoever or whatever—no, *who*ever—she'd seen.

Nothing moved on the grounds of the power plant. The wet trail she'd been following continued over the asphalt and disappeared into the bracken under the trees lining the small cliff down to the Cut.

The Cut. The lake.

Sadie sped up again, raced for the concrete stairs leading down toward the beach. A stitch in her side made her wince. She pressed her hand against it and kept going.

At the top of the stairs, she stopped at last. A rattle drew her attention to the fence separating the public part of the beach from the stretch of sand and coarse grass claimed by the power company. A mound of displaced sand marked part of the bottom of that fence. And beyond it, heading toward the water, shapes she couldn't make out. They moved too fast, with too much uncanny fluidity, for her to identify them. Too fast, also, for her to catch up.

Sadie groped for the metal railings, the peeling black paint and small patches of rust rough under her skin. In spite of the futility, she descended the steps, slowly and with more care than she'd taken in L'Arpin. The chilly sand as she crossed the Cut at least felt better underfoot than the cold concrete had.

Frowning, she stopped several feet from the disturbed sand near the fence. She moved nearer to the chain links at an angle from the pile, so when she threaded her fingers into the metal wire diamonds and held on to the fence, she still stood a good length from that spot.

Far out beyond the towering silhouette of the plant, the sky lightened in washed-out gray increments. Sadie slumped, letting her weight sag against the fence, and squeezed her eyes shut as another wave of morning sickness turned her stomach. She heaved once and then swallowed it back down, refusing to risk being seen puking on the beach at whatever ungodly hour this was.

"What are you doing?"

The shout didn't make Sadie jump or flinch. It made her freeze, remaining bowed before her exhaustion and nausea, but wound tense. Her hands tightened on the fence and her heart thumped a hard, uneven rhythm. Then she took a sharp breath and straightened, squaring her shoulders before she turned.

Bill Viago stood not far behind her, his arms crossed and a thunderous scowl on his face. Why here, on the public side of the fence? Before Sadie could speak, he took a hard, fast step toward her, and her stomach dropped. The tide of confused anger—at Bill for scaring her, at Sam for making her so easy to intimidate, at herself for being frightened—that rose immediately after surprised Sadie. She tried to hold it, anything to hang on to instead of nervousness or paranoia, but it slipped away as Bill pointed at her and barked, "Snooping around? Your boss send you to make sure he's done enough damage?"

Sadie started to fall back a step, but her bare heel hit the bottom of the fence, giving it a wobbly rattle. She forced a frown onto her face to match Bill's scowl and took a step forward instead, crossing her own arms in what she hoped looked like a less defensive gesture than it felt. "I don't know what you're talking about."

"Like hell. You tell Drye it won't work!"

"*What* won't work?"

"All the fucking water damage isn't closing my plant, and it isn't stopping the construction, so he can knock it the fuck off."

"Water damage?" Sadie repeated. She glanced out toward Lake Erie. Bill's appearance had startled her, made her forget why she'd come down here. Scanning the gray surface for any signs of life, she said, "How could Mr. Drye cause water damage in your facilities?"

"I don't know how and I honestly don't give a shit. You tell him to stop. Hey! Are you listening to me?"

From the corner of her eye, Sadie saw him reach for her arm. She sidestepped fast, turning back to him again and lifting her hands defensively. Her voice rang out high and sharp as she shouted, "Don't you dare touch me!"

The power plant overseer fell back a step, the anger dropping from his face. He raised his own hands, palms out. "Chill out, lady." His tone carried a weight of implication, as if Sadie was being unreasonable, maybe hysterical.

The anger of a moment before rose again and Sadie took a deep breath. "*You* chill out. Who sneaks up behind a woman alone on a secluded beach, corners her, and tries to grab her?"

"I wasn't—"

"You *absolutely* were. You were being *scary*. You stop that right now. And—and you owe me an apology." Sadie put her hands on her hips and straightened her shoulders. She tipped her head to give Bill the sternest glare she could manage over the rims of her glasses, a look she'd practiced to perfection in the classroom and with Izzy.

"If you hotel people would stop—"

"Cut that out. I've been there less than a month. I've seen you twice. How do you even know I work there and I'm not just a guest? Are *you* snooping around?"

"I don't snoop," Bill spluttered, voice indignant. "I'm keeping an eye out, because the damage to my facility, the cost of the repairs we might need, I *know* it's coming from L'Arpin." He scowled, and Sadie thought he was trying to find his momentum again. "So like I was saying, you better stop it."

"Me? All I do is clean the rooms, mister." Sadie sidled along the fence until she could walk around Bill without crossing into reaching distance. Over her shoulder she said, "Bother people who deserve it. And never try to touch me again."

She stormed away before Bill could formulate a response, and how much of the crawling up her spine came from the certainty that he watched her go, how much came from the fear that he'd follow her, and how much from the unsettling presence of Lake Erie, Sadie didn't know. Halfway up the concrete steps she wrapped her arms around herself and sped up a pace. She held herself together until she reached the top of the stairs, then she ran.

A delayed bolt of fear and rush of adrenaline brought hot, painful tears to her eyes. As if crying opened a path for it, the anger she'd tried to hold on to before overwhelmed her. Hatred edged the bitter wave, less for Bill than for Sam, but less for Sam than for herself for having been made so small that a perfect stranger's outburst could undo her like this.

And she knew that was wrong. She knew it wasn't fair. But as she crossed L'Arpin's parking lot, her nose running, breathing hard through her mouth, tears cold on her cheeks, she revisited over a year's worth of cringing deference—("I'm sorry." "Are you mad at me?" "I was wrong." "I must have misunderstood." "It was my fault." "I'm not mad." "What can I do?")—and hated herself for getting caught up in a man like Sam.

She slipped back into the door she'd left by. Beneath her damp feet, gritty sand ground on the smooth linoleum of the stairwell landing. The door closed behind her with a *thunk*, and Sadie leaned against the wall next to it, holding on to herself.

Her shoulders hunched, muscles so tense it hurt. She wound every bit of her body more and more taut, until the outside of her was a knot pulled impossibly tight, but the inside of her trembled and shivered. When Sadie sucked in a breath, the smallest whine escaped her, and that brought the burning tears back to her eyes. Sadie closed her eyes and took a breath, ready to push the self-recrimination down, bottle it up, and pretend it wasn't there so she could head upstairs and face her day.

Instead she paused, and with her eyes still closed she forced herself to face that loathing head-on. Hating herself for staying with Sam as long as she had would only poison her, she did know that much.

"Go away," she whispered out loud, and whether she whispered it to the memory of Sam Keller or to the weight of blame she heaped upon herself, whether much distinction existed between the two at all, Sadie didn't know.

The words didn't banish the shame and anger tearing at each other inside her chest, but they did diminish them, so she said it again, no louder but harsher. *"Go away."*

She'd remember this. She'd need to say it again and again, she didn't doubt that. But this did help.

It helped, too, to remember the way Bill Viago had stepped away from her when she'd given him a piece of her mind. With every passing second her discomfort receded and left in its place something like pride.

Sadie pushed herself away from the wall and climbed the stairs. The draining of her adrenaline left her shaky, all the aches from her slip down the stairs returned, and her damp feet slipped a little on each step, but she pulled herself up with all the haste she could muster.

When she got back to her room, Izzy still slept soundly in the little bed, easily visible in the gray of dawn that permeated the space and rendered the night-light unnecessary. That faint light didn't reach the bathroom.

Less mindful of waking her daughter now that daybreak had come, Sadie snapped on the bathroom light so she could flush the vomit and finally brush her teeth. Only then did she remember the splashing she'd heard earlier in the tub.

Sadie crossed the small bathroom in one quick step and yanked back the curtain.

The tub stood empty, and if it was damp it was probably only from her shower the night before, and if the dampness seemed to have a glimmer it was probably only reflecting the light she'd turned on.

Still, she wiped the inside of the tub with a hand towel before she did anything else.

CHAPTER NINE

Drain

For three days Sadie found excuses to skip Izzy's bath and her own showers, braiding her hair to obscure when it looked greasy. By the fourth day she couldn't stand it anymore. The sliding things she'd seen had not been in the tub, after all, but the hallway. And they'd been *leaving* L'Arpin, not coming in. And she didn't even know what they *were*. She had heard no new strange noises from the tub, seen nothing out of place anywhere in the hotel. Maybe the strangeness, if it had ever existed, had passed.

Anyway, Izzy missed bath time—splashing more than hair washing—and Sadie had finally gotten herself together enough to make a prenatal-care appointment. The nearest Planned Parenthood performed appointments and tests with payment plans even she could afford.

The receptionist signed her in, then put a privacy sticker over her name. Sadie led Izzy into an empty waiting room with frosted privacy windows. The focus on anonymity might have comforted Sadie despite having no need to hide from Sam here, but knowing its purpose—to protect women who were making their own best choices from people who had no business judging them—made her a little sad instead, and a little angry. She tried to shake the mood off, pulling a board book from her purse to read to Izzy until her turn to be seen came.

The easy normality of talking through her first prenatal appointment left Sadie with a breathless, squeezing ache in her chest. All healthy, all normal. She hoped Izzy wouldn't remember anything about the visit and talk about it to Gertie in a way that might accidentally give away where they'd been. A distraction would help. Sadie had no money to spare, but a single small hot chocolate from the gas station on the way back to the hotel wouldn't break them.

Following the clinical bright lights and sterile walls of the Planned Parenthood, and the gas station with its perfectly normal layer of grime and all the modern conveniences, returning to the dingy green halls, anachronistic huge keys, and gloomy, dim shadows of L'Arpin made Sadie tired and wary the moment she stepped into the lobby.

That wound-up fatigue followed Sadie through the gray days of November, through the burst of activity that struck L'Arpin over Thanksgiving. Though none of the many guests who checked in during the holiday bustle vanished mysteriously, the last camera incident still worried Sadie.

She knew how to shove her unease to the back of her thoughts and keep it hidden, though, so Mel's aloofness evaporated and Sadie built a congenial friendship with both her and Joe. A festive mood lightened Gertie's judgmental side, and the guests kept Mr. Drye too busy to pay too much mind to Sadie. If she had not been suffering morning sickness and a lurch in her heart at every missed call from Sam, if she had not been stretching stolen time in the free room for as long as she could, Sadie might even have begun to feel secure.

Before her shift a week after Thanksgiving, she left Izzy watching TV and stepped into the hot shower. Steam hung thick in the bathroom in spite of the whirring of the ventilation fan, condensation already beading on the unpleasant wallpaper and fogging the huge mirror. Sadie never liked stepping into the wet heat of a bathroom after someone else's shower, the sensation at once inva-sive and invaded. Breathing the hot, damp air of her own shower, however, she loved. It made her feel warm and clean through and through. She tipped her head so the hot water sluiced through her hair to run down her back, and inhaled deeply. Tension she didn't always remember she carried in her shoulders eased, and she sighed.

If the whole world were like a hot bath, how nice that would be. Lathering her hair with the hotel shampoo added a faint floral scent to the steam, not unpleasant but not quite right. With her next breath she wished she could smell something richer in the wet air, something salty and strident and pure. The steam coated the inside of her nose, her mouth. Her throat. She rinsed the sham-poo out of her hair and closed her eyes and imagined an ocean. In spite of the heat, Sadie felt a cool touch of unease shiver down her back. The image stuck in her head like a tune she couldn't shake. An ocean stretching beneath a misty sky, warm although the sun never broke through that thick cloud cover.

Sadie snapped her eyes open and tried to shake off the way her belly twisted. She'd heard of pregnancy causing vivid dreams, but never strange daydreams. It unsettled her. She almost felt she could hear the rise and fall of that ocean. But when she listened harder, the soft sound of the shower pattering down into the water mixed with the spray and the fan, and she heard nothing else.

Without closing her eyes again, she reached for the conditioner. Having her eyes open didn't really matter, though. Not when she could still taste the spray from that ocean she'd pictured. Not when she could still see the way its surface glittered in spite of the diffuse light, the way the clouds themselves seemed almost to gleam.

Letting the conditioner sit in her hair, Sadie soaped the rough hotel washcloth and scrubbed in a hurry. The steam seemed sud-denly oppressive rather than comforting. As if it tainted, not cleansed. She wondered what rippled through that ocean . . .

Forcing herself to slow so she wouldn't slip, she raised her legs one after the other, lifting her feet out of the water to wash them. Soon her pregnancy would make such maneuvers difficult, but not yet. The label on the hotel's little bar of soap had said lavender, but Sadie smelled brine and fresh breezes.

She'd heard of women craving dish soap or unused kitty litter in the throes of pregnancy, and she'd heard of scent revulsion. But why did she want this sea smell so badly?

A gentle touch stroked her calf. Sadie gasped and straightened out of her relaxed slouch, dropping her washcloth with a splash. The movement shook loose a small glob of conditioner that slid down her forehead. Sadie squeezed her eyes shut against the ensuing sting. Unseeing, she stepped forward through shin-deep water.

"Izzy," she scolded, rubbing her eyes. "How many times has Mommy told you not to sneak in while I'm showering?"

Clearing her sight, Sadie turned, expecting to see her daughter wearing her trouble-grin, peering around the curtain at her, one hand holding the plastic back and one reaching out to stroke her again.

The dropped washcloth brushed her toes. Sadie did not find Izzy invading her quiet time in the shower.

When had the water risen so high? Had she unknowingly plugged the drain?

Something stroked her ankle.

Sadie looked down, and screamed.

Tiny tentacled things swam in the water.

One wrapped itself around her ankle and another bumbled over her toes. The touch on her calf remained, a little thing with too many squirmy legs climbing slowly up her skin. Sadie screamed again and swatted at it. It came free from her leg but clung for one instant to her fingers.

"Yeeuugh!" Sadie's voice wavered, her lips pulled back in disgust. She shook her hand hard and the little thing flew off, splashing into the water.

"Mommy?" Izzy's voice carried strident alarm.

"Stay out of here, Iz!" Sadie said, tearing the curtain aside as she flailed out of the tub. Two more of the things got hold of her washcloth, twisting and twining around it.

"Mommy?" Izzy appeared in the doorway.

Another crawled up from the drain.

"No, I said *stay out*, Isabelle Miles!" Sadie shouted, voice rough and loud. Izzy burst into immediate, screaming tears.

Sadie ignored her. She fumbled for the knob and shut the shower off. The surface of the water rolled back and forth from her hasty exit. Under the water, the tentacled things bobbed back and forth as well.

"Mommy, you said *no* to me!" Izzy wailed, face furious, voice full of accusation.

"Yeah, I said no to you. Back up, Isabelle. Mommy said *back up*." Sadie reached for Izzy with the hand that had not swatted the thing away, and she gently pushed her daughter farther from the bathroom door. Izzy let out a wordless, heinous shriek at this and ran to the couch, where she threw herself face down and howled into the cushions, kicking her feet.

Sadie let her go. She lurched to the bathroom sink and stopped with her fingers trembling a hair's breadth from the handles. No slime or strange sensations marked where she'd been touched by the things. She wanted to scrub herself in scalding water nonetheless.

But what if she turned on the faucet and more of those things wriggled out?

Forget washing, Sadie had to dress, had to call someone. L'Arpin had some terrible infestation.

Oh—oh—where else *were* these things? The guests—!

Sadie yanked a bathrobe on and scrambled past a still-tantruming Izzy to snatch up the room phone. Just before she dialed the front desk, she paused. She'd never called down like that from this room. Didn't want to remind Mr. Drye that she had only *officially* been given this room for a week.

The horrible creatures swarming her tub couldn't be ignored.

But they would have to wait just as long as it took Sadie to run downstairs in person.

She dressed as fast as she could, her clothing clinging to her wet skin and slowing her. Izzy's screaming had settled down into monotonous and repetitive fake crying, and Sadie had no problem ignoring that. She picked her daughter up and all but slung the fussy toddler over her shoulder.

As she laid her hand on the doorknob, a loud knock sounded from the other side. Sadie yelped, snatching her hand back as if her touch had caused the noise, then peeked through the peephole just in time to see Gertie pound on the door again.

"Sadie? Sadie, is everything okay? Is Izzy all right? I heard such a *racket*!"

Sadie unlocked the door and pulled it open. Gertie fell back a step, eyes widening, and Sadie wondered whether the older woman's apparent alarm was for her sudden and harried appearance or for Izzy's theatrics.

"Don't run your taps, Gertie," Sadie said, and now that the immediate shock had passed, her voice came out quiet and calm. She'd fallen back into the habit of responding to a startle by making herself soft and soothing. "L'Arpin has some kind of—of pest infestation. It startled me, and I didn't want Izzy to touch them, but we're fine. It was sweet of you to check."

"Sweet? Of course I checked, Sadie. That's what people *do*."

"Right, well, thank you, anyway. I'm sorry, I'm going to run, I need to tell Mr. Drye about this."

"Of course, of course." Gertie scooted back into the hallway and let Sadie pass. Sadie hustled to the elevator, glad that Gertie hadn't offered to watch Izzy while she ran down to fetch Mr. Drye. Sadie didn't want to rely on her old neighbor too much more than she had to. As the elevator doors closed on Sadie and Izzy, she faintly heard Gertie exclaim, "Pests. Infestation!"

Sadie shook her head. The old woman had lived at L'Arpin for so long, the idea that it could be less than perfect might offend her. She hoped she hadn't upset Gertie. She might not want to need her *too* much, but she did still need her.

By the time she stepped out into the lobby with her daughter, Izzy's mercurial mood had shifted again, and Sadie blessed the quiet as she hurried up to the desk, only to find Dan seated behind it, scrolling on his phone.

"Oh, no," Sadie huffed. "It's Thursday, isn't it?"

"You're down early," Dan said, glancing at Sadie before looking back down at his phone, then doing a fast double take back up at Sadie. He frowned, and in a more alert voice he asked, "Everything all right?"

Sadie turned one way and the other, checking to be sure no guests would hear her. Then she said, "There's some sort of pest infestation in my bathtub. Coming up the drain. They crawled out while I was *showering*, Dan."

"Oh, gross." Dan pulled a disgusted face and wiggled his shoulders in an exaggerated shudder. Mocking? Or sympathetic? She leaned back and shuttered her expression in case it was the former. "I'll call Beth to go check your room, and I'll make a note for Mr. Drye."

"Great, thanks. I'll meet her in my room."

In the hall, Sadie half expected to find Gertie lingering, waiting to chat or to see what the fuss had been about. When the corridor proved empty, Sadie wasn't sure whether she was relieved or disappointed. She bustled into the room and settled Izzy into her booster seat with a banana, resigning herself to cleaning a mushy mess up when this fiasco was sorted.

Then she headed for the bathroom.

She found the tub empty. No water, no wiggling tentacles.

Sadie stared, confusion mingling with a sick embarrassment. She'd caused such a scene and now Beth wouldn't find anything when she got here.

Gritting her teeth, holding back a shiver, Sadie neared the tub and turned the water on. It poured from the faucet, and Sadie didn't engage the shower instead. She twisted the knob all the way to hot and watched as the water rose, as the first wisps of steam curled above it. The things had come out with the hot water before, after all.

By the time Beth arrived to check on the problem, the tub was full again, but only with water.

"I don't know *what* they were," Sadie said when Beth asked her for the fourth time. "They had tentacles. They were little. They liked the heat. But I don't know what they *were*."

"Or where they've gone," Beth said. She patted Sadie's shoulder. "I'll check the water heater and a couple other places. Don't worry."

Sadie bit her tongue and nodded, silently ushering Beth out of her room. Sure, Beth had promised to look into it. She'd said it the same way Sadie promised to check under Izzy's bed for monsters.

Turning to lean against the closed door, Sadie rubbed her face, sliding her fingers under her glasses and pressing against her closed eyelids hard enough to make color flower across the darkness. When she dropped her hands she had a split view—to her side through the open door, the bathroom, and in front of her through the mouth of the little entry area, Izzy squeezing a piece of banana in both fists.

How could she wash the pulped remains of banana off Izzy's hands, knowing that when she turned on the sink tiny tentacled creatures might plop out of the faucet and into their palms? Sadie shuddered. Then she took a long breath and let it out in something that was not quite a groan and not exactly a sigh, before reaching for her phone.

It may not be the end of the world, but it was time to call her mother.

On the third ring, Sadie's mother answered not with *hello* but with, "So who died?"

Phone pressed to her ear, Sadie stood with her mouth open.

After a couple seconds she caught herself, swallowed, and said, "What?"

"Well, my daughter is actually calling me," her mother said, voice just a touch too sweet, "which only happens when somebody dies, right?"

"Nobody's dead, Mom. I just need—"

"I see. Nobody's dead, you just *need* something." A low murmur came over the phone, her father's voice, and Sadie's mother pointedly answered his indistinct words. "It's Sadie. I'd ask if you want to talk to her but Lord knows if you'd even recognize her voice anymore."

Hot tears pricked Sadie's eyes, the sting drawn more by anger than hurt. She should've known better. Should've taken time to prepare herself instead of jumping into this call.

"All right, Mom," Sadie sighed. She took her glasses off with her free hand and rubbed her eyes again with the back of her wrist, then forced out the words, "I'm sorry I haven't called in a while. Things have been . . ." Her thoughts tumbled up against each other, the problems of the last couple years too many and too large to be distilled into something her mother would understand in one phone call. "Not good. It's a long story. But I—" She had to say it fast, a rush of words, or she'd never get it out, and even so her voice dropped to nearly a whisper. "I'm not sure Izzy and I are safe where we are."

As if saying it made it somehow more true, the words left Sadie twisted up inside, cold, and a little breathless. They also left a hole in the conversation, silence spiraling out over the phone. After a handful of seconds Sadie checked the screen to make sure the call hadn't dropped.

"Mom? Are you th—"

"Of course I'm here. I'm just stunned, Sadie. Stunned. Let me make sure I'm understanding this. After your father and I opened our home to you and you repaid us by making absolutely uncouth accusations and storming out—after practically cutting us off from our grandbaby, after getting engaged to a man you never even bothered to introduce us to—now you want to come back into our home, is that it?" Her father rumbled in the background again, and this time the sharpness of her mother's answer sounded much more sincere than the mocking earlier when her mother answered him. *"Exactly."*

"Please, Mom," Sadie said, and even as the words spilled out of her she didn't know if they were meant to be a real plea or an exasperated defense. She took a shaking breath and started over, leaning toward pleading. "Please. I wouldn't ask if it wasn't important."

"I'm sure. I can just guess. I know firsthand what a difficult woman you are to live with, Sadie Anne Miles." The implication stole Sadie's breath, and before she could catch her balance and find some way to respond, her mother kept talking. "I'll tell you what. If things are really bad, your father and I will come pick up Isabelle. She can have a nice long visit with us while you work out your own problems. But you marching into our home and telling us how to raise our granddaughter—"

"Excuse me?" Sadie turned her back to the room and lowered her voice to a harsh whisper so Izzy wouldn't have to hear her rising distress. "You don't get to *raise* your grandchild. She's *my* daughter. Uncouth accusations? All I did was ask you and Dad to respect my boundaries as a parent, and you refused. You flat-out refused. You tried to sneak her out to some chickenpox party, Mom! What could possibly make you think I'd trust you to respect me as Izzy's mother when I'm not there if you can't do it when I'm watching you?"

"Okay. Well. Then I guess this conversation is over, isn't it?"

"What? Wait a second—"

But her mother had already hung up.

"Damn it!" Sadie hissed, squeezing her phone to stop herself from throwing it. She couldn't afford to replace it. Couldn't afford anything. Not even a little decency from her own mother. She tried to find some depth of emotion, some rush of tears and betrayal.

What she came up with instead was an unsurprised hopelessness, as dry and insubstantial as ash.

Sadie turned toward the still-open bathroom door, glanced at the innocent water in the tub, empty of life. Beth hadn't believed her. That disbelief carried an edge, brought an embarrassed cringe to Sadie. But her own mother had all but accused her of putting herself and, worse, Izzy in danger.

Did everyone believe that Sadie was the problem? Now the emotions came, now shame surged, hot and sick in her gut and hot and clammy on her cheeks.

("*You know this isn't normal, right? You always lose your mind over nothing. People don't act like this, Sadie. Either you really think this is okay, or you're trying to get attention. So, which is it?*"

"*What? No. It's neither. I just . . . I just got upset. I didn't mean to overreact. I'm sorry.*"

"*Don't just say you're sorry. Fix it. Don't act like this, it's fucking childish.*")

Sadie's mother may have been—no, she *had* been—entirely out of line. But had Sadie deserved Beth's condescension? The water in the tub stayed smooth and crystal clear.

There would be no leaving L'Arpin yet. Still, she and Izzy would never bathe in this room again.

CHAPTER TEN

This Wave Came Without Warning

Sadie pulled a fistful of garbage out of her oversized purse—old tissues, an empty cough drop bag, an empty hand sanitizer bottle, and a snack wrapper—and dumped it in the wastebasket. Then she tucked the little bottles of shampoo and conditioner and the little bar of soap into her purse. She stuck two rolled-up washcloths in as well, then finally folded two towels as small as she could and stuffed them in last. Zipping her purse took effort, holding the bag with her knees while she pulled the tab, but in the end she fit everything.

In ten days, Beth hadn't found any sign of the things that had squirmed up her drain, Mr. Drye had made one pointed comment about how he hoped no one would cause any hysteria in his hotel, and after that no one had brought it up again.

Not directly, anyway. Gertie had asked once a day for four days straight, "Are you *sure* your baby's all right?" her fretful concern for Izzy edging into insulting by the third day.

Maybe Beth found no sign of pests because there were no pests. Maybe Sadie *was* being hysterical. Maybe nobody had ever been watching her at the Cut or in the hallways or in the shower or on the cameras that had been removed, and maybe the things that had left L'Arpin in the early light of a December morning had been nothing at all.

Maybe. *Hopefully.*

Still, hoping to speed her timeline again somehow, Sadie alternated between scouring the internet for suitable apartments and pulling the calculator up on her phone to try to rework her budget. Her moods grew unstable, and looking at these cute, tidy places either left her with a glowing warmth of possibility, of taking her future in her hands again and making plans to stop relying on Mr. Drye and L'Arpin . . . or left her miserable with hopeless envy, unable to imagine living in such a cozy little home.

This had been one of the bad days. Her eyes burned from crying in the corner near the door so Izzy wouldn't see, an activity formerly reserved for the bathroom. She felt heavy and slow, gritty.

"Come on, Iz. Time to go get all clean." Sadie held her hand out for Izzy.

In the elevator, Sadie debated whether she should remind Izzy not to mention the truck stop shower to anyone they might see. Izzy might forget herself and say something about it on their way out if they passed Mel or Gertie, or if Mr. Drye asked where they were off to. And he'd been doing *that* too much. But if Sadie did remind Izzy not to tell anyone their destination, she might do it just to be contrary.

"Can I carry you?" Sadie asked before the doors opened. She should probably minimize how much she hauled her increasingly heavy daughter around as the pregnancy progressed, but carrying Izzy to the car would be so much faster.

"No, Mommy, I want to walk."

"Please?"

"No!"

Sadie sighed, then smiled and nodded and led Izzy across the lobby.

"Good morning, Miss Miles," Mr. Drye called from behind his desk.

Flashing him a smile she hoped didn't look too fake, Sadie waved without slowing. He'd been prying lately. And she'd been answering him, even if she wasn't admitting she and Izzy were going to shower at a truck stop—he'd call her hysterical again, he'd think she was strange, he'd have second thoughts about letting her stay there, maybe about employing her—but she'd given him vague half answers. *Going for a walk* or *running errands* or *getting Izzy some fresh air.*

Not just answering him, actually. Indulging him.

"Where are you two off to this morning?"

Sadie opened her mouth to give the same kind of response as before. *Just a drive.* She swallowed the words. Because she hadn't only been indulging him, had she? She had been encouraging him.

Sadie didn't have to check her actions with anyone, not when she was off the clock. Not even someone letting her live in his building.

Instead of answering, Sadie waved and called, "See you later, Mr. Drye." She kept her voice light, casual. Respectful, even, because he *was* her boss. But she didn't give him an answer. She didn't owe him one.

Mr. Drye's pleasant expression didn't shift a bit, but as Sadie turned forward again, she glimpsed his eyes turn cold.

She almost flinched, her stomach flipping. Her steps slowed, legs heavy, and she nearly turned right around again to smooth ruffled feelings. She didn't have to plan what she'd say, the words filled her head on their own.

Sorry, she'd say, and she'd laugh as if at herself, and she'd tell him, *I know it's silly, but the things I thought I saw in the shower got my imagination going too much so we're using a truck stop bathroom until I chill out. I just didn't want anyone to worry.* Saying it had all been in her head would make it feel less real, would erode her certainty and start her wondering whether she really had seen—and felt—the tentacle-things in her tub. But it would also mollify Mr. Drye.

So she'd say it, and she'd shake her head as if admonishing her-self. Maybe she'd smile to invite Mr. Drye to join in the joke at her own expense, and then she'd use just the right amount of half-embarrassed awkwardness when she said goodbye again before hurrying out with Izzy.

If she did all that, he wouldn't be angry.

Instead, he would know business that wasn't his, and he'd feel a little superior and a little indulgent, and she'd feel guilty if she went anywhere other than where she said she'd be.

Sadie pushed through the heaviness slowing her steps, then she pushed through the door and out into the cold.

Sadie wasn't going to hand a leash over to anyone.

In spite of having to pay to use it, and the challenges of bathing with her toddler, the shower at the truck stop relaxed Sadie. She had done so little, she had merely *not* answered a question, but it felt like winning a battle. She smiled as she washed, her grin inspir-ing Izzy to giggles and silly, splashing antics. The hot water and the warmth of victory and the balm of her little girl's infectious cheer soothed away the last itchy sting of the day's earlier tears.

In the glow of the moment, Sadie decided this would be the day she'd explain to Izzy about the baby, and she couldn't stop herself from telling her daughter, "When we get back ho—to the hotel I have something new to explain to you."

Izzy cheered, because she was in a good mood to mirror her mother's, and Sadie's heart filled her whole self.

When Sadie and Izzy returned to L'Arpin she felt smooth and loose, rejuvenated. Even the biting wind off the lake during the walk from the car to the entrance didn't spoil her mood.

Gertie sat knitting in the same chair she'd occupied on Sadie's first day at the hotel. She didn't look up at the sound of the door. From behind his desk, Mr. Drye did, and when he met Sadie's gaze his eyes turned colder than the wind. His smile didn't ease that coldness, and he said, "Ah, Miss Miles, something has come up, do you have a moment?"

She didn't say *not on my day off*, and she didn't say *no, I'm with my daughter*. The resolve she'd summoned that morning, it turned out, was finite. She'd used it all up, and would have to build herself back up to any more such moments. The knowledge was bitter, and she hid a grimace as she swallowed.

"Sure, Mr. Drye. What's up?"

Sadie bent and picked Izzy up, thankful when her daughter didn't protest. Izzy had been a shy baby, never smiling at strangers. She'd outgrown that, but something in her stiff posture and her little pout whenever she saw Mr. Drye reminded Sadie of that phase. Sadie was inclined to appreciate her daughter's mistrust of her manager. Less likely she'd interrupt a conversation or say something embarrassing.

Angling her body so Mr. Drye would not be able to talk to Sadie without seeing Izzy, hoping to remind him that she was with her daughter and off the clock, she stepped closer to the desk.

"We've had some scheduling problems," Mr. Drye said. "I'm rearranging your workdays a little. You and Mel will be responsible for separate floors. She'll have three and four, and you'll take care of one and two."

Sadie understood. This was a punishment and a reminder. She had owned herself on her way out of L'Arpin earlier. Mr. Drye couldn't change that. But on the clock, he owned her actions and her time.

Or maybe she was reading too much into it. Maybe there *was* a scheduling problem, and splitting the labor in this way would help.

Sadie didn't like it. But if it was punishment, showing Mr. Drye that it worked would only encourage him. Keeping her face neutral and still, Sadie nodded. "All right. I'll remember that tomorrow morning."

Just after she pushed the elevator button, the front door opened again. Bill Viago strode in, a strange expression on his face, smug and satisfied, but still angry. Sadie faced the elevator doors quickly, in no mood to lock eyes or share words with the power plant man.

"Mr. Viago," Mr. Drye said, his voice weary and edged with something brittle. "What can I do for you today?"

The elevator doors opened and Sadie stepped in. Gertie bustled inside as well. Sadie tried not to give a start; she hadn't noticed the old woman leave her chair, much less come up behind her. Gertie reached out and pushed the button for the fourth floor before Sadie could, her lips pressed together. Just before the doors shut all the way Gertie said, her voice pitched to carry, "I'd rather not hang around the lobby when Bill Viago comes marching around in one of his moods."

Izzy still rested limp and quiet in Sadie's arms, and for a moment Sadie entertained the hope that her daughter had fallen asleep. She didn't often nap anymore, but this was early enough in the day that it would do her mood good rather than cause a cranky bedtime disaster later.

Just as Sadie tried to crane her neck to get a peek at her daughter's face, Izzy sat up straight. "What's the new thing?" she demanded.

Sadie frowned. New thing? *Oh*, right, she had decided to tell Izzy about the baby today. But the mood had been utterly spoiled since then, and they were stuck in a small elevator with Gertie as an overly attentive audience. Sadie hesitated.

"What's the new thing?" Izzy asked again, louder.

"I can't remember now," Sadie lied. She wanted to tell her little girl about the new baby, about becoming a big sister, when they were both feeling good. "I'll try to remember and—"

"Right now. Please, Mommy, puh-leeease?"

The elevator arrived at the fourth floor, and Sadie hurried out. An awkward kind of guilt prompted her to glance over her shoulder and make a lame excuse for leaving Gertie in the dust. "Sorry, I want to get her into our room before she has a tantrum."

Gertie shuffled out of the elevator, waving Sadie's words away.

"Your business is your business, Sadie. I'll just be in my room. If you need me." She stressed *need* so slightly Sadie might have imagined it.

Getting into her room and shutting the door between her and Gertie's ever-so-faintly put-upon expression came as a relief. Sadie put Izzy down and took off her coat and shoes, helped Izzy out of her outdoor gear, and stowed everything in the closet.

"Do you want to eat a banana and watch *Curious George*?" Sadie asked, sidestepping her daughter and heading to the minifridge and microwave functioning as their "kitchen."

"*No*, Mommy, what's the new thing?"

Sadie sighed. She wished she hadn't let one good moment move her to impulsivity. The idea of telling Izzy she'd be a big sister soon had been floating around in Sadie's head on and off for days, but Sadie hadn't planned a word of this conversation.

"Let's go sit on the couch and talk," Sadie said, brightening her voice and giving her daughter a wide smile. Izzy ran to the couch, and Sadie dawdled as she pulled up her phone's gallery and scrolled back, and back, and back. When she sat down on the couch next to her daughter, she'd selected a video of Izzy at a week old, but didn't press play yet.

"Did you know that you used to be a baby?"

"No, I'm not a baby, I'm a horsey!"

"You're a horsey? Wow! But before you were a horsey, you used to be a baby. A long time ago." Not so long, barely any longer than yesterday, but also *such* a long time ago. "And you came out of my body."

Sadie expected skepticism and only realized she was giving her daughter's comprehension too much credit when Izzy laughed instead. Toddlers. Sometimes Izzy seemed to understand so much, Sadie could almost forget how new she still was.

"Look, Iz, this was you when you were just a baby." She angled the phone so they both could see, then touched play. Sadie's own cooing voice came out of the video, and baby Izzy on the screen stretched and yawned and then sneezed without once opening her eyes, and that was the whole video. Sadie had hundreds just like it. August appeared in a lot of them, but Sadie had chosen one without him because she didn't want to complicate this conversation any more than she had to. Izzy often asked about her dad when she saw his pictures, but this wasn't about August, and—

The pain came hot and sharp and surprising for catching her so off guard. Sadie usually could guess when the tides of grief would rise higher again, but this wave came without warning.

This wasn't about August.

Sadie was pregnant again, having a new baby, and it wasn't about August *at all*. Last time she'd grown a life had been with him, and she'd imagined having more than one and never imagined having her next baby without August, much less without anyone.

Stalling for time, Sadie touched play again and let the video start over, then handed the phone to Izzy. "Don't touch the screen," she said, trying to keep her voice light, trying to stop it from wobbling. "Or the video might stop. That's you as a baby, Iz, think about that."

Izzy laughed and made little oohs and aaahs at the screen as Sadie pushed herself to her feet and took the three steps to the mini-fridge. She pushed aside another box of leftovers from L'Arpin's kitchen—Gertie kept saving them in moments of misguided care, and sometimes Sadie fell behind in throwing them away—to get a bottle of water. Her back to Izzy, unscrewing the cap, Sadie let the tears fall. They burned. Her throat thickened and tightened. She tried to swallow and couldn't.

Pregnant and alone with a toddler, living in a tiny room in a hotel where everyone was strange, stuck here because she had nowhere else to go, scared of her phone every time it chimed . . . Sadie had been focusing so hard on navigating all those problems, on steering Izzy safely through the storm until they could come out on the other side. She'd been thinking so much about the pregnancy in those terms, she hadn't had time to think of it in terms of not being August's baby, of not having August with her.

She ached for him. His dirty jokes and his pile of clean but never folded laundry and his smell and the way the floorboards had creaked upstairs when he'd gotten out of bed after her and his arms and the way he cut to the heart of problems and how he apologized when he needed to and his calm and everything. Everything.

Sam had reminded Sadie of August at first. But eventually his off-color jokes had turned hurtful, and his hands grabbed instead of held, and the sound of his feet on the floor above her made Sadie cringe, and he apologized only so he wouldn't have to ever change. She'd tried hiding from her grief in Sam, and when that soured she'd found herself hiding from Sam.

When the baby came, Sadie would love it as much as she loved Izzy. The baby wouldn't be part of Sam, she'd excised him from their lives. But it wouldn't be part of August, either. He couldn't be more gone than he already was, but still he *would* be. There'd be something in her heart that had nothing to do with him.

She hadn't let herself think it until now. At, of course, the worst possible time.

Sadie chugged her water bottle, drinking so fast she nearly choked. The last few drops she poured instead into her palm, rubbed her hands together, and wiped the cool damp on her face. She grabbed two flimsy, cheap tissues and layered them together, then blotted her eyes and blew her nose. She guessed she looked anything but composed, but maybe Izzy wouldn't notice.

She sat down and gently took her phone from her daughter, swiping slowly through a few more pictures, careful to skip any that showed anyone other than just baby Izzy, or Sadie holding Izzy.

"See? This was you, a long time ago. And there's me. I wasn't your mommy until you were born. I grew you inside my body." She scrolled back further, to a pregnant mirror selfie, and her free hand drifted to her belly, fingers moving lightly over what was still only a little bigger than it had been before. "Right now, I'm growing a new baby inside my body."

Izzy gasped. "Can I see?"

"Not yet, stinker."

"Please, please, Mommy, please?"

Sadie hesitated. *Please* often gave way to *right now*, and to keep Izzy quiet (first because of Sam and now because of the guests at L'Arpin), Sadie often found it easier in the short run to give Izzy what she wanted and preserve the peace. It'd cause problems someday, but for now Sadie just wanted things to go smoothly.

"Yes, let me see." Sadie opened the browser on her phone in place of the gallery and searched *14 week fetus*. She swiped through images until she found a sanitized CGI picture, and then she turned her phone back around to show to Izzy. "See? It's a baby, it's just not ready to come out and be a baby in our family yet. There's the little head, and tiny hands. Is it cute?"

"Yes! It's *so* cute! Hiiii, baby baby," Izzy said, leaning close to the phone. She repeated herself, "Hi, baby!"

"It's just a picture, not a call, stinker." Sadie slipped her phone into her pocket and took Izzy's hands. She put them on her own belly and said, "You can't feel it yet because it's so small still, but the baby is growing in my body. It'll get bigger and bigger and someday you'll see my tummy get round, and you'll even be able to feel it move one day. And then after that, when it's big enough to be a real baby in our family, I'll go to a doctor and they'll help the baby come out, then I'll come home with the baby and you'll be a big sister. This is going to be our own little baby."

Realistically, Izzy almost certainly didn't understand what any of this meant. But she responded positively anyway, cheering and clapping her hands.

The warm glow of happiness from earlier flowed through Sadie again, though tinged now with a hint of the melancholy she'd sunk into a few moments ago.

An unexpected knock at the door didn't entirely erase the smile from her face, and Sadie checked at the peephole before letting Gertie in with better cheer than when she'd bid her goodbye in the hallway earlier.

"Miss Gertie!" Izzy shouted as if she didn't see the old woman all the time. Sadie's smile slipped. She'd completely forgotten to tell Izzy that it wasn't time yet to share news about the baby. Maybe her child's understanding of the situation, lacking gravity and focused on novelty, would allow her to be distracted—"My mommy's going to come home with a baby!"

"Is she?" Gertie replied, making her voice high and excited as if to match Izzy's enthusiasm. She clapped her hands together and turned an intense gaze up to Sadie. "How *exciting*, Sadie!" She moved closer and reached out, and for a moment Sadie feared she'd try to touch her belly. Instead, Gertie took her hands, her fingers squeezing tighter than Sadie would have expected. "*How* exciting," she repeated, the emphasis shifting subtly, the brightness of her eyes changing as she seemed to search Sadie with her gaze. "How are you feeling?"

The pressure on her hands and the way Gertie held her eyes when she asked the question—the first time anyone other than the nurse practitioner at Planned Parenthood had asked her in regard to this pregnancy—hit Sadie harder than she expected. Gertie wasn't asking how her body felt, was she? She was asking how *she* felt. Her feelings. Gertie knew things weren't right with Sadie.

Well, how could she not know? Sadie was living in a hotel with her daughter and was now pregnant, with no partner. No partner, no family, no support. Her eyes stung again. She wanted some support so *bad*.

She kept her voice soft so it wouldn't break. "I'm feeling a little rough, actually, Gertie."

CHAPTER ELEVEN

Complicating, Difficult, Frightening

Mel slipped into the supply room five minutes late for their shift, wearing earrings shaped like Christmas presents and a strangely strained expression. Since their workloads had been split up, the younger woman had been quieter, but today the brightness of her eyes and the shine of sweat across her brow made Sadie think of fevers and contagious illness.

"Morning. You all right?" Sadie tried to be casual about easing a step back.

"What? Oh, yeah, no, I'm fine," Mel said, flashing a quick grin as she started loading her cart with cleaning supplies. "I mean, I feel weird, but not sick, if that makes sense? Like kinda off, but physically okay."

"Emotionally?" The image of a Big Feelings Chart from her old classroom came to Sadie's mind; she caught herself just before asking if Mel wanted *to find her feelings*. Her own mom had been an elementary school teacher and treated Sadie like a first grader her whole life—Sadie wouldn't do the same. Instead, she said, "D'you need to talk?"

Not that she had much confidence in her ability to help whatever bothered her young coworker, but she could at least listen.

"I need a favor, actually," Mel said, brightening slightly. "Could you help me with something?"

"Sure." Sadie tied her apron on.

"Can you take my shift tomorrow?"

The next day was not just the first of Sadie's two days off, it was Christmas Eve. Her first Christmas Eve alone with Izzy and, with the baby coming, also her last Christmas Eve alone with Izzy. The confused bubble of emotions she had to shove down whenever she thought about the nearing holiday would be unavoidable tomorrow.

"I'm sorry, I can't."

"You just said you could help!"

Sadie blinked and raised her eyebrows. "That was before you said what you wanted. Look, I . . ."

Sadie licked her lips and then pulled her apron tighter, using the string to highlight the small but finally noticeable change in her belly. She'd had her first ultrasound and the baby was perfectly healthy. With the second trimester she'd be moving to twice-monthly appointments, so she'd finally told Mr. Drye about the pregnancy and the time off she'd need. He'd surprised her by offering what sounded like a genuinely pleasant, almost excited, congratulations. Maybe the pregnancy, no longer a secret, would help convince Mel to calm down.

"I'm having a really hard time right now, Mel. Izzy and I—a lot's going on. This Christmas is going to be really hard." A little of the pleading kind of hostility in Mel's expression eased. Sadie plunged ahead, "And I'm sixteen weeks pregnant. I just want to take it easy on my days off."

"Oh my god, you're having a baby?" Mel didn't quite squeal, but her voice rose in pitch and her eyes lost the last of her irritation. "Congratulations!"

Congratulations. Sadie thought of Sam, thought of Izzy upstairs in a little hotel room being watched by a woman they'd met only a couple months ago. She remembered August putting together a crib in their old apartment while Sadie, pregnant then with Izzy, watched and felt her daughter's kicks. Holding the smile in place made her face feel heavy as she opened her mouth to thank Mel.

Instead, Joe's voice called from the hall. "What'd I just hear?" He appeared in the doorway of the supply closet. His normally smiling face fell into serious lines, an unaccustomed intensity glinting in his dark eyes. "Did you say you're having a baby?" His gaze flicked from her eyes to her belly and back. "You don't look it."

"Rude," Mel said, raising her eyebrows incredulously.

"What? No, it's a compliment."

"It's not, really," Sadie said. "And I wasn't ready to share the news very widely yet."

The moment the words left her mouth she wished she hadn't said them. There was no way to interpret something like that as anything but unfriendly.

And Joe's expression and demeanor were shifting now—subtly, but Sadie knew how to read such barely perceptible changes. Joe rested his weight on his back foot, fixed his gaze just a little off from her eyes. Hands in his pockets, smile forced, he hummed as if groping for something to say.

"I should probably stop sending you dinners, huh?" He spoke in a voice both low and rushed. "Drye won't let me change the menu, says guests at a lakeside hotel expect fish, but . . . but, yeah." He slowed himself abruptly, the too-bright glitter leaving his eyes. In a strangely reassuring voice, he went on, "Pregnant people aren't supposed to eat too much fish, right?"

"Only some kinds," Sadie replied, trying to keep her voice free of the uncertainty that tugged at her. She couldn't parse his behavior. It made her want to back away from him.

"Well, better safe than sorry," Joe replied. Why did he sound so relieved? He left the room in a rush, Mel and Sadie staring after him.

"I've never been pregnant before," Mel said, slow and puzzled, "but is that normally how people react?"

"Nope."

"Didn't think so." Mel grabbed the handle of her housekeeping cart. "Let's get moving before Mr. Drye comes looking for us." She hesitated. "Do you need me to, I dunno, push your cart for you, carry stuff for you? You're supposed to not strain yourself, right? I'm feeling pretty strong lately, I can lift anything you need."

Mel's offer brought back Sadie's smile, the return to normalcy soothing. They pushed their carts out of the supply closet and into the lobby.

"Thanks, Mel. I got it for now, but if I need help I'll let you know."

"Miss Miles," Mr. Drye said as she signed her skeleton key out. His tone overly solicitous, his eyes flicking to her barely swelling belly, he went on, "I've informed Miss McCann of your good news. If you need any assistance, she'll be happy to help."

She tried not to frown. So, her pregnancy was no longer a secret. Mr. Drye still had no right to spread her news around. He did, however, at least seem to have good intentions.

"I'll keep that in mind, Mr. Drye," Sadie said. She forced herself to add, "Thanks."

When Mel stepped forward to sign her key out, Mr. Drye smiled at her as he said, "I take it Miss Miles told you?"

"Yeah, it's exciting," Mel replied. She held her hand out for her key.

"How are *you* feeling?" Mr. Drye asked as he handed it over.

"Better than I must look, if you all keep asking me that."

"Well, the both of you take it easy today if you need to."

"Thanks," Sadie said. She wheeled her cart toward the elevator, with Mel close behind. Once inside, she waited until the doors closed before leaning against the wall and rolling her eyes. "Unbelievable."

"What?"

"Drye just telling people about my pregnancy."

"Don't be dramatic. Mr. Drye was just being nice."

Mel's dismissive retort stung, but before Sadie formulated an answer they reached the second floor.

"If you ever have kids, you'll understand." Sadie regretted the condescending cliché even as she said it. She all but fled the elevator.

Beth found her not five minutes later. "Mr. Drye told me your exciting news."

Each time someone new congratulated Sadie on the pregnancy, her internal flinching told her about her own turbulent feelings.

Of *course* the pregnancy was good news. Of course it was.

But it was also complicating, difficult, frightening news. That was Sam's fault, not Beth's. And it wasn't Beth's fault, either, that she knew what wasn't her business.

"Yeah, he mentioned he let you know," Sadie said. "He told me . . ." She trailed off. If Mr. Drye had given out Sadie's private news without asking, mightn't he have offered Beth's help without asking, too?

"He told you to find me if you need anything," Beth finished for her. Sadie nodded. "Good. I'll check up on you."

Sadie swallowed an irritated response. Beth probably didn't realize how condescending that sounded. After the conversation with Mel in the elevator, Sadie could relate.

"Thanks."

"You're welcome. Later, Sadie."

Normally, working alone in silence gave Sadie's imagination too much freedom. She'd imagine Sam sneaking up on her or rippling lake shadows or little things with tentacles squeezing out of taps and plopping down onto the floor or . . . well, a lot of things, none of them pleasant. After a morning of painfully awkward conversations, though, Sadie didn't mind the solitude all day.

That evening, she let herself into her room to find Izzy in her booster seat, eating a pile of cookies much too close to dinnertime. Sitting next to Izzy, Gertie was busy writing on a scrap of paper, and when she noticed Sadie's entrance she smiled and held it up.

"I made a list of baby names. Don't you love the name Violet?"

Sadie did love the name Violet, but now that it had been suggested by someone only a few steps above a stranger, she could never consider it.

Instead of saying so, she forced a tired smile. "It's a nice name," she said, "but we don't even know if the baby will be a boy or a girl."

"She's a girl." Gertie left the list on the desk as she headed for the door.

Once the latch clicked, Sadie kicked off her shoes, wiggled out of her bra with an inside-the-shirt shimmy, and let the smile drop off her face. After a moment, she unbuttoned her pants without taking them off. She didn't yet need new clothes, but she should start going through local thrift stores soon, on the wild off chance that maternity clothing in her size showed up.

Sadie gave the dwindling stack of cookies an exasperated look as she bent to check the minifridge under the desk. "You're ruined for dinner tonight, aren't you?" She opened the fridge, pulled the leftover box out, and dropped it in the trash, then sighed at the mostly bare shelves. It looked like another ramen night.

"I'm not ruined, I'm Izzy!"

"Right. Sorry, stinker."

"I'm not stinker—"

"Oh, that's right, sorry, Izzy."

"No, I'm a horsey!"

"Sorry, horsey."

She straightened, and the paper caught her eye. Gertie's slanted cursive handwriting flowed down the page in a neat column. *Violet* topped the list, but under it Gertie had written *Violette?* The rest of the names were old-fashioned—Edith, Constance, Agnes, Beatrice. None struck Sadie as a name she'd actually use. Good, then. Gertie hadn't ruined any other cute names for her.

Sadie grimaced. She hadn't been so touchy when she'd been pregnant with Izzy. This prickly irritation ill-suited her. She distracted herself by asking Izzy what she thought the baby should be named and laughed as Izzy rattled off a list of every item she could see. By the time the evening drew to a close, Sadie's sour mood eased enough to make her glad she hadn't been rude to Gertie like she'd been to Mel in the elevator.

The day of Christmas Eve dawned windy and cold, but not freezing. Sadie's phone buzzed, and she glanced at the screen with a grimace, the breath leaving her in a long, slow hiss. Sam again. Of course.

A quick check on Izzy—busy at the desk, looking through an empty toilet paper roll she played with more than any toy—and then Sadie stood, phone in hand, and made her way to the bathroom to listen to this newest voicemail.

"Hey, Merry Christmas, Sadie." Mockery tinged Sam's overly cheerful voice. The act gave way immediately to a sort of weary frustration. "I *tried* to take the blame and let you win. You could've called me even once." Sadie took a sharp breath. This sort of talk always led from *I'm so sorry* to *this is your own fault.* Why did hearing it coming make Sadie feel so relieved? "Have you ever stopped to think about what it was like when I got home and you and Izzy were just *gone*? I thought something happened to you. Did you think about the trouble you were putting me through? I called the *police* to my *home.* Public perception—!" She heard the deep breath he took, the pause, and the huff as he exhaled sharply over the phone. When he spoke again, the rising ire in his voice vanished, as cold and smooth as if it had never been there. "The cops figured out you'd left on purpose. The suitcases. You made me look like such an idiot." He gave a bitter laugh. "Haven't you put me through enough? Come home."

When the automated voice replaced Sam's, Sadie deleted the voicemail. Then she turned her phone off. If her family wanted to text holiday greetings, all tinsel and no substance, they could do that without her. And if Sam wanted to call back hoping to catch her in holiday-blues vulnerability, he could just leave another message.

Sadie stood stock-still in the bathroom, raising her gaze to the mirror. She looked small, drawn, and tired. Leaning closer, she searched her own eyes, looking for guilt, for some sign that she missed Sam. Looking for weakness, the flaw that would lead her to making a mistake like calling him even one time.

The next voicemail would be worse. Would Sadie have even realized that, two months ago? Or would she have let herself hope for something different, something better, this time? She knew the answer, and the only way to stop a sudden tide of self-loathing was to step all the way away from herself, make it distant and remote, turn it into pity for the woman she'd been. And if that pity came with an undercurrent of disgust, well, it was better than hating her right-now self.

Sadie checked her reflection to make sure she looked normal enough to keep Izzy happy and went back out into the room. She didn't turn her phone back on, just set it on the dresser, then settled down, grabbed her single daily cup of coffee, and watched slushy rain run down the window. She held her warm mug a little tighter and listened to Izzy talking to her cereal and let some of the tightness in her shoulders and tension in her jaw ease. She didn't let herself think any more about that voicemail, turning her attention instead to the cheerless little room.

She'd expected a Christmas with no garland, no lights, and no tree to seem bleak, but without the bright dressings, she found it a little easier to bear the holiday without August. Or maybe time did that. Though she didn't overflow with merriment, Sadie enjoyed a quiet stillness, something almost like calm. Considering everything, that was enough.

After an hour of Christmas specials on the little hotel room television, the phone rang. Sadie started to reach before she realized the ring was wrong, and besides, she'd turned her phone off.

The room's phone rang again.

Sadie considered letting it ring itself out, then sighed and picked it up.

"Hello?"

"Miss Miles, why aren't you answering your phone?"

"Mr. Drye?" Sadie said with a frown. "I . . . just did answer my phone."

"No, not the hotel's phone. Your phone. The contact information you put in your employee file. Your phone."

"It's turned off."

"Is everything okay?"

"Um. Yes. What is this about, Mr. Drye?"

"I need you to work today."

Sadie squeezed her eyes shut and, keeping her voice light but not tentative, she said, "I can't work today. It's my first day off this week, and it's Christmas Eve."

"Miss Ross called off. I've tried calling in everyone else, and they are all unavailable."

Sadie would have been unavailable, too, in better circumstances. Mr. Drye would have tried to call her phone, it would have gone to voicemail, and he would have been left with no second option. But Sadie and her daughter lived in his hotel. The hotel's phone in her room, connected directly to the lobby, gave him access to her whenever he wanted.

She imagined marching downstairs with the phone and dropping it on his desk. Useless—if Mr. Drye really wanted to interrupt her free time, nothing would stop him from coming right up to her room and knocking on her door. Sadie grimaced. Really, nothing could stop him from using a hotel key to *open* her door.

"Miss Miles?"

"What? Oh, sorry. Mr. Drye, I can't work today. I'm sure Gertie has plans with relatives or something, I couldn't possibly ask her to watch Izzy on Christmas Eve."

"I've already asked, she's happy to help."

"I . . . Mr. Drye . . ." Sadie stumbled over her words, then closed her lips before she could say something sharp and unwise. She needed this job, needed this place to stay. They didn't have enough money to move into a suitable apartment yet. A few more months, then she'd be able to go someplace fit to raise two children. Not yet. "It's irregular for an employer to do something like that," she said at last, keeping her voice as mild as she could.

"It's irregular for an employee to live in my hotel." Mr. Drye's words squeezed all Sadie's breath out of her. Solid thoughts spun away from her, and before she could gather a response from the frantic whirl, Mr. Drye sighed. "That was unkind, Miss Miles. You're right, of course, this is all irregular. I'm desperate. We're understaffed. The reputation of L'Arpin—the guests—the rooms must be clean. I'll pay double for the day."

Well, that changed things. Maybe Sadie could find a way to turn this into a precedent instead of a one-time occurrence . . .

"I'll be down as soon as I can."

Just before Sadie hung up, Beth's voice murmured from Mr. Drye's side of the line. Something about her tone, low and worried, gave Sadie pause. She pressed the phone tighter to her ear. Mr. Drye's voice came distantly down the line, as if he spoke while moving the phone away from himself.

"Hopefully she'll turn up fine, but if not—"

With a click, the line went dead. Dread settled heavy and cold in Sadie's belly.

Hopefully who will turn up fine? If not, then what? Sadie swallowed, her throat tight, and stared at the phone as if it would speak answers.

Who would both Mr. Drye and Beth worry about? Someone they both knew. Had Mel really called off today? She'd seemed strange . . .

A knock at the door made Sadie freeze, her grip on the phone tightening as her shoulders jumped up. The knock came again, a quick tapping, and Sadie recognized it. Of course she did. Just Gertie. Mr. Drye might've called her to let her know that Sadie had agreed to the shift. Not that she'd had much choice. But still, Gertie didn't have anything to do with that. Sadie hurried to open the door.

"Hi, Gertie, I'm so sorry—"

"Don't be sorry. I'm happy to watch Izzy if you need me to."

She rummaged in a drawer for her clothing and then hurried into the bathroom. As she had every time since the infestation of . . . whatever weird lake thing, she was sure . . . the moment she stepped in she glanced at first the tub, then the sink, then (with a shudder at the idea of sitting down and feeling a soft, unexpected touch) the toilet. Sadie changed in a rush and left the bathroom, the back of her neck tight with the now-familiar feeling of being observed. She crossed the room to kiss the top of Izzy's head.

From the corner of Sadie's eye, something moved.

CHAPTER TWELVE

What Else Might They Hide

She froze, turning her gaze to the little wastebasket. A couple of empty water bottles leaned haphazardly against each other, the old to-go container sat diagonally atop them, and empty ramen wrapping and seasoning packets crowned it. Nothing suspicious. Sadie shook her head, letting out a relieved breath, and the to-go container shifted.

Faster than thought, Sadie snatched up her daughter and straightened, turning her left side away from the wastebasket and shifting Izzy's weight to that hip.

"Mommy!" Izzy wailed as her toilet paper tube fell to the carpeted floor. "I dropped my teledope!"

"Sadie?" Gertie asked, concern coloring her voice.

Sadie didn't look at Gertie, didn't answer Izzy. She held her breath and held still and watched the to-go box.

With a soft, sliding sort of sound, it slipped farther down into the trash can. Sadie jumped, skittering back a step, but not so far that she couldn't still see inside. Couldn't still see when the gap where the flap fitted into the slot to hold the plastic box shut darkened.

Something slender wormed out of that gap. Something dark

green and slick. It wove, curling and uncurling on itself, tiny suckers glimpsed and hid and glimpsed again.

"Oh my god," Sadie whispered.

"What? *What*, Sadie?" Gertie said, her concern bleeding into alarm, the sharpness of her tone like a cold dousing. It shook Sadie out of her paralysis.

"There's something in the trash, Gertie," Sadie said, forcing her voice to stay even and low, hoping not to scare her daughter. "You should go back to your room for a minute. I'm going to get Beth. There's something in the trash." She licked her lips, her mouth dry, and her heart pounded, but the fear of that single twisting limb carried an undercurrent of vindication—no drains here, nowhere for the little thing to go. Beth would *see* it.

"What are you talking about?" Gertie moved as if to step nearer to the trash can, leaning and peering.

"Gertie! Please!" Sadie said, putting a hand out to catch her neighbor's shoulder. "It might not be safe. I'd hate for you to get stung or . . . or bitten or something. Please wait in your room."

After half a second's hesitation, skepticism clear on her face, Gertie nodded. "I'll be waiting when you get back."

Sadie nodded and herded Gertie out of her room, then hurried down the hall. Riding to the first floor, Sadie chewed her bottom lip and fidgeted, wishing the elevator moved faster.

The doors finally slid open. By L'Arpin's standards, the lobby was crowded. Mr. Drye stood behind the front desk and Beth leaned on that same desk from the other side, both of them facing Joe where he stood in the hallway leading toward the kitchen.

"There's another . . . thing, a . . . a strange pest in my room," Sadie fumbled, trying to describe it. She didn't bother crossing the lobby or lowering her voice. She didn't bother checking to be sure no guests could hear her. L'Arpin didn't deserve such considerations. The others turned to look at her. "In the trash can, in a box of leftovers. I saw a *tentacle*."

"What's a tennatle?" Izzy asked.

"Can you let the grown-ups talk, please, stinker?"

"Opay."

"You kept leftovers?" Joe asked. His voice buzzed, and for one moment his eyes widened.

"What?" Beth said, her gaze darting back to Joe.

Any hint of alarm smoothed from Joe's face, and he gave the maintenance woman a tight grin. "Well, professional concern, you know? Leftovers usually taste like shit—"

"Language, Mr. Mishra," Mr. Drye snapped.

"—no matter *how* good the food is to start with. Got my reputation to consider, don't I?"

Adrenaline crawled under Sadie's skin and vibrated in her lungs, and she nearly screamed at them then, nearly crossed the lobby to shake them, because there was *something in her room*, and Mr. Drye was worried about swearing? Joe was worried about his reputation? Instead, gritting her teeth, she said only, *"Please."*

"Certainly." Mr. Drye didn't seem ruffled at all, only impatient. "Come with us, Miss McCann. Mr. Mishra, we'll discuss your concerns more later."

The small elevator made for a tight squeeze on the ride back up, and Sadie resisted the urge to shift her weight or tap her feet so she wouldn't bump anyone.

At the fourth floor she rushed out, then stopped in her tracks. Gertie stood outside their doors, a neatly tied white trash bag lying at her feet.

"I took care of that mess for you, dear," Gertie said as Beth squeezed past Sadie from behind. Sadie moved to the side to allow Mr. Drye to leave the elevator, and then swallowed hard.

"Is that my trash bag?"

"Well, it's not mine—I recycle," Gertie said. "You really ought to separate out your plastics."

"What about that . . . thing?"

"Why don't I take that out to the dumpster for you, Gertie?"

Beth asked. Mr. Drye cleared his throat and narrowed his eyes, and she amended, "I mean, Ms. Harper."

"Of course, Bethany." Gertie stepped away from the bag and Beth crossed the hallway to scoop it up. "Thank you so much."

"But what about the *thing* in it?" Sadie repeated, her voice rising.

"There was nothing in there but trash," Gertie replied, reaching for Sadie with a solicitous frown. "Are you well, dear?"

"I'm fine. I'm *fine*. There was something in there. Open it up. I have to check." Sadie sidestepped Gertie and set Izzy on the floor. She ran her hand through her daughter's hair as she murmured, "Stay right here, stinker. Mommy's gotta check that bag."

"You will not rip open a bag of trash, Miss Miles," Mr. Drye said. "We don't want a scene in the hallway." He hesitated slightly before the word *scene*.

Sadie took a breath, an angry reply on the tip of her tongue, but what he'd said on the phone only minutes before—*it's irregular for an employee to live in my hotel*—floated through her mind. Her stomach clenched.

She shut her mouth and swallowed, breathing hard through her nose, and gave a single sharp nod. Despite the churning in her gut and the way her fingernails bit into her palm as she clenched her fists, Sadie slowed her breath, forced a mild expression, and made herself murmur, "Of course."

"We better get back to work," Beth said, the gentle pity in her voice stinging worse than mockery would have.

"Of course," Sadie repeated, something inside her deflating, leaving her feeling small and cold. As Beth collected the trash bag from Gertie, Sadie bit her tongue. She ushered Izzy back into her room with another kiss on her head, and stretched her mouth into a thin smile as she thanked Gertie. She followed Mr. Drye and Beth back to the elevator, chewing her lips.

The silence—not just awkward but thick with doubt and recrimination—on the way back to the lobby pressed upon Sadie, it pushed into her chest and made her lungs tight and made her heart thump harder.

It's irregular for an employee to live in my hotel.

She couldn't trust Mr. Drye. Probably not Beth. But she couldn't let this ruin her, either. Her and Izzy. There was no way to salvage what had just happened—asking to tear the bag open now would look unhinged, she couldn't risk it—but maybe she could find something to say to leave a different impression this morning, at least. Something to deflect from everything that had just happened. Anything.

She opened her mouth before she had a plan, and what came out was, "Do you think Mel's really sick?"

Beth froze, all but her free hand, which twitched toward Sadie before it, too, went still. "What do you mean do I think Mel's really sick?" the maintenance woman asked. Mr. Drye fixed Sadie with a steady, expressionless gaze.

Sadie didn't realize she'd started to sweat until her glasses slid slowly down her nose. She took them off and lifted a corner of her apron to wipe them, an excuse to avoid looking at Beth or their boss. She'd certainly distracted them from the trash debacle. By making them wary about something else. Not exactly ideal. Sadie groped for a way to fix this.

Mel had seemed strange the last few days. Could Sadie use that?

"I mean, it's suspicious," she said, trying to sound conspiratorial. She didn't imagine it; Beth shot Mr. Drye a quick, frowning glance. Sadie lowered her voice, adding, "I don't want to get her in trouble, you know? She's just a kid. But yesterday she tried to get me to take her shift today. And now she's *sick*. So she claims. Seems suspicious." Relief spread over Beth's face, and as the taller woman's posture relaxed, so did Mr. Drye's.

Conversely, Sadie's heart fluttered faster and her mouth dried. This conversation had confirmed . . . well, nothing concrete, actually. She couldn't go to the police accusing her boss and coworker of exchanging loaded glances. But the interaction left a chill in Sadie's gut and running under her skin. She tensed, trying not to shiver.

"I don't think Melanie would ditch you if she could be here. Especially considering your condition," Beth said reassuringly. The bell chimed as the doors opened at the first floor, but for a moment no one moved. "I'm sure she called off for a good reason. Hopefully she'll be back for her next shift." Beth didn't look at Mr. Drye this time, but still Sadie got the impression she'd added that last part for their boss's benefit.

"You're probably right," Sadie said quickly. "I'm just being paranoid."

It took effort not to cringe. What a choice of phrasing. First Beth had found nothing in her tub, now this. With the taste of the word *paranoid* lingering in Sadie's mouth, she hastened to exit, hoping she looked more casual than she felt.

Beth headed for the exit, and Mr. Drye took up his post behind the desk, and Sadie spent the rest of her day resisting the temptation to rush through her work; hurrying her way into a slipshod performance would only lead to another confrontation with Mr. Drye. Unacceptable. As her hands stayed busy spraying and wiping and vacuuming, her mind raced as if to compensate for the time she made herself take on her tasks.

The security cameras may have been removed, but Sadie could access employee records if she had enough time alone with the computer. She'd never get that time during the day, but at night? When Mr. Drye left? L'Arpin employed nighttime staff, Sadie knew, but she didn't know where they went. She'd never seen the desk manned after hours. And after that, she'd be able to check out the dumpster behind the hotel for herself.

Her plan formed, if something as slipshod as "sneak around at night" could be called such.

In her room again at the end of the day, Sadie smiled and bid Gertie good night. Then she sat and colored with her daughter and microwaved two dinners and hid her seething impatience as she waited for Izzy's bedtime.

Of course, a toddler's bedtime wasn't really late enough to get up to any clandestine creeping. By seven thirty in the evening, Izzy's soft, deep breaths filled the small room with a quiet kind of peace that usually made Sadie want to curl up and fall asleep herself. Tonight, however, her mind replayed the moment that slimy green tendril had wriggled out of the box in her trash. The memory of that moment started again, and again, and rather than fall into a loop, Sadie sat up on the bed in the dark and pulled out her phone. Scrolling forrent.com, tapping any link that listed a deposit she could afford with her meager funds, made for a grim kind of distraction. She tried very hard not to let herself think about writhing pests, fretting instead about how she would afford rent after that deposit if she left L'Arpin and the free room and Gertie's invaluable help. She copied URLs into a file with a reminder to look beyond price next—cleanliness of the unit, state of the building, googling the landlord and the neighborhood—and she added the number of apartments good research would eliminate to the list of things she didn't want to think about yet.

Nine o'clock. That should be late enough.

Sadie took the walkie-talkie, snuck out of the room, and let herself into the stairwell silently, taking the time to ease the door shut behind herself.

Sneaking downstairs in the night on Christmas Eve had never before made her heart hammer with fear rather than excitement, had never left her with a sour, dry mouth and damp palms. She should be sitting in a living room wrapping the last presents while August stuffed the stockings and ate the cookies Izzy would have left out, watching *Die Hard* in the background and arguing over whether it was a Christmas movie or not. The impossible dream made her eyes sting with tears and her throat tighten.

Now she was afraid *and* sad.

She tried to banish that hurt and fear by wondering what

Christmas Eve would have been like if she'd never met Sam, but the memory of last Christmas floated up instead.

Sam had waited until Sadie and Izzy were out of the house on last-minute holiday errands, then he'd thrown away the stocking Sadie'd had since she was a little girl and the stocking she and August had made for Izzy's first Christmas, replacing them with classy, tasteful, utterly impersonal ones. When she and Izzy had come home, tired and cold (and, in the toddler's case, fussy) to find the switch, Sadie hadn't asked if he'd found August's stocking tucked away in the attic. She'd only made the mistake of wondering where the old stockings had gone. But Sam hadn't wanted questions, he'd wanted gratitude, and he'd gone out of his way to make his disappointment painfully clear.

When anything went missing after that, Sadie had never again mentioned it. And she'd never dared to check if August's things remained where she'd stored them.

That time had been marked by a different kind of sneaking than this night—sneaking inside her skin, keeping her mouth quiet, and trying to keep her mind quiet, too, because last year, imagining a different kind of Christmas had carried the terrible risk of admitting she was unhappy—worse than unhappy.

A dangerous admission, under Sam's roof.

Suddenly the unsettling staircase and the nighttime creep through a dimly lit hotel looking for nebulous secrets didn't feel quite so bad.

Sadie reached the bottom step and paused before the door. She eased it open. Henry Drye would be waiting on the other side, his eyes hard, and in his hands . . . what? A black bag to stuff her in? A chloroform-soaked rag? Sadie had no shape to give her fears, and that made them all the larger.

But the hall stood empty.

Sadie slipped halfway through the door and then paused. There might still be someone in the lobby at this hour. Maybe she should head outside first, check the dumpster, find her trash bag and rip it open and look through it for the tiny creature she knew she'd seen inside. She eased back into the bottom landing of the stairwell. Before she turned to the exit on the other side, she took a moment to listen in on Izzy's slumber over the walkie-talkie. Nothing, all calm, all quiet.

Sadie took a breath and let herself outside.

The slushy rain of that morning had abated, but left the walkway around the hotel somehow both slick and gritty. Sadie moved with slow deliberation in the opposite direction from the main entrance. She passed windows, some aglow but many dark, and she passed the gated entryway to the closed outdoor pool. Around another corner, Sadie found the back parking lot, a part of L'Arpin's grounds she'd rarely visited. Near the center of the back wall, overlooked by no windows, the dumpster stood in its fenced-in pen.

Sadie controlled the urge to hurry, kept her eyes on her feet as she stepped with care across the slushy pavement. The dumpster's fence loomed up out of the dark abruptly, and Sadie lifted her gaze and reached for the handle to the tall gate before she saw the thick chain wound through the links of the fence, a heavy padlock dangling from it. Hung above the chain, a sign read NO ILLEGAL DUMPING.

Locked.

The trash was locked.

Sadie couldn't check it. Couldn't just go ask Beth for a key, not without a good lie and especially not with an honest explanation. Frustration temporarily pushed away the late-December chill. *Locked.* Had it always been locked? Plenty of places kept their dumpsters inaccessible. It might have always been like this. Maybe.

Or maybe Beth had locked it for the first time after throwing her trash bag away that morning.

Sadie had run right into another dead end, right into one more thing about L'Arpin Hotel that might mean nothing—or might have a sinister purpose. She didn't know, and she had no way to find out.

The irritation swirling hot and impotent within her didn't ebb as she picked her scowling but quiet, careful way back to the door she'd left by. She had to keep it leashed. She couldn't shout, couldn't vent her anger, couldn't cause a scene. With the unsafe footing, she couldn't even give in to the urge to stomp her feet. When she let herself into the hotel, she wiped her shoes on the mat just inside the door at the bottom of the stairs and forced herself to breathe, to take her time and pat her windswept hair back into place, not to leave this private little corner of the building until she had her composure.

Once she was ready, once she thought her cheeks and nose no longer looked pink from the cold, once she could keep her face calm and relaxed, Sadie slipped out through the other door and into the long, dim first-floor hallway. She walked at a smooth, steady pace, willing herself to look normal. If she saw a guest she could smile and nod and keep walking because none of them knew her, none of them knew she wasn't one of them coming or going for her own reasons.

She saw no one.

The tiled floor of the lobby amplified her footsteps. She should've slowed down, walked with more quiet care, but the urge to rush— like someone pushing her from behind—hurried her instead. She'd clattered halfway across the space when something shifted in her periphery. Something tall, mostly in shadow. Indistinct.

Sucking in a gasp, Sadie whirled in the direction of the movement.

The lobby still stood empty around her, but now Sadie noticed Joe through the front window to the left of the entrance. He stood on the sidewalk with his back to the window, bundled into a coat, shoulders hunched, and moved back and forth as if shifting his weight from foot to foot. A cloud of smoke billowed briefly around him and then swept away on the wind.

Not a problem.

She hadn't fully turned back toward the desk when a flash of light from the parking lot beyond Joe caught her eye. A car pulled in, killed its headlights, and cruised up to where the cook stood smoking. Joe hurried in that direction. Probably the girlfriend he'd talked so much about, and Sadie had more to worry about than that. She headed for the desk, expecting Joe to be out all night now that his lady had come to pick him up.

Instead, just as she slipped behind the reception counter, the door behind her banged open. Sadie fought the urge to duck behind the counter—she'd certainly been spotted by now, nothing would look more suspicious than hiding.

"Sadie?" Joe asked. She put on a friendly smile before turning to face him, her eyes catching on the hasty movement of his hand as he fumbled to hurriedly stuff something in his pocket. "What're you doing down here?"

"Uh . . ." Sadie hadn't prepared any excuses. She grimaced, her nerves transmuting into irritation with herself. What a ridiculous oversight. A distraction. She needed to distract Joe. She almost asked him about the thing in her trash can, but stopped short. If he'd had something to do with any of this, she didn't want to make him on edge. Instead, she nodded at the door behind him and asked, "What was that about?"

Joe hesitated, then grinned and gave her a wink. "Point taken," he said. "I'll mind my business if you mind yours, yeah?"

Sadie wasn't entirely sure how she'd slipped past his curiosity, but she wasn't about to question it. "Yeah."

"Well, g'night, then."

"Good night."

Joe headed off in the direction of his room near the kitchen, and Sadie waited only until he'd turned a corner out of sight before hurrying through the door to the office. As soon as she stepped into the office, she shut the door behind her and settled into the desk chair.

The near miss caught up with her at that moment. Her limbs loosened with an abruptness that made her glad she'd already sat. Her stomach flipped, her chest tightened, and a cold tremble swept over her skin. Closing her eyes, Sadie gritted her teeth and curled her hands into fists and whispered, "Stop it. Nothing happened. It's okay. You're okay."

After wasting two or three minutes finding her calm again, Sadie finally took a deep breath that did not shake and straightened in the chair, turning toward the computer.

The doorknob behind her rattled.

Sadie's shoulders hunched right back up. Had Joe decided to come back and find out what she was up to after all? Had he called Mr. Drye?

Sadie spun in her chair. She had enough time for half an idea— *dive under the desk*—before the door opened.

Lewis McCann, not Joe Mishra or Henry Drye, stood on the other side. A frown furrowed his brow, but Sadie thought he looked nearly as confused as he did accusatory.

"Thought I heard voices," he said, voice caught between gruff anger and triumph. "What're you doing here, young lady?"

"I'm worried about Mel," Sadie blurted. She followed that truth up with a lie, "I wanted to find her personal number so I can check up on her."

"Nonsense," the old gardener grumbled. "You don't belong back here. Go on back to your room."

Sadie asked, "Wait, what are *you* doing here, Lewis?"

He started when she said his name, his eyes widening briefly before the frown returned, twice as surly. When he spoke there was a quickness to his words, a defensiveness, that Sadie couldn't quite parse. "I'm supposed to be here. I work here."

"At nine o'clock in the evening?"

"Nine . . . well, what's that matter?" Lewis asked, his voice full of bluster. "You shouldn't be back here." He muttered something under his breath and turned to leave, pausing to cast her a long look over his shoulder. "I should know your name," he said. It was almost a question.

She considered not answering him, but that would look even more suspicious. "Sadie."

"Right."

He left as abruptly as he'd come, and Sadie stared after him. Her suspicions multiplied with every interaction she had in this damn hotel. Nebulous suspicions like *Lewis is hiding something, too* but also more concrete suspicions like *Lewis is going to go get Beth.*

She had to hurry. Fingers trembling, she pulled up the employee files and tapped Melanie's name with frantic speed. The screen changed. *No employee record found.* Sadie's heart skipped in confused fear. What? She double-checked the name she'd typed. *Mrlanie Ross.* A typo. Relief flooded Sadie. She fixed Mel's name and hit enter again.

No employee record found.

Sadie looked at the name again, but this time she'd entered it correctly. She jabbed the backspace button and tried *Ross, Melanie.* Then *Mel Ross.* Then *Ross, Mel.*

Nothing and nothing and nothing.

CHAPTER THIRTEEN

Not a Problem for L'Arpin Hotel

"What's this?" Gertie asked a week later, on New Year's Eve.

Sadie looked up from pulling on her shoes and frowned. Gertie held Sadie's phone, her face scrunched into an expression that walked the line between confused and concerned.

"Is that my phone?" Sadie said, straightening. She held out her hand for it.

Instead of passing it over, Gertie tilted the screen to show Sadie her own forrent.com search results. "Is this a real estate website?"

"No," Sadie said, reaching over and plucking her phone from Gertie's fingers.

"It *looked* like real estate," Gertie said, her voice a touch louder than normal, a hint sharper.

"Do you think I could afford to buy property?" Sadie asked. "It's an apartment-browsing website. I'm looking into places to rent."

Gertie opened her mouth as if to answer, then huffed her breath out and snapped her jaw shut. She crossed her arms and pressed her lips together, glancing sideways.

Sadie frowned, surprised by Gertie's unexpected intensity. "Are you okay?"

"Hmm?" Gertie turned back to Sadie, and her wrinkle-seamed

face held no trace of disapproval, after all. Perhaps Sadie had imagined it. "Of course I'm okay. It's good you're looking for someplace to stay. It'll be good for Izzy when you stop hovering over her all the time with your little walkie-talkie. And she might like a regular babysitter instead of old Gertie."

"I like you, Miss Gertie," Izzy piped up. "Can we play with Play-Doh?"

"Does your momma let you have Play-Doh?"

Sadie couldn't tell whether the old woman thought she *should* or *shouldn't* give her daughter Play-Doh.

"In any case, it would be stupid to stay here longer than it takes to afford a nice little apartment, wouldn't it?" Gertie went on. "See you in a few hours, dear."

On her way to the lobby, Sadie mulled over Gertie's words. It *would* be unwise to stay in L'Arpin longer than she had to, but wouldn't it be just as unwise to leave *before* she could afford a *nice little apartment*?

She entered the supply room and reflexively glanced at the daily schedule tacked onto the board next to the door. Right. Mel's name had no longer been crossed off on a day-by-day basis but deleted from the reprinted spreadsheet. Sadie's fretting shifted course.

Another holiday Sadie was meant to have off, and here she was, still covering for Mel. Except they weren't calling it that anymore. Mr. Drye had said only, "She quit without notice," but he hadn't seemed as bitter about that as Sadie would have expected. More distracted, almost disappointed.

Sadie felt no bitterness herself, not even disappointment. Only a nebulous worry—why had there been no employee record? did Mr. Drye lack the savvy to save former employees' records?—and an unexpected pang of hurt. Maybe Mel's age, the gulf in their circumstances and experiences, meant Mel and Sadie couldn't ever be dear to each other, but her absence left an emptiness in the place of one of the only friendly faces in Sadie's life. A goodbye wouldn't have eased the unexpected loneliness of Mel's absence, but it might have soothed the sting of hurt feelings. And if she'd just given a proper notice maybe Mr. Drye could have hired someone by now.

Sadie didn't know how long she could keep up a six-day-a-week schedule. The dragging fatigue and waves of morning sickness had passed, but the second trimester brought new discomforts—like the compression stockings the nurse practitioner had given her when a thick blue varicose vein popped up along one leg and the pads she'd had to buy for her bra when her colostrum started leaking already. She wasn't yet halfway through her pregnancy, and things would only get harder. The increased hours might prove impossible in the long run.

Mel's mysterious vanishing act also meant Sadie had all four floors of L'Arpin to herself. The excuse to spend less time lingering in each room, cleaning only what was visibly soiled and merely tidying everything else, didn't bother her too much. Less time in each bathroom and skipping over trash cans that looked mostly empty suited Sadie just fine.

And in the meantime, she'd gotten Mr. Drye to promise double pay for every sixth shift, not only the ones that happened to fall on holidays, allowing her to finalize her budget and plan the move for the first week of March.

She took her cart and started all the way back up at the fourth floor, then worked her way down. Near the end of her day, Sadie had just finished the fourth room in the last hallway when a commotion from the direction of the lobby caught her attention. A woman's voice, familiar in cadence if not in tone, growing louder and louder until it rose sharply into an intelligible phrase.

"*Tell* me!"

Sadie slipped her skeleton key into her pocket and moved closer to the wall. She abandoned her cart in the center of the hallway and made her way on quick but quiet feet toward the lobby and the voices—Mr. Drye now, speaking in the same low voice she'd heard him use on Bill Viago her first day at L'Arpin. The tone sounded at once disarming and dismissive.

Sadie stopped just shy of the point where she'd be visible from the lobby.

"That's impossible," the woman said. "She was here *all the time*. I washed her aprons every week. She was *here*."

"I'm very sorry, Mrs. Ross," Mr. Drye said, his voice soft, and Sadie's heart lurched. Of course. Mrs. Ross spoke with the same quickness to her words that Mel used. "We haven't seen Melanie in months."

Sadie's stomach sank like a stone, twisting tight. Fingers shaking, she fumbled her phone out of her pocket and opened the camera, swiping it to video mode and touching the record icon. She held the phone before her, trying to quiet her breathing, trying to still her sudden trembling.

Mr. Drye continued speaking. "To be frank, I . . . well, I'm sorry to say I only remember her because she inconvenienced us so badly. After her interview she came in for orientation"—*orientation*? L'Arpin had no orientation—"but she never arrived for her first shift. We never even had a chance to put her in our system."

Goose bumps swept Sadie's skin, clammy and cold. The trembling rush of adrenaline carried with it a hint of triumph. She *had* it, proof here in her phone Mr. Drye was covering something up.

Covering Mel's absence up.

The thin tinge of triumph soured to a guilty kind of fear, her breath hitching. The added workload, the extra money . . . Sadie had let the cloud of her own stress obscure a worry she should have clung to, should have followed. Her disquiet had been right from the start. Mel had never called off. Never quit without notice. Not if Mr. Drye would lie about it now.

Sadie had known something was off and she'd let it go. Her eyes stung, her throat tightened, and questions she didn't want to ask herself—what had happened to Mel? could Sadie have helped if she'd stayed focused? had she failed her friend?—bubbled to the surface of her mind.

Concerns for later, self-recrimination for later. For now, she had to catch what she could. Mel's mother was still talking. Sadie eased nearer to the end of the hall, holding her phone with her right hand and her right wrist with her left to try to steady the tremble in her fingers.

"She's been cleaning here for half a year," Mrs. Ross insisted, her voice caught between tearful and scolding. "She went to work and never came back, you *can't* be telling me she never worked here!"

Sadie stopped creeping and pushed only her arm out, trying to bring her phone closer to the mouth of the hallway without coming into view herself.

"I already told the police," Mr. Drye said, and Sadie sagged against the wall, covering her mouth with her free hand. When had the police come? They'd been here asking about Mel? And Sadie had missed it! "We gave her three uniforms and three aprons at orientation, we showed her around the hotel, she tried to take one of our skeleton keys home with her after the meeting and I retrieved it from her on her way out, and I never saw her again. I let them check our records, Mrs. Ross. I'm very sorry your daughter is missing. But, well, it's simply not a problem for L'Arpin Hotel. Do you need any further assistance, ma'am? Would you like me to walk you to your car?"

Mr. Drye might try to hide behind words of kindness and concern, but Sadie knew *escorted off the premises* when she heard it.

Judging by the indignant huff Mrs. Ross let out, she did, too. "The gall! I'll be back with a lawyer, do you understand that?"

"I'll be available to speak with anyone you bring back, Mrs. Ross. And I'm sorry for your difficulties."

Stomping footsteps followed, and Sadie pictured Mrs. Ross, who she imagined would look like an older version of Mel, storming out.

Without giving herself time to think about it, Sadie turned and ran back up the dim hallway. She skidded around the corner and, growing heedless of noise with distance between herself and Mr. Drye, she dashed down the next corridor. At the end, the door to the stairwell and the back exit waited.

She burst out and gasped at the bitter cold wind blowing off Lake Erie. Pausing only for a moment, Sadie wrapped her arms around herself and scanned the parking lot. From here she could see the same view she often watched out her window. Few guests parked in this corner of the lot, perhaps disliking the sight of the power plant. But there, a huddled figure hurried toward a lone car. A figure with the same long, dark hair as Mel. Her shoulders shook as she rushed toward her sedan.

"Mrs. Ross?"

The woman ahead of her froze, then turned.

"I told him I don't need an escort," she spat, her venomous tone at odds with the tears trailing shiny tracks down her cheeks. She didn't look much like Mel, now that Sadie saw her face. The eyes were the same, the hair, but other than that Mel must not have taken after her mother much at all. Except in their bearing. The way the woman stood reminded Sadie deeply of her missing co-worker.

"I'm not here to escort you," Sadie said, stepping off the sidewalk, watching for ice. She didn't want to think about a slip and a fall. "I ran to catch up with you."

"Why?"

Movement near the corner of the building caught her eye. A truck pulling up. Sadie recognized it. Beth's truck. She'd thought the wind was cold, but the wave of fear that swept her at the sight was colder still. Beth would be just as reluctant to see Sadie speaking to Mel's mother as Mr. Drye would be—they were in it together, whatever *it* was.

"I've been working here since October, and—"

"Everything okay out here?" Beth called. Sadie turned back

toward the truck. Beth had parked it a few spots down and now sat inside, calling through the open window as the engine growled and low-drifting clouds of exhaust wisped from the back.

"Yeah," Sadie said, but before she could get another word out, Beth went on.

"Is freezing out here good for the baby?"

"I'm *fine*," Sadie said.

"I'm sorry, I don't have time for this," Mrs. Ross said.

"No, please, listen, I know—"

"Sadie!"

The words *your daughter* caught in Sadie's throat, choked off by instant panic. That had not been Beth or even Mr. Drye calling her name.

Gertie shouted again, her voice high and strident. Desperate. "Sadie! *Sadie!*"

Sadie spun, eyes moving with frantic speed. Gertie wouldn't be screaming for her like that unless something had happened to Izzy. But she was nowhere in the parking lot.

"Come quick!" Gertie shouted again, and finally Sadie looked up.

Gertie had the window to her room wide open, and she leaned halfway out, waving her arms frantically.

Sadie barely heard Beth's truck door shut. Through that open window, faint at first but audible now, came the sound of Izzy screaming.

Sparing a glance over her shoulder at Mrs. Ross, Sadie took only a second to hiss, "Please wait, please, I have to talk to you." Then Izzy's screams grew louder and Sadie took off. From behind her, Beth murmured something in a soft voice to Mrs. Ross. A problem for later.

Izzy.

Sadie took the stairs up two at a time, not trusting the elevator to make the kind of speed she could with this much adrenaline buzzing under her skin. Still, by the time she reached the top her breath hurt as it whistled in and out and in and out. She reeled down the hall and threw open the door to her room.

Gertie pulled herself back inside and shut the window just as Sadie arrived. Izzy lay on the floor by the bedside table, kicking her little legs and screaming hard enough to turn her face red and sweaty. The old woman spun, her face so pale she had a greenish tint, and she pointed at Izzy as if Sadie could possibly miss her daughter's hysterics.

There was no blood, and Izzy seemed caught in the throes of a tantrum, not seizing or worse. Still, Sadie rushed to her side and dropped to her knees. She scooped her daughter up into her arms and huddled around her, pressing her cheek to the top of Izzy's head.

"I'm here, I'm here, sshh, baby, Mommy's here. Can you calm down for me? Can you calm down and use your big-girl words to tell me what happened? Ssshh, I'm here, I'm here. I can help better if you tell me what's wrong. What happened?"

Gertie hovered nearby, peppering Sadie with questions like, "What's wrong with her?" and "Does she need a doctor?" and interrupting Sadie's attempts at soothing Izzy to lean over and fuss at the little girl, cooing, "Look at Miss Gertie, sweetheart. *Oh*, you're *hurt*, aren't you? Yes. Ohh."

Her ineffective attempts to help instead prolonged the tears for several extra minutes after Sadie determined that nothing of any substance was wrong with Izzy. Every time the wailing started to subside, Gertie would ask again in a mournfully sympathetic voice if Izzy was hurt, and the screaming would kick right back up again.

Finally, Sadie stood with Izzy in her arms and told Gertie, "I'm going to check her head in the bathroom where the light is better." It wasn't, and Sadie hated the bathroom, but she needed a closed door between them and Gertie's "help." "I want to look for any bumps or marks."

"Marks? I would *never*—"

"Of course, I meant like the corner of a table or something,"

Sadie said, and whisked her daughter into the bathroom. She shut the door and then locked it for good measure, just in case Gertie took it into her head to follow them.

"Do you want to sit on the counter? Here, baby, here, sit on the counter. Can you see yourself?" Sadie settled Izzy on the counter, and almost immediately her crying slowed again. "Can I wipe your face?" Sadie asked. "You have snot on you, honey."

"No, I'm—not *honey*—I'm Izzy," the little girl protested between gasps.

"Sorry, Izzy, can I wipe your face? Look at me, look at Mommy, can I wipe your face?"

"No!"

"Okay, let's look in the mirror. See? You're all messy. Can I wipe the messy snot off you?"

Finally, Izzy nodded, and Sadie wet a washcloth from the water bottle she kept in the bathroom for toothbrushing, pretending this was a reasonable thing to have and not at all paranoid. She gently ran the cloth over Izzy's face, the cool water and soft touch soothing her daughter as it did whenever Izzy agreed to such ministrations (although if Sadie tried it while Izzy still said no, it would have kicked off another screaming tantrum).

"What happened?"

"Gertie bumped me and I bonked my head," Izzy quavered.

Sadie checked Izzy for bruises or scrapes and found nothing, while easily picturing Gertie bustling around the room—thinking she had to tidy things, or snooping idly, or even just rushing to the restroom—and shuffling into Izzy by mistake. A harmless accident, almost certainly. Still, she had to say something.

When they emerged from the bathroom, Izzy was all smiles, and Sadie kept her voice light and free of accusation as she said, "Izzy said you bumped her and she bonked her head."

"*Bumped—?*" Gertie started to raise her voice, indignation washing over her face, then she paused. "Oh, well, maybe, actually. I heard you outside and I hurried to the window to see if you were okay, and I might have—might have brushed past her on my way. I don't know. She's okay, though?"

The window. Sadie, outside. Outside trying to talk to Mel's mother.

It was Sadie's turn to hurry to the window. She slipped past Gertie and Izzy without bumping anybody and rushed to peer through the glass.

Beth's truck sat alone in the parking lot below. Mrs. Ross had left while Sadie was busy with Izzy. Sadie had no way to reach out to her again.

CHAPTER FOURTEEN

Unpleasant Reverie

"Is the apartment going to be cleaned before the next lease?" Sadie asked, stepping a little ahead of the landlord turned tour guide. Her gaze moved from the nicotine-stained walls and ceiling to the windowsill with a layer of dust and a scattering of dead bugs. She turned the light on in the bathroom and eyed the spotty mirror and the visible ring running around the bathtub. She tried to imagine letting Izzy splash in this tub, bathing the new baby here.

"The maid service left this morning," the landlord said, and Sadie could've sworn he was being sarcastic. She gave him a sharp look and he smiled, but her gaze moved past him immediately.

"What are you looking at, Iz?"

"Chock-yet," Izzy said.

"Chocolate? Wait." Izzy reached for something on the floor. "Wait, Isabelle!" Sadie lunged across the room in time to stop her daughter from scooping up a pile of tiny mouse droppings in the corner. "I'll give you real chocolate later, that's yucky stuff," she said, lifting her daughter. Izzy fussed for a moment, whining wordlessly and kicking, but Sadie repeated the promise of chocolate later in a low voice until her daughter settled.

The places she could afford were simply not the places she

wanted to have children in. The thought of the new baby looking past a crib mobile at dirty yellow walls made her grimace, and the thought of Izzy getting her hands on something diseased made her stomach clench.

An undercurrent to these fears ran swift and cold—a kind of self-recrimination that rushed through her too fast to catch and examine in any detail. The complexity of the feeling drained and left her with the bare surface of the discomfort: Plenty of parents raised children in places so much worse than the apartment she'd seen today—what made her special?

Nothing. She wasn't special, but she *was* lucky. A dubious kind of luck, anyway. She at least had options to weigh. She could settle on a place like this, dirty and infested and as much a trap as Sadie had ever seen, but she'd never have to walk L'Arpin's chilly, dim corridors again, never gaze out her window at the power plant spearing smokestacks into the sky. Or she and Izzy could stay at L'Arpin for free a little longer, and Sadie could measure the large but short-term risk of running afoul of whatever bad business occupied Mr. Drye and Beth and maybe Lewis or even Joe, too, against the long-term benefit of scraping together just enough in savings to get a safe and clean apartment.

"Thanks for your time," Sadie said to the landlord, and left without looking any further.

This had been their fourth tour of a totally unsuitable apartment. Even going with only two bedrooms hadn't made enough of a difference yet, and for a moment, while Sadie buckled Izzy into her car seat, she pictured living with a toddler and an infant in a studio apartment.

She'd lose her mind.

Car naps were Izzy's only naps these days, and she fell asleep within the first five minutes of the twenty-minute drive back to L'Arpin. As far as Mr. Drye believed, Sadie had brought Izzy with her to a prenatal checkup. She didn't want anyone at the hotel to know she was preparing to leave. Now, returning defeated, her privacy at least saved her from the embarrassment of having her failure known.

She couldn't go back there, not right away. At the last minute she turned in to the parking lot for a little playground on the far side of the power plant. She left the car idling and glanced at Izzy in her rearview mirror, wishing she could take a nap, too.

Work had been brutal the last week and a half—every day at least one room had massive puddles where no water should be. She'd called Beth to check the walls and pipes the first two times, but each time the maintenance woman found nothing. Too much like the things in the tub, too much like the tentacle slithering out of the to-go box. Sadie stopped calling.

If the increased workload from all that wet—on top of her extra hours—wasn't bad enough, the sounds of dripping and squishing footsteps in the hall and water rushing through pipes in the walls grew louder and more frequent night by night.

Sadie had sunk bit by bit into the wound-up tension and light sleep of constant vigilance. From the playground's parking lot, the power plant loomed all the larger, but at least it obscured the sight of the hotel, allowing her to relax a little.

To keep from nodding off, Sadie tried to find something interesting to look at while she waited for her daughter to wake. From here, Sadie had a view of a large portion of the plant's parking lot that had been cut off from the rest, a hastily erected temporary fence hemming in several large construction vehicles and a few piles of pipes, bricks, and lumps covered by tarps to keep off the snow. Nothing worth paying attention to, nothing that could help her stay awake or keep her thoughts from spiraling toward something a little sharper than frustration.

Izzy snored in her seat, and Sadie picked up her phone, turned the volume almost all the way down, and listened again to the recording she'd made ten days before. Mr. Drye, saying he hadn't seen Mel in months. Sadie had listened to it every day since making the video, and each time her vindication swung closer and closer to despair. It wasn't enough. If Sadie couldn't get anything more than this, she'd lose. She'd fail. Not just for herself—she'd fail Mel.

Sadie blinked hard, fending off the sting of lonesome, guilty tears. The passing days had not made the absence of one of the only kind voices in her life any easier. All that time had done was convince her that she'd been wrong before.

She couldn't show this video, Mr. Drye's words, to the police.

After all, he had said the same things to them. They already believed that Mel had never even been in the system at L'Arpin.

Sadie watched it until the end, then watched it again, the despair cold but a growing frustration hot, the contrast between them churning in her chest and guts. All she needed was one person to back her up, but Mel had never worked nights, so the strangers of the evening shift wouldn't vouch for her existence, Joe had been flat out avoiding her, and Beth and Lewis would never admit they'd ever known her. The only person at L'Arpin who had ever had Sadie's back was the one missing now.

Had Gertie ever met the younger housekeeper?

The idea made Sadie perk up, but before she could pursue it, consider all the angles, Izzy's snore turned into a snort and then a whining cry. On the rare occasion Izzy took a nap, Sadie might as well flip a coin to figure out whether her daughter would wake up full of good cheer, or full of piss and vinegar.

Fortunately, she'd parked at a playground and Izzy had a good winter coat. Though they were edging into mid-January, the temperature had stayed relatively mild that day, especially when the wind quit blowing. So, she said, "Want to go swing, Iz?"

The incipient tears dried immediately. "Yes!"

Sadie turned off the car and stepped out, unbuckled Izzy and helped her jump down, then turned her loose. The playground stood empty and waiting for her, and soon Izzy's laughing, excited shrieks rang out. This close to Lake Erie, no such thing as quiet existed—the water ran up and down the sand, the branches rubbed and clacked against one another in the wind, and somewhere nearby, cars rolled past just steadily enough that their tires made a constant hiss on the streets. No, it wasn't quiet, but it was a peaceful, steady kind of noise, and Izzy's shouts only accented that calm background hum of the world rather than piercing it.

Or maybe Sadie was biased.

She followed her daughter at a more sedate pace, telling herself her refusal to rush after Izzy had nothing to do with Gertie's implication that Sadie hovered too much, telling herself she hadn't spent the last ten days trying not to think about Gertie saying that.

She caught up to Izzy as her daughter tried unsuccessfully to pull herself properly into a swing. When Sadie leaned over to try to help, Izzy shied away, crying, "I wanna do it by my *own!*" Her voice carried much more panic than the situation called for.

"All right, drama child."

"I'm not drama child!"

"Are you Izzy, or are you a horsey?"

"Horsey-Izzy."

"Can I help you get into the swing?"

"Yes."

Sadie lifted Izzy into the swing and reminded her to hold on to the chains. Then she circled around behind her daughter so she could push her.

A figure near the power plant caught her attention.

"I'm flying, Mommy!"

"You sure are, Horsey-Izzy," Sadie said, distracted. Bill Viago stood not quite far enough away for distance to obscure his expression. Granted, Sadie had only come across the man, what, three times? But she knew for a fact she'd never seen him smile.

"I'm like a fairy!"

"Fairy-Horsey-Izzy?"

She wasn't sure she liked his smile. He stood with one hand on the huge tread of a bright yellow excavator, the other a fist on his hip, and he stared out at the lake with hard eyes. Remembering how he'd accosted her for being on the beach that November morning, she didn't think she imagined that his smile looked like he thought he owned all of Lake Erie.

"Mom*my*!" Izzy exclaimed with the particular inflection that told Sadie she had missed something.

"Right, sorry, yes Fairy-Horsey-Izzy?"

"Stop it, Mommy."

In the calm background noises of winter by the lake, the scrape of gravel still came clear enough to hear. Sadie didn't turn her gaze back to Viago, didn't care to see if he looked at her and her daughter as he turned back toward his building. She didn't want to know if it was Izzy's shout that had broken his doubtless unpleasant reverie or whether he watched them with eyes full of suspicion and blame.

"Stop it!"

"Stop what, stinker?"

Izzy, it appeared, was in no mood to be reasonable. She shouted, *"Stop!"*

When the gravel-grinding sound came again it had grown nearer, less like a scrape and more like a drag. Sadie readied herself to tell Viago she had every right to bring her daughter to a playground, settling into her most stern expression. She turned, and Bill Viago still stood where she'd last seen him, smoking a cigarette now but otherwise unchanged.

Like a cold tide, fear ran through Sadie from her head down.

The sound came again.

Sadie found its source. She stood transfixed by something that began as confusion and ran rapidly into dread.

It didn't move well. For a handful of seconds it lay in place, body jerking fitfully, long slits on its throat gaping open and closed. Without warning it lurched forward on two thin legs before half falling, its chest sliding through the gravel as its little limbs propelled it along for another moment. Something so small, hardly bigger than one of Izzy's stuffed animals, should not have inspired such abhorrence. Tiny tentacles, ineffective to help it move, writhed around its body. Its dark green coloring didn't stand out enough from the shadows when it stayed still, but the bulging and glassy-blank black eyes gleamed a rounded reflection of the dim daylight, and that gleam fixed on Viago. At the end of its face extended a slender, sharp protuberance that Sadie only recognized as a beak when the thing lunged forward again and opened wide, flat limbs that rowed at the air and the ground. Wings.

"Viago!" Sadie finally found her voice, calling a hoarse, shaking warning. This time, though, Viago must have heard the noise of the creature coming toward him, because he had started to turn the instant before Sadie's shout.

Instead, he hesitated, then spun the other way to face her. Defensive anger built itself like a wall over his features. Sucking a thin breath, Sadie pointed behind him.

The bird creature turned to her in the same moment, its movement lacking any birdlike abruptness. It nearly flopped onto its breast again before letting out a wheezing cry that almost sounded like a seagull.

At the exact same instant, Viago snarled, "What are you doing here?"

"Look! *Look!*"

The thing spread its green wings, squirming squid-like appendages making the shape unfamiliar and terrible. With frantic, awkward strokes it flapped up, banking out of sight over the roof of the plant as if deliberately hiding. Sadie's pointing finger tracked its flight.

Viago looked up.

"Did you see it?" Sadie gasped. "Did you see that?"

Viago dropped his gaze, turning a flat frown on Sadie. He flicked his cigarette down and ground it beneath his boot, then marched toward her. The power plant overseer stopped short of the hastily erected temporary fence.

Once he drew near enough to talk without shouting, he demanded, "What are you playing at?"

"Excuse me? There was—there was . . . a thing."

"A *thing*?" Viago repeated, mimicking Sadie's tone.

"It was some kind of—"

"Save it. You hotel people, always trying to fu—" He cut himself off with a glance at Izzy, an expression more cautious than chagrined crossing his face. "Ah, mess with me. Keep to yourself, lady."

He turned to stomp back across the lot in the direction of the nearest door.

"Mommy?" Izzy asked.

"Not now, Iz." Sadie leaned down to pull her daughter off the swing. It was time to go.

Rather than be shushed, Izzy raised her voice, asking in a carrying tone, "What was that monster?"

The air went out of Sadie in a rush, left her feeling squeezed empty and fighting for her next breath. From the corner of her eye, Sadie saw Viago pause. He started to turn, stopped, and picked up his pace instead.

CHAPTER FIFTEEN

Strange Implications

Sadie hustled Izzy to the car, keeping a discreet eye on Viago. He had stopped at the door to his plant and stood half in and half out, looking up toward the roof as if he now believed he might see something perched there, after all.

Could Izzy's question alone make him change his mind like that? Maybe he'd talked to her the way he had not because he thought she was wrong about what she'd seen but because he knew she was right. Viago had been a problem hovering in the vicinity of L'Arpin ever since Sadie had arrived here, and hadn't his last appearance in L'Arpin—what? a month ago?—seemed different, somehow triumphant, with Mr. Drye sounding worn down?

How was he involved with the bizarre problems Sadie faced?

She settled Izzy into her car seat, tucking her coat around her little body over top of her tightened seat straps, and then leaned close to her daughter. Keeping her head ducked over Izzy, Sadie peered up over her glasses toward where she'd last seen Viago.

Gone.

She kissed Izzy atop her head and said, "Mommy is going to go check and make sure everything is okay, baby. You stay right here."

She had to learn more. Like, for instance, if she'd imagined that creature . . . only, no, Izzy had seen it. Still, Sadie needed to see if she could find evidence that she had seen a real, honest-to-goodness little monster heaving itself through the parking lot of the power plant.

Sadie straightened, shutting Izzy in the car, and set off toward the fence. She started at a brisk walk, but the nearer she drew to the chain links, the more hesitant her steps became. The shadow beneath the looming wall of the plant gave little in the way of a hint. Whatever she expected to find there, a slime trail or a handful of green-tinged feathers or something stranger, something worse, she could see nothing in the mottled grays of the gravel in the shade. Maybe . . . maybe a patch of strange color? Or maybe just a deeper shadow or scuff in the gravel.

A little way down the fence stood a gate, and Sadie sidled toward it, her eyes darting everywhere. There were definitely laws about entering private property without permission. There may have been laws specific to power plants, even. But it's not like cops lingered around waiting for someone to trespass while looking for monsters.

Heart fluttering, breath tight and shallow, Sadie reached for the gate.

Just as she laid a hand on the cold metal latch, Viago's voice rang out. "Get the fuck away from there, lady."

Sadie flinched, turning. Viago strode back out from behind the construction equipment, his scowl tinged with triumph. Had he been hiding there on purpose? Why?

"Caught you red-handed! Trying to sneak in, up to no good. I'm calling the cops."

The same cops Mr. Drye had showed the computer records at L'Arpin. The same cops who had not bothered looking beyond Mel's absence from the files. Cops like the cops back in Finneytown who all answered to Sam and who believed every last lie about her that passed his lips. The idea of cops made Sadie's guts turn to water, but she couldn't let a guy like Viago see it, or he'd go through with his threat.

Instead, keeping her tone just light enough that any attitude she gave him would probably not also give him an excuse to lash out, Sadie said, "And tell them . . . ? That I looked at your building? That I almost touched a fence?"

Viago scowled, a flush creeping over his face. "Get outta here!" he shouted, the same way a person might shout a stray off their property. He came at her, flapping his arms.

Sadie flinched again but fought the urge to hurry away, fought a moment of embarrassed anger at being shooed like a pest, and turned to walk back to her car. Through the window she could see Izzy whining even if she couldn't hear it, probably at being left behind. When she opened the door and met the fussing head-on, exhaustion hit her all at once.

A break—from work, from fear and uncertainty and confusion and mystery, from motherhood—she wanted a *break*.

Instead, she had a small monster struggling across the ground and struggling to fly and a missing coworker and a suspicious boss and nowhere to go. And now Bill Viago, however he fit in. And his power plant. Sadie started her car while giving the construction equipment a narrow-eyed, suspicious gaze.

She backed out of the parking space, keeping her eyes on the rearview mirror more than she probably should have as she turned the car around and headed for the road. Bill Viago didn't seem as if he planned to follow her. As she watched in the mirror, he finally went back into the power plant. This time he shut the door behind himself, and he didn't emerge again.

Sadie lowered her eyes from the mirror to the road just as a bright purple car flashed past. The tangled branches of an overgrown, winter-bare bush to her left hid the car almost the instant she noticed it. Sadie's heart stuttered and her mouth dried. She leaned forward over the steering wheel. Craning her neck didn't help. She couldn't see around the branches. She couldn't tell if the car had been the right—or, really, the wrong—make and model, much less check out the license plates.

The last time she'd seen a car that particular shade of purple had been nearly three months before.

When Sam drove it to work the morning Sadie and Izzy left.

That didn't mean Sam had found the lakeside town she'd landed in. It didn't mean anything. Nothing at all.

Her head knew that, but her twisting gut didn't, her frozen lungs didn't, her hunched shoulders and whitening knuckles didn't.

She peeled out of the parking lot. It didn't make sense to speed down the tiny stretch of road, not even half a block, over to L'Arpin's lot. She told herself to slow down even as she careened in, yanking the wheel around until she navigated her car into a sloppy approximation of parking between the lines in her usual space.

On the walk into the hotel, Sadie forced herself not to look over her shoulders, not to turn her head this way and that. Sam wasn't there. Impossible. But if he was, she didn't want to draw attention to herself by looking afraid. With her free hand she pulled the hood of her coat up, hiding her red curls.

For once, entering the chilly lobby of L'Arpin Hotel let her breathe easier. Sadie paused inside the entrance and set Izzy down, her shoulders sagging. A murmur of conversation from the direction of the desk cut off abruptly at their entrance—Sadie caught the words "upsetting her" and "nasty habit" and "ruining your own" before the sudden, sharp quiet drew her attention more fully than the soft voices had. Joe and Mr. Drye stood a little too close together, the cook's expression apologetic in a familiar way. Sadie would bet the contrition masked his real feelings. She didn't care to snoop into whatever he'd been scolded for, but she could relate with the sentiment, even if she regarded him now with a thread of discomfort—he'd been avoiding her since the holidays, since Mel's absence, and however some little tentacled thing may have gotten into her trash, she'd seen it in the to-go box from *his* kitchen. She ran her hands through her hair, pushing her hood back down. Then she caught one of Izzy's hands and headed for the elevator.

"How was your appointment, Miss Miles?" the hotel manager

asked, taking care to sound casual, perhaps to save Joe the embarrassment of having been caught being reprimanded.

Sadie didn't look back at them, pressing the button for the elevator longer and harder than necessary. "Fine," she said, curt enough to make her real meaning—*none of your business*—clear.

"You seem perturbed. Are you well?" Mr. Drye hesitated just long enough that Sadie thought he wouldn't ask the next question, but of course he went ahead. "Is something the matter with the baby?"

His tone drew her around as sharply as if someone had grabbed and spun her. Had he sounded hopeful? But no, no, his expression seemed concerned, uncomplicated by any strange implications. Her suspicions must be getting the better of her. From halfway across the lobby, Joe cast her an uncharacteristically anxious glance over his shoulder as he hurried toward the kitchen hallway.

"We're all fine," she said.

The elevator chimed. Sadie tugged Izzy in and pressed the DOOR CLOSE button, pretending not to hear as Mr. Drye started to say something else.

The elevator opened onto the fourth-floor corridor, for once not empty.

Gertie stood so near the elevator that anyone coming out would have had to push past her. She wrung her hands together, wearing a frown that evaporated the moment she locked eyes with Sadie.

"You've been gone so long!" Gertie backed up a pace and Sadie took the opportunity to pull Izzy past the old woman and into the hallway. "I was worried!"

"We stopped at a playground after my appointment," Sadie said. Gertie's nosiness sometimes grated on Sadie. This time, though, the older woman's distress looked so genuine. More than that, after struggling with her guilt and loneliness in the wake of Mel's absence, and after what she had seen and what she'd thought she'd seen, Sadie found herself craving Gertie's concern.

"Not the playground by that dirty power plant?" Gertie gasped. Unlike the concern, Sadie didn't welcome the judgment.

"Believe me, we won't be going there again," Sadie said, aiming for a reassuring tone but landing somewhere closer to grim.

Almost before the words left Sadie's mouth, Gertie jumped on them. "Did something happen?" she asked. "Come, come, let's get inside"—she said this unironically, the same way she might have said it if they were real neighbors who had run into each other on a street somewhere rather than a long-term hotel guest and a not-quite-homeless young mother—"and you can tell me about it."

Gertie linked her arm through Sadie's, and for a moment Sadie thought the old lady planned to lead them, for the first time, to her own room. Instead, she shuffled right to Sadie's door and waited only until Sadie had unlocked it before pulling her—and because Sadie still held her daughter's hand, Izzy, too—inside in a rush.

"Make me some coffee, dear, and tell me what happened."

Sadie wished she could have more than coffee. No, she wished she could have a glass—a bottle, maybe—of wine. She made a weak cup for Gertie, keeping her back to her guest and watching the drips as it percolated. How much did she want to tell?

"Did something happen at the playground?" Gertie prompted.

"We saw a monster!" Izzy shouted, raising her hands like claws. She let out a high-pitched growl and stalked toward Gertie on stiff legs. As soon as her daughter said it, of course, Sadie realized she hadn't wanted to tell anyone anything about that at all. Sadie wished Izzy would stop shouting about it—how could she convince herself she'd only imagined the thing in the power plant's parking lot with Izzy insisting she'd seen a monster?

Izzy repeated, "A monster!"

"A monster?" Gertie exclaimed. If her aim was simply to humor the little girl, she did too good a job. She really sounded like she believed there might have been a monster at the playground.

And just because there *had* been didn't mean Gertie ought to be so credulous. Sadie hadn't worried about how fit Gertie might be to keep an eye on Izzy, but the thought grew large in her mind in that instant.

"Yes!" Izzy shouted, bright and excited. "A—"

If one more person said *monster* Sadie was going to scream. She hurried to interrupt her daughter.

"We ran into Bill Viago." Sadie spoke as if correcting Izzy rather than merely elaborating. Not a lie Izzy would inadvertently call her out on, but some explanation other than *monster*. "He was shouting the first time Izzy saw him. It left an impression."

"Is that all?" Gertie asked. The coffee finished brewing, and Sadie poured Gertie a mug. When she handed it over, Gertie grabbed Sadie's wrist instead of the cup. Her fingers held tight, surprisingly strong. "It's okay if that's not all. I can be here for you, Sadie." She squeezed Sadie's wrist.

"I thought I saw someone I didn't want to see," Sadie said. She cast a significant look at Izzy, trying to convey without words that she didn't want to talk about it in front of her daughter. She tugged her wrist away. Or tried to. Gertie tightened her grip, pulled Sadie a little closer.

"I want to help you, Sadie Miles," she said, and the sincerity in her eyes brought tears to Sadie's. She didn't want to talk about Sam, but she let Gertie pull her closer still, into a hug.

CHAPTER SIXTEEN

You Need That Young Woman

Sadie pushed her cart around a corner, from the lobby into the hallway that led from the kitchen and dining room at this end all the way back to Beth's maintenance room. A quick movement near the kitchen door drew her eye, and her heart surged into a shuddering rush.

Everything made her jump these days. This time it was only Joe. Whatever he'd been doing in the hallway outside his kitchen, he'd retreated back to his domain with haste. Probably the second he saw Sadie rounding the corner. Not that he needed to avoid her; the affable cook had landed himself on Sadie's list of people not to trust, people not to seek out.

Thinking it made her cringe, and she pushed her cart faster, passing the kitchen with nearly as much haste as he'd fled from her with. The list included every last one of her coworkers now, and if she hadn't seen so many strange things with her own eyes, this self-isolation would have brought the word *paranoid* creeping back into her thoughts again.

Staying confined within the dim halls and small rooms of L'Arpin, surrounded by people she could not bring herself to trust, wore on Sadie. She needed some time away, but the thought of leaving, of going out into the open world where anyone could be anywhere, brought the fast glint of purple she'd seen on the road flashing through her mind again. There'd been no further trips to the playground, only hurrying straight to and from the car any time she and Izzy had to leave L'Arpin, and though Sadie didn't have access to the guest records, only which rooms she would need to clean and when, she kept track of the customers' comings and goings as well as she could.

A grumbling roared to life and Sadie jumped, her heart lurching. When a high *beep-beep-beep* joined the deeper rumble, her momentary fright eased. Whatever construction Viago had been preparing for had begun, making a distracting racket even in the far corners of the normally hushed hotel. Sadie derived some small satisfaction from Mr. Drye's obvious fury at the constant barrage of noise, but such pleasure didn't make up for her loneliness.

She hadn't expected to want to talk about the things she'd seen, about whatever that bird had been and about the glimpse of a purple car, not ever, not with anyone. But she lacked anyone to confide in, to explain how the fear and strangeness churned her gut and kept her awake at night. Instead of talking it out, Sadie found herself trying to rationalize everything away. The car couldn't really have been Sam's. The bird couldn't really have been a monster—a seagull, tangled up in some flotsam from the lake, more like. One of those was easier to believe than the other, and what did it say about Sadie's state of mind that the image she struggled most to disbelieve was the little tendrils that had twisted and squirmed as the bird had spread its ungainly wings?

Sometimes she thought she saw things slinking along the ground when she looked out her window. Scouring social media still failed to turn up a way to contact Mel's mother, but it had given Sadie the news of a startling number of missing pets. Before she could stop herself, she imagined every one of them as a bulge-eyed, tentacled green monster. The hotel still made its constant dripping and splashing noises, and unless Sadie kept her imagination in hand each one sounded less like a leaky pipe and more like a seeking tentacle.

When Sadie did manage to banish her overactive imagination the monotony of her time in L'Arpin wore on her. Sometimes she missed teaching, missed engaging with the kids, but most of the time she just missed having new things to occupy her thoughts, especially now that she'd turned the cleaning of each room into a habitual act. On this afternoon, though, she didn't mind those thoughts. For once, she appreciated the unmindful nature of housekeeping.

Sadie had found a local food bank the week before. Not everything there worked for her—the hotel room's microwave and coffee pot didn't offer much versatility—and it wouldn't be enough to live off either way, but Sadie had spent part of that morning reworking her budget, and if she was careful she might be able to afford a suitable apartment in just a few more weeks, before the end of February.

Perhaps she could have made it even sooner if she would have quit paying to bathe herself and Izzy at the truck stop, quit buying bottled water to drink and stocking the bathroom counter with hand sanitizer and wet wipes, but these days when she ran the taps she imagined a faint glimmer in the water. Never there when she looked closer, never quite a glow, but still, after the tub incident Sadie couldn't bring herself to so much as wash her hands at L'Arpin Hotel.

Still. They'd be out of there sooner than she'd hoped. And that wasn't even the best news.

She was having another girl.

The twenty-week ultrasound that morning had been perfect—cold goo on her belly and the particular *swoosh* and *whump-whump-whump*, the baby's development on track, the black-and-white monitor, the ultrasound technician who had taken time to point out the features of the baby's little face to Izzy. And Izzy, oh, Izzy's face when she'd *seen* the baby and maybe for the very first time truly understood what was happening . . . Sadie's vision wavered with tears, and this time they were almost entirely happy.

Between her drifting mind, hazy with so much good news, and the distant but distracting cacophony from the construction at the power plant, Sadie couldn't pinpoint how long she'd been hearing the other noises before her conscious mind fixed on them.

The banging didn't stand out much from the din across the parking lot, but the sick, familiar *slap* did. Sadie's gut twisted.

Then came the scream—a strangled sound even before it choked off. Sadie's heart leaped into her throat.

She ducked into the nearest of the doorway alcoves lining the hall and pulled her walkie-talkie out of her pocket with shaking hands. It took her two tries to press the button.

Izzy's cheerful voice poured out of the little speaker in a constant chatter that ran under Gertie's quieter murmur. Whatever might be going on, it didn't affect Izzy. The relief made Sadie's knees weak, her focus fully on Izzy's voice, so that for a moment she didn't catch the sense of Gertie's words. Not until the sharpness of the older woman's tone caught Sadie's attention.

". . . want any more excuses, young lady." Sadie clenched her jaw. Did Gertie usually talk to Izzy like that? "If you deserve to be part of L'Arpin Hotel then you'll make sure it stays *nice* here, do you understand me?"

Before Sadie could fly off the handle and charge upstairs, all other considerations forgotten, Beth's voice spoke up. "Ms. Harper, I think—"

"These kinds of habits get *worse*, not better. Wait until things go missing, until you can't find something you need," Gertie interrupted, voice sharp. She hadn't been scolding Izzy, then, just being a demanding customer. Sadie wondered if she spoke to waitresses like this, too. She'd never treated Sadie that way. "I've lived long enough to know that. You ought to know it by now, too. What would the hotel be like if this went on forever, hm?" A pause, and then, "You should take care of it, Bethany. Soon."

"Me?" What problem had Gertie found with L'Arpin to make Beth sound so alarmed? "*How* soon? Ma'am, I can—"

"You know what? I think I'm going to have a word with dear Henry about this, too." Sadie had never heard Gertie's voice so firm, so hard, but when she spoke again all her sweetness had returned. "Sweetheart, Auntie Gertie"—since when was she *Auntie Gertie*?—"has to run to the lobby. I won't be five minutes. You can sit and be good for five minutes, right, sweetheart?"

Sadie's grip on the walkie-talkie tightened painfully.

Gertie was going to leave Izzy alone. The thought of her daughter, unsupervised, brought the sounds Sadie'd heard a few moments before surging back to the front of her mind. The wet slap, the choked scream—*in* L'Arpin at that moment—and Izzy would be alone.

Sadie had to make sure, fast, that the danger wouldn't spread, and then she had to get to her daughter. She shut off the walkie-talkie.

At that moment the banging and slapping gave way to a thud so loud it made Sadie jump, her shoulders hunching and her breath catching.

Moving fast, heart racing, Sadie unscrewed the wooden handle from the mop head. Inadequately armed, she tried to make herself hurtle toward the sound but could manage only a fearful scuttle. Every step drew her closer to the lobby; the ruckus should have been audible from the front desk, but of course Mr. Drye didn't come check.

Sadie reached the door where the sounds of a now-muted struggle still emanated. Beneath the violent noises came one that she hadn't heard before, one that wrapped around her heart and clutched at her throat.

Inside that room, a child cried. Another thud resounded through the door, and the cries briefly rose into a terrified yelp before growing muffled again.

Sadie grabbed for the doorknob. Locked. It rattled in her shaking grip. She snatched her key and jammed it into the lock, her skin alight with buzzing electricity.

The key turned, tumblers clicked, Sadie twisted the knob and shoved.

The door moved an inch, maybe less, before slamming into an unseen barrier.

"Right," Sadie muttered. She had survived the loss of her husband. She had taken Izzy and left Sam. She had discovered dark plots in the halls of L'Arpin Hotel. She had kept herself and her daughter safe from the strangeness within these rooms and corridors.

She could open a door.

Retreating a few steps, Sadie tightened her grip on the mop handle and shook out her shoulders, sucking in a deep breath and letting it out in a puff. Then she lunged across the hallway and raised one leg to deliver a kick with all her might.

With an anticlimactic *thwack* she drove the door into whatever blocked it again and didn't budge it even a hair's breadth beyond that. She nearly lost her balance and staggered back, her weight on her off leg, wincing at the unexpected throb of pain running up from her foot to her knee.

Sadie backed up again and tried once more. Leg still aching from the first attempt, she couldn't bring herself to put her full weight behind this kick. She accomplished nothing. The horrible *slaps* from within the room gave way to another choked cry and another terrified child's wail.

For one second, Sadie dithered. Then she dropped the mop handle, turned, and ran. She had not been to the maintenance office often, but she knew where it was. Mostly to avoid it. Now she could only hope to find it unoccupied.

Sadie skidded to a stop before the maintenance room door, tucked between the humming vending machines and the exit to the back parking lot. The door was shut, its thin rectangular window dark. She didn't give herself time to feel any relief, just used her key to let herself into Beth's space. To her right, a series of ladders in different sizes leaned against the wall, the tallest reaching to the ceiling, which in this room alone must have gone all the way up to the second floor. Directly in front of her sat Beth's desk, small and shabby compared to the one in the office behind the check-in counter, marked with coffee mug rings and home to a scatter of chewed pencils. Behind that stood a stack of wooden pallets. And to her left ran a wall covered in pegboard, tools hung neatly in their places. Sadie lunged for it, grabbing two screwdrivers. One flathead, one Phillips head. She didn't know which kind the hinges on the door would need, but she'd get into that room if she had to take the hotel apart to do it.

Sadie ran back to the room where the commotion was . . . no. No.

Where, she realized with a sinking pit opening in her gut, the commotion *had been*.

Silence lay thick upon the hallway, in its shadows and its pools of dim light. Whatever happened was done now; she knew it the nearer she drew.

Even if she'd been on time, the screwdrivers would've proved useless. These doors' hinges were all on the inside. Sadie threw the Phillips head with a small, furious cry. Too slow. She'd been too slow.

Just to give it one last try, just to know she'd done everything she could, Sadie went to the door again. She switched the flathead screwdriver to her right hand, raised it as if to stab, and then pushed the door open. It moved slowly from the very first instant, but kept moving past where the blockage had stopped her before. Sadie stepped away from the door even as she extended her arm to continue pushing it open, all at once certain that whatever impeded her progress now was hideous—another monster, a corpse, something worse.

Instead, water first seeped and then flowed through the widening gap.

Sadie jumped away as the water ran over the green carpet with enough force to push her discarded mop handle and screwdriver a few inches each. When the flow slowed, slowed, and stopped, she put a hand on the wall opposite the door for balance and leaned as far over the puddle as she could, peering into the room.

Just visible, one end of a soaking wet, rolled-up towel shoved under the crack in the door peeked out at her. Beyond that, the angle of the door and the hall, and her own reluctance to step in the water, inhibited her glimpse inside. Clothing lay sodden on the floor, an overturned shoe near one pile. The corner of a drawer pulled from the dresser, a shard of broken glass, a handheld game system with a cracked screen. She saw nothing else. Nothing but the ghost of a swirling luminescence in the water, so faint she could only make it out in the shadows.

Sadie pulled away fast.

She had to put the screwdrivers back, and then . . . then she had to get Mr. Drye and, if she didn't want to draw too much suspicious attention, pretend like she didn't suspect his involvement in all this.

That, or do the right thing—burn all her bridges, risk her and Izzy's already precarious safety, and ask him where the hell the crying child was.

She wasted an instant trying to decide. Then she shook her head at herself with a frustrated grunt and turned. Taking the long way around to the lobby wasted more time, but Sadie would damn well not step in that water. Not while it still held an ever-dimming hint of a green glow.

Sadie skidded into the lobby, still favoring the leg she'd tried to kick the door with. Her breath came hard, and she'd sweated enough that her glasses slipped halfway down her nose. Eyes wide, she clutched the screwdriver she'd forgotten to ditch in one hand. She'd directly encountered guests in L'Arpin only a handful of times since coming here, less than she would have guessed, but of course *now* a family stood around the lobby, waiting for Mr. Drye to finish checking them in.

"Miss Miles!" Mr. Drye exclaimed when he looked up at the commotion of her entrance, and for a moment Sadie could not tell if he looked excited or outraged. He blinked, the expression passed, and concern washed over his features. "What's the matter? It's not—?"

The baby. That's what he was going to say, she just knew it.

"No," she said. "Not that. But there's been . . ." She hesitated. If everything had been exactly as it seemed within L'Arpin Hotel, Sadie would have chosen her words to shield the hotel and its staff from unpleasantness in front of guests. Things were *not* exactly as they seemed, though, and Sadie knew full well that Mr. Drye knew what went on in his hallways and rooms, and so she said, ". . . an attack. There's been an attack! In one of the rooms, I heard a struggle, and a child crying."

A moment before, Sadie had been embarrassed to see the family of strangers in the lobby. Now, as the mother reached out to pull her grade school–aged son toward her and the father stepped away from the counter and toward Sadie, concern in his eyes, Sadie found herself fiercely glad of their presence. It was for their sake, not Mr. Drye's, that she went on.

"The door opened, there's water everywhere, I couldn't see all the way in but there're no noises anymore, and we need to check it out." The man frowned at her. Sadie pictured in an instant, in a flash, what would happen if he turned on her, if he thought she should have gone in. He'd say she should have gone to check on the kid herself, and she'd have to backpedal, wheedle, lose credibility. She'd stopped Mr. Drye from mentioning the baby before, but now . . . "I was afraid to go in by myself." She laid her hand on her belly, low, pushing her clothing against her growing roundness, and gave her boss a significant look. The hint of hardness in the guest's eyes vanished entirely.

"Where's the room?"

A beat of silence followed the question. Because it had not been Mr. Drye who asked it. He should have been the one, but no. It was the visitor, the mother, her voice full of urgency mirrored on her husband's face but not on Mr. Drye's.

"This way!" Sadie said.

She led them back around the long way, not giving it much thought until they rounded the last corner and the man asked, "Why didn't we just come this way?"

"I think the water is contaminated with—with something, I don't know," Sadie said. The last hints of its greenish glow had faded in her absence and she knew how that would sound, anyway. Instead, she said, "There was a smell, before. It's dissipated, I guess. But I was worried about splashing right through it."

"What are you implying, Miss Miles? The water in L'Arpin Hotel is perfectly safe."

"Of course, Mr. Drye, I just smelled something strange." Was he trying to stall? Trying to get out of going into that room with Sadie and a witness? Not if Sadie could help it. "Should we go in?"

"I should go in, Miss Miles. You stay here, where it's"—there was only the very slightest hesitation, then he said—"safe."

Mr. Drye turned to the guest. "And, sir, for the sake of our guests' privacy, I'm afraid I must ask you to remain in the hallway as well."

There it went, the chance to have a witness for Mr. Drye's duplicity slipping through Sadie's fingers.

"No," she said. "I heard *terrible* noises, you shouldn't go in there alone."

"Miss Miles, this is a conversation you and I should have in private," Mr. Drye said, his voice dropping, taking on the strained quality of someone trying very hard to maintain their calm.

"What are you talking about? We need to go in there, now. There was a *child*—"

"Yeah, man, stop wasting time," the guest said, and stepped forward as if to muscle past Mr. Drye. When he tried, though, Mr. Drye didn't budge, hardly twitched at all.

"I'm afraid I can't allow you in, sir. And, Miss Miles, this would be a good time to exercise restraint."

"Restraint! Someone was attacked, they were screaming!"

"Then *why*," Mr. Drye barked, drawing himself up tall, "have no other guests called to report the noises? Or even complained?"

Sadie fell back a step, confusion and alarm racing through her.

"What are you saying?"

"*Look* at this mess."

"Look in that *room*!" Sadie shot back. "There was a little kid in there. Where is the kid, Mr. Drye?"

"You better let me in that room," the guest said, but his voice held less conviction than it had a moment before.

"Why do you have a screwdriver, Miss Miles?" Sadie had never heard Mr. Drye raise his voice before, but he grew louder and louder now.

"I was going to try to get the door open—"

"Why did you have *two* screwdrivers?" Mr. Drye pointed at the one on the floor. "Why did you have a club?"

"A club? That's a mop handle!"

"And the screwdrivers?"

"To get into the room!"

"Did you lose your key?"

"There was something blocking the door—"

"What? What thing? There's nothing there!" Mr. Drye was shouting now, pointing at the ajar door. "You have made a fuss more than once since I hired you, Miss Miles, and I am trying to be patient, for m—" He cut himself off with a sharp intake of breath, his nostrils flaring as he squeezed his eyes shut, visibly calming himself. When he opened his eyes, he faced not Sadie but the guest. "I am very sorry for the disturbance. Please, return to the lobby while I call maintenance to deal with this mess. I'll be with you soon, and we'll discuss compensation for your trouble here."

The about-face left Sadie gaping, her heart sinking and her hands curling into tight fists. She might have rallied, but then the guest cast her a look caught between suspicion and sympathy—and the latter, she realized bitterly, only because he knew she was pregnant.

She'd lost.

"Is everything all right here, Henry?"

Gertie's soft voice, always walking the line between pleasant and querulous, came from a little way down the hall, near the corner that would lead the fast way to the lobby. Mr. Drye started, and so did Sadie. What was Gertie— Right. Leaving a three-year-old alone to come down to the lobby and complain to Mr. Drye about an employee. A hot rush of anger and worry coursed through Sadie, pushing her confused fear to the background for one instant.

The guest, shaking his head, murmured a polite "excuse me" as he slipped past the old woman on his way to rejoin his family, and the present moment surged back up in Sadie's mind.

"Just a misunderstanding, Ms. Harper," Mr. Drye replied, his voice smooth and soothing. "Everything is fine, I assure you."

"It had better be," Gertie scolded, shaking a finger at Mr. Drye. "You need that young woman."

Normally Sadie would cringe to have a customer say something like that to one of her bosses; that kind of praise made her feel servile and cheap. But this time she appreciated it, and she shot Gertie a grateful look as she turned and made her way back to her cleaning cart, careful not to stomp, not to cause any more of a scene.

The freedom to move away could not come soon enough.

CHAPTER SEVENTEEN

Oppressive Paranoia

Izzy shoved her breakfast away from herself with a wordless whine. The cereal bowl slid across the small hotel desk and bumped Sadie's knuckles, knocking her phone, with another apartment website displayed on the screen, down with a clatter.

It had been just over a month since she saw the purple car and thought she saw an impossible thing. A month of telling herself she wasn't spending all her time off work hiding out in her room with Izzy, when she wasn't taking her daughter to keep showering at the truck stop. A month of Izzy growing increasingly restless, every temper tantrum scraping Sadie's already worn nerves more and more raw, and increasing the risk that some guest would hear her screaming.

"Mom*my*," Izzy drew out the *y*, high-pitched and nasally, her fake-cry voice. "I don't *like* cereal!"

"We don't have anything else today, stinker," Sadie said, glancing up from her phone and trying a patient smile, wishing Izzy would just hush. The plan, the search for a safe way to get them out of L'Arpin Hotel, didn't include getting kicked out right before she could afford somewhere else to go.

"I'm not hungry!"

Rather than prolong the shouting by forcing her daughter to eat, Sadie capitulated. She unbuckled Izzy's booster and set her on the floor. She closed the apartment search and opened a new tab, then typed *missing family vacation NEOhio* into the search bar. The results unfurled, and Sadie scrolled down. The results had not changed since the last time she'd gone hunting for anyone who might be the family she'd heard struggling in their room two weeks ago. She swiped back up to the search bar, but before she could move on to her next set of keywords—*missing child hotel Lake Erie*, because Sadie was just worried enough about the hotel's Wi-Fi allowing Beth or Drye to snoop on her activity to avoid actually naming L'Arpin—Izzy let out another fussing cry.

There'd be no focusing for Sadie today. She closed the web browser and opened her Facebook app instead. She tapped the magnifying glass icon in the top corner and her recent social media searches opened.

Mel Ross topped the list.

Sadie had scoured Mel's page a few times a week since failing to talk to her mother, but it never helped. Mel had clearly never used this platform. She'd only ever posted one single profile picture, so outdated it featured braces, and one cover photo of three girls seen from behind wearing high school graduation caps and gowns. The friends list showed only a dozen or so people, and her page had a scant handful of posts dated years before. Mel must've made the account and then immediately switched to something more trendy.

Searching one by one through each of that handful of friends yet again took longer than it had any other time—Izzy's restless fussing never ceased, only eased or intensified through the whole long morning, until something in Sadie stretched thinner and thinner and finally snapped.

She could not take being trapped in her room, in L'Arpin, for another moment.

Without a plan or anything other than a powerful urge to get out of these four walls, Sadie abruptly said, "We've been cooped up in here long enough, huh, stinker?"

"Cooped?" Izzy repeated and, in one of her lightning-fast mood changes, she let out a shriek of laughter. "Cooped-pooped!"

"Yeah, definitely cooped-pooped," Sadie said with a snort. "Come on, let's get you bundled up."

The toddler made a lengthy production of getting into her boots and coat, her gloves and hat, only to cheerfully announce that she'd peed her pants just as Sadie opened the door. One hasty cleanup and gentle lecture later, and nearly forty minutes had passed between "let's get you bundled up" and actually stepping out into the hallway. Sadie rode the elevator down in silence, eyes closed, gathering the frayed scraps of her patience back together.

In the lobby they found Joe, his meticulously ironed and clean white chef coat almost making up for the slump to his shoulders and a shadow in his eyes that looked like worry. When his gaze landed on Sadie and her daughter, he straightened and produced a smile. Sadie dredged up a hesitant smile in return, waiting for him to make some excuse and hurry away as he'd been doing the past few weeks.

"If it's not my favorite live-in housekeeper," Joe said instead. His smile turned into a grin that carried as much self-mockery as it did good-natured teasing, though it didn't touch the seriousness still lingering in his eyes. "If only that were as glamorous for me as it sounds."

Sadie almost frowned, caught the expression, and turned it into a wry smile instead. Had she been imagining his recent aloofness? He seemed mostly normal now, if a touch gloomy.

She made herself laugh as she said, "Being somebody's personal maid would probably be a step up for me, too, honestly." *Have you been avoiding me?* and *Have you seen anything weird living in your kitchen?* both hovered on the tip of her tongue, but if something was wrong with him she didn't want him wary of her, and if not, she didn't want to make it weird. The loneliness weighed heavy enough already. Instead, she asked, "I don't suppose you'd know if there are any playgrounds near here? Other than that one by the plant."

"Hm . . ." Joe rubbed one hand over his face and then shrugged, giving the question very little time, and Sadie wished she knew any local moms she could have asked instead of just about anybody at L'Arpin. "There's a McDonald's with one of those play spaces."

Sadie suppressed a shudder. Even under better circumstances those places made her skin crawl; she hated to think about the certainty of catching some virus there these days. "Nothing outside, then," she said.

"Oh, outside? You know what's fun is looking for sea glass on the beach." Sadie raised a skeptical eyebrow, but enthusiasm finally chased the unaccustomed grimness out of Joe's gaze. "The water down at the Cut keeps the beach pretty well thawed, but people don't expect it, right? So no one else is looking for the good sea glass right now. What you do is, you go down and comb the sand for the bits of glass—from litter, right, except the lake has worn away at it until it's all rounded and smooth and pretty. You find 'em on the beach and collect a nice pile, and you can make whatever you like out of 'em."

"Ignore Jordan, Sadie," Gertie's voice called out with a chuckle that skirted close to unkind. Sadie turned to see the little old lady stepping out of the elevator, excessively bundled up against the cold. "He always thinks he can sell the odds and ends he glues those glass pieces to."

"You'll see," Joe said with a grin, but something in his voice had changed. Sadie couldn't tell if it was deference or wariness. Either way, Sadie didn't want to endure any awkwardness, and anyway, the conversation had proved unhelpful.

"Well, thanks for the suggestions, but I think we'll just take a walk."

"On the sidewalk? By the road and all the cars? The glass stuff is all silly"—was the laugh that Joe snorted before excusing himself a bit too forced? Sadie watched him go, the shadows in his eyes again, half listening to Gertie as the older woman's voice soured—"but if you *must* go for a walk today, the beach is probably safest. It's too cold to be outside, though, Sadie. I can hardly stand the thought of just going to get my pills. You can't stay out there playing, Izzy will get sick."

"You don't get sick from the cold," Sadie said, distracted.

For a moment there, Joe had been acting more like himself than he had in the weeks Sadie had suspected him of avoiding her. His abrupt departure just now seemed sharper than one old lady's dismissiveness should account for. Joe and Mel had been friendly . . . Maybe he knew something about their missing co-worker. A stretch, Sadie knew, but was there even a slender chance he knew anything worthwhile? And maybe he'd know something about the thing she'd seen in her trash can. Less of a stretch . . . but more of a risk. She didn't want to make anyone put their guard up, not even genial Joe. Probably safest only to try to get him to talk about Mel, not about his reaction to Gertie or the thing in the to-go box.

She'd have to catch him alone, though.

"No? You don't get sick from the cold?" Gertie repeated, poorly masking her judgment behind obviously false surprise.

"You get sick from germs, Gertie. Izzy's fine."

"Then why do they call it catching cold? Hm?"

Sadie suppressed a sigh and wondered if she had missed some obvious cue to help her predict when Gertie's judgmental side took over.

"I have no idea, Gertie, but it's sure misleading, isn't it?" She couldn't keep her attention from drifting in the direction Joe had gone. "Thanks for trying to help, though. Um. I don't mean to keep you, you go ahead with your day. Izzy and I forgot something. Say bye-bye to Gertie, Izzy."

"Bye!"

Sadie hefted her daughter and hurried deeper into the hotel, taking the side hallway that led to the kitchen. Joe stood at a butcher-block counter chopping vegetables, and in the moment before he noticed Sadie and Izzy and put on his bright smile, a worried kind of anger pulled at his features. Then he glanced up and it was all cheer.

"Here to sneak some snacks, or just needed a break from Gertie?"

"Do you know anything about Mel?"

Sadie could've kicked herself. She'd meant to ease into the question. But when the false smile dropped away from Joe's face and left in its wake a vulnerable, fretful look, Sadie thought maybe a blunt ambush had been the right thing after all.

Joe glanced around as if he expected Mr. Drye to uncurl from beneath a counter or step out of the pantry, then looked over Sadie's shoulder at the entrance to the kitchen. He drew closer and beckoned her nearer as well.

In a lower voice, his unblinking eyes fixed on Sadie's with unusual intensity, he said, "Mel's my friend, I know her, and I know she's gonna be fine, yeah? Just fine. But she just doesn't want to be around anybody right now. Think of it like she's on hiatus from, I dunno, everything. But she's gonna be just fine."

Sadie hesitated, narrowing her eyes at Joe. He spoke with absolute conviction, sincerity in every line of his face in a way she never saw in Henry Drye's expression.

If Mel was in touch with Joe, if Mel was just having some kind of problem she'd get over and everything was really okay, that would fix everything, wouldn't it? Wouldn't it? Sadie could let herself feel relieved, and, sure, a little hurt at Mel's disappearance—instead of so scared. Wouldn't it make things simpler? Safer? It could explain everything. Maybe Mel had even convinced Mr. Drye to lie to her mother for her. Maybe her mother was a problem. A voluntary vanishing act wasn't unheard of, after all.

Sadie could certainly understand the need to disappear.

So she tried to keep the sting of hurt feelings out of her voice, tried to keep her tone light and doubt-free, as she nodded and said,

"Okay, well, if you talk to her, will you tell her to get in touch with me?"

The cook shivered, then blinked hard and put his smile back on. "Of course," he said. "Definitely."

"Right." Sadie hesitated, eyes on the cook, groping not just for what to say but for what she *wanted* to say. Because Joe's explanation should have fixed everything, but it hadn't.

She could choose to believe Joe, to tell herself Mel was fine and L'Arpin might really be safe. She wanted to, an almost physical push in her chest urging her to just go with it and let herself feel safe.

But it didn't make sense.

Izzy squirmed in Sadie's arms, the little girl's already thin patience wearing out further. Sadie would have to think about this, have to figure out how Joe, too, now fit into it all, later.

"Thanks," she said, and left in a rush.

The moment Sadie carried Izzy outside, the pushing in her chest loosened. Her breath came easier. Big, slow snowflakes drifted down from the smooth gray sky, falling nearly straight. For once, no wind rushed off the lake, and the difference it made in terms of comfort surprised Sadie. She stood still with Izzy for a long moment, breathing in the cold and soaking in the quiet peace of snowfall, and sank the fresh doubts Joe had dropped into her as far down inside herself as she could. She needed to make room for just a little bit of peace, for a change.

Once she could move without dread anchoring her in place before the hotel, Sadie put Izzy down, took her hand, and smiled down at her. "Let's go, stinker," she said.

She led her daughter toward the sidewalk, drifting in the opposite direction of the power plant and the playground beyond it. Already her feet ached at the beginning of each day, not just after a long shift. Soon a walk like this would be painful, and if her pregnancy with Izzy was any metric to judge by, Sadie would hit a limit and give up long walks altogether in another five or ten weeks. Just in time for spring, probably.

"Not that way," Izzy said, tugging in the opposite direction.

Whether she wanted to pull her mother after her or free herself from her mother's grasp didn't make much of a difference—yanking during walks outside had been a no-no since Izzy *could* walk. Hot, rushing irritation swept over Sadie, but she forced herself to take a breath. Mood swings. Sadie wouldn't let them control her, especially not over Izzy being a normal three-year-old.

"You have to stay close to Mommy and be good when we walk near a street, Izzy, remember?"

Izzy pulled again. "I wanna go *that* way, Mommy!"

"We're going to go back *inside* if you can't be good, stinker."

"That way! *That way!*" Izzy turned so she could grab Sadie's wrist with both of her mittened little hands and yanked twice, putting her whole body into it.

The windows of L'Arpin watched like eyes, with the impassive judgment of Henry Drye. Sadie swallowed hard. She'd backed herself into a corner, giving an ultimatum so soon into their outing. Now, of course, she had to follow through and drag Izzy back inside, back to the hotel. Back to the little room and the confining walls and the unsettling bathroom.

"Please, Iz," Sadie said, a thread of desperation weaving through her voice. Another mistake. Izzy heard it, and doubled down.

"No, no, no, no, *no*! I wanna go—that—*way!*"

Sadie needed to walk Izzy back to the doors now. Scoop her up and haul her back if she had to. And she'd have to. Izzy would kick and scream and do the instinctive move all toddlers knew, arching her back and raising her arms so she risked sliding right out of Sadie's grasp. She might snatch Sadie's glasses and throw them, her new favorite tantrum misbehavior. She'd cause *such* a scene.

(*"Just ignore her. She'll only scream more if we give this behavior any attention."*

"Oh, I'm not going to give her attention. I'll give her something to cry about, that's what I'll give her."

"Please, please don't scare her. You're going to make it worse. She just needs to calm down."

"She needs to shut up! Either you take care of it, or I will.")

Izzy wouldn't learn unless Sadie endured the shrieking and crying and embarrassment. But, god, she was *so* tired, and so sick of their room, and so afraid of Izzy's toddler behavior getting them thrown out on the street.

Soon they'd be out of L'Arpin. It would be hard to find a new job then, there'd be no disguising the pregnancy and—laws or no—employers would hesitate to hire her. But she'd manage it. She could make it work. And then, once she had more control over her own life, she could focus on fixing Izzy's behavior. It wouldn't be too late yet.

For now, though, Sadie gave in.

"Fine, we'll walk that way, just hush, okay, stinker? Just hush for Mommy? We'll walk that way."

Izzy's red-faced shouting finally shut off, as abrupt as a switch being flipped. And, of course, the moment the playground came into view around the corner of the power plant, Izzy changed course in that direction.

"See the fence, Iz? We can't walk through that way," Sadie said, carefully not telling her daughter *no playground*.

After all, she couldn't *really* have seen a tentacled bird by the power plant here, could she? Izzy hadn't hesitated to call it a monster, sure, but just two nights ago Izzy called a blanket she'd dropped in a corner of the room a monster. The bird must have gotten into some trash somewhere, tangled itself up in something. Sadie had revisited this idea a few times in the last few weeks, and it struck her as truer now than ever before. Out here in the cold, diffuse light of a winter's day, snow falling like something from a cozy painting, she couldn't make herself picture a green monster with wings and tiny, writhing extra limbs. She *could* picture a seagull, tangled up in an old net or discarded holiday decorations, lurching and struggling to move over the ground or through the air because it was stuck and maybe choking on garbage. Sad. Not scary.

The moment they'd cleared the power plant's fenced-off lot, Izzy veered for the playground equipment. Just beyond the jungle gym, though, on the far side from the power plant, stretched a small, flat space of white snow that had been a field clearly intended for picnicking before the flurries started falling.

"Let's build a snowman," Sadie said, pointing at the little white-covered lawn. In answer, Izzy gave a shriek, thankfully a gleeful one, and ran in the direction her mother had indicated. By the time Sadie caught up to her daughter, Izzy was halfway through a confused jumble of a song that somehow combined "Jingle Bells" and "Row, Row, Row Your Boat" in a way that *almost* made sense.

Sadie showed Izzy how to pack the snow into a ball and get it rolling and they got to work together. Every few breaths her eyes flicked away from her daughter, first toward the power plant, then in the direction of the trees screening Lake Erie from view, then toward the road. As if somehow in the last five or ten seconds another—another trash-tangled bird, nothing more—another one of *those* might have appeared, or another rippling shadow from the water, or another bright purple car.

Izzy finished their third big snowball, and instead of letting Sadie show her how to stack it, she started a fourth. Sadie looked up again, from the construction vehicles to the trees to the exit from the parking lot. Her body didn't know whether to shiver from the cold, mild but pervasive, or whether to twist tighter and tighter with tension.

She wound up in a kind of squeezed, miserable hunch, shivers shaking her shoulder blades and her knees but failing to move her tightly crossed arms or chatter her clenched teeth. Izzy quickly abandoned her latest snow blob in favor of yet another. Each lumpy white ball was smaller than the last, but Sadie suspected that had more to do with impatience than from any instinctive understanding of fundamental snowman design.

Still, it wouldn't hurt Izzy to pretend it had been intentional. And maybe after successfully putting together the snowman she could talk Izzy into returning to the hotel, after all. Cooped up didn't sound so bad after the way Sadie wound herself up out in the open like this.

"Good job, stinker! You did them all so well! Can I show you how to put them together?"

"No, me!" Izzy shouted, and proceeded to laboriously push the lumps of snow into a more or less straight line. "Ta-*da*!" Izzy shouted, jumping to her feet and waving her arms at the line of chunks of snow. "My no-man!"

"No-man, indeed," Sadie muttered. Louder, she said, "What a *great* snowman, Izzy! I think we have some hot chocolate in the room, do you want to go back and make hot chocolate and watch a movie?"

"Hot chock-yet!" Izzy shouted. Life had grown a touch easier since Sadie had figured out how to use the little coffee maker in the hotel room to make a few things other than just coffee, including this so far very successful Izzy-bribe.

Sadie took her daughter's hand again and led her back the short distance toward the hotel. Just in time, too. A second before they moved out of sight of the door Bill Viago had stormed through the last time Sadie had seen him, it opened again and the man himself stepped out, holding a pack of cigarettes in one hand and tapping it against the heel of the other. From the corner of Sadie's eye she watched him pause and pivot to track her and Izzy's movement as they slipped out of his line of sight.

Back to L'Arpin Hotel.

She'd hoped to feel some relief from her vigilance when the familiar brick façade loomed over them, but none came. All going inside could accomplish was trading the exposed nervousness of being outdoors for the oppressive paranoia of L'Arpin Hotel and the people within it.

Speaking of the people within L'Arpin Hotel, as Sadie and Izzy stepped off the sidewalk and into L'Arpin's parking lot, she spied the small, shuffling form of Gertie crossing the street from the other direction. A pang of guilt struck Sadie; she'd thought Gertie would be driving to pick up her pills, not walking. She should've guessed, though. Had she ever seen the older woman in a car? She should have offered to drive her to the store and back.

"Gertie," Sadie called, waving with her free hand. In a softer voice she said, "Come on, Izzy, let's go help Gertie."

Gertie looked up at them, tried to wave, and nearly lost her purse. She stumbled, caught it, and shook her head, then hurried her steps. Sadie hadn't expected to see Gertie move so fast, well outside her normal shuffle, but in a moment, the older woman stepped up onto the sidewalk next to the hotel.

"Your bag is leaking," Sadie said, eyeing a dark brown stain spreading from the bottom corner of the purse. Gertie tried to catch the seepage with her hand, shifting her grip on the bag, the mess soaking into her mittens. "Let me help." Sadie reached for the bag.

"Miss Gertie," Joe called as he stepped out the front door, moving in their direction with ill-disguised urgency. "Here, I'll—"

From the way Sadie and Izzy had come, a voice rose in a shout. Sadie had heard Bill Viago yelling more than she'd heard him talking, but she'd never heard him sound afraid. The cry resolved into words that sent an electric wave of adrenaline crashing through Sadie.

"What the fuck! What the fuck is that? Help! Holy shit, someone, *help!*"

CHAPTER EIGHTEEN

Putting Words to Worries

"Gertie, watch Izzy, get her inside," Sadie said, the words tumbling fast. "Izzy, listen to Gertie. C'mon, Joe."

With that, Sadie spun and took off. She no longer harbored a younger person's illusions of immortality—bad things could happen to her, bad things *had* happened to her. But Viago screamed again and his voice rang with terror and Sadie couldn't bring herself to slow. She made her hasty, slipping way down the sidewalk for a handful of seconds before wondering if the snowy grass might give her better traction. She sank to her ankles as she ran, snow soaking her socks, freezing her skin.

"Get out here, you fucks, and help me!" Viago's voice rang out, and now Sadie could also make out a scuffling and a nasty wet slapping.

"We're coming!" Sadie shouted. She didn't think he was yelling for her, but she repeated herself anyway. "We're coming!"

Sadie skidded around the corner and froze.

Bill Viago sprawled halfway inside the cab of the excavator, leaning back on the floor by the seat, holding the doorframe with both hands. A slick green creature clung to one of his legs.

It dwarfed the sickly seagull thing she'd seen before, more than twice that size. The green color matched, and so did the slits gaping open and closed by its neck, just near a thin strip of wet-looking pink that made Sadie think of open wounds. This one clearly had four limbs—four *normal* limbs, or . . . or limbs that had *been* normal at some point but now scrabbled weak and withered against the bright yellow paint of the construction vehicle. It had the same proliferation of tentacles Sadie had seen on the other thing. These were not malformed, tiny, wriggling tentacles, though. Thick, powerful, they wound around Viago's calf and knee, reaching up toward his thigh. Viago kicked it with his free leg, and each time he struck a tentacle it recoiled and then lashed out again. When the tentacles struck the metal rather than Viago, that wet slapping noise rang out. Every time Viago kicked it, the creature let out a choked and snarling but recognizable *yip*.

It was a dog.

Or it had been one.

Sadie turned to the side and threw up in the snow. She glanced over her shoulder to ask Joe, "What *is* that thing?" But she was alone.

Joe hadn't come with her. What was wrong with him?

"Somebody get out here!" Viago shouted again. The power plant overseer's eyes fixed on the thing on his leg, his mouth gaping open with his shouts. The monstrous body heaved and Viago slipped a few inches out of the cab. He let out a shout and kicked savagely at the creature's head—Sadie could make out the canine shape of that head, though it had ragged holes instead of ears, and bulging, black-gleaming eyes.

"I'm coming!" Sadie yelled once more, finding her voice and her speed again. She ran along the fence. Finally, Viago looked up at her.

"Get help!" he shouted, kicking again with his free leg while straining to pull himself away from the writhing creature yanking at him.

Sadie threw the latch on the gate up and shoved it open so hard it swung all the way out and clanged off the fence. Chain links rattled all up and down the length of it. Sadie stooped and scooped up a cold handful of snowy gravel.

"Hey!" she shouted, still running. She threw without slowing her stride, flinging the gravel at the creature's bulbous eyes as hard as she could manage. The creature *yipped* again, paused, then shook itself and tightened its grip on Viago's leg. Sadie skidded to a stop and cast around for anything else to throw. A neat pile of short lengths of pipe lay near Sadie, and she scurried over to grab one.

"In there! Go in and get someone!" Viago yelled.

"No time!" Sadie gasped. She closed the distance between herself and the combatants in a lunge. "Oh god!" She hefted the pipe and brought it down hard on the creature's head.

The thing went still so abruptly Sadie thought for one moment she'd killed it. She leaned in just a fraction for a better look, unwilling to actually step nearer. The flash of pink she'd glimpsed earlier resolved itself now into, not a wound, but a collar, slick with some viscous secretion and half subsumed by the dog's strange new skin. She could make out only the stitched-on letters *OSI*. Before Sadie could look any closer, Viago kicked again, hard, and its tentacles unwound from his leg.

Instead of sagging, it flowed down, whirling as it descended. Low to the snow, it spread its twisting tentacles beneath it. That almost-dog face snarled at her. Then it rippled toward her.

Sadie let out a disgusted sound, half grunt and half cry, as she backed away. She swung her pipe, barely missing it this time. Those unblinking bulbous eyes locked on her. This close, a half-familiar smell rolled off it—old fish, and something subtler, rich and briny. It paused, perhaps gathering itself to attack. Sadie swung again, connecting just above the gaping slits near its throat.

It turned and fled, moving faster than something that looked so ungainly had any right to. It hauled itself, squirming limb over squirming limb, to the top of the fence, dropped down the other side, and disappeared into the trees and underbrush separating the property here from the beach.

Sadie dropped the pipe with a clatter, breathing hard.

"What the fuck?" Viago gasped, staring from his leg, soaked to the knee in some slippery-looking stuff, to the trees, the shaking of the branches subsiding abruptly.

Sadie's legs trembled and she sank down to sit on a stack of bricks before she could fall. Once seated, she leaned forward to put her elbows on her knees. She lowered her head and tried to slow her breathing, tried to slow her racing heart. The panic of a moment before felt suddenly distant, drowned by a fuzzy buzzing and a bone-deep exhaustion that struck her both at once.

"Hey, are you okay?"

It took Sadie a moment to realize Viago was talking to her. She picked her head up and watched him slide down from the excavator. His expression shifted, moving from confused to suspicious and back again.

"Fine. I'm fine. Are *you* okay? How come nobody came to help you?"

"Loud in there sometimes. Probably didn't hear me. What the fuck *was* that thing?"

Sadie tried to push herself to her feet, wobbled, and sat back down. "Don't know." She put a hand on her belly, a subconscious, instinctive gesture that she wished she could take back when Viago's eyes fixed on it.

"Are you fucking *pregnant*?" he exclaimed.

Irritation swept aside the fog left in the wake of her fear, and she scowled up at him. "What's it to you?"

"You can't do shit like that when you're pregnant! What the fuck were you thinking?"

"I was thinking *oh my god, there's a monster attacking somebody, I should help.* Which, you're welcome, by the way."

Viago rubbed his hands over his face, letting out something more than a grunt but not quite a groan. "Fuck," he said. "Sorry."

He dropped his hands and took a sharp breath as if to speak, and Sadie steeled herself for more unpleasantness. Instead, a quiet moment passed and he let the breath back out in a puff. The irritation drained out of his face and left in its wake something almost vulnerable. "That . . . *was* a killer tentacle-dog-monster, right? I mean. I saw that. My pants—" He shook his slimed leg, grimacing. "Disgusting. And I'm going to ache like fuck. That wasn't in my head. Right?"

"That wasn't in your head." Sadie had not expected to offer this kind of reassurance to someone like Bill Viago, not ever in her life. A strange feeling swept over her, not quite protectiveness of the man, not quite pride in herself for something so simple as confirming what they'd both seen, and certainly nothing so warm as affection. But not entirely unlike any of those, either.

"Well, fuck."

"Yeah."

"Look, let me walk you back to your hotel."

It was on the tip of Sadie's tongue to refuse. Viago did not top her list of people she wanted to spend time with.

He ranked above a monster, though.

"It's not *my* hotel. I just work there. I probably dislike Mr. Drye as much as you do."

Viago snorted as he crossed the snowy gravel to offer her a helping hand up. "I doubt that."

"Why do *you* hate L'Arpin?" Sadie asked as she stood. What a stupid question to focus on, but Sadie grasped for it, the distraction. She'd just run through the snow and hit a monstrous dog with a pipe. Her palms still stung with chill after grasping the cold metal. Her knees trembled, and when she tried to take a calming breath a salty, fishy smell nearly gagged her. She didn't want to talk about what she'd just seen, not yet. Maybe not ever, if the only person to talk about it with was Bill Viago. So when he hesitated instead of answering her question, she prodded. "Did somebody there do something to you?"

Viago frowned at her, but then he shrugged. Maybe he understood. "Those fuckers have been trying to sabotage my plant ever since it got built." Viago turned and spat. "When legal shit didn't work, they started breaking in and messing shit up. Loosening pipes and causing flooding, stuff like that. I can't prove it. But that don't mean shit."

It sounded paranoid to Sadie. And in that way, it sounded familiar.

Viago led her out of the construction area and toward the sidewalk. Sadie kept a sharp eye out as they walked, watching for low-moving shadows or twisting shapes or gleaming green.

"So you don't like the hotel, either?" Viago said.

Sadie hesitated so badly she nearly stumbled. All her dislike of the man came crowding back, her suspicions and her doubts. But if the thing that had attacked Viago had anything to do with the little tentacled somethings in her tub, if Beth's inability to find the "infestation" had anything to do with the disappearances and lies—a lot of *ifs*, too many *ifs*, but *what if* Sadie didn't have to be alone in all this?

"My daughter and I are leaving L'Arpin as soon as I've saved enough money to afford a deposit on an apartment. Just a couple more weeks." Sadie spoke low and fast, slowing her steps. Viago gave her a sharp glance. A suspicious glance? "Something is wrong there. Mr. Drye is doing something weird. The maintenance woman, too. Maybe more of them. I can't prove anything, either. If we had *anywhere* else to stay . . ." Sadie trailed off, trying to get her desperation back under control. Talking about her problems, putting words to worries and making her emotions real, threatened to overwhelm her. She swallowed hard, blinked her suddenly stinging eyes hard. "Well. Soon."

"Well, shit."

Sadie sighed. "Yeah."

"Listen, thanks for helping me. Don't do stupid shit like that again, though. Dangerous."

"I don't plan to make a habit of it."

They'd reached L'Arpin's parking lot, and no sooner had they stepped onto the property than the front door opened and Henry Drye marched out, his expression stormy and determined. Sadie forced herself not to flinch, but Drye didn't turn his ire on her.

"What are you doing with my employee?" he asked Viago when he drew near enough to avoid having to shout. Defensive anger snapped in his voice, and a hot rush of indignation coursed through Sadie.

She opened her mouth to remind Mr. Drye that his interest in her began and ended with how well she cleaned a room, but Viago interrupted her. "Somebody's loose fuckin' dog tried to attack me, and your employee here nearly got herself killed trying to scare it away. Remind your staff to stay off power plant property. I'm not falling for a phony liability lawsuit."

He spoke the lie with such conviction that for a second Sadie gaped at him. He took a step back from her, turning to stomp away. When his movement broke Mr. Drye's line of sight, Viago widened his eyes at Sadie and grimaced. He mouthed *play along*, then stormed away.

Sadie caught on a beat later. "See if I ever help you again," she called after him, and he waved dismissively over his shoulder without turning around.

"You shouldn't worry to help the likes of Bill Viago anyway, Miss Miles." Mr. Drye sniffed, and then with an expression of overly concerned solicitation he offered her his arm. "I was very worried when Mr. Mishra and Ms. Harper and young Isabelle came into the lobby without you."

"Are they okay?" Sadie asked, hurrying her steps to rush back to her daughter. And if that rush let her ignore Mr. Drye's proffered arm, all the better.

"What were you thinking of?" Gertie demanded the moment Sadie entered the hotel. Izzy ran to her, and Sadie lifted her daughter onto her hip. She glanced around for Joe, but he was nowhere to be seen. She'd have words for the cook next time she ran across him.

Mr. Drye followed close on her heels, and he must have heard Gertie's shouted question because he saved Sadie the trouble of trying to think of some sensible sounding answer by piping up with, "That Bill Viago"—he spat the name with considerable venom, which Sadie thought Gertie's narrowing eyes reflected— "was attacked by a dog, and Miss Miles risked her safety to help him chase it off."

"Is that what you were doing?" Gertie said, her voice no longer too loud now—in fact, almost too quiet.

How to impress on Gertie that there was something wrong, something to stay wary of, without making Mr. Drye suspicious? If that creature had something to do with the disappearances and his lies and Sadie said the wrong thing, he might know she'd seen too much. And if it didn't, he might doubt her suitability to live and work in his hotel.

Rather than the truth, then, Sadie said, "It was diseased or something. Sickly."

"Rabies?" Gertie gasped.

Sadie almost let out a hysterical laugh. Green all over, bulbous eyes, and slithering tentacles. Rabies? No. Not at all.

But if it made Gertie take care . . .

"Maybe," Sadie said, keeping her face solemn and concerned.

Even with so plausible an explanation, Sadie caught Mr. Drye giving Gertie a flat look, as if asking the older woman not to encourage Sadie.

Sadie fought a contrary urge to grit her teeth, but she didn't fight the impulse to say, "I'm calling animal control when I get Izzy back up to the room."

"Animal control?" Gertie exclaimed, one hand going to her mouth. "Is it that serious?"

"Surely not," Mr. Drye said, his brows drawing together into a brief frown, which smoothed away almost immediately.

"Definitely. That dog was dangerous."

"I want dangerous," Izzy chimed in, as if suddenly realizing she hadn't been the center of attention for some time.

"Well then." Mr. Drye didn't quite splutter, but he spoke a little faster than normal and repeated himself. "Well then, if there is an animal that might menace my guests, I should be the one to call animal control."

"But I saw it—"

"I want dangerous!"

"It's my responsibility," Mr. Drye said, raising his voice to be heard over the toddler.

"Are you sure it wasn't just a stray?" Gertie asked.

"I want dangerous!" Izzy shouted at the same moment.

"I insist, Miss Miles, I'll call the authorities—"

"Let's get dangerous!"

"—don't need to trouble yourself."

All at once, it was too much for Sadie. Her shoulders drew up, her arms tightening on Izzy. She moved back half a step, disengaging from the triangle she, Gertie, and Mr. Drye had made.

"It's fine, it's *fine*," she said, sharpening her voice the second time so that the others fell silent, except Izzy, who had begun chanting *dangerous, dangerous, dangerous.* "Do whatever you need to do, Mr. Drye," Sadie said. "Keep a watch out when you go outside, Gertie. Izzy and I are going to go to our room."

"I'd like a word with you about the dog, so I can make any necessary calls," Mr. Drye countered. Always trying to assert his authority. Always trying to be Sadie's boss, even on her days off.

Sadie still held Izzy in one arm, but she freed her other hand to lay on her belly as she said, "I really just need to go sit down, Mr. Drye. I'm all shaky, and I'm still having a little morning sickness."

Gertie threw Mr. Drye a hard look at those words, then flapped her hands at him. "You're upsetting the baby," she said, one of her ridiculous judgmental pronouncements, but this time it served Sadie and so she didn't contradict the old woman.

"We can speak about it tomorrow," Mr. Drye conceded, waving Sadie toward the elevator.

Sadie had taken only two steps before Gertie shuffled up next to her and grabbed her arm. The old woman lent surprising strength, as if she thought she needed to support Sadie. For her part, Sadie didn't necessarily want Gertie to feel as if Sadie needed her *too* much, but for the sake of putting on a show in front of Mr. Drye, she pretended to let Gertie help her to the elevator. She even let Gertie push the call button.

Just as they stepped into the elevator, the main doors opened. A tall man stepped into the lobby. His bright eyes sparkled in his tan face. Something a little less than a five o'clock shadow darkened his jaw, lightening toward salt-and-pepper at the temples. That hint of silver didn't mar his straight, dark blond hair anywhere else. Slender frame, surprisingly strong hands hidden in his pockets, the barest hint of a slouch to make him look more relatable than ramrod-straight posture would have, and features that didn't look handsome so much as trustworthy.

Sadie's breath all left her in a rush. Her head spun. Her face froze as her gaze locked on Sam Keller.

She half turned so Izzy wouldn't see him and groped for the elevator railing, unable to inhale yet, as Sam's eyes swept the lobby. He glanced at her once and winked, and she nearly lost her balance, nearly fell backward right there.

Then Sam locked his eyes on Mr. Drye in the direct, warm gaze he'd long ago perfected. "Checking in," he said.

"Of course, sir," Mr. Drye said. The elevator doors began to close. Sam didn't look at Sadie again. "Slow time of the year, you're our only check-in today. I've put you in room one-oh-three, one of my favorites."

The closing doors shut off anything else the men might say. Sadie's lungs finally unfroze, her breath coming in fast, shuddering gasps that made Gertie flutter and fuss about the baby. With a shaking finger, Sadie pressed the buttons for every floor, ignoring Gertie's confused, indignant scold when she did so.

She had to get back to her room. She had to pack and go. And she had to make sure Sam didn't know which floor she'd actually stopped on.

Sadie and Izzy's time at L'Arpin Hotel had run out.

Last October

Smooth the Way

"Sadie? What the fuck is this?"

The pregnancy test.

Sam's voice had come from the direction of the bathroom. She'd taken the test two days before and stuffed it into her tampon box and just . . . left it there. The stupidity of it had struck her hard, driving the breath out of her. Sadie froze, her hands tightening into fists on the little pair of bright pink pants she'd been folding.

She'd put Izzy's clean, unfolded pants down on top of the dryer and the word *escape* had floated across her mind as it had been doing ever since she saw those two little lines on the test. Her mouth had gone so dry that when she licked her lips her tongue only rubbed over the skin and did not wet her lips at all.

"Sadie!" Sam had shouted, and Sadie jumped, one hand rising to her throat and the other to her mouth. "Can you hear me?"

"Yes," she'd said, and the word had come out cracked and soft. She tried to swallow but couldn't and then raised her voice, and this time she shouted, "Yes, Sam! I'll be right there, I'm in the laundry room."

On her trip from the basement up to the bathroom, Sadie had

paused only long enough to make sure Izzy remained in her room, quietly building towers out of her blocks. "It's almost time to get ready for stories, Izzy. We'll get your pajamas when I come back in here." Sadie had tried to sound normal and Izzy hadn't looked up from her construction, so she must've managed it. From the entrance to Izzy's room, Sadie'd had a clear view down the hallway to the bathroom, but through that open doorway all she glimpsed of Sam was his shadow.

Had she ever done anything as difficult as forcing herself to hurry down that hallway? She'd find Sam standing there, the cabinet under the sink open, her tampon box ripped into, wrapped tampons on the floor, damning pregnancy test clutched in one of his hands.

Escape.

He must have heard her steps in the hall, because before she'd entered the bathroom, he said, "Want to tell me what this is?"

Sadie had paused in the hallway, just for the merest hint of a moment, not enough time to even have a full thought—only the idea, only the word *lie* and the barest outline of the concept of a fictional long-ago miscarriage she'd simply never told him about. Not a plan. But the closest she'd get to one.

"What is what?" she'd asked, stepping into the bathroom, her face stiff and still, her breath caught in her throat.

The smell of peppermint had overwhelmed her before the scene registered. Sam, standing by the sink, had crossed his arms and watched her with a stony, cold face. The cabinets hadn't been open after all, the tampons still safely tucked away, and he held nothing—not her pregnancy test, not a thing.

The relief that had struck Sadie nearly bowled her over.

He hadn't found it. He didn't know yet. She still had time.

Escape.

The danger of even thinking the word so near to Sam, with his eyes on her, already angry, drained all that relief right back out of her. He nodded down, toward the cabinets, toward the cause of his ire.

Every surface from Sadie's waist down had been covered in pale blue toothpaste. A pile of toilet paper next to the trash can had been mute evidence of Izzy trying to wipe her hands off after making the mess.

"Well?" Sam had demanded.

The urge to laugh that had welled up in Sadie at that moment would've been just as dangerous as that word—*escape*—that had been following her around for two days. Sadie had bitten her lips to keep it back and, rather than answer right away, she'd turned to the linen closet tucked into the corner opposite Sam. Rummaging for a hand towel to clean the mess up with had given her enough time to control her face, so when she turned back to Sam she could say, "She must've gotten in here while I was downst—"

"Are you smirking at me?" Sam's interruption had not been loud, but it had vibrated with insulted anger. Sadie's face had gone cold, her stomach twisting into a knot and sinking so fast she felt nauseous. Or maybe that was morning sickness. Didn't matter. What mattered was that she must not have wiped the inappropriate look all the way off her face after all.

"No, Sam, of course not," she'd said, cringing at the way her words had come out in a breathless gasp rather than a casual reassurance.

It hadn't taken Sam a full stride to cross the small bathroom, and then his fist was in her hair, her head yanked back, throat exposed, weight off-balance.

"Please," she'd gasped.

"Mommy!"

"Go to your room, Izzy!" Sadie had shouted, tears springing to her eyes as they hadn't a moment before. Her daughter shouldn't have to see this.

"Let go of my mommy!"

Sadie had reached up, digging her fingernails into Sam's hand, trying to disentangle her hair. She'd had to twist, had to strain, to see her daughter. Izzy had run full tilt down the hall to throw herself at Sam, tiny fists bouncing off his legs as her high voice, distorted by fury and the tears of an incipient tantrum, shrieked something with the words *no-no* and *my mommy* in it.

Sam didn't kick Izzy. Not quite. He shifted to the left and raised his right leg, then shoved sideways.

Not a kick. But Izzy had gone tumbling just the same and Sadie found her voice in the kind of scream that left her throat raw.

"Let go of me right fucking now, you asshole!"

She'd grabbed her own hair, below Sam's fist, easing the pain in her scalp, and then simply dropped herself to the floor. Sam hadn't expected the move, and with a last painful yank on Sadie's red curls, he'd lost his grip.

Izzy had sprawled on her back in the bathroom, howling and kicking her legs. Huddling over her daughter, Sadie had pulled her up to sit and run her hands over Izzy's back, the back of her head, her arms and legs. Nothing broken, nothing bloodied, but relief hadn't loosened her limbs again. Fury had coursed through Sadie.

"Get up for Mommy, Izzy, and go to your room. Please," she'd said, and then Sam had her by the back of the neck, pulling her up. Sadie writhed, lashing out at him with her elbow.

"Did you just fucking hit me?" he shouted.

Escape.

He had to be mollified.

"No," Sadie had gasped. "No, it was an accident." Izzy had kept wailing and she hadn't budged at all, and the rage coursing around in Sadie's chest, chasing the fear and being chased by the fear in turn, had crystallized all at once and at entirely the wrong person as Sadie's patience broke—*why* wouldn't Izzy do as she was told? why wouldn't she let Sadie keep her safe?—and she screamed, *"Is-abelle Miles, Mommy said go to your room!"*

And of course the screaming hadn't helped. It had made everything worse. Sam had shaken Sadie, hard, and had growled, "If you don't get her out of here or shut her the fuck up, I will."

"Let go, then," Sadie had said, remembering at the last second to make the words a plea rather than a snarl. Mollify Sam. Pacify Sam. Smooth the way, clear the path, make it possible. *Escape.* "Please?"

His fingers had loosened on the back of her neck, and Sadie had collapsed to kneel next to her daughter. Izzy's face had turned bright red, shiny with tears and snot, her eyes swelling from the crying and her mouth open as she screamed and screamed. Guilt stabbed Sadie right through, so sharp it felt like she really might die, and her own eyes had filled with hot tears.

She'd done this. She'd gone to Sam and she'd stayed with him all through as bad as it got, and now Izzy thought she had to save her mommy and her mommy screamed at her for it.

Escape.

Sadie pulled her daughter into her arms and whispered in her ear, "It's okay, Izzy-baby. It's okay. Mommy's sorry. Mommy's sorry. I shouldn't have screamed." She'd continued the litany until Izzy's screams trailed off, her body growing pliant and still rather than tightly wound squirming. Calm. *Calm.* Sadie hadn't been able to get Izzy to behave any other way, but she needed to convince her daughter to go, now, to hide out safe in her room until Sadie came for her after—after Sam was done. "Will you go to your room now, please, stinker?" Sadie had asked. "It will help Mommy if you go to your room and wait for me, and I'll come and get you when I can. Okay?"

Izzy had sniffled and snorted and then nodded, and Sadie's back had crawled with the looming presence of Sam just waiting, waiting for Izzy to be out of the way before he did whatever he wanted to do now, all because she'd made the wrong face about a toddler mess that anyone else—that *August*, and the pain swamped her at the thought—would have taken a picture of and laughed about on Facebook.

"Go wait in your room now, okay?"

"Opay."

"I'll make it all better," Sadie had promised, and Izzy had nodded and trusted her mother to make it *all* better.

Escape.

CHAPTER NINETEEN

You're Safe in L'Arpin

Sadie stood with her arms crossed tightly across her chest, one hand gripping the opposite elbow, the other hand raised to her mouth. She chewed her thumbnail, frowning as she stared down at the sleeping shape of her daughter. Her mind buzzed, a prickly, restless blank. That fuzzy panic had carried her through the rest of the afternoon, through making another subpar microwave dinner for Izzy, through bedtime. Every sound beyond her walls and door made her gasp and flinch, filled her with the certainty that Sam waited just outside. Trying to think, trying to plan their next step, had failed, fear shaking coherence apart any time she started to string more than one idea together. She only had gut instinct to go on now—wait until night, until it would be easier to slip out, and *go* before he found their room.

Sam.

Samuel Keller, mayor of Finneytown, Sadie's ex-fiancé (although she hadn't officially called off the wedding, had she?), the new baby's father.

In L'Arpin Hotel.

Sadie took a shuddering breath, then another, another, and then she was hyperventilating again. She stumbled backward from the pull-out bed, covering her mouth with one hand and groping behind herself for a chair with the other. She collapsed into the little desk chair, her legs shaking, her guts turned to water.

They had to get out. Again.

They had to get out again.

Sadie lurched right back to her feet, pressing her hand harder against her mouth for one second before she dropped both arms to her sides. She looked at Izzy again, made herself take a slow, steady breath. Another. Her thoughts still ran in circles, jittery, all edges, no focus, except that *they had to get out again.*

Action. She needed an action to go with that. Getting out. It meant packing.

Right. Packing. Sadie could do that in the dim shadows, she didn't need to turn the light on. She knew, after all, that whatever didn't make it into the suitcase could be replaced and whatever couldn't be replaced could be done without. She'd managed it just fine before.

If "just fine" meant finding herself and Izzy stuck in a nefarious hotel that her ex somehow *still* found her in.

She pulled her suitcases out of the closet, working by feel and by the surprisingly adequate glow seeping through the window from the parking lots below. It didn't matter right now whose things went in which suitcase, didn't matter if nothing stayed neatly folded. The idea that she would pack her bag and then Izzy's bag, so tidy, separating their clothes and belongings and making folded little stacks within, that was an idea for a planned leaving. It was an idea for the moments before triumphantly exiting L'Arpin for the last time to drive to the new apartment she was *so close* to affording. Her throat constricted.

Sadie paused to take a deep breath, to calm herself down, and instead, all at once her eyes stung and she sniffled and then she choked on a sob. If she hadn't already been kneeling on the floor next to Izzy's little suitcase, she might've collapsed. Instead, she folded over her knees, clamping her hands hard over her own mouth. She squeezed her eyes shut tight, but it didn't stop the burning or the tears.

She'd stuck it out in L'Arpin through so much, through uncertainty and disappearing guests and a missing coworker and a suspicious boss and *monsters*. She had let herself feel *trapped* here in spite of all that because she could have held on just long enough to get her and Izzy somewhere better.

Sam Keller showed his face *one time* and Sadie's whole plan shattered into worthless scraps to be stuffed into the luggage with the rest of her and Izzy's lives.

"Pathetic," she hissed at herself, and the cracked whine in her whisper set off another round of sobs that she muffled into her sleeves, mortified at the thought of waking Izzy like this.

A soft tap at the door nearly made her scream. She sat up too fast and bumped the desk chair, then fumbled to grab it before it could in turn bump the desk.

The tap came again, a fraction less soft.

If she didn't answer, would he keep knocking? Would he stop tapping quietly and start pounding? What if being so far from Finneytown emboldened him, let him drop the mayoral act and wreak whatever public havoc he wanted? What would Mr. Drye do if his troublesome employee's ex-fiancé caused a crisis in the halls at night?

"I know you can hear me in there, Sadie Miles."

Sadie sagged, the relief coursing through her its own kind of burden, heavy enough to bow her shoulders. Not Sam. Gertie.

"You don't want to leave me standing out here all night, do you?"

Of course she didn't. She also didn't want Gertie's tapping and talking to wake Izzy. She snatched up her walkie-talkie and hurried to the door. Even though she knew it wouldn't help, knew nothing could disguise the marks crying must have left on her face, she rubbed her eyes hard before peering out the peephole. Just in case.

Gertie stood alone in the hall. Well, of course she did.

Sadie slid the door chain out of its slot and unlocked the dead bolt, trying to do both quietly enough that Gertie wouldn't hear. She had relied on the doorknob lock all the time she'd been here, until tonight.

For once, she didn't wish the hallways had better light as she slipped out and shut the door behind her, hoping the shadows disguised the mess she knew she looked. She held a finger to her lips as she met Gertie's concerned eyes with a brief and quickly broken glance.

"What happened today, Sadie?" Gertie asked, not lowering her voice at all. The older woman's eyes were round with distress, her furrowed brows deepened the nest of wrinkles on her forehead, and she stood wringing her hands together. "Are you okay?"

"I'm fine," Sadie said, putting on a smile that didn't tremble at all yet still failed to mask her blotchy face and red-rimmed eyes.

"Don't lie to me," Gertie said, a hint of indignation creeping in with the concern in her voice. Her voice rose, just a little, but the risk of standing in the hall talking, much less shouting, drawing attention, made Sadie's skin crawl. Gertie went on, "I'm not stupid. I can see—"

"Can we—can we go into your room?" Sadie interrupted. In the months she'd known Gertie, the older woman had never invited her or Izzy into her own room. For Sadie's part, a blend of self-consciousness and respect for Gertie's privacy had prevented her from inviting herself in. Even if that was what Gertie had done from the start, bustling into Sadie's life.

The request might have caught Gertie off guard. At any rate, she fell silent for the briefest moment, and when she spoke again her voice had softened once more. "Why, yes. Sure. Come on in."

Gertie stepped to her own door, withdrawing her key. It was bigger than the other guests' keys, bigger than the skeleton key Sadie used during her shifts, and more old-fashioned. Gertie must have first come to live in this room before locks had been updated, and held on to hers. Why had she locked her door when she'd only been just outside?

Gertie pushed her door open. No light spilled out, the room lay in darkness. She slipped inside. The last bit of her to disappear was her hand, waving for Sadie to follow her. The darkness swallowed Gertie like deep water, and irrational dread washed over Sadie. No dark fancies attached themselves to the dread, Sadie didn't find her imagination diving into the room ahead of her and coming up with horrible possibilities. Somehow that made the cold weight in her gut all the harder to shake.

Sadie tried to take a breath, couldn't manage more than a little gasp, and then plunged after Gertie into the darkness.

Which abruptly was not dark at all. Gertie stood by a lamp, turning a little key that made the flame within the graceful glass grow. That explained the darkness. It would be unwise to leave a fire burning alone in the room—even a little one, even for only a few moments. Still, next to the archaic gas lamp sat a normal hotel-ugly electric lamp, turned off. Near where Sadie stood by the entrance, the light switches on the wall tempted her. If she flicked them, would they turn on? Of course they would, but *would* they?

Sadie couldn't help herself. She reached out and turned them all on at once. Light flooded the room and Gertie blinked hard, flinching a little. She ducked her head and said, "Those lights hurt my eyes, Sadie. Turn them off."

"Sorry," Sadie said, doing as she'd been asked and casting the room into warm-glowing lamplight again. She managed that deep breath, now, the one that wouldn't come in the hallway. If Mr. Drye and Beth had been making her paranoid before, seeing Sam might be pushing her over the edge. There was nothing frightening about Gertie's room.

"It's no problem," Gertie said, flapping a hand. She settled down on the sofa, a match for the pull-out one Izzy slept on in their room next door, and patted the cushion next to her.

Sadie shook her head. "I'd rather stand." When Gertie looked hurt, Sadie added, "I'm too keyed up to feel comfortable sitting right now."

Well, that did it. Sadie had been too hasty not to make Gertie sad, too quick to give an excuse, and now she'd lost the flimsy shield of pretending everything was fine.

"What's going on, Sadie?"

Sadie chewed her lip for a moment and then laid it out with as few details or specifics as she could. "Izzy and I left a bad situation a few months ago. It was right when I found out I'm pregnant. The . . . the bad situation showed up at the hotel today."

"Oh, Sadie," Gertie said, her voice soft and full of pity. Sadie barely managed not to sneer at the tone. Pity never helped anyone, but neither did ill will when she might need real help soon.

"We have to go, Gertie."

"*Go?*" Gertie replied, the pity on her face washed away by a wave of alarm. Gertie pushed herself back to her feet and drew nearer to Sadie, her movements too quick, too precise. Not just alarmed, Sadie realized. Agitated. "What do you mean, go?" she asked, reaching out to wind her thin fingers around Sadie's wrists in a tight grip. Sadie tried to gently disengage, but Gertie's grasp tightened. She pulled Sadie a little closer to herself and repeated, "What do you mean, *go?*"

Sadie pressed her lips together to stop them from trembling. She was a shattered vase held together with string; she couldn't hold Gertie together, too. This time she twisted her wrists out of Gertie's hands, not concerned with gentleness.

Gertie fell back a step, her wide eyes flashing. For an instant Sadie took the look for fury, then Gertie blinked. Tears glimmered, tracing twin tracks down her lined face. Gertie took another step back, and when she drew in a breath her chin trembled. She raised shaking fingers to her face, pressing her hands to her cheeks.

"Oh, but don't go," Gertie said. "I would—I would miss you. I would miss little Izzy. Henry wouldn't let anyone do anything to you, Sadie, not here. You're safe in L'Arpin. I'll tell Henry to fix it, he'll do it tomorrow. You just . . . you go get Izzy and you bring her in here, you'll both stay with me, and when the bad person leaves everything will be fine."

Unbidden, the image rose before Sadie's eyes, of Gertie in the doorway shaking a finger in Sam's face, and how fast Sam would go right through the little old lady. Gertie's loneliness, always obvious but now heartbreaking, added a weight of guilt to Sadie's shoulders. But if Sam hurt Gertie because of Sadie, how much worse would that guilt be?

"No, Gertie. Thank you, but no. We have to go."

"When?"

When, indeed. Right now, probably, but Sam would expect it. He'd be watching. He might have done something to her car.

So far he'd glimpsed her only once, through closing elevator doors and wearing a coat that was big enough to—hopefully, *hopefully*—obscure the signs of her pregnancy. So far he didn't know which room was hers, but it wouldn't be long before he'd find out. He was good at charming people. And he'd see her without her coat, or in better light than the dim hall, or he'd notice the shape of her body in spite of it. He'd know about the baby and he'd never, never let her get away.

Her only saving grace was that he might not know she was not a guest but an employee of the hotel—he might not realize she had access to the staff-only areas and the computers and skeleton keys. She could find out how long he'd booked the room for, and plan her next steps. He wouldn't expect that. He'd expect her to make a hasty mistake instead.

If he had to check out tomorrow, Sadie could maybe spend a day or two planning something better than *drive into the night with no destination*. If Sam had booked his room for even one more day, Sadie could spare only as much time as it took to wake Izzy and then calm the inevitable storm of sleepy tears so they could get out undetected.

"I have to figure that out," Sadie whispered. She repeated herself a little louder, meeting Gertie's eyes again. "I have to figure that

out. Right now. Can you please go sit in the room with Izzy while
I do?"

"Do what?"

"I have to check the schedule."

"You're thinking of work at a time like this?" Gertie scolded.

"What? No. I need to see when his room is scheduled for a checkout cleaning. Just—just, here, here's my room key." Sadie pulled it
out of her pocket, not the skeleton key Mr. Drye kept behind the
desk but the one for her door alone. She pressed it into Gertie's palm,
and before she could pull back, Gertie closed her fingers over Sadie's
hand. She squeezed. Tight. Too tight, the metal of the key biting into
Sadie's fingers. "Ouch, Gertie, stop that!" Sadie exclaimed, yanking
her hand away.

"Sorry, sorry, I'm sorry," Gertie said, reaching out to pat Sadie's
hand. "I didn't mean—I'm just—it's lonely, I'll miss little Izzy."

"We'll keep in touch, okay? All right, Gertie? Please just watch
her. Please don't wake her up. I'm trying to keep her *safe*," Sadie
said, desperation crackling in her voice. She slipped her hand out
of Gertie's and hurried for the door. "Just wait in my room, okay?
Don't let *anybody* in but me."

She hurried out the door, leaving it open behind her as she turned
toward the stairs. Her ankles twinged a little, her knees ached, but
the idea of the elevator made her shudder. The stairs were quieter.
The stairs were harder to get trapped or cornered in.

CHAPTER TWENTY

Strange Mood

Sadie moved down the stairs as lightly as she could, hands on the banisters to either side, arms stretched out. She paused at the landing, her breath caught in her throat, and listened. Silence below. She leaned out and peered down. Empty. At the next landing, she repeated the quiet caution.

When she reached the first floor, her heart hammered so hard she thought her whole body ought to shudder from the force of it. Her hands trembled and her breath shook as she crept toward the door to the first-floor hallway. She couldn't take the fastest route—it led right past Sam's room. Her gut twisted at the thought of him standing just beyond door 103, leaning against it, his forehead touching the wood, one hand on the knob, eye to the peephole.

Watching for her.

Well, he wouldn't see her. Just like when she'd raced to get those screwdrivers two weeks before, Sadie would have to take the long way around.

She let herself out of the stairwell and into the hallway, her mouth sour and her brows drawn together. She turned toward the corner that led away from Sam's room and set off at a quiet run.

Even avoiding Sam's hallway, every alcove in the corridor made her breath shiver. Would Mr. Drye leap out of one of those doors? Beth or Lewis?

But the way stretched clear ahead of her. She was going to make it.

Just before reaching the lobby, she paused to flatten herself against the wall. Leaning out just far enough, she checked that Sam wasn't waiting there for her, that Beth wasn't doing any late-night repairs, that Mr. Drye had left on schedule.

No sign of him. Any of them. Sadie didn't sag with relief. The back of her neck tingled, and her skin crawled.

Had she ever experienced fear like this, running across the open stretch of the lobby in the dark of night? Her eyes darted from the fireplace to the desk to the hallway entrances gaping open and dark around her. The short hallway that led to the supply room and the pool had never felt so much like a sanctuary.

Until movement through the glass door to the pool courtyard drew her eye. Her blood froze in her veins as she snapped her head in that direction.

Joe stood by the pool with one hand in his coat pocket and the other holding the stumpy remains of a cigarette he was just finishing. Sadie had no time to run into anyone right now, especially not someone she may not be able to trust. She didn't catch his attention, merely slipped into the supply room. Once inside, she shut the door behind her quietly without yet turning on the light, and then knew with terrible certainty that Sam waited in the dark there for her already, that he stood just behind her and watched with eyes accustomed to the shadows, that he would be grinning and reaching when she turned—

She flipped the switch with a gasp and spun.

He wasn't there. Sadie leaned back against the door, breathing hard, sweating as if she'd run a race. Her heart pounded panic-fast, and time skewed and stretched as she calmed herself down enough so when she straightened her knees wouldn't give.

She crossed to the schedule hanging on the wall and ran her finger down the room assignments. "One-oh-three," she muttered, "one-oh-three . . ." Sam's room wasn't listed on the next day's chart. "Damn." She flipped to the following page, and the next one after that, all the way through the end of the chart's two-week period. His room number didn't appear on any page.

Dropping the sheaf of papers with a flutter, Sadie ran her hands through her hair. Could Sam have checked into L'Arpin for more than *two weeks*? Why? He wouldn't need that long for—for whatever he planned. Could it possibly be a coincidence that he'd wound up here? That he'd come this far north for some other reason and landed in L'Arpin in a simple, cruel twist of fate?

No. Impossible. There had been no surprise in his eyes when he'd seen her in the elevator. He'd come here *for* her. So why such a long stay?

Unless his room number had been left off the schedule by mistake. It happened sometimes. Sadie chewed her lip. She needed to see the records of check-in and checkout times and guest information. That meant she had to access the computer. Depending on how Mr. Drye ran his hotel's IT, that might be accessible from the office computer *and* the front-desk computer. But if the manager of L'Arpin Hotel kept up with the digital times the way he did with the door keys, she might only be able to get that info at the front desk.

Out in the open, clearly visible, easily cornered.

Even if room 103 had been in place on the schedule, Sadie knew she would have gone to the computer anyway. She would have double-checked. This didn't really change anything.

She pulled the walkie-talkie out of her pocket and turned it on, making the act of checking on Izzy with Gertie an excuse to delay leaving the supply room. The speaker gave her only a quiet rustling, probably Izzy shifting in her sleep or Gertie snooping around a bit. No emergencies. No excuse to hurry back to the illusory safety of her room.

Squeezing her eyes tightly shut, she took several deep breaths and tried to still the quake in her knees and ease the tightness in her belly.

It didn't work. No matter. No more stalling.

She flicked the light back off with the door still shut, so no illumination could spill out into the dim hallway and give her away. For a moment she held the doorknob, her palms tingling and her chest tight, as her imagination tried to run away with her. She was out of time for *what-ifs*. Sadie eased the door open far enough to peer out.

From the other side, Sam shoved it the rest of the way.

He moved with deliberation rather than speed—the door didn't slam into her, but it did push her stumbling to one side as he crossed the threshold. Once she'd cleared the door, the danger of a serious impact past, then he moved like a flash. One of his hands found her arm, the other her mouth, and he yanked her out into the hallway with him before she could think.

He hadn't let the door strike her. His caution wound cold threads of terror around her heart, around her lungs, until she couldn't breathe.

He knew.

He knew about the baby.

Sam pushed her back against the wall without releasing her arm or her mouth. Sadie rolled her eyes in the direction of the door to the pool, where she'd seen Joe Mishra only a few moments before. But now that she needed him—needed *anyone*—he'd finished his smoke and gone on his way. Sam's grip on her arm tightened, painful. Sadie's eyes darted back to his face. Her arm would bruise, but he took as much care as ever not to mark her face. The hand over her mouth was a warning more than anything else.

Don't make a scene.

He leaned close, closer, until his forehead touched Sadie's. He never blinked, never took his eyes away from hers. Sadie breathed hard through her nose, pressing herself flatter against the wall.

She wedged her free arm between her chest and Sam's, her fist near her throat, pushing her elbow into his solar plexus. But not hard enough to make him think she wanted to hurt him.

She did want to hurt him.

But he couldn't think that.

When he gave her an almost sad smile, the warmth did reach his eyes. He'd always been good at that. Sadie looked away, turning her gaze toward the end of the hallway. The idea of Mr. Drye or Beth or Lewis appearing seemed suddenly very appealing.

"Hey, hey, hey," Sam said, his voice soft and coaxing and full of good humor. Sadie closed her eyes and tried to slow her breathing. She'd seen him like this only a few times before. Strange moods, when his customary sharp, snide kind of everyday condescension evaporated and left in its place something more concentrated, more pure, almost indulgent. This was when he most thought he loved her. It was when he was the most dangerous. "Look at me. Sadie, babe, look at me."

She did. He dropped his hand from her mouth and cupped her cheek.

"Get off of me, Samuel Keller," Sadie hissed.

His expression didn't change as his fingers dug into her arm, a vicious squeeze. Sadie tried not to wince, but the pain must have flashed across her face anyway, because he made a low hushing sound, his tone soothing, his other hand stroking up her face to push back her hair. He didn't loosen his grip, though.

"I don't think that's a very respectful way to talk to me, Sadie, do you?" he asked, his voice patronizing.

All the old answers tumbled around in her head, tried to spill out of her mouth at once.

No, Sam. I'm sorry, Sam. I didn't mean it like that. I'll be more careful. I'll be quieter. I'll smile and I'll hush and I'll nod when you need me to. Please, Sam, please.

"Fuck you, Sam."

The words fell into the narrow space between them like stones into silent water. If Sam hadn't kept his punishing grip on her right arm, if his other hand hadn't frozen in the act of pushing back her hair and then tangled it into his fist instead, she might have loved the way his smile dropped away into shock.

Anger followed. Sam tightened the fist in her hair, pulling her head back, forcing her face toward the ceiling. She gasped but didn't cry out, didn't give him that. When he leaned closer to her, trying to press his body along hers, starting to whisper, "You ought to be—" *then* she did dig her elbow into his solar plexus. Hard. "Bitch!" he exclaimed, pulling away.

Away. She'd driven him back. Not far back, but still. Back.

Months. She'd been away from him for months. All the doubts he'd fed her, all the promises that she'd never survive without him, she'd put the lie to it all. And she'd prove him wrong about this, too—she wasn't his to touch, to hurt.

Sadie drove her knee up. Sam might have been surprised, but he wasn't slow. He twisted at the hips and her knee struck his thigh. The blow made him hiss but didn't make him clutch himself or fall to the floor.

He grabbed her, pulling her hand away from her throat and her arm away from her chest. His grip shifted and he bent her wrist back, the smile gone and in its place an expression not of rage but of sorrow. She knew what he'd say next and opened her mouth to cut him off.

"Why do you make me—"

"I don't make you do *anything*, Sam Keller!" Sadie didn't mean to yell but he'd pulled her wrist too far, the pain drove her voice up into a cry. She tried to turn her body, tried to angle herself to relieve the pressure. He let go of her right arm and clamped his hand over her mouth again, harder this time. Forgetting himself, maybe. Maybe enough to make a mark.

The sound of the elevator bell chiming in the lobby froze them both.

Sadie sucked a breath through her nose and tried to scream.

What came out was something like a hum, but high in both pitch and volume, surprisingly loud. Sam shifted his grip on her face to cover her nose as well. She grabbed his fingers with her free hand but he torqued her wrist farther back and tears sprang to her eyes. From the lobby, whoever had come down on the elevator made a racket. A thud and a screech, stumbling steps, low muttering. A thin, high sound briefly rose above the mutter, then a hiss and a grunt. Whoever was out there, drunk or high or something worse, they made too much noise to hear the tiny sounds Sadie managed around the suffocating hand on her face. With more muttering and staggering, the unseen elevator person's presence receded from the lobby.

Desperate, Sadie dropped her hand from Sam's fingers and pounded her fist on the wall as loud as she could. Sam pulled her face forward and then slammed her head against the wall, hard enough that her knees turned to jelly and she sank downward. Her lungs burned.

Rather than let her go or hold her up, Sam sank down with her, squatting above her. He shifted, settled his weight on her thighs. Leaning close to whisper in her ear, he said, "We should settle this in private, Sadie. We don't want a scene, especially not with the baby on the way." He dropped her wrist and put his hand on her belly, and his touch made her flesh crawl. She couldn't pull away, couldn't shout, couldn't *breathe*.

She could bite.

Sadie sank her teeth into Sam's palm. He dug his fingernails into her face. She bit harder and reached up to rake his eyes with her own fingernails. He didn't let go, yanking himself away from her, until she tasted blood.

She spat at him.

"It's not even your fucking baby," she lied.

Sam laughed as he swiped at the bloody spit on his button-down shirt, smearing the hint of red over his chest. Then he lunged forward again, grabbing Sadie by both arms and rising, pulling her to her feet.

"Bullshit," he said. He shook her hard, paused, then shook her again and repeated, "*Bullshit*, Sadie."

This time when she kneed him she struck home, and he staggered back with a wheezing gasp, doubling over with his hands between his legs. Sadie struck him with her knee again, aiming for his jaw.

He toppled, and she ran.

Sadie slapped the elevator button as she ran through the lobby, then turned the corner into the far hallway. If the timing didn't line up Sam would miss the elevator distraction entirely, or see it standing open and know she'd run on, so she didn't slow. From somewhere behind her a furious shout rose, and Sadie gritted her teeth as she dodged around the next corner. She paused at the stairwell and opened the door silently, easing it shut again so that it didn't close all the way. If the elevator trick did its work she wouldn't want the sound of the door to draw him here after all, but if he did get this far, maybe he'd see the door ajar and think she'd taken the stairs. Sadie ran halfway down that hallway and then pressed herself into one of the alcoves lining the corridor, a guest room door just behind her.

She waited. Beat by beat her racing heart slowed, slowed, and her pulse stopped rushing in her ears. Her breath came smoother. But her hands never stopped shaking, the tension in her shoulders and her back never unwound, she never unclenched her jaw. Swallowing hard, Sadie leaned around the alcove and peered up and down the corridor. The door to the stairwell, at the corner she'd come around, still stood slightly ajar. Sam hadn't come this way.

Or he had, and he'd been clever enough to disguise the signs of his passing.

Either way, Sadie had to get back to Izzy. She'd been gone too long, and she'd learned all she needed to know. They had no time to plan a more stable exit. They had to flee in the night.

Sadie's hard-won semblance of calm fled the nearer she drew to the doorway. For a moment before she pushed it open, she stood in the crux of the two halls, visible to anyone down either corridor. Then she slipped into the stairwell and shut the door behind her as silently as she could manage.

Straining her ears, she heard no hint of Sam above her. Slow and silent, she started her climb. By the time she reached the fourth floor she wanted to scream just to relieve the terrible tension bearing down on her, dragging cold nails up and down her spine, curdling her breath in her lungs.

She pressed her lips tight together and let herself out into her own hallway.

From here she could not see her door. She could only see the bright rectangle of light spilling out of it onto the green carpet of the hall.

CHAPTER TWENTY-ONE

Look at Them

"No," Sadie said, reeling down the hallway. "No, no, no, no. Get *out* of there, you—"

Through the open door the room, brightly lit but otherwise untouched, was empty.

"—asshole . . . Izzy? Izzy!"

Sadie lunged inside, then froze. Impossible uncertainty robbed her of strength. She shook herself, and her gaze flew around the room. Nothing. No one. No sign of Izzy or Gertie. Searching the room wouldn't turn up anything, Sadie knew it, but she *had* to check.

"Are you hiding, baby?" she asked, voice trembling. She dropped to her knees and lifted the blanket, peering under the bed. She twisted to peer under the desk, then under the pull-out sofa's mattress. "Izzy, Izzy, Isabelle, where *are* you?" Sadie moaned. Then, with a gasp, "Gertie!"

Gertie must have taken Izzy to her room. Maybe she thought it was safer, after what Sadie had said before disappearing into L'Arpin. Sadie scrambled for the door when a shadow beyond the rectangle of light stopped her in her tracks. Her heart leaped—*Izzy!*—even as her belly sank—*Sam?*—until Gertie stepped farther into the bright illumination, only her face still obscured by the shadow, saving her eyes from the irritation of the too-bright light.

"Where's Izzy?" Sadie yelped.

"Izzy," Gertie gasped, "woke up." She gasped again, bending to put her wrinkled hands on her knees. The neck of her nightgown hung askew, revealing one thin shoulder. The old woman continued speaking through labored breaths. "She wanted—you—I couldn't—" Gertie swayed, and Sadie hurried closer. She caught Gertie's shoulders. Closer, eyes adjusting to the dimness, she could pick out the wild wideness of Gertie's eyes, the unshed tears and the way her lip trembled. Gertie straightened, clutching Sadie's forearms, desperation lending her an almost painful strength. "I lost her—she was too fast for me—the elevator, I couldn't get there."

Sadie shook her head. "Where'd she go, Gertie?"

"She said she was looking for her mommy," Gertie said, the word *mommy* sounding petulant and ridiculous in Gertie's querulous old voice.

Panic stole Sadie's ability to push aside her irritability. Maybe Gertie meant well, maybe she'd tried her hardest to catch Izzy, but she'd lost Sadie's little girl. While Sam was somewhere in the hotel, full of that almost cheerful rage that scared her the most.

"But where did she *go*?" Sadie resisted the urge to shake Gertie.

"The elevator, I said! I didn't get there in time, I can't take the stairs, by the time the elevator came back up she wasn't on it anymore!"

"Oh my god."

"I went down anyway, hoping I'd find her—"

Sadie let go of Gertie's shoulders and stepped back. Gertie clung all the tighter to her arms.

"—I came back here, thinking, maybe, but she's not, and I'm sorry, Sadie."

"Let go, Gertie."

"I'm so sorry."

"I said *let go*, Gertie!"

Sadie wrenched her arms out of Gertie's grip and stepped back, half expecting the older woman to stumble and girding herself against guilt if Gertie fell. Gertie didn't so much as waver, and Sadie shook herself. Without another word, she turned.

"Wait!" Gertie pointed past Sadie, not down the hall but into Sadie's own room. Sadie spun, her heart leaping, her eyes raking the scene for Izzy.

Still empty.

She rounded on Gertie, tears of helpless terror springing to her eyes at last. *"What?"*

"Do you hear that?" Gertie asked. She made a strange face and pointed again. Not into the room. At the window. The same window that Sadie had looked out of to witness a guest fighting for her life in the pool months ago. Different sounds caught her attention now. Furtive, soft, hard to hear. They shouldn't have been audible at all. She hadn't noticed before, but the curtains fluttered more than the heater could account for.

The window.

"Oh my god, why is the window open?" Sadie asked in a low voice, a new and more terrible horror shaking her. What if—?

She nearly fell over the suitcases she'd left on the floor as she raced for the window, knees weak, her stomach not just knotted but heaving like a ship at sea. She put her hands on the sill and leaned out and looked down and did not see the terrible thing she had feared she'd see there, and she collapsed under a wave of relief that drove a sob from her.

A touch on her shoulder made her scream, but Gertie's voice at her ear stilled Sadie's cry.

"Oh, oh, oh, Sadie, *look* at them."

Sadie looked.

She saw nothing and moved to stand, but Gertie put a hand on her shoulder and leaned over, pressing Sadie's chest against the windowsill. Halfway out the window, Gertie pointed. Sadie followed the gesture and gasped.

Monsters squirmed through the shadows and the snow, converging on L'Arpin Hotel.

"Look at them," Gertie said again, her voice a whisper.

They varied in size and shape. There, another thing that might once have been a seagull. There, an animal that still mostly looked like a cat. More dogs, a trio of things that might once have been raccoons or perhaps possums. Writhing tentacles, undulating bodies, bulging eyes. Dark in color, little more than movement within the shadows. Except in the power plant's parking lot. There the bright lights kept them to the edges, but at those edges the things gleamed, reflected. Or, and this was worse, they glowed a glow all their own. Scattered among the monsters came animals that simply looked like animals, but the light in their eyes matched the glow in the monsters, and Sadie knew that they were all part of the same *thing*.

And then—bile rose in Sadie's throat—and then she saw among the creatures, people.

Not many. The people mostly weren't like the monsters. Mostly. There, though, a woman with white hair and bulging eyes and not a stitch of clothing on her body emerged from the trees lining the little cliff down to the beach. And there, an otherwise average-looking man who moved in his own soft glow. Three more came from around the corner of the power plant. One of them had tentacles as well as arms. None wore clothing, their skin gleaming as if they'd just had a swim.

Sadie put her hands over her mouth to stop herself from throwing up and pulled away from the window. She turned her back to the sight and breathed hard through her nose, trying to banish the horrified nausea. Tears pricked her eyes and she squeezed them closed.

Monsters. Sam. And Izzy missing.

Sadie removed her hands from her mouth, swallowed hard, and wiped her eyes, then pushed herself to her feet.

"Hide or something, Gertie," she said, shoving past the old

woman without casting her a second glance. Gertie didn't matter, not now. Only Izzy mattered.

Gertie called something after her, but Sadie didn't wait to listen. She burst out of her room and ran for the stairs.

Sadie didn't bother with quiet now. Let Sam find her, let him try to get between her and her daughter.

The monsters were coming.

She slammed through the door to the stairwell and pelted down to the third floor. Izzy might've pushed any buttons in the elevator. She could be anywhere. Oh, god, she could be *anywhere*. She could have gone outside. The thought nearly made Sadie throw up again, but she swallowed it down. No. No, there was no way Izzy would wander out into the cold, she hated the cold, she didn't have her coat or her hat, much less shoes. She was in L'Arpin somewhere. Sadie just had to find her.

Before anyone or anything else found them.

"Izzy!" Sadie shouted as she burst out into the third-floor hall-way. She raced around the square layout of the halls, turning corner after corner until she arrived back at the stairs. No Izzy.

She crashed back through the door into the stairwell, and this time she was met not with silence but with a muffled bang from below. All the way below, the first floor. From the door to the parking lot.

"Oh, god," Sadie whispered, and then she rushed down to the second floor and out into the dim, green corridor. "Izzy!" she shouted as she set off again. *"Please!"*

She couldn't breathe, couldn't think. Should she knock on doors? Should she rouse the whole hotel? Call the police? Her phone was back in the room, she didn't have time to go get it. But—but yes, maybe she should wake everyone up. Her little girl was missing. They might not care about that. Monsters at the door might concern them. If anyone would believe her before they saw the things with their own eyes.

She couldn't force herself to slow, though. Couldn't stop running.

Her daughter was missing and her body moved in search and *slowing* was not an option.

"*Izzy, where are you?*"

When she reached the stairwell again, the sound of glass breaking met her ears before she even opened the door. She shoved through anyway. She would have to just get past whatever it was. She had no choice. She needed Izzy.

From the second-floor landing the door to the first-floor hallway lay out of sight behind the angle of the stairs, but Sadie had a clear view to the door leading to the parking lot. The narrow, rectangular window writhed with slick green tentacles pushing through where the glass had been. Glittering shards littered the floor. One of the tentacles touched the handle, then wound around it. Whether by chance or design didn't matter, the door opened and something spilled through onto the floor. It moved in a confusion of grace and clumsy thrashing, the flailing limbs of whatever it had been jerking out of sync with one another even as the tentacles flowed and pulled it into L'Arpin. A terrible smell rolled in with the thing, wet and overwhelming, a choking smell almost familiar—almost a sea smell—but wrong in a way that made her body rebel, down to her bones. She threw herself backward and slammed the door.

The elevator.

"*Isabelle Miles, where are you?*" Sadie screamed as she raced back down the hallway, terror squeezing her heart, winding her thoughts tighter and faster.

Izzy didn't answer, but finally Sadie's shouts roused the first guests at L'Arpin Hotel. As she flew past, doors opened to either side of her. Men, women, families peered out into the hallway that looked exactly the same now in the early night as it did in full daylight or deepest midnight. Voices followed her as she ran. *What's going on? Are you okay? Shut up, lady! Is that glass breaking?* And more and more, blending together, none of them her daughter.

She skidded to a stop before the elevator and pushed the button.

Out of sight around the far corner, the sound of the stairwell door crashing open momentarily silenced the voices. In the hush, the slick slide and slap sound of what Sadie knew were tentacles was audible for only a moment before the first scream. A wave of shrieks and hoarse cries followed that first one.

"Come on, come on, come *on*," Sadie hissed, pressing the elevator button again.

Doors slammed as people retreated back into their rooms, but from behind some of those doors more shouting joined the cacophony. Sadie pressed herself against the elevator door, staring past the handful of guests—mostly men, straightening their shoulders—who stepped out of their rooms, turning toward the sounds.

Until the thing came around the corner on four thin, ungainly legs. It staggered, fell sideways against the wall. It dragged itself along, prongs gouging the glossy, watery wallpaper.

The door opened behind Sadie. She stumbled backward into the elevator as something that could not decide whether it was a deer or a squid or a fish or something *worse* gave up on legs and sank to the floor, unfurling too many thick tentacles to count. Grace replaced clumsiness, and it poured itself down the hallway as the elevator doors closed.

They didn't quite cut off the fresh screams.

Sadie pressed her hands over her ears. What had changed? What had *changed*? Whatever Mr. Drye had been doing—wherever those things had been hiding—why come out in the open *now*?

The elevator stopped at the first floor. The doors parted. All the lights went out, and the muted hum of the heating system dropped away.

For a second the sudden darkness lay on L'Arpin in silence. Into that silence, thin and muffled, drifted a cry Sadie knew better than her own voice.

"Isabelle," she gasped.

The silence ended, slick dragging sounds and screams covering that little wail.

She lunged out of the elevator and stumbled to an immediate halt. In the lobby some illumination filtered in through the empty panes of the double doors and the windows flanking them. The unpleasant white glow of the power plant's lights caught on the sharp, glittering edges of broken glass in the frames and scattered in the water on the floor below them. A deep puddle pooled under the windows and before the doors, growing thinner and shallower as it stretched across the lobby toward the openings to the corridors.

Trails.

Whatever had come through here hadn't lingered.

At its deepest the water swirled with an illumination of its own, green and ghostly faint. Did tiny shadows move within that barely perceptible luminescence? Sadie shivered and skirted around the edge of the lobby.

Izzy's cry had not come from the direction of the supply closet, but Sadie dashed there first, anyway, though she'd left Sam writhing in pain in that little corner of the hotel.

A low shadow huddled on the floor. For one heart-stopping moment Sadie thought it was Sam, still there. The breath squeezed out of her and her legs wobbled, her headlong rush nearly turning into a tumble as she skidded to a stop.

But that wasn't Sam. In the pale light filtering through the glass door to the pool courtyard, Sadie could see the bulk of a coat and the shape of the body within. The length of the limbs was wrong, and shadows alone could not account for the darkness of his hair and on his jaw. Something reeked, her pregnancy-heightened sense of smell picking up the distinct scent of chlorine and something richer, something almost meaty. She parted her lips to avoid breathing through her nose anymore. Her breath whistled in and out of her open mouth as she inched forward, her legs trembling. On her next step her foot slid, and she threw her arms out to brace herself against the walls.

Water on the floor. But not glowing. That chlorine smell. Pool water. And barely visible in the uncertain light, something darker staining that once-clear water. The second smell. Sadie swallowed hard to avoid throwing up.

Her heart racing so hard she thought it would shake her off her feet, Sadie leaned closer, and at last the figure resolved itself.

Joe Mishra lay dead before her, soaked through with pool water, his throat slit wide open.

Electricity raced through Sadie's nerves, ice flooded her veins. She jerked upright and reeled backward. She slapped her hands over her mouth to cut off a scream.

No monster had done that.

Hyperventilating, Sadie scrambled away from the body, her eyes stinging. She threw herself into the supply room.

Had Sam done that to Joe? Or Mr. Drye? Were actual, real, slimy monsters not enough? Sadie had to find Izzy. They had to get out of L'Arpin. Should have gone weeks ago. Months! She'd wasted too much time on indecision and the mistake proved deadly.

Sadie shook herself. Self-recrimination later. No time for it now. Izzy needed her.

She reached for the light switch before remembering the power loss and let out a soft curse, her voice trembling with terror growing to border on hysteria. She held her hands out and moved by feel, searching for her mop, for the sturdy wooden handle she could detach from it. If her fingers touched anything slick and slimy first, if tentacles wrapped around her wrists, she'd scream and scream and never stop. Her skin crawled, her lips drew back in an unseen grimace.

Her hand brushed a mop handle.

She pulled it out and used her foot to brace the mop head while she twisted the handle loose. Dubiously armed, she wasted no more time. Somewhere on this floor, Izzy had been calling out for her. She'd tear the hotel apart room by room if she had to.

Without letting herself look at Joe's bloodied, wet body again, Sadie ran back out through the lobby. She avoided the faint glow of the water as she passed it. The door behind the front desk shuddered in its frame. It opened. No one moved through it, but below the level of the desk, the sound of quick slick sliding spurred her steps yet faster.

She ran down the first guest room corridor off the lobby. Here, the open doors she passed had flashes of movement within, where screams let loose. Sadie didn't want to look at any of it, but each time she passed she had to peek inside, had to check if she could see Izzy or hear her voice among the cacophony. Monsters moved through the screams, some as horrible as the deer had been and some looking so normal until she saw how they grappled with the people within, how they paused to watch her run by.

They all watched Sadie run.

At the corner near the stairwell door, Sadie caught the faint sound of Izzy's cry again.

"Izzy!" she shouted. "Isabelle!"

She rounded the corner. Another door gaped open to her right. The maintenance room. Something moved within. The strange watery smell rolled from that darkness, more powerful than anywhere else.

Instead of bulbous eyes watching her from the shadows, a shape lunged out at Sadie.

Sam's hands latched onto her arms. She shouted as he threw himself back into the dark room, dragging her with him.

"Sam, *stop*!"

He half turned, dragging her off-balance, and shoved her. She reeled and struck the ladder leaning against the wall with a clatter, the rungs digging into her back. Dropping her mop handle, Sadie snagged a grip on the side of the ladder, just stopping herself from falling.

"Not now! Not *now*!"

"Shut up," Sam said. Somewhere out of sight a soft hushing sound repeated, and louder than that but farther away the sounds of scattered struggles continued, but right in front of her Sam's heavy breathing drew nearer to her face.

She could barely see the shape of him moving in the blackness. "Can't you see what's happening? Can't you—" Sam gave no warning. Pain flared in her jaw and her grip slackened. She slid down, the rungs of the ladder rumpling her shirt and raking her back.

"Don't try to distract me, bitch," Sam snarled. Sadie drew her legs up as far as she could, tucking her elbows down. Sam's kick struck her knee instead of her belly and she cried out.

He'd never been so careless before. Back at home—no, not home, back at Finneytown, back in Sam's house—he never would have risked something happening that couldn't be glossed over. Never would have risked kicking a pregnant woman as she huddled on the ground.

Out of control. He'd go too far. He'd go too far this time and he might kill her. The knowledge shot through Sadie, bitter cold and sharp.

What would Izzy do if Sadie died? The mere question closed Sadie's throat, choked her, filled her eyes with burning tears.

Sam kicked her again. Sadie shouted and recoiled. Putting her hand down to pull herself away, her fingers curled around the fallen mop handle.

Gritting her teeth against the pain, Sadie moved fast. She snatched the length of wood up in both hands. The tears filled her eyes but the darkness rendered sight moot anyway. Listening hard, Sadie swung.

The handle connected with a solid *thwack* that jarred her fingers. Sam let out a grunt and a string of curses. Sadie drew back to strike again. This time when the blow landed, Sam must have been ready. When Sadie tried to pull away for another swing, the handle didn't budge. Then Sam yanked it toward him. Sadie tried to hold on but was pulled forward, and she had to let go or risk sprawling face down on the floor.

The shushing noise stopped, replaced by a low grind. Footsteps neared her, stopping when a hard sole landed on the fingers of Sadie's right hand. The pressure grew and Sadie bit her lip to stop a pained gasp.

"Who the fuck do you think you are, Sadie?" Sam asked, his voice low and rich with trembling rage.

He reared back, raising the mop handle.

Even as Sadie flinched, she frowned. Why could she make out his movements now?

"You did this to yourself," Sam said. The faintest green glow caught in his hair, illumination from behind, from the back of the room where no light should be.

A new shadow unfurled behind Sam. It moved forward, and the glow grew, as if something had been blocking a light. Sam stood silhouetted in sickly green, his face a deep, blank shadow until he started to turn. Then, in profile, Sadie saw his furious surprise turn to panic.

Something long and thick whipped out from the shadow behind Sam and wound around the mop handle and his wrist. It twisted tighter and pulled. The sickening crack preceded Sam's scream by a bare second. As if in response to his cry, Izzy's voice wailed from somewhere behind Sam and the shadow figure, from somewhere within that light.

Sadie scrambled to her feet as three more tentacles unfurled from the thing still holding Sam's broken wrist. She pressed herself against the ladder, her eyes caught on the sight of the silhouetted monster coiling strong limbs around the mop handle, pulling it from Sam's limp grip and snapping it in two before dropping it. The tentacles wound next around her ex-fiancé's neck. Her gaze may have been trapped, but Sadie's body was not. Though she could barely blink, she could sidle around the perimeter of the room. Inching closer to that glow, she followed the sound of her daughter crying and whoever was with Izzy *shush, shush, shushing.*

Sadie had moved far enough around the room now, the tableau

of the creature attacking Sam no longer stood in stark silhouette. Though the glow cast everything in sickly green, details resolved themselves. Bulging eyes, writhing tentacles, weakened arms and legs. Gaping gills, slick-gleaming skin. Round, kind face. Long, dark hair no longer pulled into a smooth ponytail. Sadie sucked in a breath, freezing at last in her shock.

Sam thrashed, desperate, capable of only a terrible spluttering gagging noise, held fast by the tentacles of Melanie Ross.

CHAPTER TWENTY-TWO

Full of Bright Promise

The light dimmed. Or did it? No, gray crept over Sadie's vision. She took a shuddering breath, cold pouring over her, her hands trembling and her throat constricting. Her mind skipped off the truth of what stood before her, and her thoughts scattered into terrified scraps as time stretched and ran and—how long had she been stuck there listening to Sam make painful, wet gurgles? How long had she stood frozen, unable to draw a breath herself—how long had her own lungs been burning, watching Mel commit a murder?

No, no, no, that was all wrong. Mel was sweet, she was a little immature, she was funny, she was not a *killer*.

"Stop! Stop it!" Sadie's voice came out high and cracked.

Mel turned toward her.

Sadie's legs wobbled, rubbery. She groped behind herself, seeking any support. Dimly green-lit, her own reflection gleamed within that bulbous gaze, as if she stood before herself diminished and confined.

The tentacles binding Sam loosened and he drew a hacking, raspy breath. His hands shook as he yanked the limbs off his neck, gagging and gasping for air. He reeled back until his thighs struck

Beth's desk and then he froze, holding himself up on it. His eyes darted from Mel to Sadie and back, wide with panic.

Mel hardly seemed to notice. Her mouth opened, closed, and then her lips drew back from her teeth. When she moved a clumsy, stumbling step on withered legs, the paralysis in the maintenance room broke. Sam stumbled away, tripping and sprawling. Mel lurched toward Sadie, arms lifting half-up, fingers trembling as she reached out. Sadie staggered closer to the source of the light—a door hidden in the floor, rough stairs, and that glow—but then Mel dropped to her tentacles and flowed toward Sadie. Sam scrambled to his feet, gave Sadie one wild look over Mel's shoulder, then turned and fled.

Mel didn't even glance at him. One writhing limb flashed out, and almost before Sadie registered the cold, slick touch on her wrist the tentacle wound around her hand, her arm, up to the elbow, and pulled.

Sadie gritted her teeth, braced herself for the break of bones, just like Sam. Instead, Mel dragged Sadie off her feet. More tentacles surged forward to join the first, catching her arms and bracing her chest and her hips, slowing her fall. One cupped her chin and forced Sadie to look into those unblinking, gleaming eyes. Mel drew her lips back again.

"Sadie," she croaked. "It's . . . it's not . . ."

"Sadie!" a voice cried, and in almost the same instant, the jagged point of half of the broken mop handle drove down into Mel from above. The splintered wood speared through her back. For an instant all of Mel's tentacles tightened on Sadie's body, drawing a ragged gasp from her. The monstrous young woman turned, several tentacles releasing Sadie to whip out at her attacker. A key ring fell to the floor and slid away, then a baseball cap. Sadie tried to look up, to see who fought Mel, but one of her old coworker's slick tentacles still held her chin fast.

"Don't," Mel seemed to gag on the words, "you—"

The second half of the mop joined the first, plunging into the thing that had once been Sadie's friend. Mel let out a sound that was not quite the scream of a human woman, then went limp all at once. A putrid stench, sickness and rot and stagnant water, wormed into Sadie's nose. Shuddering, she slapped the loose tentacles off her body. She scrambled away, pushed herself clumsily to her feet, and turned.

Beth stood over Mel, breathing hard, her cap askew, her back to the steps leading from below up to the strange, secret door. Whatever spurted from Mel in place of blood splattered Beth, but beneath that the maintenance woman was already soaking, and a darker stain had been splashed across her front, the green light rendering it nearly black.

She turned to Sadie, her expression difficult to read in the dim light and deep shadows. Hard, and concerned, and something Sadie couldn't discern. She stepped past Mel's mutated corpse as if it was nothing, reaching out for Sadie.

Sadie pushed herself back. "Don't touch me," she said, aiming for sternness but landing somewhere nearer panic. Beth's eyes widened, then narrowed, and Sadie fumbled to add, "I mean—I mean I'm okay. Please. I need space. I'm . . . I'm gonna be sick."

From the hallway, the noises slowed and dimmed. From behind Beth, in the glowing room beneath the maintenance office of L'Arpin Hotel, Izzy's voice rose.

"*Mommy!*"

"What—" Gertie's voice trembled from behind Sadie, then cut off so sharply that Sadie spun, expecting to see some fresh horror taking the old woman. Gertie stood, hands gripping the doorframe to either side of her, the pure dark hallway behind her. She stared down at the huddled form of what had once been Mel, lips pressed together, eyes wide. In the strange, dim light she looked pale and wasted and full of grave stillness. Her eyes flashed up, and in a hard voice that did not tremble, she asked, "What did you do, Bethany?"

"Don't—don't worry, Gertie," Sadie said, forcing herself to

straighten. She'd left the old woman alone at the top of L'Arpin to face all of this, there'd been no time to waste before, no other choice. But now she had someone else, someone who could help. Gathering her thoughts gave Sadie direction again, and she turned to push past the maintenance woman while adding, "Beth, get her out of here."

"I ran into—" Beth hesitated, then rushed on with just a hint of strange emphasis, "—a *guest*. He was leaving from here." She glanced at Sadie and then quickly away, lowering her voice as if embarrassed. "He said, uh, 'Get the fuck out of my way, it's gonna kill that bitch for me.' I ran in here and she—" Beth pointed at Mel, but Gertie cut her off.

"She is not a problem." Gertie stepped delicately around the stinking thing that had been Melanie.

"Not anymore," Beth said. "How did that slip past you?"

Sadie's stomach twisted, but she swallowed hard and tried to ignore it, ignore the crawling up her spine as she said, "Beth, please, there's no time, get Gertie out of here while I find Izzy."

Beth didn't look at Sadie. Her eyes stayed locked on Gertie. She looked nervous. Well, of course she looked nervous. Tentacled lake monsters had overrun the hotel. But . . . why hadn't she looked nervous before?

"But you've killed her, how could you do this?" Gertie's voice rose at last, less panicked than Sadie would have expected. More angry.

Tears sprang to Sadie's eyes—her body, reacting to the truth before she was ready to acknowledge it. She could only run from it, first with her words as she interrupted this hideous, calm conversation to repeat, "Get *out* of here!" Then with her feet, slipping past Beth and plunging down into the light beneath L'Arpin Hotel. Down the stairs, down toward Izzy.

"You miscalculated," Beth said, her voice defensive.

Sadie did not ask *miscalculated what?* She only descended. With every step she took the stairs grew less smooth, less even, and the sickly glow brightened. Lacking banisters, Sadie put her hands to either side, trailing her palms along the rough walls.

From above and behind, Beth's voice followed Sadie for a fleeting instant, echoing, ". . . ing what you asked, *please* don't . . ."

Sadie couldn't listen to this. "Izzy!" she called.

"Mommy!" Izzy wailed, and then fell to wordless crying.

The tears that sprang to Sadie's eyes burned in hot contrast to the ice still piercing her heart, her guts. "I'm coming, baby, stay still!" Anything could lay at the end of this secret staircase. If Izzy tried to come to her, if she fell or got lost— Sadie shook her head, couldn't quite banish the terrible images that ran through her mind. "Don't move, okay?"

"Opay!" Izzy called back, her voice still tearful but growing less hysterical. "Opay, Mommy, I can't move!"

The walls under Sadie's fingers grew slick before she noticed the heaviness in the atmosphere. Sadie snatched her hands away, rubbing her fingers on her pants. Moisture, warm and pungent, hung in the air. From behind her came the scrape of shoes on stone and murmuring voices made unintelligible by echoes and by the growing sound of water running over stone somewhere below.

The stairs turned a corner, and Sadie stumbled to a stop at the entrance to a cavern.

Her eyes found Izzy first. Sadie's little girl lay in the far corner, curled on her side, bound hand and foot but—as far as Sadie could tell—unhurt. She turned her attention to the space she'd found her daughter in.

Long, wide, not small but nevertheless cramped, with its low ceiling and uneven floor. A spring burbled in the center of the stone floor. Light poured from the water, brighter in the churning eddies, dimmer near the calmer edges, swirling and green and unsteady in the way all things full of vitality are unsteady. The water burbled from a crack in the ground and ran in a smooth-worn channel across the chamber, plunging into a hole that Sadie guessed, unless she'd gotten too turned around, ran north. Toward Lake Erie.

At the opposite wall a strip of dry stone remained, and Sadie made for that. The closer she drew to the water, the more she wished she could avoid breathing the mist spraying from its agitated surface. Her vision swam, the edges full of warm oceans under impossible skies. Her open mouth tasted the same sea wind from the shower the day of the little tentacled creatures. The roar of shifting tides cut under every other sound in the chamber, even Izzy crying louder the nearer Sadie came, even the footsteps descending the final stairs behind her.

Sadie threw herself to the ground next to her daughter at the same moment that Beth and Gertie emerged into the chamber. Sadie grabbed the knots on the rope binding her daughter's wrists, but she kept the two women in her peripheral vision.

They should have run when she told them to.

Now they stood, so still and calm, watching Sadie. She pulled the rope away from Izzy's wrists carefully, fury churning in her chest at the sight of the red rope burns on her baby's skin. The ankle rope followed, and Sadie stuffed the bindings into the waistband of her pants rather than drop them and risk tripping herself up.

She gathered Izzy into her arms and straightened, turning to face Beth and Gertie.

Months. She'd been here for months. All the time she'd been watching out for Mr. Drye and Bill Viago, while Gertie fed her, bit by bit, companionship and trust—had it all been a lie?

"You should have run," she said, voice weak and almost pleading. She clutched Izzy tighter and grimaced and made herself say it again. She only meant to firm her voice but instead the words came in a shout. "You should have *run*, but you didn't! Oh, no. No, no. It's you. You're doing this."

Gertie smiled at her, a gentle smile full of bright promise.

CHAPTER TWENTY-THREE

Can I Tell You a Story?

Izzy buried her face in Sadie's shoulder and sobbed. The familiar wet mess of tears and snot soaking Sadie's collar, the way Izzy's fingers caught in Sadie's hair as she wrapped her arms around Sadie's neck, her warm weight in her arms and on her hip, anchored Sadie against the unbelievable strangeness of the cavern and its spring and the old woman walking toward them, Beth trailing behind her.

Gertie didn't shuffle. She didn't hunch her shoulders or reach toward the wall for support. Standing straight, she seemed tall, though Sadie still had several inches on her. She stepped right down into the swirling waters of the spring, and when she spoke it was her voice but it held no hint of quaver or querulousness.

"Izzy, sweetheart, don't cry," she said, her tone light and soothing.

"Don't you talk to her," Sadie said, holding Izzy tighter. "You talk to me."

"You're scaring her." Gertie's eyes flashed at Sadie, and a little of the sharp judgment Sadie was used to bled through into her voice. Izzy tightened her grip on Sadie's neck, her whining cry rising. Instantly, Gertie lowered her voice and spoke to the little girl again. "Can I tell you a story, Izzy?" she asked, stepping closer through the water. She took on a storytelling tone, like a librarian reading to a ring of eager children. "I know little girls like stories about magic worlds. Can you imagine a magic world all covered in water, all warm as a bath and bright as a night-light, even after sunset?" She bent and ran the tips of her fingers through the bright water, trying to catch Izzy's eye with an inviting smile.

"Listen to Mommy, stinker," Sadie whispered in Izzy's ear. Whatever Gertie had to say, she didn't want the old woman infecting her daughter's mind with some dangerous delusion. The edges of Sadie's vision crowded with the flash of sun on water and glittering sea spray and shadows moving dark and deep, and she whispered "Listen to Mommy" again, because worse than a dangerous delusion would be Gertie pouring a dangerous reality, drop by drop, into Izzy's ears. "Just keep listening to me, we're going to be okay, Mommy's got you." Sadie kept up the whispered litany, but she couldn't keep herself from hearing what Gertie had to say.

"Isn't this nice, sweetheart? Wouldn't it be good to make the whole world this nice?"

The clumsy flight of the seagull, the choked snarl of the dog, the graceless stumble of the deer. Sadie held those memories between her and the bright images pushing into her vision with every breath of the damp air. Melanie's face, teeth bare, eyes unblinking and inhuman.

"What are you talking about, Gertie?" she ground out through gritted teeth. Sadie kept her head near Izzy's ear and at the sudden change in volume Izzy flinched, whimpered louder. Sadie went back to shushing her child as Gertie stepped forward, eyes bright and smile beatific.

"I'm talking about a miracle, Sadie, listen to me. My name wasn't always Gertie Harper. We Americanized it when we came here, oh, *such* a long time ago. It was easier to get along here as Margret Harper, little Gertie, than Marguerite Arpin. When my father built the hotel—"

"*What?*"

Gertie continued as if Sadie had not interjected, "—in 1842, I was six." Sadie shook her head, her whispers falling silent as she struggled to make sense of what had just come out of Gertie's mouth. She snapped her jaw shut and shook her head again, but Gertie only laughed. She spread her wrinkled hands and smiled. "I'm *finally* old." She stepped closer, her laugh dying with a soft huff, and looked down at herself. She repeated, "Old. But not infirm. Not dulled by time. No."

"Do you need these theatrics, Ms. Harper?" Beth asked.

Gertie and Sadie both turned to look at the maintenance woman. Her hat had been knocked off in the struggle with Mel in the room above, and Sadie only realized she'd never seen her without that cap when she noticed how little hair Beth had. As if she felt Sadie's gaze, Beth ran her hand over her scalp and then winced as it came away trailing a tangle of what few strands were there. Visible through the patchy hair, Beth's scalp gleamed green.

"Why don't you go find your father, Bethany?" Gertie said, her tone subtly shifted. She sounded not gentle and patient, but like a woman forcing gentleness and patience.

Beth hesitated, glancing from Gertie to Sadie and back. She shook her head. "Not yet. You might still need my help." Though she scowled, jaw clenched, her voice trembled for an instant when she said *help*, and did Sadie glimpse a glitter of tears in the maintenance woman's eyes?

"Oh, dear, no thank you. I don't need help."

"Then why did I have to—" Beth cut herself off, sucking in a breath. Her hands moved, elbows bending, and she stopped just shy of touching the front of herself as if she'd been about to try to wipe away the dark stains there.

The water soaking her, the dark splash on her front. Oh god— "*Joe?*" Sadie asked, her voice catching. "Beth . . . you didn't . . . ?"

Beth didn't answer right away, glanced first at Gertie. The old woman pouted, an expression of long-suffering patience, and gave Beth an approving pat on the arm. The gesture seemed to strengthen the maintenance woman; she stood straighter, some of the doubt cleared out of her eyes. To Sadie, Gertie said, "It needed to be done."

"But why?"

"I won't share L'Arpin with the unworthy."

If Gertie's voice rang with the fervor of a zealot when she said *the unworthy*, Beth's voice trembled with the worship of a convert as she added, "We don't have room here for drug addicts."

"You *what*? You can't—you can't—" Too many horrified protestations crowded Sadie's head and she spluttered, then sucked a trembling breath and tried to stay calm, tried to reason with these unreasonable people. "Drugs don't make someone unworthy. You don't get to decide who's *worthy*, Beth. Joe is—was—he's a good guy."

"Sweetheart," Gertie said, her voice gentle, almost tender. "I'm the one who decides who's worthy. Beth"—Gertie turned to Beth then—"just needed to see for herself how it feels to follow the right path. Now, speaking of who's worthy, I told you to go find your father."

"Okay. Yes. Don't drag this out, Gertie. You'll scare them too much."

Gertie flapped a hand at Beth, saying, "Go on, Bethany." Without further hesitation, Beth turned, crossed the cavern, and disappeared back up the stairs.

Sadie listened to Beth's steps grow fainter and fainter. She stood straighter, shifting her weight from one foot to the next, and tried to think past the impossible idea of Beth slitting Joe's throat.

Because if this wasn't a trick—if Beth had really gone off to look for Lewis—Gertie may be more capable than she'd been pretending, but still Sadie could probably give her the slip and escape L'Arpin and the monsters and any further strange claims Gertie might make.

"Poor Bethany. She didn't turn out as poorly as a few of the others, but the changes are souring now. Might take Lewis bad, too, but still better than losing yourself and dying. Dear Lewis, he's already so confused. We'll help him, though, best we can." Gertie tutted and shook her head. "Henry, now, he was special. Like I'm special. And he"—Gertie's voice turned savage, her eyes flashed in the green light—"he might have outlived me."

"Did something happen to Mr. Drye?" Sadie asked. Then, her belly twisting, she saw a different possibility in the fury in Gertie's eyes. "Did you do something to him?" With a cold rush through her bones, Sadie realized she had no doubt that Gertie, smiling little Gertie, who had been so helpful and so kind, could absolutely do something hideous to Henry Drye. Or to Sadie. She backed up, but it was only one step before her heel touched the wall behind her.

Perhaps seeing Sadie's stalled retreat, perhaps remembering Beth's warning, Gertie smoothed the anger from her face and smiled again.

"That's no matter. It's no matter right now. And Beth will be just fine, so don't you worry about that, either. Because even if she changes a little—"

"A little!" Sadie exclaimed. "Is that what happened to Mel?"

"*Even* if she changes a *little*, Beth will live longer, she'll be stronger, she'll save her father. We'll save her father, and we'll help you, too, dear."

"I don't understand *any* of this!" Sadie edged toward that strip of dry stone, toward the only path to the stairwell. "And I don't need any help, Gertie!"

"We—my friends—well . . ." The conviction in Gertie's eyes shone strong even as she stumbled over her words. After a moment her smile turned wry, and she chuckled. "I'd only make a mess of explaining what you'll understand so well, so soon. It's hard to put into words." Gertie's moment of levity passed, earnestness flooding her voice again as she said, "Everyone needs help. I've helped you so much already, haven't I? Trust me to help you now. I have been so *blessed*. I want that for you, for everyone. All you have to do is step down into the water with me."

"Even if that water can . . . can change us," Sadie said, the words sounding much less impossible than she would have thought, after all she'd seen, "what makes you think it'll be good for us?"

"You're not listening, Sadie Miles," Gertie scolded, for a moment sounding less like a strange would-be savior and more like Sadie's old neighbor. "My father built the hotel when I was *six*. When we found this spring, he had the idea to turn L'Arpin into a health resort. We bathed in the waters and felt so . . . *alive*. Wholly and beautifully alive. But before we could open the cavern to guests, my family soured same as Bethany. We had to carve the channel to the lake while they could still pass, then stage the boating accident . . ." Gertie's gaze turned sad and fond, and she turned as if to gaze past where the water flowed through the hole in the stone.

Toward the lake.

Sadie took the chance and quickened her pace as Gertie kept talking, her voice pensive, as if for a moment she spoke more to herself than to her captive audience. "They're well out there. Especially as the waters warm. And I've been in communion with my friends for the better part of two centuries."

Sadie reached the narrow, dry ledge above the spring just as Gertie turned back to her. "We're leaving, Gertie. Marguerite. Whatever. We're going."

"You *can't* go," Gertie said, a hint of the desperate pleading of earlier that night crawling back into her voice. "You can't, we're *close*. I—I want to help you. But I also want you to help everyone. You see? You"—her gaze flicked from Sadie's face to Izzy, from Izzy to Sadie's belly, and terrified understanding stole Sadie's breath and left her gaping—"could be the turning point."

"You want my baby."

"We've tried so many times, pregnant guests or babies and children, but if it's too sudden, it goes bad. Henry let you *live* here, though. It should have worked, but you never . . . Why? Why did you never drink the water, never eat anything Jordan sent you? It would have been slow, it would have been *safe*. You and Izzy and the baby, and I never would have had to bring in—"

Gertie cut herself off, an expression other than beneficent surety crossing her face for the first time. Guilt, nearly fear.

"Bring in . . ." Sadie murmured, and Beth's voice spoke from memory: *You miscalculated.* "Sam. You found Sam, you told him to come here. I thought Mel, the post online about the party . . . How did you even *know* about him?" For the briefest moment, Gertie's eyes flicked from Sadie to Izzy, and then back again. The look on her face in that tiny instant, satisfaction with the barest hint of guilt, gave Sadie her answer. After all, how many times had she left Izzy, who may not have known their address or phone number but definitely did know Sam's name, alone with Gertie? Beyond that, Gertie must've filled in the gaps herself, just by knowing about Sadie's circumstances. Then all she'd have to do was find him. "But I don't understand. Why did you bring Sam here?"

"You should have come to me for help," Gertie said, her voice sad, shaking her head. "I thought you trusted me enough for that, Sadie."

"You don't get to guilt me for not trusting you when you called my ex here and tried to—to poison me!"

"It's not poison—"

"Whatever!"

"Mommy, stop screaming!" Izzy wailed, beginning to cry again. Sadie tightened her arms around her child and tipped her head down. She kept her eyes on Gertie, who watched with a tender expression that turned Sadie's stomach, while she shushed her daughter. She swayed a little from side to side, rocking Izzy. All the while, her heart raced and her mouth was dry, and she slowly, slowly, slowly used the back-and-forth rocking of her daughter to surreptitiously edge closer to the exit again.

"Would you stop that," Gertie said, patient exasperation coloring her voice. "It's not safe for you upstairs. I can't always control what I've called."

For a moment Sadie thought she still meant Sam, then realization washed over her. Of course.

"You summoned the monsters."

"They're not *monsters.*"

"But why now?" Sadie asked, groping for any questions, anything to keep Gertie talking, to stall her and keep her from acting. "Only because your plan to drive me into your arms backfired?"

"You know why, young lady. I can't . . . you can't just leave. Not now, not yet."

All the horror happening in the dark up there in L'Arpin Hotel . . . for her? No—for her baby?

Gertie stepped nearer, the water swirling around her legs. Sadie dropped all pretense and carefully set off across the only dry path.

"Stop being so stubborn!"

"No yelling!" Izzy cried out.

"Hush, stinker, hush. And you—you stay away from us."

Rather than stay away, Gertie moved faster, wading effortlessly toward Sadie and Izzy. She shook her finger as she came, scolding even now, "I didn't think you were so selfish, Sadie. I didn't think you'd turn your back on all the good we can do for the world. All the good I can do for your *baby.* Help me, Sadie. Help me help you. Help me help *everyone.*"

Sadie reached the far end of the narrow area and turned to run.

Gertie lunged, and for all she looked so frail, Gertie was much faster.

CHAPTER TWENTY-FOUR

You're Something Else

Gertie came at them fast.

So fast that cold fear poured through Sadie. Everything about the woman had been a lie, down to the way she moved. Sadie took a stumbling step and realized she wouldn't make it.

She shifted Izzy's weight, set her daughter down, pajama bottoms bright against the drab stone floor.

"Run to the stairs and wait for me. If I say go up, go up and hide!"

"Arright, Mommy."

"Now, Izzy!" Sadie said, turning. She brought her arms up just in time, blocking a blow Gertie aimed at her jaw. *"Now!"*

"*Opay!*" Izzy shouted, and the patter of her retreating footsteps struck Sadie's heart with a blend of hope and dread she'd never imagined before. She begged for Izzy to escape without knowing who she begged, and she reeled with the terror of knowing those may have been her last words to her little girl.

No time for hope. No time for terror. Only Gertie, grabbing Sadie's shoulders, her hands so strong. Sadie tried to shove her away, but her grip on the old woman's wrists did nothing. Gertie pushed and Sadie surged against her.

"Don't make me do it this way," Gertie said, her voice regretful, almost sad, and not labored at all by the struggle.

"I'm not making you do anything!" Sadie said, her own voice high and tense and breathless. She let go of Gertie's wrists and shoved hard at her chest instead. At the last moment, she pulled the blow, just a little. No matter how it felt, it looked like she was trying to beat up a little old lady, and she couldn't quite force herself to lean into the violence.

Until Gertie recovered and shifted her grip, leaning back. She dragged Sadie forward a step. Toward the water.

Sadie's reservation shredded beneath the whirling, sharp-edged fear of that green glow. She kicked Gertie's knee as hard as she could, throwing herself backward at the same time. Gertie shouted and lost her grip at last. One of Sadie's sleeves tore, leaving a long scrap in Gertie's fist. Sadie reeled backward and fell hard on her tailbone with a cry.

"Careful!" Gertie gasped, hurrying toward Sadie again, her posture softened all at once with solicitous concern.

Of course. They didn't need Sadie, they needed the baby. She scrambled backward toward the stairs in an awkward scuttle. When Gertie drew near she lashed out in another vicious kick. Gertie reeled from the blow, staggering the three steps back until she splashed into her otherworldly stream.

Sadie pulled herself to her feet, turning before she'd made it fully upright.

"That's enough!"

Sadie stopped in her tracks, her heart squeezing and her breath rushing out of her all at once.

Beth McCann stood on the bottom step. She pressed Izzy's back to her front, an arm across the little girl's belly holding her up, the other hand covering Izzy's mouth. Izzy kicked and squirmed, she raised her arms and stiffened her body the way she did whenever she wanted out of her mother's grasp, but Beth held tight.

A step behind her, Lewis peered over his daughter's shoulder.

His eyes sharpened from confused fear to anger. He shoved past Beth, and then everyone was speaking at once.

"Listen to Gertie, or else," Beth said.

"What are you *doing*? Put that child down!" Lewis scolded. In one hand he held a sharp-pronged gardening tool, faintly glowing green wetness staining its end. His other hand he lifted, shaking a finger at his daughter. "What's the meaning of this?"

"Give me my daughter, Beth," Sadie tried to speak over Beth and Lewis both, without raising her voice in a way that would scare Izzy or upset her captor. She held her arms out and moved slowly toward them. "Give me my *daughter*, Beth, *please*. Now."

Sudden guilt flickered in Beth's eyes, but her gaze darted from Sadie to her father, from her father to Gertie. Gertie gave her head a tiny shake. Beth's jaw clenched, her throat moved as she swallowed, then she looked back at Sadie. The hardness on her face still didn't reach her wide, sad eyes, but her voice held no doubt when she answered, "No. Turn around and listen to Gertie now, Sadie."

"Bethany Elizabeth McCann, you put that child down!" Lewis shouted.

Sadie dropped her hands and any pretense at calm.

"Give Izzy to me *now*!"

She charged at the larger woman but only made it two stumbling steps before Beth moved as well. She didn't retreat before Sadie's fury; she leaped closer to the spring. Sadie skidded to a stop.

"Don't." The word came out faint. Sadie sucked a breath and tried again, but like in a nightmare, her voice wouldn't come. She only mouthed it again: *Don't*. And *please*.

Beth had to shift her grip on Izzy to hold the child out over the water. Sadie reached for the wall, staggered by a swooping, sick sensation, like the floor was falling out from under her.

Then Izzy took a deep breath, her legs pinwheeling, thrashing. Her expression full of a kind of terrified wrath, she screamed, *"I want my mommy!"*

Izzy's voice freed Sadie's, and she bellowed, "Don't you dare! Don't you *dare*! I'll burn this whole place to the ground!"

"Sadie, please, listen to me. If you just calm down you'll see . . . this is a gift." Gertie gestured to Lewis, who shot her a confused glance. "No one has to lose themselves to the fog of age."

The gardener's face darkened like a storm cloud. "Why you— leave me outta whatever the hell this is!"

For all Gertie claimed to care about Lewis's well-being, she blithely ignored his offended exclamation. "What about the mothers who have babies that aren't well? I could—*we* could save so many people."

"What about Mel's mother?" Sadie shot back. "Did you see her, when she was here begging Mr. Drye to tell her about her daughter?"

She tried to use the distraction of the conversation to edge closer to Beth, but the maintenance woman gave a sharp shake of her head. "Ah-ah-ah," she said, leaning farther out over the water.

"Bethany!" Lewis shouted, something like horror and something like tragedy ringing in his voice. She winced but ignored him.

Splashing drew Sadie's attention back to Gertie in a hurry. The older woman stepped up out of the water, her skirt hanging heavy and wet from the thighs down. Sadie backed up as Gertie stepped close again, but Beth made another "ah" noise, and Sadie gritted her teeth and stilled her feet.

"It doesn't have to be frightening, Sadie." Gertie reached out to brush a lock of Sadie's red hair from her face. Sadie slapped her hand away and Gertie shook her head with a disappointed *tut*. In a stern voice, she went on, "But it *does* have to happen. You, the both of you"—she gestured at Sadie's belly, fingers stopping just shy of a caress—"will help us understand how to get it right every time. *Think* about it, Sadie. No more illness, no more fear of aging and dying. How much more pure will the world be when we're free from the shadow of poor health and short lives, when we can turn to making everything warm and soft and beautiful?"

Sadie shook her head. Gertie had convinced herself—or nearly two centuries of exposure to this uncanny spring had convinced her—that these mutations would save not just human life, but human social ills? The impossibility struck her. Gertie's shining eyes, the open and honest love suffusing Gertie's face, scared her more than naked ambition or pure malice would have. Gertie *believed* what she said, it danced in her gaze and her voice. Something had *made* her believe it, in spite of all the monstrous evidence.

And Sadie would have to go along with this. She shot an anguished look at her daughter, and then turned pleading eyes to Beth one last time.

Beth wouldn't even meet her gaze.

But Lewis did. He caught Sadie's glance and scowled, then nodded once.

His daughter must have caught the gesture, because she turned to him, already saying, "Dad?"

He jumped at her.

"Wait!" Sadie gasped, pushing Gertie aside. Perhaps unprepared for resistance now, the old woman stumbled back a step.

Lewis didn't knock Beth back or make her drop Izzy into the water. He wasn't gentle, no time for that, but he grabbed Izzy around the waist and yanked her out of his daughter's grasp. Teetering on the edge of the dip into the spring, he spun awkwardly and dumped a screaming Izzy roughly onto dry stone before toppling backward into Beth's midsection.

The McCanns fell into the water with a pair of shouts and a single splash. Izzy screamed again and Sadie dove for her. Beth and Lewis struggled to their feet at the same time, Lewis shouting even as he spit out a mouthful of luminescent water.

"How could you threaten a little girl, Bethany!"

"It's for you," Bethany said, her pleading edged by anger. "I can't watch you . . . you remember Mom, how hard . . . it's for *you!*"

"No," Lewis said. "No. My Bethie would never." He gasped a trembling breath. Sadie gathered Izzy up into her arms, casting a look back at the gardener. He gasped again. Weeping, Sadie realized. Her heart ached, but he was beyond help, and she had Izzy back. "My Bethie would *never*. You're—you're something *else*."

Sadie backed toward the stairs. If Lewis tried to follow them, she'd have to lose him, too. He'd saved Izzy, but he'd choked on a mouthful of that terrible water. He wouldn't be safe for long. Sadie turned to run. She'd only reached one step when she heard a sick sound, wet and cracking and slick. Gertie's scream followed the noise, and Sadie couldn't help herself. She turned.

Lewis stood in place, his shoulders shaking so hard she thought he'd knock himself over. He watched Beth fall, his gardening tool jutting from her throat. She made a terrible, wet noise, a gurgling keen, and then she splashed into the water, enclosed in its light.

Lewis howled but didn't move.

Gertie wailed and did move.

She leaped back into the water, landing half on Lewis's back, and bore him down.

Sadie didn't look back again. She ran up the stairs with her daughter, tears stinging her eyes, her throat tight, terror beating at her breast. The echoes of violence and shouts from above held less horror than the sound of the drowning below.

Especially when the sound from below ceased. Any second now, Gertie would follow Sadie and Izzy up from the glowing pit.

CHAPTER TWENTY-FIVE

Its Writhing, Grasping Way

The green glow of the chamber below dimmed the higher Sadie climbed. She blinked against the gloom. The illumination reached just far enough to pick out the gleaming, sinuous lines of Mel's tentacles—their writhing forever stilled—and her death-mask face. Sadie stumbled through the shadows, covering Izzy's eyes with one hand.

"Don't look, baby," she whispered.

"Opay," Izzy whispered back, tightening her arms around Sadie's neck and pushing her face against her mother.

With her hand on the doorknob Sadie paused. Panic twisted in her chest, slithered up her spine—Gertie would ascend those rough stairs any second.

But the fear rooted her feet to the floor, too. What monsters might wait just outside? Writhing mutations? Sam Keller? L'Arpin staff, enthralled by Gertie?

"Please," the no-longer-querulous old voice drifted from behind and below, breaking through Sadie's trembling indecision.

She steeled herself and slipped out of the room just as the old woman's voice grew louder, a scuffle clarifying into footsteps from around the doorway. The dark corridor stretched empty to either side, and Sadie forced herself to draw a ragged breath.

Out here the sounds of struggle and fear had muted into sporadic bursts of thumps and blows, a solitary scream, and the hiss of running water from too many directions. Beyond the edge of the doorframe, out of sight of the maintenance room, Sadie's hesitation gripped her again. Which way to go? Where did safety lie?

Gertie's voice came clearer, "Don't strain yourself, Sadie. I would feel, oh, just *horrible* if you hurt yourself. You only need to understand."

Gertie sounded so sincere, but also much too near. And Sadie had heard more than enough. No time for dithering. Whether toward safety or peril, Sadie had to move. She lurched forward.

The green carpet in the hallway *squished* underfoot, and she leaped back only to land in something that not only *squished* but splashed, just a little. Water seeped out of an open door behind her, a little to her left, but Sadie could pick out no swirl of glow, not even a hint. She swallowed hard and surged forward again anyway, seeking drier ground, unable to take the risk. She'd burn these shoes, these pants, later. If she had a chance.

The ceiling reverberated with an impact from the floor above and Izzy yelped. In the wake of her little cry, the bumps and thumps and scrapes all fell still at once. The near silence came on so suddenly that Sadie stumbled to a stop, clutching her daughter as she spun in a fast, tight circle. Wide eyes adjusting slowly to the dimness, Sadie picked out myriad shadows as they shifted, then slid nearer.

Through an open door into a guest room, a silhouette lifted itself into view, so covered in tentacles as to be unrecognizable. From the direction of the stairwell around the corner at the far end of the hall, back the way she'd come, a human figure materialized—Sam, drawn by Izzy's familiar little voice?—but no, no, not Sam, Sadie realized as it stepped nearer. A suggestion of tiny writhing limbs marred its outline. Not Sam, not even really a human.

"Sadie," Gertie called as she stepped out of the maintenance room, putting herself between Sadie and Izzy and the person-shape. From behind Gertie, the shadowed almost-human repeated the old woman, choking out Sadie's name in a drowning victim's voice.

Sadie dashed away from them. Breathless with dread that Sam might have fled in this same direction, she ran for the corner that would lead to the lobby, to the exit.

"Please!" Gertie called and the drowned voice echoed.

A small shadow slithered out of a room to Sadie's right. She whirled to deliver a kick that sent the creature—from the size and the squeal, it had once been only a rat—flying into the opposite wall.

With ten feet between her and the corner, one of the few guest room doors that had been shut flew open. It struck the wall behind it with a *bang* that made Izzy scream. Sadie jumped back, her heart pounding so hard she thought she'd shake herself off her feet.

Bill Viago barreled through the doorway, a crowbar in one hand, something dark and wet slicking the end of it. Blood stained the side of his face and the ragged, flapping edges of a tear down the front of his shirt. He favored one leg as he turned toward Sadie, his eyes huge and his lips drawn back in a grimace.

"What the fuck is going on?" he shouted.

"You're not welcome here, young man!" Gertie shouted, nearer. The choked voice couldn't keep up with all those words, mumbling. From somewhere farther away another voice groaned a ghastly approximation of the same exclamation. "This isn't for you!"

"Viago—" Sadie gasped, rushing toward him.

A mass of tentacles and bulging eyes tumbled out of the room next to the doorway framing Viago. Sadie recoiled with a disgusted cry from this thing, which had clearly once been two creatures. A cat, perhaps, and a raccoon, but whatever it had been before, now it was gnashing teeth and slick limbs, and it threw itself at Viago.

"Yeeurggh!" Sadie's shout, disgusted and terrified, distracted the creature. It turned toward her just as she reared back. She leaned just enough to grab the handle of the door it had come through, then threw her weight back. The door slammed on it with a sickening, wet squelch. It went limp but still twisted its slick limbs around itself. Sadie kicked the door again and again, until its tentacles stopped writhing.

"You stop that right this instant, Sadie Miles!" Gertie cried.

"Fuck!" Viago shouted.

"Don't say those words!" Izzy scolded, picking her head up from Sadie's shoulder as if she had not just been sobbing onto her mother's shirt.

"Just *run!*" Sadie said, and she put action to words. She dashed past Bill Viago, who didn't hesitate to turn on his heel and run at her side.

"Give her to me," he said, reaching for Izzy.

"No!" Izzy wailed, wrapping her arms and legs tighter around her mother, throwing Sadie's balance off. She stumbled, and Viago caught her elbow.

"I can carry her!"

"*No!*"

"You're not helping," Sadie grunted at him.

They rounded the corner. The lobby still gleamed with wet trails, the light from the power plant's parking lot still illuminated the space more than the rest of the darkened hotel. Glass still glittered. In front of the desk, Henry Drye lay dead of a crushing blow to his skull. His single remaining eye fixed on the chandelier, unseeing gaze only barely reflecting myriad dull glitters. Sadie covered Izzy's eyes again.

"Fuck this," Viago groaned.

Sadie's shoulders tightened into a defensive hunch even before she thought the name *Sam*, but she spun toward the door. She stopped in her tracks with a short, sharp cry, her arms tightening on her daughter.

Steep slopes or steps should have made a deer balk, but this thing was no longer a deer. Its tentacles had gotten the monster to the fourth floor in the first place. She shouldn't be surprised it had found its writhing, grasping way back down, too.

Its spindly, once-graceful legs splayed on the floor, the tentacles writhing around it. It turned its head to aim one bulging, lidless eye at Sadie. The antlers seemed to shine in the reflected light, wickedly sharp and slime coated. The illumination picked out the green in its hide, and when it opened its mouth, there came the luminous glow Sadie would never forget. If she survived this night.

"Please come back, Sadie," Gertie's voice came from nearer than Sadie had realized. "We need to do this gently." The drowning voice echoed her. Sadie looked over her shoulder as Gertie stepped into view, still mostly shadowed in the hallway's gloom where the corridor met the lobby. The old woman hesitated there, then held out her hand. "Please. Let me help you, Sadie. We—I don't want to make this difficult."

The deer bellowed, its grunting voice thick and clotted and broken into strained syllables. It was trying to echo Gertie's words.

The young woman with the white-blond hair and huge eyes stepped past Gertie, pausing only when Gertie put a hand on her wrist. "Give her a moment to think, Annie," Gertie whispered to the woman. The guest Sadie had seen in the pool on her first day in L'Arpin. She stood nude, her skin only tinged with green, her eyes wide and black but not lidless.

"She's the one who can fix us?" The woman didn't quite ask, didn't quite accuse. "Her baby, if this goes right, we'll learn how to fix it all?"

Gertie hesitated, and Sadie leaped into the beat of silence in the older woman's insecurity.

"Do you really think that? She told me herself, she wants to learn how to make that, all *that*"—Sadie waved from the young woman to the deer-thing, throwing her arm wide in a gesture meant to indicate all the monsters of L'Arpin Hotel—"go right *from now on*. You . . . I don't think there's any way to fix you . . ."

The silence stretched.

"Maybe not," the guest—Gertie had called her Annie—said, but subtle movement drew Sadie's eyes to Gertie's lips. The old woman mouthed the words an instant before the drowning voice spoke them. "But if it's perfected, we can help everyone. I won't have to hide anymore."

Some weight of understanding settled on Sadie. The wistful sorrow in every line of Gertie's posture when she'd looked at the watery tunnel as she explained how her family had been forced to flee into Lake Erie. The longing when she spoke of helping everyone. Her lips dictating Annie's voice: *won't have to hide anymore.*

Nearly two hundred years alone, convincing herself she brought a gift no one understood.

Pity churned, sick and sour, in Sadie's gut, but it did not move her.

"Follow me," she whispered to Viago.

Then she turned and ran for the short corridor that led to the pool courtyard exit.

"Grab her," Gertie said, the frustration in her voice tinged by sadness. "Gently!"

Sadie pulled Izzy's head down, hiding her little girl's face as she rushed past the body of Joe Mishra. Viago vaulted the corpse without breaking stride. The glass door loomed before them. Sadie didn't have her skeleton key, it was tucked away behind the desk wherever Mr. Drye kept them.

"Smash it!" she screamed.

Viago leaped forward, swinging his crowbar in a vicious arc. The glass shattered with an almost musical tinkling. It crunched under Viago's boots as he careened through, and under Sadie's shoes as she followed.

Beneath the sliding tentacles of the coming deer monster, it did not crunch so much as *whisk* with a sharp sliding sound, quickly muffled under squirming, wet weight.

The cold wind of a February night stole Sadie's breath and made

Izzy whimper and burrow closer to her mother's body. Viago's breath puffed in curling clouds as he cursed and ran toward the gate at the far end of the courtyard.

Sadie followed, a shiver already tightening the muscles in her arms and shoulders and down her back. As she ran, she glanced at the smooth snow. No footprints. No sign that anyone had gotten out here ahead of them. Though the frigid air stung her exposed skin, leaving the moist warmth and rotting water scent of L'Arpin was worth every cold-burning lungful. Perhaps the chill helped more than just to clear that taint away; the sounds of pursuit slowed. Sadie risked a glance—the tentacled deer flailed with less fluidity, lurching forward in fits and starts. She traced its path with her eyes and put on another burst of speed.

"It's heading for the pool," she gasped at Viago. The snow that lay on the skeletal branches of the shrubbery melted as it fell onto the gently rippling water. A haze of mist drifted just above the surface, and the depths carried a hint of green light. Within the small courtyard, there would be almost nowhere out of reach of those grasping tentacles if it got into the heated water and reached out for them.

"Sadie, you *gotta* gimme the kid," Viago said, and reached for Izzy again.

Izzy wailed, Sadie's steps faltered, and then she pushed her daughter away from her body. "He's a good guy, Izzy. He'll run faster with you. Be good." Viago grabbed her and they ran again. Sadie hated the sight of her daughter's frightened face peering over a stranger's shoulder, reaching for her around his arm, but when Viago sped his steps she matched his pace, and they flashed across the courtyard.

"No!" Izzy cried, "Mommy!"

"I'm—I'm chasing you, it's a race, help him win!"

Viago grabbed the gate handle as a loud splash sounded behind them. He threw the gate open. The ripple of water grew. Viago and Sadie sprinted through. A tentacle grazed her ankle, but failed to hold, and she slammed the cold metal shut behind her.

"Fuck me!" Viago shouted, veering hard to the left, to the north.

Sadie's gaze flew over the assembled creatures closing in on the hotel, coming from the direction of the power plant and the road more than the lake.

"They must have been moving to surround the building," Sadie gasped. "The ones that came straight from the water to L'Arpin didn't get cold enough to slow down."

"Doesn't matter why they're out here," Viago grunted as the crowd of things, some more normal and some more heinous, turned eyes that either blinked or could not, either moved or bulged pure black, toward Sadie, Viago, and Izzy. "What matters is getting past!"

"This way!" Sadie shoved Viago in the direction of the stairs leading down to the Cut. The only clear path available drove them to the last place she ever wanted to see.

CHAPTER TWENTY-SIX

Night Still Stretched Before Them

Sadie followed half a step behind Viago and Izzy, crossing the parking lot as the sluggish monsters pulled themselves after. A low purple shape caught her eye—Sam's coupe, gathering a coat of snow. No sign of him. He'd fled from Mel, but had some other monster of L'Arpin caught him? Did he hide still in the dark rooms of the hotel? Or was he out here, waiting for her?

Her distraction caught up with her; Sadie's feet slipped on the parking lot's slick slush. She pinwheeled her arms with a shout, catching Viago's attention. He turned to her just as she caught her balance, and she waved him on.

They ran, sliding but never quite falling, until they'd crossed the lot. The snow was not quite ankle deep, a danger only where it had turned the pavement slippery, and on the frozen grass they got a greater and greater lead on their pursuers.

Viago stopped short at the top of the steps leading down to the beach. Sadie nearly plowed into him, skidding to a halt a breath behind him. Had he seen something down there? Someone? Wide-eyed, Sadie leaned to peer around him, but nothing dangerous waited on the sand at the bottom of the stairs. Viago thrust the crowbar into Sadie's hands, and shifted Izzy's weight to free one hand to hold the railing.

"They're solid ice," he said over his shoulder, and began to descend as hastily as he could without taking a terrible fall. Sadie followed suit, the metal railing freezing her palm.

They'd neared the bottom when the first rustle of underbrush above heralded the arrival of the monsters. Viago tried to hurry his steps. His foot slipped out from under him and he fell backward with a shout.

"Izzy!" Sadie yelled, reaching her free hand for her daughter, knowing she couldn't catch her.

Viago moved fast, though, curling his body and wrapping his arms around Izzy, keeping her shielded atop his torso as he slid the last few feet down the steps in a painful-looking, bumping rush.

"Isabelle!" Sadie tucked the crowbar awkwardly under her armpit and held the railing with both hands now, descending sideways as fast as she could. When her own feet slipped out from under her she wrenched her shoulder, holding herself up.

"Did we win the race?" Izzy asked from below.

Viago groaned. "Yeah, kid, we won."

"I'm not a kid, I'm a horsey."

"Sure, whatever."

Viago clambered to his feet as Sadie reached the bottom step.

"Can you run?" she asked.

"I fucking better be able to. C'mon, the gate."

Sadie's gaze caught on the surface of the lake. Farther from shore, a thick layer of smooth, white ice stretched to the horizon. Between the arch of floodlit sand to the east and the rocky pier to the west, a semicircle of thawed water churned. Here, at least, the water didn't glow, but brief flares did light the shallows and the depths. Bioluminescence, creatures in the lake. Like lightning, they illuminated a submerged scene in bits and pieces. Creatures that roiled beneath the surface. An occasional tentacle reaching into the air before retracting quickly, as if unable to stand the dry or the cold or both. Things flashed, darting, fast. Things slid along the bottom. Things pressed toward the tiny waves and then receded before they could break the surface. A trio of figures like people, but not, watched with bulging eyes that gleamed with every flash.

"Look at that," Viago said, his voice grim.

"I am."

"Not the lake. *That.*"

He pointed and Sadie turned to follow the gesture. The holes in the cliff wall, the ones she thought on her first trip here must have been related to the power plant, the ones that had released a tiny trickle of water then, now gushed twin streams that glowed as they flowed to the lake. Where that water met Lake Erie, the creatures that could not surface surged in a tentacle-twisting, thick crowd.

That water cut a path between Sadie, Viago, and Izzy and the fence leading into the power plant's property.

"We'll have to jump it," Sadie said.

"Fuck."

"Mommy!" Izzy screamed. Sadie's gaze snapped to her daughter, then in the direction of her daughter's horrified gaze. The strangeness on the beach had distracted them. Even slowed by cold, the creatures that had come from L'Arpin drew too near, sliding down the cliff or off the steps and onto the snowy sand.

Among them came a child-sized creature, nearly human. Only a green sheen to its skin, only a shiny blackness to its eyes, only the slow weakness in the cold, marked it as anything other than a normal girl of seven or eight. Was this the child Sadie had heard crying in the barricaded room? Her heart had ached for that unseen child then, and the way the little girl reached for Sadie now sharpened that ache into something nearer to heartbreak.

"To hell with that creepy-ass shit," Viago muttered, eyes fixed on the child as it neared.

Then it croaked her name. "Sadie." She shuddered at the sickly thickness of its voice. "Please come back, Sadie. I'm trying to be patient, but we need you." It spoke not with Gertie's voice but with her inflections.

"Gertie—" Sadie gasped, cut herself off, then swallowed and opened her mouth again, searching for the right words. The child-thing paused. If Sadie tried to plead now, tried begging, tried to find a way to make Gertie Harper—Marguerite Arpin, whoever she was—see this madness for what it was, Gertie would hear it through her monsters. She would hear it, and if Sadie could just find the right words to reach the part of Gertie that really was a sweet old lady trying to help people, help her family . . .

But no. If she did that she'd be caught up, stalled, she'd fall right into a trap of her own making.

"Fuck you, Gertie." Sadie grabbed Viago's free arm, and as the child shouted with Gertie's fury, they fled together.

The luminous stream ran in a channel several feet wide, letting off a faint mist. Sadie pointed to where it narrowed and Viago veered in that direction. Even there, on snowy sand, cold and terrified, more than four and a half months pregnant, it looked like a daunting leap.

Hesitating would doom her, would doom Izzy and the baby who didn't even have a name yet.

The terror clawed up her throat as she leaped, and she had to let it out in a strangled cry, still clutching Viago's arm as he jumped by her side. His longer legs gave him better clearance, and his forward foot hit the sand on the far side a second before Sadie's. He gave his arm a yank, pulling her forward a fraction, saving her from slipping backward into the water when the ball of her foot hit the sand but her heel didn't quite reach.

"What now?" Sadie shouted.

"The gate, there!" He pointed to where the fence met the flaky stone of the cliff, at a gate she hadn't noticed when she'd come before. "Take her back." He took his crowbar back and shoved Izzy into Sadie's arms as they fled across the sand, freeing his hands to dig in his pockets until he produced a key ring. Sadie expected a panicked fumble. Instead, Viago moved with fast but steady surety, selecting a key and sliding it into the lock even as they skidded to a stop. He pulled the gate open and shoved Sadie and Izzy through, crowding after them and slamming it again. It wouldn't slow the creatures for long, but they'd regained a bit of their lead.

Viago led them to a metal door in the side of the building. As he unlocked this one, Sadie cast an anxious eye over the power plant. Brick and steel, with large windows made up of hundreds of palm-sized panes of glass, thick metal frames like a grid between each pane. The creatures had surged easily through the wooden doors and simple windows of L'Arpin, but this might hold them off for a while.

Viago yanked the door open, and the three of them burst through into the darkness. He slammed the door. The scrape of the dead bolt sliding home was the single most comforting sound Sadie had ever heard.

"What were you doing at the hotel?" she asked, gasping.

"I saw those . . . things breaking in and came to see if I could help," he answered, sounding much less out of breath than she was in spite of carrying Izzy for most of the frantic run. "That fucker Drye tried to strangle me in the lobby. But I—" He hefted his crowbar, and Sadie widened her eyes at him, giving her head a single sharp shake and then throwing a significant glance at Izzy, crying softly in her arms. "Uh, right. Well. You know. Come on, there's an office this way."

He led them along the wall for a moment until they reached an interior door that opened onto the kind of banal, well-lit hallway Sadie might have expected to find in any office building or perhaps a high school. Linoleum floors, cinder block walls painted white, drop-tile ceiling with flat fluorescent lights. She'd never loved such a mundane sight as much as this.

"I was trying to call the cops when Drye caught me. He smashed my phone," Viago said as he led Sadie and Izzy down the hall. In the brightness of it, the dry warmth of an environment-controlled building, the quiet as they moved farther from the exterior and what lurked without the building, the events of mere moments ago took on a surreality that left Sadie shaking her head.

"This is unbelievable," she said.

"Damn right it is. That's why when we call the cops we're gonna have to think of some story to get them here. There's my office."

Bill let them in and shut the door behind them. Without turning on the light, he moved around the room, pushing the few chairs and a filing cabinet against the door. Sadie crossed cautiously to the window. From here she could see only a few out of place, huddled shadows. The creatures, motionless, watching and waiting but not sure where to attack. Sadie made sure to keep to the side of the window, peering out only cautiously.

As adrenaline waned, pain grew. Or her awareness of it grew. Her lower back ached so badly that Sadie had to grit her teeth against a small grunt that tried to escape her. Her feet, her ankles, her knees all throbbed. She wished she could sit down, but the chairs had all been shoved against the door, and they seemed much less appealing there. She did lean over to set Izzy down.

"What time is it?" she asked. It must surely be near dawn by now. Whatever else Gertie would risk, being exposed by anyone coming and going in the cold light of day couldn't possibly be acceptable to her.

"Shit."

Sadie glanced around, her eyes finding a clock. At the sinking realization that it was not yet ten o'clock in the evening, she thought Viago had cursed because of how much night still stretched before them.

Then he slammed his office phone down with another curse.

"No phones?"

"They cut the lines. I don't know how!"

Sadie let out a bitter laugh. "Gertie has been lonely and planning something like this for . . ." She hesitated. How much would he accept at this point? ". . . for a long time, Viago. And she has a lot of, uh, help. She probably cut off the gas station and the houses nearby, too. Just to be safe."

"The little old lady?" Viago demanded.

Sadie stood in silence for a moment, watching Izzy curl up on the floor under the desk. The resilience of toddlers always astounded her. Maybe if they survived all this, Izzy would be okay. Instead of answering Viago, she said, "Do you have a blanket or anything in here?"

He pulled his heavy canvas jacket off and handed it to Sadie. She spread it over Izzy and murmured a comforting hush until the little girl closed her eyes.

"Do we need to whisper?" Viago asked when Sadie straightened.

"Can't hurt. And yeah. That little old lady. She's behind all of this. Drye answered to her. She secretly owned L'Arpin and everything."

"What does she want you for?"

Sadie hesitated, her hands going to her belly and her gaze going to Izzy. "It's difficult to swallow," she warned him. And then she told Bill Viago everything that had happened over the course of that uncanny evening.

At the end of it, he stood silent as Sadie's heartbeat picked up, slowly at first but faster and faster. Would he laugh at her? Call her a liar? Turn them out to save himself?

He didn't do any of that. He turned to the phone and tried it again, muttering, "We gotta get you out of here." He put the receiver to his ear, then pressed his lips together and narrowed his eyes. He clicked the button several times, his scowl only deepening. "Phone's still not working."

"Did you expect it to?"

"No."

"Do . . . do you believe me?"

Viago rubbed his hands over his face and let out a grim approximation of a laugh. "A harmless old busybody just sicced a pack of fucking sea monsters on us. I don't have to believe shit, I saw it."

The relief that coursed through Sadie took her by surprise, and she reached behind her, finding a low bookshelf to support her weight as her knees wobbled and her breath rushed out of her.

"Oh, shit, are you okay?" Viago asked, looking from Sadie's face to her belly.

Sadie couldn't help it. A near-hysterical laugh bubbled out of her.

"No," she said, rubbing her eyes with her free hand. "But I'm not hurt."

"Fair. Let's figure out how to get the hell away from here."

Sadie opened her mouth to agree, but her skin crawled with the remembered touch of Mel's tentacle cupping her chin, and the little girl's croaking voice echoing the unseen child's cry, and Mrs. Ross's despairing face turned away from Sadie, and Sadie said, "Not yet. We have to stop Gertie. She'll just do this to more people. She wants to spread this as far as she can." Viago hesitated, a frankly skeptical frown drawing his brows together. Sadie straightened and asked, "Do you really want all that going on next to your power plant forever? Do you think she'll ever leave you alone, after this?"

". . . Fuck. Okay. We need to figure out how to stop this. Hang on." He hurried to his desk, slowing when Sadie hissed and pointed at the sleeping toddler curled up beneath it. With exaggerated care, he slid a drawer open and pulled out a tablet. Angling his body to block any glow from showing through the window, he turned it on and immediately slid the brightness all the way down. After a moment of tapping and swiping, he gestured for Sadie to join him at the desk.

Viago had split the screen, one half showing an aerial view of the two properties, L'Arpin seeming small next to the power plant and the lake to the north of both, and the other half a blueprint. Sadie leaned onto the desk and something hard in her pocket pressed against her, making a hissing staticky noise. She jumped, her heart leaping into a race and electricity firing under her skin, before she remembered the walkie-talkie. With a frustrated huff, she pulled it out and set it on the desk, then leaned back over Viago's tablet.

"Is that L'Arpin?" Sadie asked, touching the blueprint. When the image went into full-screen mode, she snatched her finger back, and Viago grunted before he flipped it back to split screen.

"Yeah. When all the trouble with them started, all the . . ." he trailed off, his eyes widening. "Shit, I thought all that stuff was just petty power-tripping manager-type bullshit. The break-in, the . . ." He turned to meet Sadie's gaze. ". . . the water damage."

"This whole place could be compromised," Sadie murmured. "Oh *no*. What will you do?"

"Fuck if I know. I'll figure it out if we get out of tonight alive and, y'know, ourselves."

Sadie shuddered and nodded.

"So. Where's that cavern thing?" Viago asked.

Sadie leaned over the tablet, frowning at the busy lines and notes of the blueprint until she found the front door. From there, her eyes traced the path to the maintenance room. She pointed, careful not to touch it this time.

"That's good," Viago said, using two fingers to zoom in on the picture. "Where in the room was the staircase?" When Sadie pointed again, he said, "Right by the outer wall. That's good. That's *great*, actually. A cavern under that wall there, it'll weaken the whole structure. They were fucking stupid to build it like this. We're gonna watch a couple YouTube videos about operating construction vehicles, you and me." Sadie couldn't tell if he grinned, or bared his teeth. "If we can take down this wall and collapse the cavern, maybe we can seal the spring. Probably damage the hotel enough they'll never be able to reopen." He looked delighted at the idea, then worry replaced his smile. "Do you think the monsters will go back there?

To, like, rest or hibernate or whatever. How do we get them all in there to kill them?"

"We won't be able to kill them all," Sadie said, turning a dark gaze out the window, into the night populated by a deadly old lady and an out-of-control ex and squirming, sluggish monsters. From here, she couldn't see the lake, but she knew now what lurked beneath those waves. "But without new . . . contaminated water? Cursed? Whatever, without that they can't make more of themselves, or they would've been reproducing for nearly two hundred years." She looked back at Viago. Her mouth was dry, her heart fluttering, and she had to force her next words out around a lump of fear in her throat. "And I think I do know how we can kill a lot of them. Kill Gertie." She stepped back from Viago, squaring her shoulders, hands on her belly. A shiver marred her posture. "Because I know what they want."

CHAPTER TWENTY-SEVEN

Into the Dark Maw

"Izzy!" Sadie screamed as she ran down the sidewalk along the front of the power plant. The snow fell, wide, soft flakes moving in thick swirls, reflecting the streetlights and parking lot lights but obscuring her vision nonetheless. "Izzy, please, where did you *go*?"

She fought through the instinct to keep her voice down. The point, after all, was to be heard. But not by her daughter, who waited safe and sound in the power plant with Bill Viago. She needed to catch Gertie's attention—but that purple car still parked in the lot filled her with the dread of catching Sam's attention as well.

Sluggish slithers met Sadie's ears and her heart leaped into a gallop. She nearly faltered, terror bringing stinging tears to her eyes. "Isabelle Miles! It's not safe to hide from Mommy!"

She had to show Gertie what she wanted to see. But she had to do it without arousing the old woman's suspicion. If she simply ran screaming into the teeth of the trap, the risk of alerting Gertie to the subterfuge skyrocketed.

If Gertie thought Sadie'd lost Izzy in the panic and the flight, everything might go to plan. From the sounds of pursuit, muted by the softening effect of the snow, it seemed to work. The trick meant she had to linger, though, drawing the monsters in but, second by second, risking drawing Sam along with them.

Forcing herself to run back into the dark maw of L'Arpin Hotel's broken front door took all of Sadie's strength. The shadows within didn't shift, not yet. But as she plunged from the streetlight and snow glow of the night back into the humid, unlit warmth of the hotel, she couldn't shake the feeling of being swallowed.

She also couldn't escape the terror that she'd find Sam Keller, or the deer-thing, or the mutated guests, or some *worse* monstrosity waiting just within those shadows.

The lobby was still.

Sadie carried Viago's crowbar in both hands, its surprising weight tiring but comforting at the same time. She couldn't be caught too early, or by the wrong person. As she ran for the stairs, her will faltered and her voice failed her. Surely she had Gertie's attention now, and where Gertie's attention turned, so turned the focus of the creatures. That was all she needed. Screaming like that only increased the certainty that Sam would find her again—a disaster that carried not just the personal threat but could also doom the whole plan.

In the stairwell, Sadie encountered the first creature, a nearly normal beaver but for the bulging eyes. It charged her, and with a scream more of terror than battle lust, Sadie brought the crowbar down on the thing's skull. She left it twitching in her wake as she ran up the stairs. Gertie would expect Sadie to check her own room first. Gertie would expect Sadie to hope that Izzy had gone somewhere familiar and easy to find.

Sadie would have to hope Sam wouldn't have the same expectations, would have to hope Sam never learned her room number, because she had to give Gertie what she expected for just a little while longer.

On the top floor she forced herself to begin screaming again. From here, all she had to do was lure every monster in L'Arpin downstairs while avoiding her ex-fiancé.

Easy.

"Izzy! *Izzy!*" At least she didn't have to think of any convincing lines. She didn't need to find her daughter, but if this failed she would still never see her little girl again. The knowledge ate at her guts and twisted her heart and choked her voice into something like a sob as she called Izzy's name again, knowing full well Izzy couldn't hear her.

In their room, Sadie threw herself at the desk and snatched the other walkie-talkie up. She shoved it into her pocket and pushed herself back to her feet. At the last moment, she paused and grabbed her purse, too, with her phone and keys already tucked inside. If this worked, she wouldn't be able to come back for it. And if it didn't, well, whether she had it or not wouldn't matter. She turned toward the hallway once more.

The bathroom door banged open. Sadie let out an unfeigned scream and yanked it closed again without looking at what lay waiting within. Water seeped under the crack in the door, and Sadie ran back out of the room into the hallway. With a splash and a slipping sound, something followed. Sadie glanced over her shoulder. Whatever the tentacled mass had been, she couldn't identify it now. She didn't try. Only turned her eyes forward and ran again.

Near the elevator, something moved. The power had not been restored to the building, and Sadie's eyes adjusted slowly after the bright night outdoors, but she made out a shape coming at her.

Something cool and slick wound around her ankle. With a strangled yelp, she turned and swung the crowbar in a vicious arc at a medium-sized creature emerging from another door. A bird again, maybe the same seagull she'd seen before. The crowbar hit its side with a crunch. It let out a strange shriek and collapsed away from her. The tentacle on her ankle loosened and Sadie kicked free. She didn't head back for the stairs. Each floor of L'Arpin formed a connected square. She ran away from the stairwell at first, still howling her daughter's name, dodging around the small creature by the elevator. Each hallway presented a length of doors. Most hung open, letting in the corridors' only hint of light from their windows and the streetlights beyond them.

Down the first hallway, a single creature emerged from a room in the wake of her screaming dash.

Around the corner, down the second hallway, a door swung slowly open as she neared. Her heart skipped a beat and she veered as far from the opening as she could within the narrow hall. She didn't think she could go faster, but as the first tentacles slipped out onto the floor, she found an extra burst of speed.

A mass of shadow that writhed and squirmed waited for her in the center of the third hallway. She swung at it with the crowbar. The weight of her weapon pulled her arms, swung her off-balance, even as she batted the creature to one side. She stumbled with a cry, nearly dropped the crowbar, and caught her balance.

She rounded the final corner. In the fourth hallway before the staircase, three monsters came at her together. Fear slithered up her spine, filling her mind with a buzzing whirl. One of the creatures, very small, scrambled up the nearest doorframe. With a choked chitter, it leaped for Sadie, tentacles twisting through the air. She ducked, sucking in a whining breath. It plopped somewhere behind her.

Sadie straightened, still running. She lifted the crowbar above her. A possum hissed as it scrambled toward her, its unpleasant little body almost entirely unchanged. It dodged the crowbar as she brought it down, gouging the carpet. Sadie stumbled as she wrenched the bar up. The possum jumped at her. Sadie let out another disgusted, frightened cry and kicked its face. She brought her heel down on it, hard, and ran right over top of the thing.

The last monster reached her then, something mostly human. He gasped through his wide-open mouth as gills gaped soundlessly along the sides of his neck. When he reached for Sadie, she raised her arms to protect her throat. He grabbed her wrists, his grip strong but not painful. "Come to the spring, Sadie," he gasped. "I'm waiting for you. We can make this easy."

He began to pull Sadie. Perhaps he expected her to resist, to draw back from him. Instead, she lunged into him, slamming her forehead into his nose.

"Owww, my god," Sadie shouted, pain flaring across her own face even as the grip on her wrists loosened. In such close quarters she couldn't lift the crowbar, so she just kept running, pushing him backward with her. She twisted her left wrist free and grabbed a fistful of the collar of his shirt. Sticking her left leg out to tangle his, she bulled forward and yanked him to the side, tripping him up. She stumbled over him as he fell and nearly dropped the crowbar. Something swiped down the back of her shirt and she lunged forward.

The stairwell door stood ajar before her.

She slammed through it, kicking it shut behind her. She wanted to be chased, yes, but she didn't want to be caught. If she was trapped in the chamber with Gertie and her creatures when the time came . . . it would still end.

Panic clawed at Sadie's breastbone, at her spine, at her throat. She ran down one flight of stairs and let herself onto the third floor.

Empty first hallway. Behind her, the stairwell door opened again as her pursuers poured through.

Empty second hallway.

One fast-flowing cat-creature leaped from a doorway in the third hallway. Sadie barely dodged it, kept running.

Nothing in the fourth hallway.

Most of L'Arpin's horrors must have waited on the top floor, in case she returned to her room.

Back into the stairwell. Down another flight. At the second floor, she opened the door and merely screamed for Izzy, not pausing as she would have to listen for a response if she really didn't know where her daughter was. She clattered down to the first floor—the floor where Sam's room was, the last place he might wait for her. Instead of heading into those hallways, she let herself out the back exit, onto the slippery sidewalk.

The sluggish creatures that had been out in the cold too long had drawn nearer. Sadie ran a frantic circle around the perimeter of L'Arpin, sticking to the grass near the sidewalk where she could, slipping over slick pavement where she couldn't. Her lungs burned. A stitch cramped her side. Her knees creaked and popped with every step, the joints aching so fiercely she wanted to cry.

The cold may not have affected her like it did the lake monsters, but she was slowing nonetheless by the time she careened back into the hotel.

She pushed herself to keep up her stumbling run. First floor. Almost done. The maintenance room. She had to get to the maintenance room, and she had to go the long way. It dragged the danger out that much longer—gave Gertie extra moments to put it all together, extra moments that turned the crawling on the back of Sadie's neck into a painful buzz as her panic mounted and mounted—but Sadie could not force herself to go past room 103.

In these corridors, chaos had marked L'Arpin more than anywhere else. Glass crunched underfoot, already dark light fixtures shattered. Doors hung open, contents of rooms strewn about. A familiar housekeeping cart lay overturned in the center of one hallway, its contents spilled across the floor. Sadie spied a box of hairnets and two pairs of gloves and snatched them without slowing her stride. She separated a pair of hairnets from the rest and shoved them and the gloves into her pocket while discarding the box.

The monsters chased her, but she'd put enough distance between them that she had whole seconds, now and again, during which she couldn't see them around corners. Her heart leaped at the realization.

She had a chance.

The maintenance room door was not one of those standing open.

She ran for it.

The moment of truth. If Gertie waited in the room rather than the subterranean chamber, it would all end for Sadie tonight. If

Gertie even stood on the stairs where she could see the room, the game would be over. If Sam waited there to catch her, to slow her, she would be done for.

Viago would finish it either way, but it would take only one person in the exact wrong place for Sadie to be caught up in the destruction when it came.

Sadie's hands trembled. She dropped the crowbar with a dull thud on the carpet and leaped to the door. The creatures began to round the corner behind her. Hand shaking, she twisted the handle and threw open the door.

Empty.

Relief nearly made her swoon.

And there, glittering where they'd been dropped during the fight between Beth and Mel—Beth's keys. Sadie snatched them up and turned to the stack of ladders leaning against the wall. She didn't give herself time to think about whether they were sturdy there. Whether they would topple under her weight. Whether the bottom feet would slide out and send her down the wall as she climbed. Whether she could climb fast enough, twenty-three weeks pregnant.

She could only try.

Sadie clambered up the largest ladder as fast as she could. The keys bit into her right fist. Her shoes, slick with snow, slipped on a metal rung. She clung with her arms until she regained her balance.

She neared the top just as the door slammed open again.

Sadie froze.

Trapped atop a ladder and fully exposed, she watched as the monsters surged through the room. If any of them looked up, her escape would fail. If the ladder shifted or fell or if she made a noise or dropped the keys or a million other things that could happen, she'd fail. If whatever senses Gertie gleaned from her horde weren't too overwhelmed by the multitudinous rush—if she figured out the ruse before they reached her—Sadie would fail.

Failure meant an absolute best-case scenario of death.

She wanted to squeeze her eyes shut and make it all go away, but she had to know the moment the last monster descended the stairs. So, she made herself watch, eyes wide, breath frozen in her lungs, during the interminable, eternal seconds it took for the creatures to race through the room and down the steps.

None of them looked up at her.

Her whole body shook as she hurried down the ladder. Any second now, they might realize they'd been tricked. They might come barreling back up the stairs. Sadie made it to the floor and forced herself to turn her back on that looming stairwell. She scampered out of the room with the skin on the back of her neck crawling so terribly it made her want to claw her own flesh.

She shut the door quietly and jammed three keys at the lock before she found the right one.

Rough hands grabbed her shoulders.

CHAPTER TWENTY-EIGHT

Hard, Sharp Violence

Sadie screamed.

Sam spun her and shoved her back against the door she had just locked. How long could that door hold?

His right hand held her shirt only weakly, the fingers loose, the angle of the wrist wrong where Mel had broken a bone disarming him earlier. His left hand, though, squeezed, fingernails digging into her even through her shirt. Sadie gritted her teeth and pressed her lips together, swallowing a second cry.

How well did sound carry down to that cavern? How much had Gertie already figured out? Sam let go of her shirt with his injured hand and put that elbow on her throat instead.

Sadie choked, tried to shove Sam. He didn't budge, he leaned nearer.

"Shut the fuck up and collect yourself," he said, as if he'd found her crying in their room or in the bathroom. "We're getting the fuck out of here. Together. Now." The burning rage he'd radiated earlier had burned out, as it always did. He spoke as if he'd never been about to beat her on the floor with a mop handle. She scrabbled at him, scratching his hands, balling her fists and striking his face, but he barely flinched. And all the while she tried to draw a full breath, and all the while she waited for the door behind her to shudder, to splinter under a deadly onslaught. Sam put his face right in Sadie's and scolded her, "We don't have time for an outburst right now! I *know* you, Sadie Miles, and there's a reason you didn't let that thing kill me, so cut these bullshit games and let's *go*."

He spoke as if they would leave together and things would go back to normal. Cold rushed through Sadie's veins, leaving a trembling shudder in its wake, but when the cold drained, it left her not hollow but hard. Frozen solid inside. Maybe she should've let Mel kill Sam. Sadie would never go anywhere with him, not ever again, but he was right about one thing.

They didn't have time.

Accustomed now to the darkness, Sadie could faintly make out the bruising on Sam's wrists, on his throat, where Mel's tentacles had nearly killed him. Like the rope burns on Izzy's wrists. The rope burns—the ropes! Sadie still had the ropes.

She yanked one out from where she'd shoved them into her waistband. She raised her hands, twisting the rope between them as soon as she'd cleared Sam's grasp on her neck. Then Sadie threw the rope over his head, pulled, and crossed her arms. The angle worked against her, she had to push her arms in their opposite directions rather than pulling out to tighten the rope, but the ploy did its job.

Sam let go of her, leaned back. Sadie released the rope before his backward jerk could pull her off-balance. She followed through with the momentum, though, and for the second time that night headbutted someone so hard she saw spots. Her forehead struck Sam in the jaw and his body went loose, limp. His weight carried him back into the wall opposite the maintenance room door. He sagged down and came to rest on the floor, expression slack and eyes distant.

Sadie hesitated for half a breath, then reared back and kicked him in the face, aiming for the same place she'd just headbutted.

His eyes rolled back and then fluttered closed. His chest rose and fell, but other than that, a stillness settled over him.

He could just stay there.

Sadie turned in the direction of the lobby and tripped over something long and hard. She caught herself on the wall and looked down. Viago's crowbar, one end still slicked with the gory evidence of violence. Moving fast, shaking so hard she dropped it the first time, Sadie bent and lifted the crowbar, wiping the handle down with the hem of her shirt, leaving the incriminating mess at the other end.

She put it in Sam's hand, closed his fingers over the handle, then fumbled her phone out of her purse and took a pic.

If Sam happened to survive what would come next, she'd make sure he never came after her again.

But only if Sadie survived what came next, too. How fast could an excavator move? How much had Gertie and her monsters figured out by now? Sadie couldn't answer those questions, but she could push herself for one last burst of speed as she left L'Arpin Hotel—hopefully for the last time.

She fumbled the walkie-talkie out of her pocket as she ran. Viago still had its pair. "Now!" she gasped into it. "I got as many in as I could! I'm clear! I locked the door, but I got slowed down, you gotta go *now!*"

A few tentacled creatures still dragging themselves sluggishly through the snow turned to follow her. They struggled, slow with cold. She ran across the parking lot, back toward the power plant. From here, distance combined with the muffling quality of the thick snow to mute the sound of a construction vehicle growling to life.

The cold stung her face, her hands. She tried to put the walkie-talkie back in her pocket but dropped it. It let out a crack as it skittered away across the snowy parking lot. Sadie did not stop to retrieve it. With clumsy fingers, she pulled the hairnets and gloves she'd snatched from the cart out of her back pocket. She tucked her hair into one of the hairnets as she drew even with the power plant.

The excavator rumbled toward her, Viago at the controls, Izzy on his lap. She dashed up next to the huge machine, flinching before the noise. Viago stopped the vehicle and lifted Izzy out the door to his side, setting her on one large tread. Sadie snatched her down.

Izzy wrapped her arms around Sadie's neck, and Sadie squeezed her daughter hard, burying her face in her little girl's hair. Viago's jacket, large enough to be a blanket, still draped Izzy's little body, and she was warm and heavy and soft. The tension in Sadie's chest and gut and shoulders unwound all at once, and Sadie couldn't hold back the tears—of terror but also of beautiful, desperate relief. She bit her lips to muffle her sobs as she cried onto the top of Izzy's head and wished for all the world that she could just sit down and hold her baby and shut out the rest of this night.

"The bulldozer is turned on for you already!" Viago shouted over the rumble of the excavator's engine. Sadie jumped at the sudden intrusion into her welter of emotions. She turned her teary gaze up to him and Viago blinked at her, then shifted his eyes away from her face. "Just follow me," he added, still loud but less gruff.

Sadie gave him a thumbs-up and stepped back from the machine as it set off again. It picked up speed as it drew away from her, but not much. The YouTube tutorial had said it would trundle along at just under twenty-five miles per hour. The bulldozer would be even slower, around ten miles per hour. Viago had to get a head start in the excavator, though, because it required a more precise hand at the controls. Sadie would have to hope she and Izzy could catch up in the second machine fast enough to help if Viago needed it.

Sadie rounded the corner to find the bulldozer not only running but also pulled out of its space in the construction area and pointed in the right direction. She hurried to it and set Izzy down long enough to tuck her daughter's hair into the second hairnet, gathering the material together and tying a little knot to give it a more snug fit. She pulled the adult-sized rubber gloves over Izzy's little hands.

"Keep these on," she said, tugging them as far down Izzy's arms as she could and tucking them into Izzy's pajama sleeves. She pulled the second pair onto her own hands.

Viago had been right when he'd said the police would never believe them about the monsters. She wasn't sure she could count on them to believe even if they found bodies in the rubble. She wasn't sure she'd trust the authorities to care, in the face of the property damage they planned to do. Hopefully the hairnets and gloves would be enough to prevent any evidence of Sadie and Izzy's involvement.

Once outfitted, she hoisted Izzy, ignoring a twinge of fear that all this carrying and climbing would hurt her, hurt the baby. She could give in to those terrible worries after she finished with the last of the necessary business of this long, hideous night.

She clambered onto the tread, then yanked the door handle. It didn't budge and Sadie pulled again, throwing her weight into it, suddenly certain that Viago had accidentally locked it and her part of the demolition would be impossible. The door opened with an abrupt jerk that nearly sent her and Izzy tumbling. Only her tight grip on the handle saved them. Heart hammering, Sadie ducked into the cab and settled Izzy on her lap. She hesitated then, looking over the controls, mentally rehearsing the steps she'd watched in that single YouTube video.

Then she twisted the throttle knob to point to a little white silhouette of a rabbit and listened to the tone of the engine change. She took Viago's jacket from Izzy and turned it backward, pulling the arms up over her shoulders and tucking them behind her back, hoping that would suffice to keep Izzy in her lap. She licked her lips, braced her feet on the footrests, and pushed the joystick that controlled the movement of the bulldozer.

With a lurch, the machine rolled forward and she pulled the lever back, abruptly slowing it.

"Ohhh, god," Sadie muttered under her breath, snatching her hands off both joysticks. "I don't know . . ."

"It's too loud!" Izzy cried, covering her ears.

It was too loud. Sadie wished she had earplugs or headphones. She wished she was somewhere else entirely.

She grabbed the joysticks again, gritted her teeth, and set off. In fits and starts, speeding and slowing and turning in sharply angled bursts, Sadie drove the bulldozer away from the power plant. She turned it toward L'Arpin.

A cacophony of sound, a crunching and a rumbling and a screeching, reached her even over the thunder of the bulldozer. Viago, tearing L'Arpin apart with the excavator. Sadie forgot hesitation and pushed the dozer to its measly high speed, leaning forward as much as Izzy and her own belly allowed, eager for her first sight of the destruction of L'Arpin.

The view didn't disappoint.

Sadie caught the moment the excavator's arm came down, tearing through brick like it was nothing and plunging like a spear into the earth below. The excavator's arm lifted again and the whole machine backed up a few feet, then the arm speared down again, into the snow-covered flower bed between the sidewalk and where the wall had been. It broke through, pulling chunks of pavement and soil down with it. Viago brought the arm up and down, again and again, and Sadie pictured the cavern with the glowing spring collapsing in an explosion of hard, sharp violence.

Even at top speed, minutes passed before Sadie and her bulldozer joined Viago at the site of the destruction. She plowed forward, lowering the blade too fast. It clanged onto the ground, shuddering the entire machine, and then *screeched* forward, throwing sparks to either side as she scraped loose rubble toward the hole. Viago drove his excavator out of her way, but not so far that he couldn't continue his demolition. He stabbed the arm into the earth again and again, moving farther every time, while she followed in his wake, shoving, filling.

Sealing.

Viago stopped only when the excavator's arm failed to penetrate as far as before. Waving for Sadie to back up, he moved closer to the hotel again, and stabbed in once more. He kept up the process until every attempt to bring the arm down ended in a failed spearing. Making sure he'd gotten every inch of that terrible cavern. Then he drove the excavator all the way out into L'Arpin's parking lot, making room to let Sadie finish filling in all the rubble.

When it was done, she turned off the machine and let the silence settle not only into her ears but also into her bones, which continued humming with the vibration of the bulldozer for another few moments as she and Izzy scrambled down and away from the ruined building.

Viago jumped out of his excavator and met them halfway.

"Come on," he said. His mouth moved wide, exaggerated, as if he shouted the words, but they came at Sadie in a muffled mumble. Her ears felt like they were stuffed with cotton, and Izzy stuck her fingers into her own ears, rubbing hard. Sadie pulled her daughter's hands away and then followed Viago.

"Where are we going?" she shouted. Even her own voice sounded muted.

"Gotta check that water," he called back, leading her toward the Cut.

Sadie's stomach flipped. Of course, he was right. But what if they reached the beach and the green-glowing water poured just as strongly from that crack into the lake as it had earlier? What if they got there in time to see Gertie pulling herself through the opening in the stone, her monsters pouring out before and after her?

What if it wasn't over at all?

Viago started down the steps with more care than he'd used before, and he didn't fall this time. Sadie watched him descend, and the moment his shoulders sagged and he stopped on the stairs to lean against the railing and let out a ragged laugh, Sadie sank down to sit on the ice-cold concrete step.

She rested only for a moment, only as long as it took to gather her strength, then pulled herself back to her feet and followed Viago the rest of the way down.

A plume of dust, half-settled already, fell around the openings in the rocky cliff face. The stream of glowing water flowing down the sand had already narrowed, shallowed. As she watched, the trickle ran itself out. No new water poured from the stone to join it.

"We did it," she whispered. Then she grabbed Viago's arm and shook him. *"We did it!"*

"Watch out," he said, drawing away, and she remembered belatedly that he'd been hurt struggling with Henry Drye or some other monster. He narrowed his eyes at her, but his stare lacked its old anger. She grinned at him, and a moment later he snorted.

"Yeah," he said, "we did it. We fucked that hotel up."

CHAPTER TWENTY-NINE

Done Borrowing Trouble

"All right, come on, you have to get out of sight," Viago said then, waving for her to follow him as he turned toward the fence.

"What?"

"I said get out of sight. There're a million places to tuck yourselves away in there"—he pointed at his power plant—"but we have to move fast. The phone lines are probably still down, but people have their cell phones, and we weren't exactly stealthy."

"What—what do you mean?"

He paused, giving her a surprised look over his shoulder. "Do you want to be here when the cops show up? Let's go. I'll tell them I haven't seen you since you fought off that . . . that rabid dog or whatever we said it was. Once the heat dies down, we can figure out our next moves."

"What will you say about the bulldozer, and—"

"That gardener, his name was McCann, right?" Viago huffed something like a laugh. "Knew keeping tabs on the hotel fucks would come in handy one day. Yeah, McCann. I'll tell the cops Drye killed his daughter, and McCann came here, stole the excavator and drove it into the building, then came back and did the same for the bulldozer, and got caught in the destruction because he didn't know what he was doing, and died."

"That will not work," Sadie said, voice flat.

Viago shrugged. "Sounds fine to me."

"Are you serious right now, Bill Viago? That *will not* work. A—a—a cursory glance at the hotel will disprove that whole story," Sadie said, stammering in her haste to convince him.

"What are they gonna think? That some pregnant lady nobody's seen for weeks and the power plant overseer did it?"

"You are *on record* hating L'Arpin and everyone in it! They'll think *you* did it all by yourself."

"Nah," Viago said, but he sounded less sure.

"Yeah. What do you bet Drye filed a report every time you came to L'Arpin, just to have a paper trail in case something bad ever happened?"

"Did he?"

"I don't know! But doesn't it sound like something he'd do? Listen, Viago. We can't just hide out in your power plant, we have to get out of here."

Viago hesitated for a long moment, eyes turned up to the cloudy sky and jaw clenched. Finally, he heaved a heavy sigh. "We'll see."

"We'll *see*?"

"We'll see," Viago repeated. "We need time to figure out what we're going to do next; running off half-cocked isn't going to solve any of our problems. So come inside and I'll find some closet nobody uses and you two stay in there and keep your mouths shut while I shake the cops. Then we can talk about if it's time to get lost or not."

He meant together.

The realization struck Sadie, and she gaped at him for a second. She was so tired of carrying everything on her shoulders—no support, no fallback, no relief. The thought of following him into that building, letting him guide the next steps and handle the cops and make a plan together after that, tempted her. And that temptation stuck in her throat, impossible to swallow.

It turned bitter in an instant.

Viago may not be as bad as she'd thought at first. But he was not someone she wanted to tie her fate to. Tired or not, Sadie didn't want to tie her fate to anyone other than her children, not ever again.

"No, Bill."

"What?" The incredulity in his voice pricked Sadie, a guilt she shoved way down. He blinked at her, brows drawing together. "What d'you mean, no?"

"I mean, no. But also thank you. Thank you for coming, for helping put a stop to all that—"

"People needed help," Viago said, waving a hand. "Anyone who's not a total fuck would've done the same."

Sadie had her doubts about that, but didn't voice them. "Still," she said, "thanks. But Izzy and I are going to get out of here, and we're never going to look back. And you should really do the same."

Viago shook his head, whether in refusal to flee or in disbelief at Sadie's answer. "Fine," he said, and then repeated himself. "*Fine. Good luck out there.*" Sadie thought he meant the words, but couldn't really tell. He gestured at the icy concrete stairs. "What're you waiting for, a hug? Go, if you're gonna go."

And that was that.

Viago turned on his heel and marched across the sand. He didn't pause at the gate for longer than it took to let himself through and lock it behind him, and he didn't look back as he returned to the same door he'd led Izzy and Sadie through not long before. He shut it hard behind him.

"Pain in the ass," Sadie muttered to herself, caught between exasperation and a thin, exhausted kind of humor.

"What's a pain inna ass?" Izzy asked.

Sadie looked down at her daughter's curious little face, safe and bright and beautiful, and a storm of relieved laughter burst out of her. She hugged Izzy so tightly the little girl squeaked, then eased her grip and laughed until tears ran down her cheeks.

"It's a not-nice word for a not-nice person," Sadie answered at last, setting off back up the stairs toward the parking lots. "We won't say it again."

Walking to her car, parked safely in the lot on the far side of the destruction, felt unreal.

They had no packed bags, no clothing but what they wore. Sadie had her purse, she had her keys and her phone. Nothing else. She unlocked her car and leaned over to put Izzy in her seat.

"It was a mistake staying in Ohio," she said, talking to herself but directing the words at Izzy. "We'll figure out something better. We'll leave this whole state, go somewhere without even one single lake in it. A desert, maybe. I'll get a new teaching license there. Might be hard, but it can't be harder than all *this*." She tugged, tightening Izzy's car seat's straps. Then she leaned forward and kissed Izzy's forehead. "Mommy will figure it out."

Straightening sent a jolt of pain through Sadie's pelvis and her back and she winced. Her wince turned into a tired smile as the baby kicked once, twice, and then pushed with some little, still-forming limb before going still. Sadie eased herself carefully into her seat and buckled the seat belt. She started the car and navigated around the rubble to pull out onto the street. She didn't bother looking back at the hotel, or at the power plant.

Driving to the highway along the main road would be faster, but in the distance, sirens wailed and red-and-blue light grew visible before the police cars themselves. She'd have to be evasive, probably best to pull straight across the road onto a back street and lose herself in the tangle of a suburban development. Going slow would put her on edge, but she'd drive the speed limit and draw away from L'Arpin at what would feel like a crawl.

"Mommy, what's that cloud?" Izzy asked as Sadie drove toward the nearest side street.

"What cloud?" Sadie asked, distracted, humoring her daughter only to prevent a tantrum.

"*That* cloud. Over there."

Sadie glanced in her rearview mirror. "Huh," she said. "February's awfully early for a mayfly swarm . . ."

She trailed away, watching the dark cloud of insects, disquiet growing cold and hard in her belly. Then she shook her head sharply and turned her eyes back to the road. She was done borrowing trouble.

"It's pretty," Izzy said. Sadie snorted. Izzy had once called dog poop near a sidewalk "beauty-bull," so this proclamation about an unseasonably early swarm of mayflies, or whatever they were, didn't surprise her mother. Then Izzy added, excited, "I like their light!"

Sadie glanced more sharply into the rearview mirror, her heart lurching and her breath going out of her in a rush.

A hint of green shimmered within the swarm.

Sadie abandoned stealth and sped into the quiet streets of the sleeping lakeside development. It was well past time to get herself and Izzy as far away from the Cut as they could go, forever.

Acknowledgments

First of all, my thanks to you, the person who just finished reading this book. I hope that you loved Sadie and Izzy!

Thanks and love forever and always to my entire family, especially to my own children who inspired so much of the toddler behavior in this book, to my stepson for never acting bored when I wanted to talk about writing for too long, and to my husband who always believed that my writing would work out even when I doubted myself.

Great big thanks to my spectacular agent, Chris Bucci, for seeing the potential in my book and helping me make it stronger, for the work he put into getting it out there, and for answering every one of my seven billion questions and concerns with the same thorough care and patience with which he answered the first. And thanks also to the team at Aevitas Creative Management.

Thank you so much to my editor, Michael Homler, for working with me to make this book shine, and for championing it and bringing it out into the world. Thank you so much to Olga Grlic for creating this incredible and striking cover—it's even better than I had dreamed. My thanks also to everyone at St. Martin's Press who worked on *The Cut*: Madeline Alsup, Stephen Erickson, Sara LaCotti, Shawna Hampton, Kiffin Steurer, James Sinclair, Alisa Trager, Soleil Paz, Ken Diamond, Judi Gaelick, and the whole St. Martin's team; I can't say how much I appreciate the work you've put into this book.

To my wonderful beta readers, early readers, and critique partners—whether you read the whole book five times or helped me fix the mess that the first three chapters used to be or double-checked the continuity after revisions, this novel would not be what it is without your time, your help, your insight, your talent, your encouragement, and your kindness: Briana Una McGuckin, Erin Hardee, Erin Adams, Rose Black, AS Crowder, Beth Sobel, Alice Ball, Hester Steele, Kara Allen, Tia Tashiro, and Audely Benson.

I have had so many amazing friends who have helped keep me sane through the years of writing, querying, submitting, and publishing: Mo and Erin (the gestalt entity known as MK Hardy), Briana Una McGuckin, Erin Adams, Hester Steele, Dave Goodman, Alex Fox, Meg Quisenberry, Tony Gagnon, Marty Amos, Branden Hershberger, Robert Rodriguez, Amanda Farrenholz, the Inklings, the Pitch Wars class of 2020, and my Pitch Wars mentor, Roxanne Blackhall.

A special shout-out to Antonio Lopez A., for being the first person to (repeatedly) suggest I try my hand at writing horror, years ago.

Finally, to anyone who has believed in my writing and offered encouragement of any kind, from the bottom of my heart, thank you.

About the Author

Amanda Farrenholz

C. J. Dotson possesses the statistically average number of body parts for a human being to have. She and her husband, stepson, and children (all of whom also appear human) share a cabin in the woods with more bugs than she would ever like to see. In her limited spare time she enjoys reading, video games, painting, baking, and decorating cakes (with . . . questionable success), and petting her dog and two cats. Visit her at cjdotsonauthor.com or cjdotsonsdreadfuldispatch.substack.com.